MARK OF THE MEDALLION

THE WIZARD ACADEMIES
BOOK 1

MIKE SHELTON

Mark of the Medallion

Library of Congress Control Number: 2019919792
ISBN: 9781733510448

Salem, Oregon

Sign up for my email list to get further news and information on my books and giveaways at:
http://www.michaelsheltonbooks.com

Cover Illustration by Gordon Napier

Map by Robert Altbauer

ACKNOWLEDGEMENTS

Thank you to my readers, editors, and family (especially my wife Melissa) for their continued support and help in bringing these fun and adventurous fantasy books to life. My inspiration for writing comes from you!

Mark of the Medallion is a work of fiction. Names, characters, places and incidents are the products of my imagination and are used fictitiously. Any resemblance to actual events, locales, or persons, living or dead, is entirely coincidental. I alone take full responsibility for any errors or omissions in this book.

-Mike

Books by Mike Shelton

WESTERN CONTINENT BOOKS:

The Cremelino Prophecy:
The Path Of Destiny
The Path Of Decisions
The Path Of Peace
The Blade and the Bow (A prequel novella to The Cremelino Prophecy)

The Alaris Chronicles:
The Dragon Orb
The Dragon Rider
The Dragon King
Prophecy Of The Dragon (A prequel novella to The Alaris Chronicles)

The Dragon Artifacts:
The Golden Dragon
The Golden Scepter
The Golden Empire

The Wizard Academies:
The Mark of the Medallion
The Search for the Medallion
The Power of the Medallion

GEMSTONES OF WAYLAND BOOKS:

The TruthSeer Archives:
TruthStone
TruthSpell
TruthSeer
The Stones of Power (A prequel novella to The TruthSeer Archives)

MAPS

WESTERN CONTINENT
Forgotten Lands
KINGDOM OF FINN
KINGDOM OF ARC
SUR
TWIN CITIES
MAR
WIZARD SCHOOL
THE REALM
TEAN
ANIKARI
WIZARDS CONCLAVE
CITY OF ARC
DENIR
BELOR
EMPIRE OF GILDAN
CYRENE
CITY OF GILDAN
WIZARD ACADEMY
KHAZER
JOR
BLUE SEA
HASARI
TURG
THERA
MAHLI
AMAN
ISLES OF VORWYTH
NORTH SOLSHI
THE CITADEL
ELVYN
RALEEZ
WESTRIDGE
LOR'L
SOUTH SOLSHI
CASSIAN
ALARIS
MALLEK
TILLIMOT
QUENTIS
MARGARID
GAZIR
Bay of Ghazi
WIZARD SANCTUARY
RH
2019

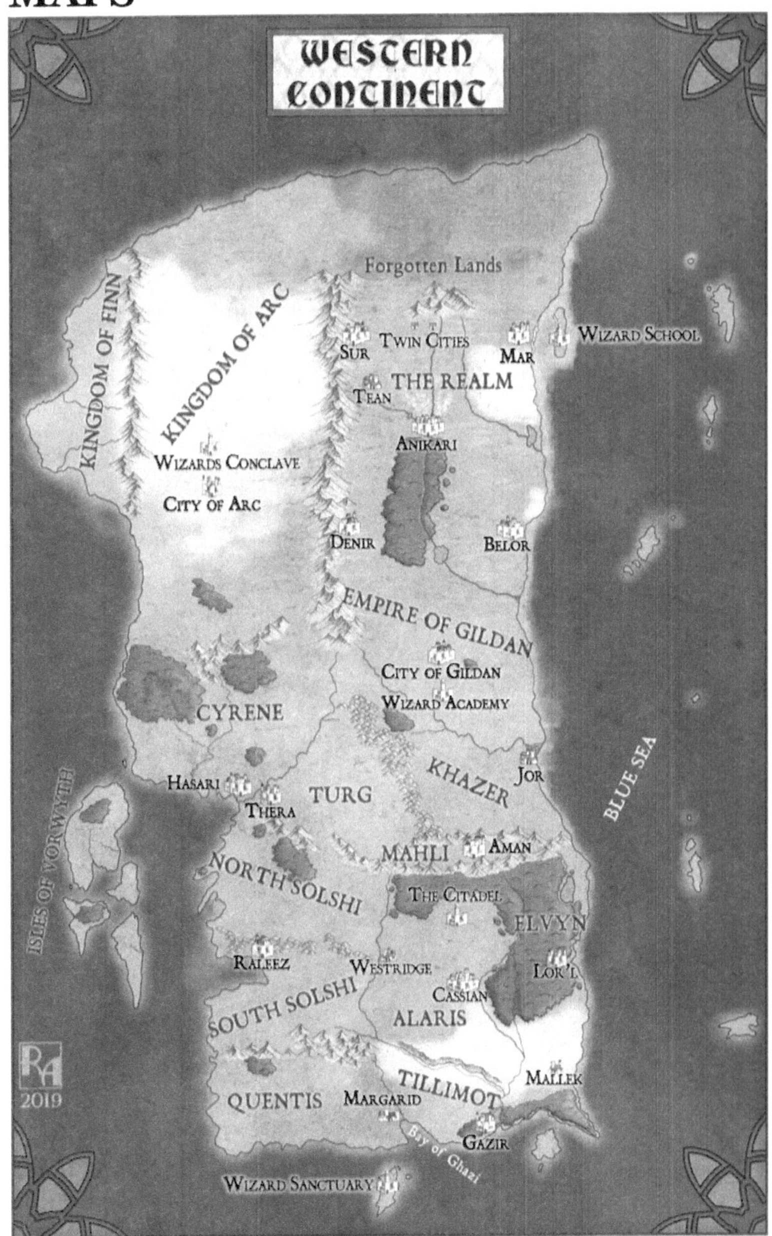

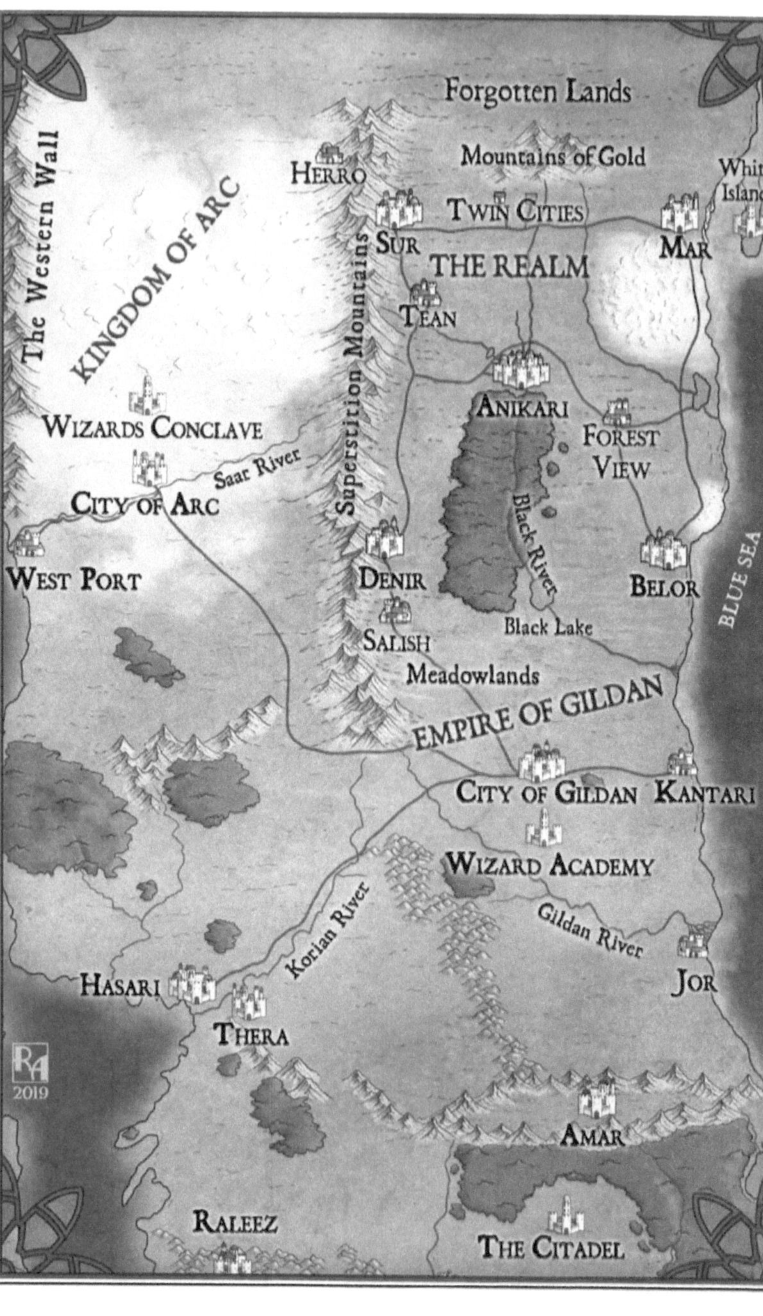

Forgotten Lands
Mountains of Gold
White Island
HERRO
TWIN CITIES
MAR
The Western Wall
SUR
THE REALM
KINGDOM OF ARC
TEAN
Superstition Mountains
ANIKARI
FOREST VIEW
WIZARDS CONCLAVE
Saar River
Black River
CITY OF ARC
DENIR
BELOR
WEST PORT
SALISH
Black Lake
BLUE SEA
Meadowlands
EMPIRE OF GILDAN
CITY OF GILDAN
KANTARI
WIZARD ACADEMY
Korian River
Gildan River
HASARI
JOR
THERA
AMAR
RALEEZ
THE CITADEL
RA
2019

CHAPTER ONE

Kyril stood on top of the sturdy stone wall, spread his thin arms out wide from his sides, and jumped into the air. He thought he could fly. He closed his eyes and for a few brief moments felt the hot wind ruffling his dark hair. But gravity had a way of teaching Kyril a hard lesson, and he hit the ground with a thud.

Sprawled on the grass, he cradled his right arm in his left and winced at the pain radiating from it. Blood welled up from a scrape on his forearm. He glanced around the garden of the Gildan Wizard Academy hoping no one had noticed his failure—but wishes were not being granted that day. And worst of all, it was Bale Nabhani, the bully of the academy, who had observed his attempt and subsequent failure.

Kyril shook his head to clear his mind of the foolish thoughts of flying. He knew it didn't make sense, but for a brief moment he thought he could do it—fly, that is. Something or someone in his mind convinced him to at least try, but now the thought seemed reckless and irrational at best. He would definitely need to investigate this delusion of grandeur—but first he needed to have his arm tended to.

Striding up to Kyril in long, heavy steps, Bale smirked, wrinkled up his broad nose, and then threw back his head and laughed. From Kyril's perspective on the ground, Bale loomed even larger than normal. With short black hair, a face even darker brown than his own, and deep-set brown eyes, he glared down at Kyril.

"Kyril Siravan, what in the emperor's name did you think you were doing?" Bale sneered and shook his head. "Are you really that stupid?"

"It's none of your business," Kyril croaked and felt his own face heat up. He tried to turn away and stand up. As he did so, he got tangled in his burgundy wizard's cloak, jarring his injured arm, forcing a yelp of pain from his lips. Teeth clenched against the agony, Kyril managed to get to his feet.

"You're the fifth person I know of to try something stupid this week," Bale said with a condescending laugh "Is everyone going crazy but me?"

Kyril scowled at Bale, but didn't hold his eyes for long. Even though Kyril was a wizard apprentice, and Bale had no affinity for magic, he was still afraid of the school bully. Bale was of mixed heritage from a minor barony in the south of Gildan. He got his larger stature and darker skin from his father. His family's strong ties to the emperor came from his mother's side. Even as one of only a few non-wizards at the school, he outranked Kyril who was from a poor family, and a recent orphan at that.

"I'm not crazy, Bale," Kyril said under his breath, more to convince himself than to cater to Bale's accusation. But he barely believed his own words. Only an hour before he had been studying on a bench in the gardens of Gildan's finest Wizard Academy, when the thought came to him that maybe he could fly. And why not? Wizards could do lots of things couldn't they?

Kyril ran a hand over his thick black hair, which hung slightly over his ears, watching as a few leaves floated to the ground in the stagnant, hot, and humid summer air. He turned toward a sizeable group of palm trees, planning to take a shortcut through the garden to get away from Bale and head to the healers. As he did so, he caught a glimpse of the myriad of domed buildings north of the Wizard Academy in the city of Gildan.

Without warning and making almost no sound, Bale jumped around the trees and intercepted him, moving faster than his size should have allowed. He weighed at least twice as much as Kyril did. But then, he always had been small and thin, and Bale—well, he surmised that Bale had never been small or thin. Kyril stifled a laugh at the thought and tried to move around Bale's hefty frame once again.

"What's so funny?" Bale asked. He moved closer to Kyril and planted his feet on the ground.

"Nothing." Kyril shook his head and peered down at his feet, glancing at Bale's as he did so. The bully's feet were gigantic; matching the rest of his muscular stature.

Kyril wanted to get away and see to his arm, but Bale stood his ground and loomed over him. Bringing up his meaty hand, he pushed on Kyril's good shoulder, but the jolt still sent waves of pain through his other arm.

"Ouch!" Kyril blurted, his voice coming out in a high shriek.

"You're not very smart, Kyril," Bale said in a deep, mocking voice. "I'm not sure how you ever got into the academy in the first place."

"Bale!" came a loud female voice from behind the palms. "Bale Nabhani, leave him alone."

Bale jumped at the voice and Kyril turned to see Sylvonna Hickory marching around the trees. Her blue eyes were stern and her short blonde tresses shook around her head. While as thin as Kyril, she was many inches taller. Her lighter skin marked her as being from outside of Gildan.

"This is none of your business, Twig," spat Bale, using the offensive insult to both her skinny frame and her last name.

"Hello, Sylvie," Kyril said, feeling relief at the arrival of a friendly face.

However, with that relief came a bit of heat to his face. Sylvie was one of the more powerful—and in his opinion, one of the most beautiful—women at the Wizard Academy. At sixteen, she was a year older than Kyril, and upon arriving almost a year earlier as part of a student exchange program from the Wizard Conclave in the Kingdom of Arc, she had become Kyril's friend—something that he didn't have many of. They didn't spend an overly large amount of time together, but she was always polite to him and treated him with respect, despite the fact that they were studying in different wizard disciplines. He was an apprentice wizard of the mind, and she was a full wizard of the earth.

"Saved by a girl again, apprentice," Bale said. "You are pathetic."

Sylvie ignored Bale's taunt and moved closer to Kyril.

"What happened to your arm?" Sylvie asked.

He shook his head at his own foolishness. Maybe Bale was right. He was stupid, at least in regards to trying to fly. What had gotten into him? He knew he couldn't fly—no wizards could, unless you counted the dragon riders down south, but they used dragons for their flying.

With thoughts of dragons in his head, the idea of flying once again overtook him, and he found himself moving backward toward the wall.

"Ky!" Sylvonna called to him. "Where are you going?"

Kyril blushed and shook the silly thoughts from his head. "Nowhere," he said.

Maybe he was going crazy. For a moment, he felt another presence in his mind. Could someone be trying to influence his thoughts? He glanced around the gardens and saw no one suspicious in the vicinity. Surely, it wasn't Bale. Concentrating harder to push the thoughts from his head, he began to feel his left hand grow warm. With Sylvie and Bale in a staring match, Kyril risked a quick glimpse down at his scarred palm. He could have sworn it glowed for a moment.

"The fool jumped off the wall, flapping his arms, and tried to fly." Bale laughed loudly, pulling Kyril's attention from his hand. "What an idiot."

Sylvie took three quick steps to stand in front of Bale. Even though she had to look up a few inches to meet his eyes, he was the one that reluctantly backed away. Levels of power meant a lot in Gildan, and even though Sylvie was still in school, she was a full wizard, while Bale was not.

Bale put his hands up in front of him. "No need to get testy, Twig. But someone should look into all the weird things going on around here lately. Unfortunately, Kyril isn't the only stupid apprentice who is crazy lately."

Sylvonna glanced from Bale to Kyril, and then back again to Bale. "What are you talking about?"

Kyril was interested also, and took a few steps closer to the other two.

"Maybe you've been too busy being a high and mighty wizard to notice," Bale said with contempt, "but yesterday a student thought he was a dragon and almost burned up a classroom. The day before a woman ran into a wall, thinking she could go right through it. And just this morning two students in the practice yard almost impaled each other with swords that they swore were only blunted ones."

Sylvonna glanced at Kyril and he just shrugged. He hadn't heard about any of these events. But then he did tend to keep to himself. He had been admitted to the academy almost two years before as an act of charity after he lost his family in a fire, and didn't have a lot of friends.

Sylvie pursed her lips then spoke matter-of-factly. "We have a problem at the school, it seems."

"You think?" Bale blurted out.

Sylvie's blue eyes flashed in his direction, stopping him from saying anything more.

"You are dismissed, Bale," Sylvie said.

Bale opened his mouth wide and his eyes even wider. His fists clenched tight. "You go too far sometimes, Twig." But without another word he turned around in a huff and began to walk away. After a dozen feet, he twisted his head back around.

"Hey Twig, make sure you don't let the boy try to fly again."

"What a fool," Kyril mumbled under his breath.

Sylvonna furrowed her brows at Kyril, and he took a step back wondering what he had done. Sometimes wizards were hard to figure out—and women even harder.

"What?" Kyril said, louder. "He is."

"He's still from a noble house," Sylvie said. "The house of Nabhani is a very mighty one in Gildan, is it not?"

Kyril nodded his head. *Too powerful.* Families like Bale's teased poor orphaned boys like Kyril. Someday, he would get back at them. He clenched his fists, but pain stabbed out from his shoulder and down his right arm. His head felt light and he wavered on his feet a bit; Sylvie moved quickly to support him.

She grabbed his left hand to steady him. Before letting go, she turned over his hand and stared at the rounded and patterned scar that marked his palm. Her eyebrows furrowed for a moment as if thinking of something.

Kyril grabbed his hand away and put it behind his back. "Can I go and get my arm looked at now?" He didn't want any questions about the burn mark on his hand right now. He knew Sylvie had seen it before but so far she hadn't said anything about it.

Sylvonna recovered and smiled. "Of course. Healer Joelle from the Realm should be able to fix you up." With one last glance down at Kyril's hidden hand, she turned and led the way across the gardens.

Kyril tried to keep up with the young wizard, but her legs were longer than his and he had to almost run to reach her side. The white stone structures with domed roofs of the Wizard Academy sat amidst tall palm trees swaying in the afternoon breeze. The gardens were one of the jewels of Gildan, with plants imported from the southern kingdoms of the western continent in which they lived.

Kyril took a deep breath, and the fragrant perfumed flowers of the garden drifted by him. He smiled. Others stopped talking and gave nods of respect to Sylvie as they passed by. Kyril hoped that someday they would notice him too.

CHAPTER TWO

Walking through the door of the south wing of the Wizard Academy, Sylvie was awed—for at least the hundredth time. Having come from a small farming village at the edge of The Kingdom of Arc's desert, she'd spent a few years in the Wizard Sanctuary in her home kingdom before coming south. But Gildan and its academy, with its fragrant gardens, spacious domed buildings, and numerous wizard apprentices, was far larger and grander.

At twelve, she had shown a strong affinity for magic and just recently, at barely sixteen, had been named a full wizard of the earth.

With only a moment's thought she could feel the power of the earth flowing beneath her feet. She wondered if wizards of the mind and heart felt the same way. Their powers came from internal forces, while hers came from the things all around her; the rocks, the dirt, the trees, even the air filled her to the brink of almost bursting with power. It had taken a lot to not use that power to lash out at Bale. But at the core of her beliefs she truly believed what she'd told Kyril and so had tried to treat Bale with respect even though he hadn't returned the favor.

Sylvonna glanced over at Kyril and wondered what had gotten into him with this business of jumping off a wall. Usually a quiet and unassuming young man teased by many, Kyril rarely stepped outside of his comfort zone—at least from what Sylvie had seen. Having been a stranger to the ways of Gildan when she arrived, she had somehow gotten Kyril to open up and explain the cultural nuances of Gildanian life to her—some of which was far different than those of Arc.

The hallway they walked in was brightened by candled chandeliers high overhead every ten feet. The carpet that ran the length of the hall was soft and thick beneath Sylvonna's feet. Here in Gildan, luxury was common.

"You all right, Ky?" Sylvie asked with concern.

Kyril nodded and mumbled, "I'll be fine."

"Joelle will fix you up."

"I'm sure she's too busy for me," Kyril said. "She's become quite renowned after healing the emperor's son last month. I'll be fine with anyone that will help me. I don't need any special attention."

"She'll see us," Sylvie said as she walked with quick steps down the long hallway. "She's a friend of mine."

Three older gentlemen approached them down the hall and Kyril started fidgeting next to Sylvie. He took a step toward a nearby side hallway, but she softly touched his unhurt arm and guided him back.

"Oh no, you don't," Sylvonna said under her breath. "There's nothing to worry about."

The two of them stopped a few feet before the men passed them by.

The man on their right had the tan skin typical of those from Gildan, long grey hair, and wore a heavy blue cloak over his thinning frame. He was a wizard of the earth like Sylvie, and was the current headmaster of the Wizard Academy. Next to him stood a broad-shouldered man. His hair was also grey, but it was cut above his ears, and his face held a day's growth of beard. The man on the other side of him was shorter and bald with lighter skin than the other two. A red birthmark accented his forehead. Sylvie didn't like how the man's beady eyes seem to take everything in.

"Commander Brashir." Sylvie nodded her head first toward the man on her right. "Nice to see you." Kyril stayed behind her and out of the corner of her eye, Sylvonna saw him nod his head while keeping his eyes focused downwards.

"Wizard Sylvonna Hickory," the Commander said in greeting, then glanced over at Kyril with furrowed eyebrows.

"You know Kyril Siravan, don't you?" Sylvonna asked with a smile to the Commander.

Before the Commander could answer, the bald headed man nodded his head slowly and then let a small grin cross his face. "Ah, yes, one of our wizard of the mind apprentices, if I've heard correctly."

Both Sylvie and Kyril glanced at each other in surprise.

With a wave of his hand, the Commander introduced his companion on his side. "This is Targon Qureshi, a brilliant wizard of the mind," he said. "He has recently taken more interest in our school apprentices and is searching for someone to mentor."

"And this," said Wizard Targon with a flick of his head to the bald headed man, "is my faithful scribe, Gamal Turami."

A flash of what Sylvie thought was annoyance flashed briefly across Gamal's face, but without any other words he just tilted his head slightly toward Sylvie and Kyril.

Sylvonna smiled. "I am Sylvonna Hickory, wizard of the earth."

"A visitor from the Kingdom of Arc," the Commander explained to Targon.

"Ah…I see," the wizard said, turning his attention back to Kyril.

Sylvonna took a step forward to resume their walk. "We're going to the healers," she said as she moved past the two male wizards.

Brashir frowned and reached out and touched Sylvonna's arm, signaling her to stop. He watched Kyril, but addressed her. "How did it happen?"

Kyril let out a long breath, but Sylvonna answered instead.

"He fell off a wall," Sylvonna said, and tried to take a step away.

The Commander nodded and mumbled, "There have been a lot of strange things going on around here lately."

"An unfortunate accident, I am sure," Gamal said with eyes that bore into Kyril's. "Whatever were you doing up on a wall?"

"We need to get him to Joelle," Sylvonna jumped in again, saving Kyril the embarrassment of answering.

"Yes, yes," the Commander said. "Of course."

Before passing him, Targon put a hand lightly on Kyril's shoulder. "Please ignore my scribe, he's not very good with people. But please come see me when you are healed, son."

Kyril appeared surprised but nodded his head and continued walking with Sylvie.

"They make me nervous," Kyril said when they were out of earshot.

Sylvonna laughed. "The Commander is nothing to be afraid of. He cares for his students. I'm with you on the scribe though. But Wizard Targon seemed to take an interest in you. That's good, Ky. He's a powerful wizard of the mind. That may help you with the other students."

Kyril only grunted.

"Sylvonna!" came a loud shriek from a doorway to the healer's room.

"Joelle!" Sylvie ran a few steps and hugged the red-haired woman. "How is the famous healer?"

Joelle laughed. "I'm not famous, Sylvonna. Now you, you're one of the youngest wizards of the earth in quite some time. Me, I'm just a lowly healer who happened to help the emperor's son. It was nothing special. I'm just glad I could help."

Sylvonna laughed along with her friend. Being from Belor, a southern city in the Realm, Joelle was freckled-faced, redheaded, and liked to talk a lot.

Turning toward Kyril, Sylvonna said, "You know Kyril, right? He had an accident."

Kyril blushed. "Healer Joelle…I…I…" Kyril didn't know what to say.

"Just call me Joelle," she said. "Now, what happened and what can I do for you?" She ushered the two inside the room.

Walking farther into the room, Sylvonna's nose twitched with the scent of herbs. Half a dozen beds lined the walls and two large shelves near the back held what were obviously herbs, ointments, and potions for healing.

"I haven't seen you out with the other students much," Joelle turned to Kyril. "I'm from the Realm, so I don't have many friends here either. I know how that can be. Also I'm a wizard of the heart, and people are nervous around us—you know, they wonder if we are manipulating their emotions. What type of wizard are you? Oh, silly me, I can tell by your burgundy cloak you are a wizard of the mind. I wonder if your power works like mine…"

"Joelle…" Sylvonna put a hand on her friend's arm.

"Oh right. I'm sorry. Too many questions."

Sylvie gasped as she gazed around the room and noticed all the beds were full. "What happened?"

Joelle shook her head. "I wish I understood. It seems that strange actions by many of the wizard students have followed with injuries." She motioned Kyril over to a stool in a far corner.

She was worried about Kyril. For some reason he was one of those people that got picked on more often. She realized all he wanted was to be accepted and wondered if this was just a way of getting attention. But peering around the room she recognized some of the others there with strange injuries and began to think maybe something strange was really going on with these delusions of grandeur.

Peering around again, she tried to determine if there was any common element to those being healed. There were both men and women; some were apprentices like Kyril, while others were full wizards like Sylvonna.

Joelle visually inspected Kyril's arm and then gave him a questioning tilt of her head.

"I think it's broken," Kyril said.

Joelle opened her mouth to speak, but Sylvonna jumped in. "He fell. Nothing more than that."

Joelle's right eyebrow raised for a moment, but she seemed to take the hint and didn't push any further. Instead she began talking about something else as she reached over and took Kyril's arm in her hands.

"Have you lived here your entire life, Kyril?" she asked. "In the city of Gildan?"

Kyril shook his head. "Less than two years. I lived in the meadowlands below the foothills of the Superstition Mountains—west of here."

Joelle smiled. "I'm from Belor. Have you ever been there? Well, probably not. It's out of the way for most people here, unless you want to cross through the Everlasting Meadows. Ahhh, what a beautiful sight, though. It's lovely there. I love sitting on the city wall and looking west at the meadows. Some people wanted to build a new town out there, but Governor El'Han stopped them. Our governor is a friend of the king of the Realm, Darius DarSan Williams. Did you know the two grew up together?"

Joelle finally took a breath. Sylvie glanced at Kyril and he smiled back, amused at the healer's chatter.

"There," Joelle said, and with a tender touch placed Kyril's arm back in his lap.

"There, what?" Kyril said.

"I healed it." Joelle laughed, her voice seeming to carry a hint of relaxation to those around her.

"You did all that while talking?" Kyril said in disbelief. He tentatively rubbed his left hand over his right arm and smiled. "It's warm."

"Talking is a distraction to the pain," Sylvie laughed. "It helps others to relax and me to heal."

Kyril glanced from Sylvie and then back to Joelle for confirmation.

Joelle nodded her head and blushed a bit. "Well, I do like to talk, but Sylvie's right, it actually helps me heal people. And since you have your own wizard powers, you will heal even quicker. You should still wear a sling for a few days to make sure you don't bump it. The bones are mended, but it still may be bruised and tender."

Kyril considered his arm once again and touched it with his palm—the palm that Sylvie had seen the scar on. The mark had a pattern on it that Sylvie would have loved to study more. She also could have sworn she saw it glow for a moment back when she first found Bale teasing him. She'd never heard of something like that before.

Joelle handed Kyril a small packet. "Mix these herbs with a cup of water and drink it twice a day for three days," Joelle instructed. "It will help to replenish your energy and make sure your body is strong enough to continue healing itself. Be careful with your arm for a few days, but soon it will be as good as new."

"Thank you, Joelle," Kyril said with a bit of nervousness.

"You're welcome," she said, smiling broadly at Kyril.

Sylvie watched both of them blush a bit and then cleared her voice to bring Joelle's attention back.

"What about all these other people here?"

"Accidents," Joelle said as she pursed her lips. "All of them. I think they all must be related somehow." She glanced at Kyril before continuing. "People are thinking they can do things that they shouldn't or can't normally do, or else they are seeing things that aren't really there."

Kyril's face went even more red and he turned his attention back to the room. Sylvonna watched him as Joelle droned on about the other injuries.

"That's it!" Kyril said with excitement in response to something that Joelle said about all the people she was healing.

Joelle stopped talking and both women turned to him.

"What's it?" Sylvonna asked.

"The mind," Kyril said. "Everyone that I've heard about that has been hurt has been a wizard of the mind."

Joelle's eyes went wide in recognition of what Kyril had deduced.

Sylvie glanced around the room once again to confirm Kyril's findings. Sure enough, all the current patients either wore or had sitting next to them a burgundy cloak—the color of a wizard of the mind. Joelle was called away to help someone else and she bid them farewell.

"We'll talk later," Joelle said to Sylvie and Kyril, her eyes lingering a moment longer on the young man.

Joelle walked off to help the other healers, and Sylvonna turned to Kyril. "We need to find out what's going on! Why is it just infecting wizards of the mind?"

"Before I jumped, I felt a pressure on my mind," Kyril offered up. "Almost like some entity or someone was trying to get control of my mind."

Sylvie thought for a small moment and then made up her mind. "I'm going to go and talk to the Commander. He may have some ideas. Want to come along?"

"Oh, no," Kyril said. "I need to rest."

Sylvonna smiled knowingly. She knew how uncomfortable he was around the leaders of the school—and anyone with more power than him. It reminded him of how insignificant his own was. She peered down at his left hand again.

"Ky?" she asked, but then thought better of it. She hadn't figured out how to ask the question yet. She knew he was sensitive about it and tried to keep his scar hidden. "Never mind. Go get some rest."

Kyril smiled. "Thanks for your help, Sylvie."

"You're welcome," she said, "but you shouldn't let Bale and the others bother you so much. You'll be a influential wizard someday, I know it. Then they'll be coming and asking you for help."

Kyril let out a puff of air with a small laugh. "I don't know, Sylvie. It seems like you might be the only one to think that. There's nothing I have that anyone wants."

CHAPTER THREE

Kyril avoided Bale for the next two days, but he still couldn't avoid the taunts of others.

"Hey, bird," yelled out a classmate as Kyril finished his dinner. "Get off the ground yet?"

The crowd around the cruel apprentice snickered. Kyril blushed and tried to ignore him.

"Watch out, he's a powerful wizard you know," teased another. "He might lay an egg on your head and knock you down."

This brought a larger following of guffaws and chortles, and Kyril left the room as fast as he could. He ran a hand over his eyes and tried to forget everyone else. But maybe they were right. Maybe he would never amount to anything and should just leave the academy. He was young enough to still take on another non-wizard apprenticeship. There was nothing wrong with being a laborer, baker, or tailor.

Kyril walked into his room, which he shared with three other apprentices, and sat on the edge of his dormitory bed. The low summer sun streamed an orange and yellow glow through a western-facing window. He was the only one there—the others in his room had joined in an after-dinner game of blackball out on the southern lawn. Originally called black forest ball, it was played at the edge of the rumored evil Black Forest when youth used to try and throw a ball to the edge of the evil forest without going in. Today, it was played on a lawn or patch of dirt with a line drawn to which one tried to roll a ball without it going past the line.

Kyril, still feeling anxious about his fall, had declined the invitation. Well, it wasn't so much an invitation, but his roommates had felt sorry for him and told him he was welcomed to join.

He noticed their relief when he'd declined. He admitted to himself though, his arm was only a convenient excuse for something that he didn't want to do anyway.

He rubbed his left hand over his arm where it had broken. There was no pain and only a slight spot of bruising left. He used his familiar, rough scar to scratch an itch on the arm. He brought his hand out in front of him and turned it over, palm facing up. A thick scar sat centered in his palm, consisting of three circles, one inside the other. Six straight lines came from the center at equal intervals and made their way out to the edge of the scar. At three points there was another faint bump in the skin.

Bringing his other hand forward, he ran his fingers delicately over the mark while his mind went back to that fateful day almost two years before when he had received it.

He had been out running an errand for his father—picking up a few chickens from a neighbor down the road in the meadowlands.

Down the lane toward his home, he saw smoke rising in the air, more than would be normal for their house stove. He knew something was wrong and tried to run faster, but he only fell down and twisted an ankle. By the time he arrived, his entire house was in smoldering embers on the ground, and his family—his mother, father, and younger sister—were nowhere to be seen.

Moving as fast as he could to the edge of the destroyed home, he noticed a small flame still spreading toward their barn. He didn't know what to do. It would take too long to get water from the well and he wasn't strong enough to beat back the flames on his own. As he stood there watching the flames move closer to the barn—where their wagon, chickens, and extra food was kept—he spied a metal object among the embers of the house.

It was his mother's medallion. He had only seen her wear it once when she had run out of the house searching for his father one night. He had been late coming back from a journey and she had been worried. Upon finding him and bringing him back, she'd put the medallion back into a wooden box. A box that now was in ashes with the rest of the house.

He reached down with his left hand and grabbed a hold of the medallion. The painful moment came roaring back to Kyril's mind. The scorched medallion had instantly burned his hand and stuck to it. He remembered turning around trying to figure out what to do as the flames reached the barn.

"No," he had yelled out.

In response, the medallion flared to life and his entire hand lit up. He jumped back in surprise finding it hard to believe what he was seeing. He held his hand out in front of him, the pain almost too much to bear.

In apparent response to his wishes and with the power of the Medallion, a wind came from the west and pushed back the flames from the barn, extinguishing the rest of the fire. Still in pain and barely coherent, Kyril ran into the barn and stuck his burning hand down into a bucket of water. The medallion fell off as the cool water swirled around his red swollen hand.

With a roar of agony, he fell backward and fainted.

The next thing he remembered was waking up in the home of the town healer. His hand was bandaged and throbbing with pain. The town healer, a friend of his family, arranged for Kyril to stay with a distant relative in the large city of Gildan, the capital of their empire. With only a bit of money from the sale of some leftover items in their family barn, Kyril rode with a merchant out of the meadowlands.

On the way there, some bandits tried to steal the merchant's goods. Without knowing how it happened, power in his hand had flared once again and scared off the bandits.

With evidence now that he might be a wizard, the merchant soon dropped him off at the Gildan Wizard Academy, the largest magic school in Gildan.

Now, two years later, he was still an apprentice and had shown only minor abilities; a fact that seemed to get him teased more and more. His wound had healed, leaving only a scar, and no other sign of magic had erupted from it since arriving in Gildan. At least until that morning after jumping off the wall.

He knew he had seen his scar glow—and he thought that Sylvie might have seen it also. He really didn't want the attention, but maybe…just maybe he would be accepted by others if he could show an increase in his wizarding abilities.

Standing up, Kyril poured himself a cup of water then began pacing the room. As he did so he wondered if he could use his newfound powers to teleport himself somewhere different. His mind began working speedily, calculating what he would need to do. He felt his hand grow warm again and the power of his mind expanded.

"Kyril," a soft, faint, and deep voice whispered in the back of his mind. "Kyril, come to me."

Kyril moved toward the door. Without paying much attention, he stepped out into the hallway and crashed right in to someone, his cup of water spraying out in front of him and drenching the other person.

Kyril snapped out of his thoughts and refocused his eyes around him.

"Kyril!" An angry voice met his blank stare. "Now look what you've done."

It was Bale, his face red with anger. Before Kyril understood what was happening, Bale reached out with his meaty fists and pushed Kyril to the floor.

Shaking his head to clear it further, Kyril tried to make sense of what had happened. The last thing he remembered was being in his room. He had been thinking about the medallion…and then things got confusing.

"You've ruined my shirt," Bale bellowed down at him. "I've been summoned for a meeting with my mother and one of the emperor's advisors. What am I supposed to do now?"

Kyril glanced around. No one else was in the hallway.

"Twig isn't here to save you this time." Bale sneered, took a step closer to Kyril, and kicked him hard in the ribs.

Kyril tried to roll away but Bale kicked him again. "You'll pay for your stupidity this time. You weren't even paying attention coming out of your room. Trying to fly again?"

"Fly?" Kyril croaked, getting up on his knees. Now he remembered what he had been thinking about. He had thought he could possibly teleport somewhere. He put a hand to his head and tried to stop the throbbing. He *was* going crazy! He would never have thought of that on his own.

"Are you listening to me?" Bale roared. He brought a leg back to kick Kyril again, when in defense Kyril pushed his left hand out in front of him. White power blazed forth and caught Bale on the inside of his leg, changing his trajectory enough to miss Kyril's head and only kick the side of his shoulder.

Bale stopped and peered down at his leg with rounded eyes. When he glanced back over at Kyril, he wiped a streak of sweat off his broad forehead. "Now you've burned a hole in my pants. Why, you little pathetic…"

"What seems to be the problem here?" came a deep voice behind the two of them. A voice that Kyril thought sounded familiar.

Peering around Bale's muscular body, Kyril spotted the burgundy-robed wizard Targon Qureshi, the wizard of the mind that he'd met the day he had broken his arm. Standing behind him was Gamal, his scribe. The man had a surprised but pleased look on his face.

Bale turned himself around and upon seeing the wizard, pointed back at Kyril. "This apprentice has no respect for others. I was on my way to an important meeting, when this whelp poured water on me and then burned a hole in my pants.

Who's going to pay for this? Not him! He's poorer than the dogs begging at the back door!"

Targon took a step closer and motioned Kyril to stand up, then turned his attention back to Bale with a sneer. "And who are you, sir, to treat a wizard this way?"

"A wiz…?" Bale stuttered. "He's just an apprentice, and not a very good one at that. It's against the rules to use magic against someone else in the school and he…"

"Enough." Targon waved his hand in the air and Kyril felt a breeze blow by him. "I'm sure it's just all a misunderstanding. Accidents do happen."

"Accidents?" Bale spat. "You mean you aren't going to do anything about this?" He motioned to his wet shirt and burned pants.

"And what is this important meeting you were off to, Bale Nabhani?"

Bale's eyes opened wide for a moment with surprise. "How did you know my name?"

Targon ran a hand down over his thin beard. "It's our job to know about all those who don't treat wizards as they should."

Bale stood speechless for a moment, then his face reddened. "I was summoned to an important meeting at the palace. I'm to get my first assignment…"

Gamal stepped out from behind Targon. He dug his hand into a pocket, produced a few coins, and tossed them out toward Bale.

"Maybe this can help, son," said the man.

Bale faltered from his anger for a moment as he tried to grab the coins before they hit the ground.

"Ahh, very good, Gamal," said Targon. "Yes, what a great idea."

"And if you go by the school's tailor we will send word for a new pair of pants to be made for you," Gamal said with a smile.

"At least someone knows what's important around here," Bale mumbled.

Kyril gazed around at the three men. With offer of money for a new outfit, Bale appeared to be somewhat satisfied, but Targon's forehead was furrowed as he glared over at Gamal. Targon caught Kyril looking at him and resumed a more pleasant expression. He walked closer to Kyril and put his arm around his shoulders.

"My scribe, Gamal is always so helpful," Targon said to Kyril.

Kyril caught a short eye roll from Gamal, but Bale cleared his throat and all three turned to him. He gave a short bow to Targon, ignoring both Gamal and Kyril in his departure.

After he was out of sight, Targon slapped Kyril on his back—almost knocking him over.

"Well done, Apprentice," Targon said. "Well done indeed. Now let's talk about how we can make sure that boy or anyone else never bothers you again."

CHAPTER FOUR

The next day at lunch, Kyril walked into the dining room by himself. Smells of fried chicken and vegetables wafted toward him and he smiled without realizing it. Memories of home ran through his mind in no apparent order. Most of them had to do with his mother's cooking. They had been poor and usually ate vegetables and watered-down soup, with the occasional fish caught in a nearby river. But a special day—a birthday, harvest time, and the new year—would bring a plump chicken to their table. Food at the wizard school was so much more plentiful than it had been at home, and he tried not to take it for granted.

Lost in his thoughts, he felt himself falling forward onto the hard marble floor. Before he knew what was happening, he flung his hands out to stop his momentum and just missed smacking his head on the ground.

"Watch your step," said someone behind him.

A ruckus of laughter sounded off to his side. He turned his head and saw a few of Bale's cronies next to him, one with a foot stuck out just a bit farther than the rest. Kyril knew he had been tripped. Some of the kids were apprentices, while others were like Bale—rich nobles who'd come here to train for high-ranking government positions.

Bale stood off to the side, clearly enjoying the scene, but not participating in it fully. His jaw, however, was clenched tight and his eyes threw daggers in Kyril's direction. He was obviously still angry about yesterday.

Kyril slowly began to lift himself off the floor when Sylvie walked over from one side while a group of three strolled over from the other. Sylvie stood with one hand on her hip and the other stretched out in front of her, power crackling up and over her fingers.

"None of you deserve to be wizards," Sylvie said. "This kind of behavior was never tolerated at the wizard sanctuary in Arc."

"Then go back home, sweetie," said one of the male apprentices of the group. "I don't remember inviting you here."

Sylvie reached her hand down to continue helping Kyril up, but at the last minute he pulled his hand back and stood up himself. Sylvie furrowed her brow at him as if asking why he wouldn't accept her help.

Kyril shook his head in revulsion at Bale and his group of cronies and felt his hand began to heat up again. He closed his eyes for a moment to mentally push the power back down. It wouldn't do any good for him to lose his temper here. When he opened his eyes back up, three others in burgundy robes—two apprentices and a wizard—reached Kyril's side and turned and faced the group that had been teasing him. The wizard, a male a year or two older than Kyril, stood out in front.

"Get back to lunch and leave Apprentice Kyril alone," the wizard said.

Kyril thought he recognized him but couldn't place the name for a moment. His hair was dark, pulled back into a ponytail, and he stood a few inches taller than Kyril. His brown eyes flashed angrily around the room as he waved a hand to dismiss everyone.

"Jordan Quereshi," Sylvie said to the wizard. "What brings you over to the apprentice dining room?"

Jordan smiled at Sylvie. "Don't worry about it, Wizard Sylvonna," Jordan said very politely, his perfectly straight white teeth showing. "No need to busy yourself in our doings here, Arcanian. And I could ask you the same question."

Kyril heard a few female sighs in the room and realized they were all attuned to Jordan. His high cheekbones, smooth skin, and slanted eyes—more so than other Gildanians—gave him an exotic appearance. It was rumored one of his grandparents was an Elf from Elvyn.

Sylvie's blue eyes grew round and turned to Kyril. "You all right here, Ky?"

Sylvie regularly dropped by the apprentice dining room a few times a week to say hi to Kyril. Up until now, she was usually the only one who even noticed Kyril at all—unless it was to tease or trip him.

Kyril nodded. "I'm fine."

"You want to join me for lunch today?" she asked.

Kyril glanced from Sylvie and back over to Jordan and the other two with him.

"He's going to eat with us today," Jordan said matter-of-factly.

I am?

"Oh, all right." Sylvie seemed a bit disappointed and Kyril felt a bit of guilt rise up inside of him. She'd befriended him when others wouldn't. But now, his own kinsman and classmates were asking him to eat with them. She quietly said goodbye and walked away.

After she'd left, Jordan slapped Kyril on the back. "Come on, let's meet the others."

"The others?" Kyril said.

Jordan pointed at a long table in the back. Five other apprentices; three women and two men waved them over. With the other two alongside Jordan, Kyril joined the table, making them nine altogether. It was the most people that had ever paid him attention before—either before or after coming to the academy.

With a quick glance backward, he noticed both Bale and Sylvie watching him. Both had a look of concern on their faces—though Bale's appeared more angry, while Sylvie seemed like she was trying to puzzle something out.

After introductions around the table and a few bites of chicken and a butter-smothered roll, the conversation turned quieter and Kyril had to strain a bit to hear what was being said in whispers around the table.

"Someday, men like Bale will not bother us anymore," said a woman at the far end of the table. "His kind will be put in their place."

Kyril thought the woman's name was Altia. He was sure she'd originally had dark hair but it was now died auburn, and was shaved on one side and long on the other. With her painted lips and eyes, it was hard for Kyril to turn away.

"Wizard Targon says it will be soon," said Jordan.

Kyril tore his eyes from Altia and nervously glanced around the room. But no one else seemed to be paying them any attention. He wondered what Jordan meant.

Another man to Kyril's left slapped him on the back. "Good thing you're with us now, Kyril."

When Kyril didn't answer right away, the man's hand gripped his shoulder a little too tightly. "You are with us, right?"

Kyril peered around the table, his eyes lingering just a moment longer on Jordan, the only full wizard in the group.

"Settle down, Anson," Jordan said. "Kyril just met Wizard Targon last night. I'm sure once he gets to know us better, he'll be on board. But give the man a chance to finish his meal."

Anson removed his hand and Kyril let out a deep breath. He was thankful for Jordan's intervention. But was puzzled about their conversation, and how they knew he and Targon had met so recently. It must have showed on his face.

"Don't worry," Jordan said with a broad smile. "You'll see that what we do is for the good of all."

"What *are* you doing?" Kyril squeaked out the first words since sitting down at the table.

"Wizard Targon says that we wizards should be the rulers," Jordan explained. "And not just all wizards, but certain ones…ones that have the power and intelligence to rule."

Everyone nodded their heads and smiled at Kyril. It made sense what they were saying—at least to a degree. Those with the aptitude to rule should be the rulers. It shouldn't be based on bloodlines or family nobility.

"The emperor is a wizard," Kyril said out loud, still trying to put everything together. He didn't expect them to be talking badly about him. That would be treason.

"Yes, Emperor Alrishitar is a great wizard and a kind ruler. But he still gives too much credence and power to those…" Jordan glared across the room at Bale, "those that are not wizards. But I'm sure he will understand. He is one of us."

One of us? Kyril thought. What did that mean? He glanced around the table and then twitched for a moment as he realized what they were saying. Everyone at the table, and Wizard Targon, and the emperor, were all wizards of the mind.

"It is your right, Kyril," said Altia with a fervor in her intelligent eyes. "Wizard Targon will teach you and you will be a great wizard like the rest of us will be."

Kyril didn't know about that. He wasn't sure anyone could make him a great wizard. He was just hoping to someday be competent at best. Greatness was not in his future—he was certain about that.

A few more enthusiastic words were said from others on the subject, and then the chime sounded, signaling them to prepare for their next class. Kyril stood up and began taking his tray of dishes to the appropriate place next to the kitchen when Jordan caught up with him once more.

"Tonight, we are having a meeting with Targon. You should come with us."

Kyril caught Bale's eye once again and he turned back to Jordan.

"Thanks for helping me today," he said. "I would be happy to attend your meeting."

Jordan smiled and walked away, while Kyril continued to his own class. Even the thought of studying the history of the Western Continent, his next, and usually least favorite class, couldn't keep Kyril from smiling. He had finally found a group of friends that accepted him. To him that was magic in and of itself.

CHAPTER FIVE

Sylvonna walked out of her afternoon class, Understanding Geology, with thoughts of going outside to the back of the school and trying some new things that she had learned. Although apprentices were prohibited from using magic without permission, as a full wizard she had no constraints put on her. And as a visiting wizard, she loved to put into practice the new things she was still learning.

The Wizard Conclave in the Kingdom of Arc was much smaller than the Wizard Academy in Gildan, and although she enjoyed her classes there and loved High Wizard Danijella Anwar, a lifetime idol of hers, she had to admit that she was learning quite a bit of new things here in Gildan. She had taken a liking to Gildan, both as a student and as an instructor to younger apprentices. Their approach was much more organized and strict than she was used to, but their knowledge of magic was also broader.

Lost in her thoughts, she missed a door swinging out in front of her. She squealed out something unintelligible and jumped to her side, narrowly avoiding a collision.

"Ky!" she called out as she saw him leaving the room behind a few other apprentices.

Kyril turned toward her and moved out of the rush.

"Are you still alright after today?" she asked out of concern. She knew that Kyril was a relatively weak apprentice from a poor background. She had been drawn to him ever since she arrived.

Kyril's face scrunched up a bit. "Why wouldn't I be?" he asked more curtly than usual.

"I'm just worried about you. Bale and the others seem to have it out for you."

"Not for long," Kyril mumbled under his breath as his eyes darted down the hallway.

"What does that mean?" Sylvie said. What was going on with Kyril?

"Nothing," Kyril mumbled again, but then he peered up at her. "I have new friends now, that's all. And Bale isn't going to bother me much longer."

"Kyril!" Sylvie put her right hand on her hips, while she held a notebook in her other. Her short blonde hair—a style made popular by the High Wizard of the Wizard Conclave, swirled around her chin. "Don't do anything stupid. Jordan might be all smiles and good looks, but be careful. I don't want to see you get hurt."

"I'm not going to get hurt, Sylvie," Kyril said, settling down a bit. "It's just…for the first time, I have some friends."

Sylvie frowned and Kyril jumped backwards a step.

"I mean, *we* are friends, Sylvie. And I'm so grateful for that. You've always been here to help me. But I need to learn to help myself and I think they can help me do that."

Sylvie smiled. Kyril wanted so much to be accepted. Maybe this would be good for him. "I understand. Meet me for dinner?"

Kyril smiled. "Sure." Then he turned to go.

Sylvie reached out and grabbed a hold of his hand. "Just be careful, Ky."

Before she let go of his hand, she felt the rough scars underneath once again. She had seen them before, but it wasn't until the other day that something in the back of her mind had been tickled at the shape she saw there. She turned his palm over in her hand.

Kyril's face grew nervous and he pulled back his hand away from her.

"Where did it come from?" Sylvie asked for the first time.

Kyril moved to put it under his robe, but before he did she could have sworn it began to glow. "It doesn't matter." He looked down the hall and shuffled away. "I have to go."

After a few steps, Sylvie called out to him. "See you in the dining room."

There was no response back, but Kyril walked faster.

Sylvie stood there for a moment deciding what to do. She turned around and ran right into Bale. The suddenness of the action caused him to drop his books, and papers splayed all around them.

"Twig," Bale spat. "Why don't you ever pay attention to where you're going?"

Sylvie croaked out a sound. It was true. She often let her thoughts run away with her and she didn't pay attention. But that didn't give him the right to talk to her like that.

"You were the one to run into me," she said instead.

His eyes grew large and his dark face grew darker.

She held herself straight and began to walk away. After a few steps she turned around, waved her hand in the air, and all of Bale's books and papers rose up effortlessly in the air. She gathered them together and brought them to his outstretched hands.

"Don't do me any favors," Bale growled at her.

Sylvie knew he resented not having magic. She smiled sweetly at him and waved her hands once again. The papers and books jumped out of his hands and fell once again to the floor. A small crowd standing around them laughed.

"If you say so," Sylvie said, and she turned and walked away.

"Sylvie?" said a voice beside her. It was Joelle.

"What did you do?" she said, her wild red hair floating around her head like she hadn't done anything to it that day. "Are you all right? Was that Bale?"

Sylvie smiled, but then felt bad. "I'm sorry. It's just so hard sometimes not to use magic around him. He is such a bully."

"But aren't you the one usually saying we should still show respect for him—he is from a noble family and will someday be a leader in Gildan. That's what you're always telling us."

Sylvie let out a deep sigh. It *was* usually what she said, but after her words with Kyril she hadn't been thinking clearly. She was worried about her friend and had taken it out on Bale.

"You're right, Joelle," she admitted. "I shouldn't have taunted him. "

"I was in the palace this morning healing someone, and I saw him leave the spymaster's office," Joelle said with a low voice. "Have you ever seen the spymaster himself? I wonder if it's someone we know. What would Bale be doing in there?"

Sylvie laughed. "I'm sure I don't know, Joelle. How do you have so many questions inside of you?"

Joelle shrugged, her green eyes going wide and her lips turning into a mischievous smile. "Just curious, I guess."

It was then that Sylvie remembered Kyril's palm. She linked her arm through Joelle's. "Do you have some time to help me?"

Joelle peered around and lowered her voice. "You mean…something secret? You know I don't like to get involved in things…"

"I need to go to the archives," Sylvie stated. "I know you use them a lot for your healing research. Can you help me there later tonight?"

"Yes, I can," Joelle said, appearing relieved at a favor so simple. "And there's a wonderful man that works there too. Have you ever met Hasani? He's a year older than us, but very very smart. He knows where everything is. What is it we are searching for?"

Sylvie just nodded her head a few times as Joelle continued to ramble on. Soon the two parted ways, Joelle off to the healing center and Sylvie outside to practice her magic.

"Meet me at eight bells," Sylvie said with a wave of her hand.

Joelle waved back and left Sylvie to head outside.

Looking around, she was happy that she would be alone for a bit. Joelle was a good friend. That they were both from other kingdoms had brought them together soon after Sylvie had arrived, but her constant talking did wear on Sylvie's nerves sometimes.

CHAPTER SIX

Out behind the east side of the academy at the back of the gardens sat a massive stone wall, a small quarry of rocks, and a clear area for wizards of the earth to practice. Sylvie walked out onto a wooden deck and stood gazing down into the deep hole that had been dug out by students over many decades. Closing her eyes for a moment to still her mind, she brought her hands up in front of her and imagined the powers residing in the earth itself.

She felt the veins of energy around her. The trees, rocks, earth, and stones—even the ancient academy itself—held power. The very air around her was filled with particles of power unseen by most. She brought all this inside of her and felt a swelling of energetic magic deep down. Her toes tingled and her chest heaved as she thought about the pile of stones on the other side of the hole.

Opening her eyes, she pointed at the rocks and raised one up into the air. It was the size of a pig or sheep. Then she brought up another rock and then another. Soon she had four, each bigger than the preceding, swirling in the air across the pit from her. She laughed with glee and reached out for one more.

A sound alerted her to someone behind her, but she ignored them for the moment and kept her focus. It was most likely only another student. After lifting the fifth and biggest stone into the air, she brought it into the center of the others. Now, to put into practice what they discussed earlier in her advanced class. She clapped her hands with a burst of energy, and all four rocks zoomed with sudden speed into the middle rock.

Just at the point that seemed all the rocks would bash into tiny pieces, she used her power to melt the middle one. As the other four met its tremendous heat, all of the rocks began to meld together and form into one. The new humongous stone now hung over the hole in the ground. Sylvie struggled in her mind with the sheer weight of it. She thought about High Wizard Danijella back home and how it always seemed so easy and natural for her.

Become one with the earth. Her mentor's words raced through her mind.

But Sylvie had never understood that part of it. She knew where she stood on the deck, and she could see and feel the hefty rock in front of her, but they were still separate entities.

"Close your eyes," said a soft male voice just over her shoulder.

It was so easygoing and smooth—and she sensed no danger, and so she complied.

"Contemplate the rock—everything about it. Its material, size, shape, and location. Where has it been? What animal has stepped over it? Where did it come from? See it in your mind," the voice continued.

Sylvie didn't recognize the voice, but its soothing nature lulled her into doing his bidding. The voice was male, but not quite deep enough for a full grown man yet. He spoke slowly and simply, allowing her to completely understand his directions in the Gildan language—not her native tongue. She could now clearly see the rock in her mind. It was huge—at least 20 feet across.

"Now see the rough edges. Think of this rock sitting in an immense river, water running over its edges for hundreds of years. Feel each drop of water sliding across the rock," the voice continued.

She now saw the water rolling over the rock, smoothing away its roughness. It was thrilling. She was really doing something amazing.

"Now take a deep breath and become the water," the man said, moving to stand by her side.

Sylvie did as he instructed and something shifted inside of her. She found herself flowing with the water. She could feel the rough edges of the rock beneath her melt away. The power of the water surged through her and became one with her. She was part of the water and part of the rock.

She giggled with delight as the reservoirs of her power increased, filling her to the brim. She felt invincible. Nothing could touch her. She pulled more and more water to her and the rock began to crumble under the pressure.

"I can do anything," she sighed with euphoria.

Then a darkness spread across her inward vision and she felt herself falling, the large rock crumbling on top of her.

A hand grasped hers from beside her and she opened her eyes. The rock in front of her had shrunk in size, and was now as smooth as a round ball. There was no evidence of water around her. Breathing hard, she turned to her side and watched as the man, a bit younger than her, raised his hand in front of him and lowered the new rock carefully to the floor of the quarry.

Sylvie, feeling lightheaded, brought her hand up to her head. The man next to her, still holding her other hand, helped her to the ground.

They sat in silence for a moment. Sylvie watched him out of the corner of her eye. He sat cross-legged, his thick black hair sitting nicely above his brown face and eyes. He was good-looking without being too pretty and his features were small and he held his head in a regal manner. The man's clothes were of fine silk, appropriate attire for the hot summer days in Gildan. A golden band sparkled on his wrist and without a doubt Sylvie realized who he was.

"You're Prince Zaidan Alrishitar," Sylvie gasped, and she moved to stand up in his presence. Doing so brought another bout of lightheadedness and she stumbled on her feet for a moment.

The prince was instantly at her side, and steadied her. She turned to him and he smiled, his white teeth perfect and bright.

"Wizard Sylvonna Hickory." Zaidan bowed his head slightly as his mouth curved upward. "That was an amazing show of talent. I'm not sure we have many earth wizards in Gildan with such abilities."

"Except you, of course," Sylvie said, feeling a bit self-conscious around the prince.

Prince Zaidan was the second child and first son of the emperor of Gildan. If she remembered correctly, he would soon be fifteen, as she had heard mention of a party being planned in his honor. In Gildan, one was recognized as a full man or woman at that age.

The prince's eyes sparkled as if he held a secret, but he waved a hand in the air, dismissing Sylvie's claims. "You are more powerful than I am, I've just had more specific training with my tutors than you."

"A perk of growing up in the palace I presume," Sylvie said, smiling back at him. "Well, thank you for your help. But what happened at the end there when I lost control?"

Zaiden's smile turned into a frown. "You almost burned yourself out. Well, you weren't that close yet. But if you would have continued you may have been hurt. I pushed you too hard. As wizards of the earth, we must be careful not to bring too much of the earth's power into us."

Sylvie smiled and nodded her head. "So that's what the High Wizard meant. Wizards of the mind and heart pull their power from within, but those of us with powers of the earth pull from outside of us and it's a big earth…"

"…with lots of power," the prince finished her sentence for her. "I know of the High Wizard you speak of; Danijella Anwar. She is a friend of my father's. We've met before and I've heard stories about how much power she can hold, though I don't know whether to believe them all."

"Oh, it's all true, Zaidan…" Sylvie had forgotten for a moment who she was talking to. "I mean, my Lord…Prince…"

Now she was making a fool of herself. Her face heated up and with her light skin and blonde hair, her skin would be as red as a tomato.

"Not to worry," Zaidan said, ignoring her embarrassment. "Zaidan is fine. It is my name, you know."

Sylvie let out a puff of air and tried to regain control of her thoughts.

"Can I walk you back to the building?" he offered.

Sylvie nodded and they walked around the south lawn, through the gardens, and back toward the south entrance of the academy. Before they reached the building, Zaidan stopped, put his hand gently on Sylvie's arm, and brought her from the main walkway behind a small group of miniature palms.

His hand felt warm on Sylvie's skin and she thought she felt a trickle of magic in his contact. He was tall for his age and, although younger than her, stood eye-to-eye with her. His dark brown eyes held hers for a second longer than would normally be comfortable, but she did not blink.

"I need to ask you something sensitive, Sylvonna. I'm asking now as a prince of Gildan." Zaidan's face grew serious as his hand dropped away from Sylvie's arm. A light breeze blew through the foliage around them, masking their conversation from others in the gardens. She wondered if Zaidan had done that with his magic.

"Yes?" Sylvie said.

"You are trusted by my father and the royal family," he continued. "You came to Gildan very highly recommended by your High Wizard. But I'm afraid there are others here in Gildan—and even in the academy itself—that are intent on undermining my family's authority and the peace of Gildan."

Sylvie listened intently. What did Prince Zaidan want from her?

"There is a group of wizard extremists gaining strength. Their goal is to have only wizards rule, and to afford them the highest rights in society. This group abhors those without magic and think that those without should only be servants to those with wizard abilities."

"How horrible." Sylvie put her hand to her mouth. "I know many good people that aren't wizards. It's our responsibility to help and serve, not to be overlords and tyrants."

Zaidan ran his fingers through his thick hair and smiled. "I'm happy to hear that. Those are my father's thoughts also."

"But why are you telling me this? What are you asking of me?"

"They won't be paying attention to you. We would like you to look around and see what you can find. Be another set of eyes and ears," Zaidan instructed. "Let us know—me know—if you hear or see anything suspicious. Anything that seems irregular or could help us in managing this uprising."

"You don't know who is leading them?" Sylvie asked.

Zaidan shook his head. Then he waited a few moments while a group of apprentices headed out to the lawn area. Sylvie noticed some of Kyril's roommates, but not Kyril himself. The observation did not surprise her as he rarely joined them outside for activities. However, thoughts of Kyril, along with what Zaidan had been saying, brought a few things to her mind. However, until she had further proof of anything, she would keep things to herself. Kyril was her friend.

"We know there is a high-ranking wizard leading the group. But don't know for sure who it is, or even more importantly what they are planning," Zaidan said. "But we hear they have started recruiting in the academy."

Memories of Jordan befriending Kyril popped into her head. Something else she would need to figure out.

"I understand," Sylvie said with a slight bow of her head. "I will let you know if I hear or see anything."

Zaidan seemed to relax once his message was delivered. "I'm sorry to drag you into this. But any problems here in Gildan could of course spill over to Arc and the Realm. We must all work together."

"I agree," Sylvie said.

"Now, let's get you back inside before anyone sees us hiding behind these trees and rumors begin flying around." Prince Zaidan's eyes sparkled with mirth and he smiled broadly. He acted older than most typical fourteen-year-olds. Of course, a prince of Gildan was anything but typical.

"We wouldn't want your royal reputation stained by speaking with a foreigner from the crude kingdom of Arc, now would we?" Sylvie said with as straight a face as she could muster.

"No. No. I didn't mean that!" Zaidan said. His arms waved around and he stumbled on his words. "I would never speak of you that way."

Sylvie laughed as they returned to the walkway heading to the academy. "Prince, I was joking. Please accept my apology if I offended you."

Zaidan appeared relieved and wiped the sweat from his forehead. "It is quite refreshing to speak to someone like you, Sylvonna Hickory. We are too formal sometimes in Gildan. I look forward to meeting with you again. Please keep me informed of your progress."

They stood for a moment at a crossroad of the walkways. Sylvie bobbed her head to the Prince in farewell and they turned and walked their separate ways. Before they went too far, Sylvie turned back around.

"Prince Zaidan, thank you for the lessons today."

Zaidan turned his head and smiled. "My pleasure."

Sylvie entered the academy with a silly grin on her face. That was one of the most stimulating conversations she had taken part in in quite some time. Many of the students at the academy ignored her—or at least didn't pay her any special attention. Being a foreigner in the school was more difficult than she had thought. The instructors accepted her well—she learned fast and had exceptional talent—but the students shied away. Except for Joelle and Kyril she had few real friends.

But now, she had spoken with the prince of Gildan. It lifted her mood as she headed toward her room to rest and clean up a bit before dinner. She was excited to see Kyril, but didn't know how or even if she should bring up the prince's concerns to him.

CHAPTER SEVEN

Kyril's roommates had just left to go outdoors and join in a few yard games before dinner, but as usual, Kyril didn't join them. Instead, he sat in his room thinking about his new friends—Jordan and the others. For some reason thoughts of his family came to him and he brushed away a tear. It had been difficult since they had died.

Kyril sighed and found himself running his fingers over his scar. Once again, a tingle of magic coursed through him and lit up his palm, highlighting the raised mark. He didn't know what it meant for sure, but something made him connect his strange visions of grandeur to the power that was now emerging from him. Each time he had thought about something—walking through walls, flying, teleporting, his scarred palm grew warm. But each time he also felt something else in his mind, almost like another presence. Someone urging him on.

A knock sounded on Kyril's door, shaking his thoughts from him. He wiped his eyes once more, making sure they were dry before answering. He opened the door and was surprised to see Altia, one of Jordan's friends from lunchtime and one of the most exotic women he had ever seen.

Altia was an apprentice wizard just like Kyril. She was shorter than he was and currently wore dark red painted lips. An attractive dress fit her snugly at the waist.

"Hello, Kyril," Altia said with a gleam in her eye, as if she was aware of the effect she was having on him.

Kyril felt his cheeks warm and he searched for what to say.

"Wizard Targon Qureshi requests your presence at dinner tonight," Altia said.

Dinner? With a powerful wizard? Kyril didn't know what to think of that.

"Kyril!" Altia's eyes flashed at him after he didn't answer for a few moments. Kyril noticed the eyeliner around her eyes, which seemed to accentuate her frustration with him.

"Are you sure he wants me?" said Kyril finally. It was the only thought in his head. Well, the only one beside Altia. He was having a hard time concentrating on anything else.

"Of course, you," Altia said. "Why else would I be here?"

Why else indeed. A woman like Altia would never come seeking Kyril out for friendship on her own.

He took a step toward the door.

"Is that what you're wearing?" Altia said, from behind furrowed eyebrows.

"What's wrong with this?" Kyril pointed to his burgundy apprentice robe. It hung loosely over a tan shirt and brown pants.

"Seriously?" Altia said. "You're meeting His Excellency of the Mind tonight and you want to wear that? It's a wonder you're actually a wizard at all. Maybe you belong with them after all."

"Them?" Kyril was having a hard time following Altia's accusations. What was wrong with what he was wearing? It's what all the apprentices wore.

"*Them.*" Altia waved her hand around the room as if Kyril should understand. "Those that don't have magic. Those that aren't wizards. Those that we will rule someday."

Ah, now Kyril understood. She thought they were better than those without magic and that they should be dressing up to meet with Targon, one of the most powerful wizards of the mind. Finally something was getting through to his brain.

"Kyril, you're gawking again." Altia rolled her eyes. She pushed into the room. "There must be something else for you to wear in here." She began rummaging through the wardrobes and emerged with a high collar white shirt, black pants, and a very deep burgundy robe with gold trim. Each garment had been grabbed from a different wardrobe.

"Those aren't mine!"

"So?" Altia said, thrusting the clothes toward him. "Put them on. They're nicer than yours."

Kyril took them from her and obediently went to the back of the room behind a changing screen.

When he emerged a few minutes later, Altia reached her hand up to his head. He flinched away for a moment but held steady as she finger-combed his hair to the side—different from his normal, messed-up look.

"Better!" she exclaimed. "You look nice."

Kyril swallowed hard and tried not to blush at the compliment. Altia took his right hand and pulled him out of the door. Kyril turned toward the dining room, but Altia pulled him the opposite direction.

"You don't think we're meeting wizard Targon in the academy dining rooms do you?" Altia said.

Kyril shook his head. "Of course not," he lied.

"We are going to his private chambers in the north wing," Altia informed him.

As they neared the door to leave the living quarters, he heard a voice call out behind him.

"Kyril?"

He pulled on Altia's arm to stop, turned around, and saw Sylvie standing down the hallway, waving. Kyril groaned. He just remembered that he had told her they would meet for dinner.

"Come on, Kyril," Altia said as she pulled him along. "We'll be late. You don't want Wizard Targon to be angry at you, do you?"

No, he did not want any wizard to be angry with him. But right now one was going to be. Either Targon or Sylvie. She began walking toward him, but Kyril only waved and said, "I'll see you tomorrow, Sylvie."

Sylvie's face fell and Kyril felt bad. But she was his friend and would understand. It wasn't every day that you got to have dinner with a wizard of the mind like Targon and be pulled there by a beautiful woman.

Walking to the south wing, Kyril caught quite a few stares from other boys. They would gawk at Altia, then him, then back again. Kyril laughed at their expressions.

"What's so funny?" Altia asked.

"Oh, nothing," Kyril answered. He was definitely enjoying the attention.

Soon they arrived at a set of ornate, carved double doors. Small frosted windows were inlaid in each one, transparent enough to see activity on the other side, but not enough to see who it was. Altia slowly opened up a door and popped her head in.

"Altia. Kyril." Jordan came over to them and opened the door wider. "I'm glad you made it. It's almost time to eat."

Jordan led them closer to the table while Kyril glanced around the room. It was big enough to fit dozens of tables, but only two were situated up front. A fireplace, currently not in use in the warm summer evening, and a set of comfortable sofas and chairs filled one wall, while a dark bookcase and a few tables and chairs covered another. Expensive-looking artwork hung on the walls in between.

Something smelled good and Kyril's stomach rumbled.

Out of a door in the back strode wizard of the mind, Targon Quereshi. Long silk robes of various shades of burgundy billowed around him. His eyes were sharp and he nodded his head or shook hands with everyone in the room. His manner was easy and comfortable, and he appeared to slide through the room without seeming to take a step. He approached where Kyril stood with Jordan and Altia.

"Ahh, Apprentice Kyril. So good of you to come," Targon said as he took Kyril's hand in both of his. "I've been meaning to get to know you better."

Kyril swallowed hard. "Thank you, sir."

"And Altia, you're ravishing as always," Targon said, turning his attention to Kyril's side. "Quite a handsome pair you two make, side by side."

"I...uh..." Kyril stumbled for a moment. He didn't want Targon to think he and Altia were together or anything.

But then Targon winked at him to show him he was teasing, and Kyril relaxed.

Targon then turned to Jordan and grabbed him into a one-armed hug. "Always a pleasure to see you, Wizard Jordan."

Jordan offered back a simple greeting.

"Let's eat. I'm hungry," Targon announced to the room. With a wave of his hand, platters of food lying on long tables in the back of the room lifted up into the air and made their way to the two long dining tables.

Kyril rarely saw such uses of magic. In the academy, they were taught to use magic only when necessary to help someone, to stay safe, or if normal physical labor wouldn't work. Targon must have noticed Kyril's wide eyes and open mouth.

"Nothing is too minor to use magic for, Kyril," Targon said as he motioned Kyril to the front of the table. "It's a part of who we are. Those that try and suppress it do not have our best interests at heart."

That makes sense.

Targon offered Kyril a place of honor next to him, though Kyril saw a brief frown run across Jordan's face when he had to sit farther down the table. Kyril felt a bit embarrassed with everyone staring at him, and braced himself for dirty looks, but they never came. Only greetings and congratulations. It was the most surreal experience he had ever had. They were actually all happy to be around him.

Wizard Targon sat, and everyone else followed suit. Soon steaming plates of spiced chicken, fried vegetables, and fresh local fruits were transferred around the table—once again through magic. Both apprentice and wizard alike used their powers.

When Kyril had quickly drained his glass of pomegranate juice, Targon turned to him.

"Would you like some more?" he asked with a twinkle in his eye.

Kyril did like the juice. "Yes, sir."

"Well, then bring it to yourself." Targon waved his hand toward the juice at the other end of the table.

Kyril's stomach fell. Normally apprentices weren't allowed to actually use much of their magic outside the classroom, and especially not for such mundane things.

"It's fine, Kyril," Targon urged with a soft voice. "Like I told you, we wizards shouldn't be shamed or shunned from using our powers. It's our right. Our powers give us privilege."

Kyril's arm shook as he lifted it into the air and pointed at the pitcher of juice. Conversation stopped and he felt a dribble of sweat running down the side of his face.

"It's all right, Kyril," said Altia from down by the juice. "It's wonderful to use our powers."

Kyril took courage from Altia and with a quick thought, summoned the juice to him. It lifted off the table and raced toward him without finesse. Before Kyril considered what was happening, Targon flicked his fingers and the pitcher stopped moving, the juice sloshing out and spilling onto the plate of his scribe.

Gamal jumped up from the table, accidentally taking a tablecloth with him which proceeded to pull numerous other plates and dishes from the table. The scribe slipped on juice that had sloshed on the floor, and went down with a plate of food hitting his bald head.

The room went silent as Targon—with magic of course--finished moving the pitcher of juice safely away from the edge of the table. Gamal twisted his body around on the floor, detangling himself from the tablecloth, plates, and food. The man, at least thirty years older than Kyril, slowly stood up. The birthmark on his forehead appeared more red than normal.

Slinking back in his chair, Kyril didn't know what to expect. How would Targon treat him now?

A soft glow surrounded Gamal as he deliberately pointed his finger toward Kyril. It seemed that fire blazed from behind his dark eyes. Kyril felt the blood drain from his face and his body became numb—he had no idea how to react. In response, he felt his palm warming, and he shoved it under his robe, but not before he heard a few gasps from others in the room.

"Enough, Gamal!" Targon stood up and glowered at his scribe. "Kyril is our guest here."

Gamal turned his head slowly toward Targon, anger clearly etched across his face. Kyril felt something flitter through his mind and didn't know if it was the work of Gamal, Targon, or if it was his own doing.

Gamal obediently lowered his hand.

Immediately Kyril felt his mind relax and his palm returned to its normal temperature. Everyone at the table was still watching him.

"I'm sorry," Kyril said to Targon with lowered head. "I'm sorry to have spoiled your dinner. I will leave now."

Kyril stood and pushed his chair back from the table. He had ruined everything. His chance to be accepted. His chance to learn more. His chance to have real friends.

"Nonsense," Targon said with a wave of his hand. "It was just an accident. I was the one who asked you to bring the pitcher down here." The wizard turned to his scribe. "Gamal, please accept my apology. I will relieve you of your duties the rest of the evening. You may go and clean up."

Gamal took a few deep breaths and his demeanor seemed to appear more relaxed. He spared a quick glance at Kyril, during which Kyril thought he felt a quick flash of darkness in his mind, but then the scribe turned back to his master and bowed his head.

"You are most gracious, Wizard Targon," Gamal said. "You are correct in saying it was an unfortunate accident. Please forgive my outburst. I was out of line."

The words were said as if by rote, but Kyril detected a note of sarcasm hidden behind them. Gamal was Targon's right-hand man, and being a scribe to such a powerful wizard must have some power of his own. Kyril felt gratitude for Targon. The wizard had saved him from sure retaliation from the scribe.

Gamal took his leave and Targon called in some servants to clean up the mess. He waved at Kyril to resume his seat, and then he sat back down himself. During the entire exchange with Gamal, nobody spoke and the room remained silent.

"Well, that was fun," Targon said with a full smile as he leaned back in his chair. "Our newest member here does have a flair for the dramatic."

Everyone laughed, and Kyril felt his face flush. However, within a few moments, conversation resumed to normal.

As others continued chatting with each other, Targon leaned over to Kyril and whispered, "I should like to know more about you Kyril Siravan. You intrigue me."

Kyril's head swam and he had a hard time thinking clearly. Why would he be of interest to such a mighty and esteemed wizard?

"The power you apparently hold is unique." Targon lowered his voice as he glanced down at Kyril's left hand. "We have been searching for you for a long time."

CHAPTER EIGHT

An hour later, Kyril left Targon's dining room in the north wing of the Wizard Academy, and made his way back to his dorm room alone. He silently hoped that Altia would escort him back, but Targon kept her and Jordan there for something as the others left.

After his debacle with the juice pitcher, the rest of the dinner had gone well. All there, whether wizard or apprentice, male or female, and regardless of their own personal backgrounds, seemed to enjoy each other's company. Targon appeared to take a personal interest in Kyril, asking him about his hometown and family. Of course, upon finding out about the fire, he expressed his deepest sympathies.

Before leaving the dinner, Kyril had been invited back to see Targon again the next afternoon in his study. He said he had some special activities to discuss with Kyril, and Kyril was already looking forward to it. The entire evening had been exciting, and Kyril walked with head held high and a new bounce in his step as he entered his dorm room.

One of his roommates, Behn, a new apprentice wizard of the earth, spoke to him as he entered.

"Hey Kyril, there's a note for you." Behn pointed to a bulletin board onto which a small envelope with Kyril's name was tacked.

"From who?" Kyril asked.

"It was here when we got back in," said Sayid, a small boy of about ten from eastern Gildan.

Kyril wasn't sure the boy had any wizard powers, but he came from a long line of wizards and so he was sent to the academy early. Sayid was told that his powers would become evident any time now. The third roommate, Tal, glanced up from a book his was reading. He, like Kyril, was a wizard of the mind, and was the most studious of the three. He was from a noble house that hadn't had a wizard in the family for decades. He wasn't a bad sort, but did tend to peer down his nose at others from time to time.

His roommates were all younger than him and all in all seemed to ignore Kyril for the most part. It didn't bother Kyril much; he was used to it. He understood he was put in with the younger group because of his, so far, minor wizarding skills.

Grabbing the envelope off the board, he turned it over and then opened it up. A small device fell out into this hand. He looked it over for a moment. It was grey and lightweight and appeared metallic with a few small buttons on it. Moving over closer to one of the lamps, he read the hastily written script of the note. It contained directions to go to a shed in the far corner of the property that night, and to activate the device with his magic. The note wasn't signed, but appeared to be quite urgent.

"Who's it from?" asked Sayid.

Kyril shrugged his shoulders. "Doesn't say. Just left me some strange instructions.

"Maybe it's from a girl," laughed Behn.

"I doubt that," said Tal from his bed, still reading and not looking up.

Kyril ignored him.

"Hey!" Tal did move his head up and looked at Kyril for the first time that evening. "That's my cloak!"

He took it off and handed it back to Tal, who had now dumped his book on his bed and was standing next to Kyril. Although Tal was a few inches shorter, Kyril began to back away, but then thought otherwise and moved closer.

Tal had definitely not been expecting that.

"I had dinner with Wizard Targon Quereshi and needed to look my best," Kyril said. "No harm done."

"And those are my pants and shirt," said Behn. "This is not your personal closet here, Kyril. What's gotten into you?"

"Well, Altia said it would look good on me and…"

"Altia?" Sayid said. "You mean a *girl* put you up to this? Gross."

Behn laughed and pushed Sayid back onto his bed. "Someday, you'll grow up and discover girls, Sayid."

"Oh and you know so much about them?" Tal punched Behn in the arm playfully. "You're what? Two years older than Sayid here?"

"And a lot better looking," Behn said with a laugh, then turned to Kyril. "I guess it's all right, if it was for Altia. Though I don't know why she gave you attention."

Kyril just shrugged, not wanting to give any information on what he had been doing. The group had been told to keep things secret. Only select people were invited.

"I've got to go out again." Kyril held up his note

"Altia?" Sayid teased.

Kyril shook his head. "Just something I have to do."

"Not with my cloak you're not," Tal said, and sat back on his bed and resumed his studying. "And don't take it again. It's worth more than your entire wardrobe." His eyes flashed hard at Kyril to emphasize his point. "I mean it, Kyril. You take one of my things again and I'll charge you with stealing."

Kyril swallowed hard and nodded. He didn't need his roommates anyway. He had new friends. He reached into his cupboard and grabbed a new change of clothes. In a few minutes, he was dressed in his own worn-out clothes.

The summer sun had just set and curfew was at the next bell, so Kyril needed to hurry. He skirted around the side of the building and walked down a stone pathway toward the east side of the academy. He could see the deck and huge hole where the wizards of the earth studied their craft. A hint of jealousy swam through his chest as he realized he would never be strong enough in magic to move large rocks. He'd hardly been able to move the pitcher of juice, and Targon had had to save him from that.

Thoughts of the powerful wizard put his mind at ease. Maybe Targon saw something in him that Kyril hadn't seen yet. The mighty wizard wouldn't spend his time mentoring him if he didn't see potential, right?

With a new smile on his face, he passed the deck and moved into a dense thicket of palm trees next to an old stone building that the gardeners used to store their tools. The note had said to go inside and wait. He glanced around him and hesitated a moment. A foreboding impression suddenly hit him. What was he doing out here?

He was intrigued however, and with a bit of newfound confidence from his meeting with the great wizard he pulled on the handle of the shed. Kyril flinched as the door gave a small squeak, glanced around once again to make sure no one had heard him, then moved inside.

With only the light of a partial moon shining through a dirty window, Kyril could hardly see anything. He tripped on something and began falling forward. He put his hands out in front of him and knocked into what felt like a shelf. Something fell and crashed to the floor.

Kyril froze.

In the quiet, he heard faint footsteps walking outside the thick wooden door.

He held his breath until they went away. Holding the device out in front of him, he wondered how to activate it and what it would actually do. He turned it around in his hand and felt a small button on one side. He pushed it in and at the same time tried to direct his feeble magic toward the device.

Nothing happened. All of a sudden he felt very foolish. Maybe it was all a joke. It did seem like something that Bale or one of his followers would do.

All of a sudden, he felt the device shake slightly and a soft glow appeared around it. Kyril jumped a bit, hitting his back against another shelf. He transferred it to his left hand and immediately felt a stronger connection. Without warning, a light emerged from the device and the hologram of a hooded face stood in the air in front of him. In his surprise he almost dropped it.

"Took you long enough." The voice was a deep whisper, but in the still air, Kyril heard it clearly. The person sounded like he was disguising his voice—making it deeper. So Kyril tried to do the same.

"Sorry," Kyril said. He groaned at how stupid his voice sounded. "I wasn't sure how it works. What is it?"

The other person ignored his question. "I am to deliver a message to you. A message from the office of the spymaster himself."

"The spymaster?" Kyril said louder. The man was known throughout Gildan as a firm supporter of the emperor in bringing miscreants, thieves, and others intent on trouble, to justice. What did they want with him?

He slapped his hand over his mouth with surprise and then lowered his voice and tried to disguise it again. "Is this a joke?"

Someone was definitely pulling a prank. If not Bale, then maybe it was something that Sylvie had come up with to get back at him for being rude to her. Or Jordan and his new friends.

Kyril tried to keep from laughing. Whoever it was, they were doing a great job. "All right, I'll play along. What does the *spymaster* want with me?"

"This is serious," the voice said, clearly angry about Kyril's attitude. "I don't know who you are, but on behalf of Emperor Alrishitar, the spymaster is requesting your service."

Kyril tried not to laugh again. Off in the distance, he heard the evening bell ring. That's what this was all about. They were keeping him out past curfew and now he was going to get into trouble. Maybe this wasn't a prank of his friends. His stomach fell. Maybe it was as he first thought—Bale or one of his cohorts.

He pushed on the door to open it. If he hurried, he could make it inside before he got into trouble. The door crashed into something as Kyril pushed it open.

"Hey, what are you doing?" came the voice again, clearly more angry.

"It's curfew," said Kyril matter-of-factly.

"I have my orders," said the voice. "This is my first assignment. Now just stop and listen."

Kyril's heart began beating louder. Whoever was on the other side of the device must be a new apprentice for the spymaster. "All right," he said softly. "But hurry."

"You will report back to me on everything you hear about Wizard Targon Quereshi. Everything. What he talks about, where he goes, and what he is planning."

Kyril's heart stopped beating and sunk into his chest. What was going on? This was way beyond a joke now. He tried to breathe but his breaths were coming out in ragged bursts.

"Did you hear me?" came the low voice. "I am your handler. You will report to me and I will report to the Spymaster and he will report to the emperor. This is his command."

"You're asking me to spy on Wizard Targon? But why?"

"I'm not *asking* you."

What could he do? He was in no position to not obey the orders. But he could hardly talk to those his own age and now he was being asked to spy on a powerful wizard. Why had they chosen him for this? It didn't make sense. He stilled wondered if it was a prank.

"Maybe you have the wrong person," Kyril stammered. "I'm not sure I'm cut out for this."

"I don't know who you are," said his handler, "but this is important to the Empire of Gildan and to our Emperor."

Kyril groaned but let the apparition of the man continue to speak.

"You must not tell anyone about this and you must be extremely careful that Targon does not find out. He is dangerous and if he suspected you of anything…"

The rest of the sentence was left unsaid. Kyril understood the implications. He reached a hand out to steady himself against the shelf and knocked a pot down. It hit something else and then the ground, both *clangs* interrupting the quiet night.

"Who's there?" came a faint voice closer to the academy.

"Fool!" said his handler from the other side of the device. "You're going to get us both caught. You better not mess this up for me."

"For you?" Kyril said. "I'm the one that's going to get caught in the shed!"

"Worse than that if you mess up this assignment," said his handler. "Neither of us are to know who the other is, though I suspect that is part of my test in this assignment rather than from some overall need. But be careful around Targon. He mustn't suspect you to be spying on him. And get me my information soon!"

"You don't understand," Kyril said. "Targon is not dangerous." Targon was his friend.

"Hey, is someone there?" came the outside voice, louder and closer now.

"You need to go," said the handler just as the second bell rang. "There is a key to the academy hidden under a rock next to the back door."

Kyril heard footsteps running toward the shed.

"I'll contact you," were the handler's last words before his magical face disappeared, leaving Kyril all alone once again.

Slowly, he pushed the door open. In the darkness, the faint moon left a silhouette of a man barely thirty feet away. With his heart racing and sweat lining the edges of his hairline, Kyril took off running toward the academy's back door. He heard footsteps behind him, but Kyril was much faster.

In short order he arrived at the back of the academy. Leaning down by the side of the door, he noticed a rock that had recently been moved. Underneath it lay a key. A key he stuck into the locked door and turned, then proceeded to walk into the hallway of the women's side of the academy.

CHAPTER NINE

S after dinner that evening, Sylvie met Joelle in the academy's library. She stood in the front foyer just inside the decorative double doors, looking down the long rows of books.

"Fascinating, isn't it?" Joelle said. "So much grander than the Wizard School on White Island."

"Much bigger than the one in the Wizard Conclave in Arc where I was trained too," Sylvie said in a whisper. "Who would have thought there were so many books? How will I find what I am searching for?"

"Hasani will help us," Joelle said with a twinkle in her eye. "He's very handsome! You'll love him."

Sylvie restrained herself from rolling her eyes. "Joelle, we're not here to flirt. I need to find answers."

Joelle pouted for a moment but pulled Sylvie forward. Soon, an elderly woman approached them.

"May I help you?"

Sylvie opened her mouth to ask her question, but Joelle blurted out first, "Is Hasani here?"

The librarian sighed and nodded her head. "He does seem to attract the women."

"He's so exotic," Joelle said with a sigh of her own.

"Who's exotic?" came a deeper voice, accompanied by a man walking out from behind a nearby shelf.

Joelle blushed and Sylvie almost choked with amusement at her reaction. Hasani was indeed exotic and quite a rare sight to see north of the Mahli Mountains to the south. His dark skin was even darker than Bale's and his hair was tied into small braids that hung down to his shoulders. Tied at the end of many of the braids were multicolored ribbons. His brown eyes were intelligent but held a tint of mirth in the way he watched them. His nose was broad and his lips a bit thicker than her own, but they fit him well. He stood a few inches taller than Sylvie and wore a burgundy robe.

Hasani bowed his head to the two women. "Hello Joelle. Are you feeling alright?" He smiled as he spoke.

"Oh, yes. Quite fine," Joelle said. "Never felt better. How are you? You look great. I mean good. I mean…"

"It's just that your face is flushed and I was wondering if you were ill," Hasani said with a wink at Sylvie.

Joelle flushed even brighter at his remark.

"Now, Hasani," said the librarian. "Don't tease the girls so."

Hasani laughed and extended his hand toward Sylvonna. "Forgive my manners. I am Hasani from the kingdom of Mahli, wizard apprentice of the mind and librarian scholar in training."

"Not that he needs much training," said the librarian with a hand on Hasani shoulder. "He's a natural at remembering where everything is at. Seems to be a trait from wizards in Mahli."

"I'm Sylvonna Hickory from Arc, a wizard of the earth," said Sylvie.

After shaking her hand Hasani clapped his own together. His dark eyes full of delight. "A full wizard already. You must be very strong."

Now it was Sylvie's turn to blush at the man's praise.

"And such beautiful hair," Hasani said, turning back to Joelle, he continued. "And yours, too, Joelle. To think there are more hair colors in this world than black was one of my greatest discoveries upon leaving Mahli. I've now been both south and north of my tiny kingdom. The world is such a wonderful and beautiful place."

He said the last words while glancing back and forth between Joelle and Sylvie.

"Enough chatter," said the librarian. "I'm sure these lovely ladies have a reason for being here?" she said in a way that implied she hoped they weren't just here to visit with Hasani.

"Yes, we do," Sylvie said, gaining control of the situation.

The librarian took a step away. "Then I'll leave you in my apprentice's capable hands. I have other wizards to help."

After she walked away, Hasani beckoned the two women farther into the library. Sylvie was once again enamored by not only the amount of books, but by the ancient architecture itself. The foot-wide crown moldings were carved by hand into beautiful and intricate designs. In the corners, the swirls turned into various mythical shapes. There were dragons, a phoenix, and even one of the famed Cremelino horses. That such magical things existed in the world amazed Sylvie. She had seen her High Wizard's famed Cremelino horse, a beautiful and magical creature of pure white and lightning speed.

"Sylvonna?" Hasani's voice brought her back to the task at hand.

"You can call her Sylvie," said Joelle. "It's what we all call her. Well, except for Bale and other mean people. They call her 'Twig.'" Joelle covered her mouth realizing she had said too much. "Sorry," she whispered to Sylvie.

Hasani only smiled at Joelle, but turned up a thick eyebrow at Sylvie.

"Sylvie is fine," she said, answering his unasked question. After a brief pause she decided to say what she had come for. "I'm searching for a book about magic artifacts--specifically medallions."

"What does this medallion look like?" Hasani asked.

Sylvie tried to remember what she had seen and felt on Kyril's hand. "It fits inside a palm and seems to have two, maybe three circles, inside one other. There are lines coming from the center and out to the edge." Sylvie paused for a moment but couldn't think of anything else at the moment.

"Do you know anything else about it?" Hasani asked. "That's very vague."

"I…think I've seen a similar one once before—whether in a picture or in real life, I can't seem to remember." Sylvie said with a shake of her head.

Hasani appeared deep in thought for a moment as they waited for him to answer. "Follow me." He crooked a finger at the two and with long steps hurried down an aisle of books. At the end, he turned right, and passed by four other aisles. Then he took them up a short flight of stairs where they passed by so many more aisles of books that Sylvie lost count.

They finally stopped at one, and walked down to almost the end. Hasani then pointed to a shelf. "You might find it here. There are books sorted by which kingdom they came from. But it's hard to know its origin with your description. There's a table over here," he said, pointing a few feet away. "You may use it while looking through the books."

"Thank you, Hasani," Sylvie said.

Hasani bowed his head. "My pleasure."

"You aren't staying with us?" Joelle asked with pleading eyes.

"I must help my other patrons, and then I am going to check into one of the locked rooms for your medallion." Hasani winked and smiled. When he turned to go, his braids swished mesmerizingly around his neck.

Sylvie heard Joelle sigh as he walked down the aisle and out of sight.

"Joelle!" Sylvie said, trying to get Joelle out of her daydream. "Are you going to help me?"

They both grabbed an armload of books, brought them to the table, and began flipping through the pages.

"Why do you care about this specific medallion?" Joelle asked.

"I…I saw it somewhere and I think it's important." She wasn't ready yet to confide that she had seen and felt it on Kyril's hand—a hand that she swore had glowed. But she suspected he might be getting into trouble and wanted to help him

For the next few hours they poured over various books, both ancient and new. Once or twice they thought they found it, but Sylvie didn't think it seemed quite right. Hasani returned twice more to check on them, bringing a few more books from other parts of the library.

"It's getting late," Joelle said with a yawn. "I have the first shift in the healing room tomorrow."

Sylvie hated to leave, but she agreed with Joelle. "I'm teaching a class of apprentices in the morning also, and need to finalize my preparation."

They began to close up the books and take them back to the shelves. After a few minutes though, they realized that they didn't remember where they had taken them all from.

Joelle let out a long breath of air. "Do you enjoy teaching?" she asked.

Sylvie smiled. "I do. I really do." Then she paused and scrunched her nose up a bit. "Except when I get the know-it-alls who think they know more than me."

"Do they?" Hasani came around from behind a shelf.

Both girls jumped in surprise.

"What?" Sylvie asked, confused.

"Do the apprentices know more than you sometimes?" Hasani said with a sparkle in his eye.

Sylvie didn't know where he was going with the question and only shook her head. "I don't know. Not usually."

"But there are apprentices that know more than wizards, they just haven't finished their studies yet, or proven themselves," Hasani said.

Sylvie then remembered that Hasani was an apprentice himself. She hadn't meant to hurt his feelings or anything. She pursed her lips, trying to figure out what to say.

Hasani burst out laughing. "I'm just joking with you Sylvonna. Is she always so serious?" he asked Joelle.

"When it comes to her studies and magic, yes she is." Joelle said with a smile.

"Not like some people I know." Sylvie glared playfully at Joelle, who was twirling a long strand of curly red hair around her finger.

"What? Me?" Joelle said, then turned to Hasani. "Do I not take my magic seriously? Who told her that? I came all the way from the Realm to study, teach, and help train healers here in Gildan. I can be serious when I want to."

When Joelle took a breath, Hasani laughed again, his voice carried musically, echoing off the nearby shelves and walls. It was then that Sylvie noticed another sizable book in his hands. It appeared old, and he held it with care.

"I'm sorry, Hasani," Sylvie said. "We need to go. I'm sure it's almost time for the curfew bell to ring."

Hasani nodded but put the book down on the table in front of them. He glanced around him to make sure no one else was nearby. "I'm not supposed to have this, but I think you might want to see it before you leave." He tenderly ran his fingers down the side of the book and then flipped it open.

Sylvie gasped. She couldn't keep her eyes from the yellowed page. "That seems like it could be it." It had the right shape and size, but it would be hard to know without asking Kyril more about it.

Joelle let out a squeal of delight at the news. "Finally."

Hasani put a finger to his lips and both women went quiet. Before anyone could speak again, the first curfew bell sounded.

Joelle sighed deeply and caught Sylvie's attention with her gaze.

Sylvie stood up and then put a hand on the edge of the table to steady herself. On the outside she was trying to be calm and obey the rules. As wizards, she and Joelle could stay out later, but Hasani needed to get back to his room soon.

"Hasani," said the librarian as she came around the corner. "Oh!" she exclaimed upon seeing the two women still in the library.

"We were just leaving," Sylvie said, glancing at Joelle.

The librarian gazed at the pile of books on the table and then her eyes widened when she saw that one that they had recently been looking at.

"You aren't supposed to go down there alone," the librarian said with a stern gaze. "You know the rules, Hasani. This book shouldn't leave the basement."

Hasani had the good grace to smile broadly. "I was just trying to help out these nice wizards." He handed the ancient book carefully back to the librarian. "I'll take care of the other books first thing in the morning. I promise."

The librarian shook her head and then let out a sigh. "Fine. Fine. Now off with you before you get caught after curfew."

Just as the three turned to go, a deep, quiet voice sounded behind them.

"Excuse me."

All four turned to see who it was.

"Scribe Gamal," said the librarian, appearing a bit perplexed. "What can I do for you at this late hour?"

Gamal scrutinized the three young wizards and frowned. Sylvie didn't care for Wizard Targon's scribe. The man, with his bald head and beady eyes, always seemed as if he knew something they didn't. She supposed that's what happened when you were a scribe and scholar for your entire life.

"We were just leaving," Sylvie said.

Hasani bowed briefly to Gamal and then followed Sylvie and Joelle down a long aisle of books. Turning a corner, the three stopped for a moment and eyed one another.

"That man has been coming in here every night for the past three days searching for something," Hasani said.

Sylvie furrowed her brow. "I don't like him."

"Me neither," added Joelle.

Hasani bid them farewell and headed off to the men's dormitory, while Sylvie and Joelle began the short walk to their personal rooms—small, but singular rooms that were given to full wizards.

As they turned the last corner, the final bell rang. They'd almost reached their rooms, which were adjacent to each other, when they heard a sound down the hall. Peering into the dim light they saw the outside door crash open and a figure run inside.

"It looks like a man," Joelle shrieked.

Sylvie instantly called upon her power and thrust her hands out in front of her, bathing the dim hall in a bright light. Running toward them was none other than Kyril. His normally brown face was pale and his eyes appeared shocked and worried. After almost running into the two women, he slid to a stop and ran his fingers through his thick hair. Sweat dripped down the side of his face.

"Sylvie!"

"Kyril, what are you doing here?" Sylvie asked. "What's wrong?"

"Are you hurt?" Joelle appeared sympathetic to his possible plight. She reached her hand out toward his. "Do you need a healer?"

Kyril snatched it back, but not before a glowing light spread across it.

"I need to go." Kyril began to jog away.

"Kyril, what's going on?" Sylvie asked again.

"Nothing. Nothing," Kyril said without turning around. "Need to get to my room before someone sees me."

Then he was gone and around a corner. Sylvie let the lights dim again, and both she and Joelle stood there for a moment in silence.

"Something's not right here," Sylvie said.

Joelle nodded her head. Before anything else could be said, a door opened farther down the hall and a woman walked out of her room. She was at least a decade older than Sylvie and one of the elder instructors at the academy, a wizard of the earth like herself. The woman didn't say anything but glanced back and forth down the hall looking for the source of Kyril's footsteps. Without another word, both Sylvie and Joelle stepped into their own rooms.

CHAPTER TEN

The next day was their weekly day off from classes. That didn't mean that Kyril didn't have schoolwork and studying to do, but at least he could do it on his own schedule. He stayed in bed a bit longer than usual, and then found himself pacing the floor of his dorm room when Tal came into the room from his morning meal.

"Kyril!" Tal said after being in the room for only a minute. "I try not to get into your business, but could you please stop that pacing? You're driving me crazy."

"You're just like the rest of them," Kyril said. His frustration level was at an all-time high. "Noble born—you think we should all bow to you."

"Now you're just being foolish," Tal said. He blocked Kyril's way across the room.

Kyril huffed and moved to go around him, but Tal blocked his way once again. "Kyril, you need to stop this. I don't know what's gotten into you. You know, everyone is beginning to talk about you more."

That got Kyril's attention, and he stopped mid-stride and frowned at Tal. "What does that mean, Tal?"

"It means there is strange talk about you," Tal said firmly. "Jumping off of walls, glowing hands, running through the halls late at night, secret meetings with Wizard Targon."

Kyril put his hand to his head and took a deep breath. He turned around and went to his bed, sat down, and tried to think for a minute to himself. Something that seemed to be more and more difficult these days.

"Everyone wants to tell me what to do. Everyone wants me to be someone I'm not," Kyril said, peering down at the floor.

"Has Bale been bothering you again?" Tal asked.

"He tries, but my new friends are always there. Always!"

"Isn't that good?" Tal asked. "Don't you want friends?"

"Of course I want friends," Kyril said, hands clenched together. "But I've never had them. So why do they want to be friends now? Why can't I stand up to Bale on my own without them? I am a wizard—even if only an apprentice."

"Bale is…" Tal began, but couldn't seem to find the right words to say.

"You're a noble Tal, and a wizard." Kyril stood up. "That should put you on higher footing than Bale."

Tal shook his head. "You don't understand things, Kyril. Bale's family is close to the emperor. That gives them strength."

"What about our strength?" Kyril shouted. "Doesn't being a wizard count for something?"

"Being a wizard means we serve the people. You know that. That's what we're here for. Soon, you and I will go to our first assignment, and as wizards of the minds and scholars, we will advise leaders and do research."

"But why should we only advise leaders?" Kyril shot back. "Why shouldn't we be them?"

Tal's dark eyes opened wide and he watched the door as if expecting someone to come in. "That's dangerous talk, Kyril. Where did you hear such things?"

"From Wizard Targon Quereshi," Kyril said. "You're a wizard of the mind. You should come and meet him."

Tal shook his head. "You're going to get yourself in trouble. You should stay away from him."

Too late for that, thought Kyril. But he was torn between the excitement he felt around Targon and his group, and the recent instructions from his handler to spy on him.

"He's got grand ideas for us!" Kyril became more animated as his hands flew around him and his voice grew louder. "Jordan and Altia and…"

Tal burst out laughing and took a moment to contain himself.

Kyril couldn't see what was so funny.

"That's what this is all about, isn't it?" Tal said as if the understanding of some great secret had suddenly dawned on him. "Taking our best clothes, being out late at night, trying to impress your new friends. It's all about a girl—you're trying to impress Altia."

"What?" Kyril blurted out. He could feel his face heat up and a dribble of sweat rolling down his left temple. "No. That's not it at all."

Tal laughed again, and Kyril was just about to jump toward him when the door opened and Sayid and Behn walked in.

Kyril stopped mid-stride, and both he and Tal turned toward the door.

"What's going on here?" Behn said. "Your face is all red, Kyril." He brought up a hand in front of him and waved it around a few times. A cool breeze stirred from his hand and filled the room.

"Behn!" Sayid said. "You're not supposed to use magic like that here."

Behn only shrugged. "Who's going to tell?" Then he turned with a scowl to Kyril. "No one here is going to tell, *are they?*"

Kyril just shook his head and headed toward the door. "I need to go."

The cool wind died down behind him. Stepping through the threshold, he slammed the door closed behind him. He stood by the door and tried to regain his composure. Other apprentices walked by, giving him strange looks and then turning and whispering to their friends. Behind the closed door he heard Tal laugh and mention Altia's name, and then his other two roommates joined in the laughter.

How could he ever go back there again? They would tease him forever, especially Sayid, who was too young to even understand half of it. And it wasn't Altia that was causing him to change. It was Targon. Targon, one of the greatest wizards of the mind in Gildan—and the man that the spymaster and emperor wanted him to spy on.

He slammed his fist against the stone wall, earning him additional attention from passersby. Without knowing for sure where he was going, he took off running, his burgundy cloak billowing out behind him. He ran through the boy's hall, out the door, and up the paved walkway toward the north part of the academy buildings.

The sun was warm on his face and the nape of his neck began to sweat. The scent of sweet summer flowers drifted by him as he ran through the gardens. In the soft breeze, droplets of water from nearby fountains dashed his warm skin. Coming to the far north end, he paused a moment to catch his breath. Glancing up in front of him he saw the large domed palace of the Emperor Mezar Alrishitar. It stood on a hill in the middle of the city overlooking the sprawling people of Gildan.

Once his breathing slowed, he opened the door and stepped back inside. There were fewer people here, and he was able to walk down the hallway for a minute without anyone bothering him.

Turning a corner, he slowed down and walked more casually, enjoying the solitude and taking time to observe the lifelike gold-framed paintings that lined the hallway where only the most powerful at the academy lived.

Now he was having second thoughts about what to do. He stood for a moment studying a beautiful painting. It was of a young man in his early twenties. By his brown skin and hair color, he could tell he was from Gildan. The man sat atop a grand Cremelino horse, the famed magical white horses that ran faster than anyone could imagine and spoke to their masters' minds. The man's hair was tied back behind him with a gold band and his hand was outstretched in front of him. A brilliant light of multiple colors swirled out from his fingers.

"It's quite an amazing likeness, isn't it?" said a voice behind him.

Kyril's heart missed a beat and he flinched. He hadn't heard anyone approach.

"Wizard Targon," Kyril said, turning to him and bowing his head.

Targon only smiled and continued to study the painting himself. "It's our emperor, Mezar Alrishitar, when he was younger. The King of the Realm gave him one of the magical Cremelinos. Isn't it a magnificent show of power?"

"Yes," Kyril said. The painting appeared so lifelike. "I wish I had that kind of power."

Targon turned his head and peered down almost six inches at Kyril. The man's wrinkled face was soft and held a hint of kindness. "And what would you do with that kind of power, Kyril Siravan?"

Kyril hung his head for a moment. Thoughts of Bale teasing him rushed through his mind followed by the memory of Tal's mocking attitude. Why couldn't his roommate comprehend how Kyril could like someone like Altia? Even Sylvie probably was only his friend out of pity for him.

He quickly repented of the last thought. It hadn't been fair to Sylvie. She had been a good friend. But the rest never respected him or treated him well.

"If I had that kind of power I would show everyone how powerful I was," Kyril blurted out. "Then they'd know who was really in charge of things.

However, instead of ridicule, Targon only put his arm around Kyril's shoulder and squeezed in a friendly gesture. Kyril felt confidence and assurance like he had never felt before.

Targon leaned his head down a bit. "And what would you do for that kind of power?"

"Anything," Kyril said without any hesitation. He was tired of being bullied. "Anything."

CHAPTER ELEVEN

An hour later, Kyril leaned back in the hard wooden chair he had been sitting in, listening to wizard Targon and a few of his other followers. He was sobered by what they spoke about. He hadn't realized there were so many injustices going on around them. Thoughts of his handler's warning about Targon rushed to the forefront of his mind and he put a hand to his head to stop a building headache.

"Kyril," Targon said from across the room. "Are you feeling all right?"

"Yes, I'm fine," Kyril stuttered after a moment.

Targon left a small group of wizards and walked to the back of the room where Kyril sat. He squatted down on his haunches so that he was at the same level as Kyril.

"If something is bothering you, you can tell me," Targon said. "I value your opinion."

"My opinion?" Kyril said. *No one ever has ever listened to me.*

"Of course," Targon smiled broadly. "I listen to all my apprentices and wizards."

A distant warning went off in Kyril's head as Targon said *my wizards*. He hadn't pledged himself to the man…or had he? Had his actions showing up here been construed as loyalty to Targon?

"You have doubts about what we do?" Targon asked.

Kyril turned his head, expecting the wizard to be angry, but instead he met kind eyes that held compassion for him. No one had ever treated him that way. More often they gave him pity or frustration. Did Targon really care about him?

"I do care about you, Kyril," Targon said. "As does everyone else here." He waved his hand around the room. A few other wizards and apprentices looked over and caught Kyril's eyes. They nodded their heads at him and smiled.

"How did you know what I was thinking?" Kyril moved up to the edge of his chair and Targon stood up.

"Come, let me show you something." Targon reached his hand out for Kyril's to help him stand up from the chair.

Without thinking, Kyril stuck out his left hand and Targon took a hold of it. As Targon brought him up from his seat, Kyril's hand began to glow. Kyril groaned at the timing and snatched his hand back and into the folds of his cloak.

Targon's eyebrows rose up in a question, but nothing was said. He only turned and beckoned Kyril to follow him. Kyril felt as if everyone in the room was watching him—but in reality he knew they weren't. He just hoped they hadn't seen the glow of his marked hand. He wondered why it had responded to Targon the way it had.

Targon stopped for a moment and filled up two glasses with a sweet smelling juice, one for Kyril and one for himself. After handing one to Kyril, he continued toward a door at the far end of the room. Kyril followed, stopping only once to take a sip of the juice. However, before his lips touched the rim, Targon turned around.

Kyril paused, and Targon reached a hand back and softly wrapped his fingers around Kyril's glass. Instantly, Kyril felt it grow cool to his touch.

"Now try it," Targon said. "It's much better chilled."

Kyril did as the wizard suggested. The cool juice—a mixture of grape and something else, he guessed—tasted wonderful on the hot day. Targon opened the door and the two of them entered a large study. As Targon closed the door, Kyril glanced around while taking a few more sips of juice.

With a flourish of his hand, Targon waved the drapes open, and light spread throughout the tidy room. A shiny mahogany desk sat in front of the window with a comfortable-looking chair tucked in behind it. Another small table and three chairs sat in the middle of the room on a rug with patterns of circles and diamonds. Bookshelves lined one side of the room, while cabinets with other decorative items lined the other. It was to these cabinets that Targon walked.

Kyril took a few steps closer as Targon reached up to a high shelf and brought down a medallion on a chain. It was as black as night, and seemed to even repel the sunlight. But the blackness was so deep and pure and beautiful in its own way.

Targon brought it down closer and held it out in front of Kyril, and something inside of him flared to life. He struggled to breathe for a moment, but then the feeling receded, leaving only his left hand warm under his cloak. He realized he had never seen the black medallion before, but there was something familiar about it.

"You've seen it before?" Targon asked.

Kyril shook his head. "Never, but it is beautiful."

"Yes it is," Targon said. "I made it myself. But it is not complete yet."

Kyril felt his face scrunch up at the information. "What do you mean?" he ventured.

"When I was a young boy I had three cruel older brothers. One had some slight talent for a few magical acts—mostly skills that helped him to steal from and bully others. The other two were mundane—no magic at all. But because they were older and bigger than me, they picked on me. You know what that's like, right?"

Kyril nodded his head. *Yes I do.*

"Their friends had powerful fathers. A banker, a local magistrate, and a nobleman who had inherited all his money. As a young boy, all I wanted was to be with them—my older brothers." Targon dangled the medallion in his hand and its swinging back and forth drew Kyril's attention.

"As I grew older I began to realize I had stronger powers than any of them—of anyone in my village. But I had to suppress them. If they knew that I was different from everyone, they would pick on me more, and I wasn't strong enough yet to fight back. So, I ran away."

Kyril couldn't take his eyes off of the medallion as it continued to swing back and forth. Its darkness attracted him, but something inside him also pushed back. He glanced up at Targon who appeared momentarily annoyed, but then a smooth smile replaced the expression.

"Where did you go?" Kyril asked.

"At the southern tip of the Superstition Mountains is the headwaters of the Korian River. I stole a small boat and took it south to Hasari, down in Cyrene."

Kyril had never known anyone that had gone to any of the united territories before. Targon continued swinging his medallion in front of Kyril, but Kyril was too interested in the wizard's story to look at it anymore.

"And what happened there?"

"The people there accept magic for what it is. Power." A bright gleam filled Targon's eyes. "Those with more power and magic are respected more and sought after. With the help of a local wizard I learned to control my powers. By the age of seventeen, I was stronger than he was."

"What happened to him?" Kyril was caught up in the story.

Targon looked down at the medallion and it stopped swinging. He took the medallion and set it on one of his open palms. With his other hand, he ran his fingers lovingly over it. Without turning his head up, he glanced up at Kyril with his eyes.

"My master was no longer needed and he knew it," Targon said in a chilling voice. "Soon after, I started the crafting of this medallion."

Did Targon kill his master? He didn't dare ask. If he did, there must have been a good reason. Maybe his master had tried to hurt Targon. Maybe he had been jealous of his powers.

"Then I returned home to Gildan, a full wizard with amazing powers." Targon glanced up and locked onto Kyril's eyes.

"Did you go back to your family?"

"Only for a short time," Targon said. "I had unfinished business there." Targon began to swing the medallion again. The blackness seemed to sap the light from the room. "I continued to strengthen the medallion with what it needed.

Kyril wanted to ask what Targon meant, but wasn't sure how to frame his question. Thoughts of the black medallion brought up his mother's medallion in his mind, and with it the memory of his burned hand.

There was a knock on the door and Targon put the medallion back on the top shelf of the cabinet. "This is our secret, Kyril," Targon said with a voice of warning.

The wizard took a few long, quick steps to the door and jerked it open.

"I was not to be disturbed," Targon said in a voice that instantly gave Kyril a headache. "Someone will pay for this."

Kyril searched for another way out when he heard Targon arguing with Gamal, but he couldn't see one. There could very well be a secret door, but if there was, it wasn't obvious. Targon turned back to Kyril and fire danced in his eyes.

"Stay here," he ordered. "I'll be back in a moment."

And the door shut.

Kyril's heart was going to jump out of his chest. He downed the rest of the juice, but his throat still felt dry and his head ached from Targon's outburst. Looking up at the shelf, he noticed other artifacts and decorations. Many were black like the medallion. He paced the room for a moment and was just about to head to the door, despite Targon's warning, when the wizard came back inside.

With a deep breath, Targon was once again all warm smiles. "I'm sorry about that Kyril. Sometimes things need to be taken care of quickly."

Kyril only nodded.

"Don't be worried," Targon said as he walked up to Kyril and put a hand on his shoulder. His fingers squeezed a little too hard and Kyril bit back a groan. "I told you my story because I trust you, Kyril. I feel as if we are kindred spirits. Something has drawn us together."

Targon's eyes traveled to where Kyril's hand was still tucked inside his cloak. It lingered there for a moment as if Targon knew about the mark there, but he stayed silent on the subject and eventually turned away.

"Soon we will both have our rightful due, Kyril," Targon said with a flourish of his cloak. "Soon!"

* * *

Kyril left Targon's suite and walked to the nearest door out of the academy buildings. It was hot, but he didn't care. He needed to get away and be alone for a while. He had a lot to think about. Targon's black medallion worried him. And his own power welling up inside of him worried him even more.

Before he had gone far, he heard his name being called behind him. He turned around and saw a young apprentice girl approaching. He recognized her, but didn't know her name.

"Kyril Siravan?" the girl said.

"Yes?"

"I was told to give you this." The girl handed him an envelope. Upon seeing the writing on the outside, his heart dropped.

The girl turned and started to walk away.

"Who gave this to you?" he asked.

She stopped and twisted her head back toward him. "I'm not sure. It somehow ended up in my hand when I left the library."

Kyril shook his head, wondering what that meant. The girl went on her way, and Kyril walked a bit farther around the side of the school before opening the envelope.

It said that his handler wanted to talk to him again, that very night after dark. *Why does it always have to be after dark?* Kyril grumbled. Why couldn't they talk in person? It was hard trusting someone he never even met.

"Ahhh!" Kyril yelled out as he crumbled the ball of paper in his hands. Without paying any attention he started running, heading around the nearest corner…and he ran smack into someone. They both fell down hard on the ground. He shook his head a few times to get his bearings back and then glanced at who he had run in to.

"Kyril," exclaimed Sylvie with a smile. "I've been meaning to talk to you."

"Sylvie," mumbled Kyril. Not the person he wanted to talk to right then.

CHAPTER TWELVE

"Where are you going in such a hurry?" Sylvie asked once they'd both stood up and dusted themselves off as best as they could.

"I…I…" Kyril stuttered. He didn't even know where he was going himself.

Sylvie gave him a sympathetic smile that he wasn't in the mood for. He took a deep breath and tried to steady his mind. He was a wizard of the mind, wasn't he? The discipline was fated to rule the world, if he believed Targon.

"Kyril, what's this?" Sylvie said. She took a step and reached down to pick up a balled-up piece of paper from the ground. "Did you drop it?"

"Give it to me!" Just as Sylvie's fingers touched its edges, he snatched it from her and stuffed it into his pocket.

"What is wrong with you, Kyril?" Sylvie had both hands on her hips. Her short hair bobbed angrily around her red face. "You've done nothing but be rude to me lately. What have I done to deserve such treatment?"

She was right, but Kyril also knew he needed to start standing up for himself. He shook his head to clear it. Targon was getting to him. He realized that. But the powerful wizard had some good points. His fingers still held the balled-up note tightly inside his pocket. He thought about the contents and winced at what he had been asked to do. He guessed now was as good a time as any to start playing the part.

"Sylvie…" he began, and then he knew what he must do. Though it would hurt him horribly to do it. "I've found some new friends."

Sylvie's eyes went wide, then Kyril watched as moisture formed at the edges. He couldn't bear to see her cry and turned away.

Sylvie's hand reached out and took his—the one with the scar. He tried to pull it away, but she held on tight. He pulled harder and she stomped her foot hard next to his. The ground shook and rocks buckled out of the ground under him as he struggled to keep his balance. He realized how angry and hurt Sylvie must be to use magic like that.

Still holding onto his hand, she turned his palm over face-up and ran her fingers softly over the scars. It was an intimate gesture, and Kyril felt something stir deep within him.

"How did it happen?" Sylvie asked.

Kyril averted his eyes from her question. He couldn't meet her gaze. He steeled himself once again and used his mind to block his feelings. In response to his negative thoughts his palm flared up with a brilliant bright light, the lines and rings of the scar forming a pattern in the air above his outstretched hand.

Sylvie let go and took a step back. Her eyes once again went as wide as saucers, but she said nothing.

Kyril was overwhelmed with the feeling that he could transport himself away from Sylvie. It was the same feeling he had when he thought he could fly, but something was different this time. The power was deeper. The voice in his mind was clearer now.

Sylvie was still staring at him, and without thinking he swirled his hand around, so the brilliant light formed patterns in the air. Soon the light formed a wall of bright colors around him and with a final mental push, he leapt away from Sylvie.

"Kyril!" came the faded echo of a forlorn cry. "What have you done?"

The lights around Kyril blinked out and he found himself a few hundred feet away from where Sylvie stood. He'd actually transported somewhere! He turned to run again, but someone stood behind him and he skidded to a stop.

"Jordan," Kyril said. "Were you following me?"

"Targon asked me to keep an eye on you," Jordan said, his sparkling white teeth grinning back at Kyril with a gaze that didn't appear as friendly as it used to be. "Seems he was right to do so. You've been hiding things from us Kyril."

Kyril frowned for a moment but then remembered what he had done and smiled. "I did it," he said softly. "I transported. Targon was right. I do have something special inside me."

A look akin to jealousy appeared—and then quickly disappeared—from Jordan's face. Kyril saw something move out of the corner of his eye, and he turned and watched Sylvie walk away across the yard from him. Her shoulders were slumped. Kyril took a step toward her, but Jordan put out his arm and stopped him.

"She doesn't understand," Jordan said. "Those of earth and heart don't understand what we can do with our minds."

"I guess," Kyril said, still conflicted about his feelings toward Sylvie.

For the second time in the last few minutes, someone reached down to the ground to grab the paper that had once again fallen out of Kyril's pocket.

"What's this?" Jordan said as he picked it up. He began to unfold it.

Kyril panicked. The note would condemn him for sure. Targon, Jordan and all those with him would banish him out of their group. Or worse.

"Give it to me!" Kyril snatched the paper away from Jordan.

With a quick uncontrolled thought of Targon, the bright light once again encircled his left hand. Before Kyril could think of anything else, the light flashed brightly and once more he transported. This time, upon opening his eyes, he let out a loud groan before leaning over and almost vomiting.

Pushing the nausea away he stood straight and glanced around before groaning out loud.

He was in Targon's office; the very place he recently left. If he got caught in here alone, he would be in even bigger trouble than if they had found the note.

He took a step toward the door, but something on the cabinet shelf caught his attention. It was the black medallion that Targon had been holding. He knew he shouldn't, but with a quick scan of the room, he took three rapid steps and reached for the medallion.

With his hand hovering over it, he hesitated. A burning in his own hand caused him to stop and pull away. The outline of his scar glowed faintly. When he moved it over the black medallion, a faint glow showed that same pattern on the black medallion itself. He hadn't noticed that before.

With his unmarked hand Kyril picked up the medallion and turned it over. There was nothing etched on the other side; only a smooth surface met his fingers. He shivered with thoughts of how Targon had made the medallion and why it had the same markings as the scar on his palm.

He realized now what he needed to do. He needed to find the medallion that had belonged to his mother. The very same one that had burned his skin. He wasn't sure how he would get away from the academy, but eventually he would.

Hearing sounds at the door, he put the black medallion back and once again stretched out his hand and thought about being back in his own room. Lights flashed as he heard the doorknob click. Just before transporting, he saw Targon beginning to enter the room. A voice called to the wizard, and with hand still on the doorknob he turned away from the room as Kyril disappeared.

A moment later he ran into his own bed and fell over. Luckily, none of his roommates were around.

CHAPTER THIRTEEN

"Sylvie!" Joelle tapped her hand on the tabletop. "Sylvie, are you listening to me?"

"What?" She had not, in fact, been listening.

It was evening, and they were once again sitting at a table in the library. Hasani was supposed to have met them there almost a half hour earlier, but he had not shown up yet. They were going to study the book he had found. Sylvie hoped it would give her some insight into what was bothering Kyril. She worried about his new friends.

"What do you think of Wizard Targon?" Sylvie asked, instead of responding to whatever Joelle had been talking about.

"Targon?" Joelle's eyes open wide in surprise at the change in subject. "He's one of the most powerful wizards of the mind in Gildan. I've heard he is quite outspoken about the emperor's openness to those who are not wizards. But that's about it. I did heal his scribe Gamal one time—he came to the library the other night when we were leaving. Now *he's* creepy."

Joelle shivered and wrapped her arms around herself.

"What do you mean?" Sylvie asked.

"I was healing him because he had a dislocated shoulder—wouldn't tell me what happened," Joelle began. "I had the feeling he was doing something he shouldn't have been doing. I went to push up his sleeve to take a look at the rest of his arm and he swatted it away—but not before I saw a swirling tattoo. He stared at me with his big eyes and told me just to heal his shoulder."

"I don't trust Targon or his group," Sylvie said. She didn't know if she should say anything yet to Joelle about her conversation with the prince. "And now they've wrapped poor Kyril up in something—I just know it."

Joelle smiled and appeared to relax a bit, after her words about Targon's scribe. "That's what you're worried about? Kyril? I'm sure he'll be fine. Maybe this will be good for him."

Sylvie only grunted. She wasn't sure about that. Something was going on. It was too coincidental that the prince came to her about his suspicions at the same time that Kyril had begun acting strangely. And the way he transported right in front of her? That wasn't a common wizard power—especially for an apprentice.

"I don't like not knowing what's going on," Sylvie said, more harshly than she'd intended. "Where's Hasani, anyway?"

Joelle flinched at her outburst, but then glanced around the room and shrugged her shoulders.

"I'm going to find him." Sylvie stood up and took a step away from the table when the librarian came running around the corner.

"Something's happened to Hasani," the librarian said. Leaning over, she put her palms to her knees, trying to catch her breath.

Joelle jumped up, her unruly hair waving around her face as she raced to the librarian's side. She put a hand on her shoulder and looked over at Sylvie with worried eyes.

"What do you mean?" Joelle said.

The librarian took a few more seconds, and then stood up straight. "The room is unlocked, and papers are scattered everywhere."

"What room?" Sylvie asked, glancing around to see who else was in the library. At this time of night, the final hour before curfew, most of the wizards and apprentices headed outside for a respite from the daily heat.

The librarian gave them both a hard, knowing eye. "Don't think I don't know what goes on around me in my library."

Sylvie backed up a step and pursed her lips.

"Have a seat," Joelle offered the woman, her healer instincts kicking in. "Can you breathe all right? Do you need anything?"

The librarian swatted Joelle's arm away. "I'm fine. Now what did you have Hasani searching for?"

Sylvie and Joelle glanced at each other. Finally, Sylvie spoke.

"He was helping us find some information on a medallion. Nothing special." Sylvie shrugged and tried to appear casual about it.

The librarian peered up at Sylvie, and Sylvie felt once again like an apprentice. The woman was old enough to be her grandmother, and her powers of the mind, especially in remembering things, were legendary. She eventually stood and crooked her finger at the two young women.

"Come with me," she said, and began walking away from the table.

Joelle and Sylvie had to hurry to keep up. The three walked in silence through rows of books, finally arriving at a stairway that led down beneath them. The librarian paused for a moment and tilted her head as if listening for something. She took a step down and then stopped again and turned and looked back up at the two young women. She studied them for a moment as if deciding something.

"I can trust you two, can't I?"

"Of course," Sylvie said without hesitation.

The librarian huffed and turned back down the stairs. "We shall see about that," she mumbled. "This is not usually a place for foreigners."

Joelle and Sylvie glanced at each other once again and both shrugged their shoulders. Sylvie had no idea what was going on. They followed the librarian down the stairs, and the lower they went, the mustier it became. A mixture of old paper, ink, and stone pervaded her senses. At the bottom of the stairs, they turned a corner and Sylvie put her hand on the roughhewn walls. Two torches set in the wall lit their way down a narrow walkway.

As they walked, the librarian's pace quickened, but she constantly glanced back behind them. At the end of the hall they came to a thick iron door. It sat partially ajar and, with only a slight push from the librarian, it opened enough for them to enter.

Light flared from the librarian's hand, lighting the space in front of them. The room into which they entered appeared to be more of a lobby than anything else. Three groups of chairs sat around the room, and six doors surrounded them. One door beside them was open and light spilled out of it. It was to this room that the librarian motioned Sylvie and Joelle to follow her.

Coming to the door, they all peered inside. Joelle gasped and covered her mouth with her hand. Books and papers were scattered about, but it wasn't the mess that horrified them. It was the blood dripping on the floor and splattered over some of the torn pages that caught their attention.

Sylvie could hardly believe what she was seeing. She followed the drops of blood from inside the room to where they led out the door and following them across the small lobby she could tell they ended at a closed door on the far side.

"I suspect that Hasani was here to bring you back the book he had shown you last night," the librarian said. Her lips were tight, and her voice brokered no argument from Sylvie or Joelle.

"You think the blood…is…Hasani's?" Joelle managed.

"I don't know," the librarian said. "You tell me."

Sylvie didn't understand. But Joelle nodded and walked forward. She squatted down on the ground, pulling her long green robes up so as to not touch the blood. She hesitantly reached forward and ran her right pointer finger across one of the bloodstains.

"It's still moist," Joelle said.

"Then whoever did this hasn't been gone long," Sylvie pointed out. Light flared around her and she turned toward the far door. "Where does that door go? We have to go after them."

The librarian ignored Sylvie and turned back to Joelle. "Tell me. Is it the boy's blood?"

Joelle raised her finger to her lips, and with a flick of her tongue, tasted it. Sylvie scrunched up her face at the thought of tasting someone else's blood.

"It's male." Joelle closed her eyes with a look of determination.

Sylvie hadn't known about this type of ability before—she was amazed. Could Joelle tell whose blood it was?

The seconds dragged on. Every moment they wasted, Hasani could be falling deeper into danger. "Joelle?" she said, prodding her friend.

Finally, Joelle opened her eyes and shook her head. "It's not Hasani's."

The librarian let out a breath of held air and wiped moisture from her eyes. "Thank goodness. But can you tell whose it is?"

"There is not a lot here," Joelle said. "But I do know it belongs to someone older, someone with wizard abilities, and someone from Gildan."

"How can you tell all of that by a drop of blood?" Sylvie exclaimed. "That's incredible."

Joelle shrugged. "It's a gift I have. Every kingdom, race, sex, and age of people have a slightly different structure to their blood. With enough of it, I could tell more."

"So, it's not Hasani's blood, but Hasani is missing," said the librarian.

Sylvie recognized the churning thoughts of a wizard of the mind. They thought things through. That's where their power came from.

"But did someone take him?" Sylvie asked. "Who has access to this room?"

"From the library, only me, Hasani, and the heads of each wizard discipline." The librarian appeared deep in thought.

"Targon!" shouted Sylvie. She didn't trust that man.

The librarian shook her head. "It's possible, but he is not a head of any wizard class, only a very strong wizard with a growing following. Someone would have needed to give him a key."

"Or he could have stolen it," Sylvie said. She took a moment to peer around the room. "What's missing?"

The librarian walked around the small room—Sylvie guessed it was about eight feet squared. A table sat in the center with what appeared to be usually four chairs around it—two of which were currently on the floor. Three shelves of books covered all the walls but the one where the door was. At least a third of the books were scattered over the table and across the floor.

Joelle moved over closer to Sylvie and put a hand on her arm. "We have to find him."

Sylvie nodded, but before she could say anything, the librarian came back to them.

"There is only one book missing," she said.

"Are you sure?" Sylvie asked. How could the woman tell with all the mess?

"I know my library, wizard!" she answered back firmly. "The book Hasani showed to you two the other night—a book he shouldn't have taken out of here."

"What book?" Joelle asked, still holding on to Sylvie's arm.

"The Western Codex. An ancient book about powerful magic and magically created relics."

"The medallion…" Sylvie said under her breath.

"What did you say?" the librarian asked.

Sylvie's mind, however, was already on another task. She stepped back into the lobby and began following the drops of blood to the door on the opposite side of where they had entered.

"Where does this door go to?" She stopped, touched the cool steel, and then turned back around.

The librarian's face went pale and she shook her head a few times.

"Where?" Sylvia repeated, her voice growing louder.

The librarian sighed. "To the palace. Behind this door is a secret passageway that leads to the palace itself."

Joelle's eyes went wide before, to Sylvie's surprise, she grabbed a staff that had been left by the doorway, perhaps by a forgetful old wizard in the past. She pushed past the librarian and put her hand on the door.

"We need to find Hasani," Joelle stated.

Sylvie agreed, and together, all three of them opened the door and entered the dark tunnel.

CHAPTER FOURTEEN

The sun had just set, and the curfew bells would sound in an hour—plenty of time for Kyril, Altia, and Jordan to complete their task. Currently, the three of them were walking in the shadows of a small lane than went north between the Wizard Academy and the city of Gildan. Soon after entering the city, they headed in the general direction of the palace. Sitting up on top of a small hill, it was hard to miss. A few other people hurrying to get home passed their way, but none paid them much attention. Students were a regular sight around this part of the city.

Kyril turned his eyes to the side and watched Altia without being obvious. The shaved side of Altia's head faced him, so he could clearly see her dark eyes and painted lips. His heart skipped a beat when he saw her lips twitch upwards just a bit.

Did she know he was watching her?

Without any warning he stumbled and pitched forward. Arms flailing to the side, he tried to catch himself. Just before he thought he would fall for sure, Jordan snagged his arms and righted him back to his feet.

"Thanks," Kyril mumbled.

"You have to pay attention, Kyril," Jordan scolded. "This is serious business for Wizard Targon. What were you thinking?"

"Yes, what were you thinking?" Altia said clearly mocking Kyril "You do know the plan, right?"

Kyril continued walking forward, keeping his burning cheeks away from his companions. He knew the plan. It was to be his first assignment for Targon. The wizard had gone over it again for the second time with them earlier that evening. It wasn't the plan that bothered him; it was his handler who he had told the plan to the night before. What would they do with the information?

"What does he want with a stupid book anyway?" Kyril asked.

Jordan grabbed him by the arm and pulled him to a stop. Kyril tried to wrench his arm back, but Jordan hung on tightly. Altia moved in closer and Kyril glanced back and forth between the two of them.

"Are you questioning Wizard Targon's intelligence?" Jordan said. "Because that would be a very bad mistake to make. He's taken you into his confidence and is trying to help you—trying to help all of us get what we are due."

Kyril's gut clenched and his knees shook. But he couldn't let his weakness show. His handler told him to make sure they went through with the plan. He couldn't let Jordan or Altia suspect him.

It took all he had, but he glared back at Jordan. "Are you questioning my loyalty?"

It was quiet for a moment. A bird flew overhead and cawed, and the voice of a mother calling for her child echoed in the distance. Kyril breathed heavily and tried not to faint.

Then Altia swatted Jordan's arm away from Kyril and started laughing. "Oh, Kyril. You are definitely a one of a kind. Who thought you had it in you? Let him go, Jordan. Kyril doesn't have the strength to stand up to Targon. Why would he cross him? I'm sure he knows that we all work for the same purpose."

Jordan scowled at Kyril and Altia, then turned and began walking toward the back wall of the palace. Altia hung back a few yards with Kyril and grinned at him.

"What?" Kyril asked, not comfortable with her gaze.

"You do know Jordan is a wizard of the mind, don't you?" Altia said. "He's not like us apprentices. He could have taken you down before you knew what was happening. He is Targon's nephew and was raised by him from a young age, and I don't think he likes the attention you have been getting from his uncle."

Kyril wiped moisture off his forehead and groaned. "Really?"

Altia nodded, and her bright lipstick caught Kyril's attention again.

"Kyril, focus," Altia said.

Jordan twisted to look at him with questioning eyes, but the others only smiled at him, and he grunted and continued walking at a quicker pace. "He takes these missions seriously, doesn't he?" Kyril asked.

"And why shouldn't he? We all do." Altia grew serious. "I know you're new to this, Kyril, but we are so close to getting the admiration we deserve. Targon is working on a way to make us all more powerful and more respected. But he has been distracted lately and we need to get back on track."

"And that's why he needs the book," sighed Kyril. But he wasn't sure that everything Targon did was for them. He had much to gain himself if he found a way to be more powerful.

Soon, they came to the last row of houses behind the palace wall. From his vantage point, Kyril could see the large domes rising up above them. A perfumed scent of flowers from the famed gardens on the other side of the wall drifted across Kyril's senses.

Jordan led them to one of the smaller homes and knocked on the door. It opened only a crack and Kyril saw a beady set of brown eyes watching them. Soon, however, it opened fully, and a small man barely as tall as Kyril beckoned them inside.

"Jordan," said the man, reaching around and giving him a big hug. "It's been a while."

Jordan smiled and nodded as he returned the embrace. Pointing beside him, he said, "You know Altia. And this is Kyril, a new recruit."

The man chuckled in a way that made Kyril wonder what the man knew that Kyril didn't.

"Name's Oden, my friend," said the little man. "Nice to have you in the company."

Kyril gave a short nod to the gentleman but said nothing.

"I presume you are here to use the doorway?" said Oden to Jordan.

Jordan nodded his head. "Yes. We shouldn't be gone long."

Even though Kyril had no idea what was going on, Oden seemed to understand and led them through his small house to a back room. On the back wall was a bureau of drawers. Oden motioned the three of them over, and they proceeded to scoot the heavy piece of furniture out of the way. Behind it was a small opening.

Holding out his hand for Altia, Jordan motioned her forward. "Ladies first."

Altia gave a mock scowl and then turned her head to Kyril and grinned. "He always sends me first. It's less about ladies first than it is about having someone in front of him if there is trouble."

"In you go." Jordan swatted Altia on the behind as she crawled through. Kyril felt a bit of anger and resentment flare up in him, but he pushed it down and followed. Jordan took up the rear.

"One hour, and then I close it up," said Oden.

Kyril stood up. It was dark, but soon Jordan brought forth a light from his hand and Kyril noticed they were in a rough, narrow tunnel, which was only a few inches taller than Kyril. Jordan had to keep his head down a bit so as not to scrape the top of it.

It dawned on Kyril what they were doing. They were breaking into the palace. He shook his head and took a step back.

"Come on Kyril." Altia took his hand and pulled him along. "Everyone is afraid their first time. You'll get used to it."

Kyril held back a sneeze—the air was musty and warm in the tunnel. He hoped he would never get used to it. This was not a business he planned on being in for long.

"Just stick to the plan and nothing will go wrong," Altia said. "It never does."

Kyril shut his eyes for the briefest of moments, and for at least the tenth time in the last hour asked himself what he was doing.

Soon the tunnel came to what appeared to be a dead end. Kyril began to panic. Maybe the plan was to dump him here and get rid of him.

"What's going on?" he asked. "Why is it blocked?"

Jordan laughed and Kyril took a step back. Altia was now behind him and she pushed him forward toward the rock wall.

"Don't kill me," Kyril called out in fright. "I'll do better next time."

With the hard push from Altia, Kyril was flung into the hard rock wall. He put his hands up to guard his face, but instead of crashing into the wall, his feet continued to carry him forward into another tunnel, this one much wider and seemingly better cared for. He spun around and saw the rock wall still standing there, now behind him. Then Altia and Jordan came walking through the wall as if it wasn't really there at all.

Jordan threw back his head and laughed. "I never get tired of that."

Altia grinned at Kyril.

"What was that all about?" Kyril asked.

"It's a spell that Jordan cast on his first mission," Altia explained.

Jordan shrugged. "It's not that difficult. In the dark rock tunnel, seeing a wall of rock is not out of the ordinary. I just spelled your mind to think you saw it there."

Irritation rose up inside of Kyril. "That's not very nice. I don't want people messing with my mind again."

"Again?" Altia asked. She pushed a lock of hair behind her right ear and gave Kyril a questioning look. "You mean this has happened to you before?"

"Not exactly," Kyril said. He didn't want to talk about it. It made him feel foolish.

"When?" Jordan probed.

"Never mind," Kyril said. "It doesn't matter."

"It may," Jordan said. "Has someone else manipulated your mind recently? Maybe they are spying on us through your mind."

The truth was far closer than Kyril wanted to admit. Sweat ran down his cheek and he wiped it off with the back of his hand. Did they suspect him?

"Kyril?" Altia said. "Are you all right?"

Kyril took a deep breath. He had to give them something so they wouldn't suspect him. "Alright. Over the past week I've felt the desire to do…things…that I shouldn't be able to do, but something in my mind—or someone—convinced me it was possible."

Altia and Jordan shared a glance between them that Kyril couldn't decipher. They knew something that they weren't telling him.

"What happened?" asked Jordan.

"Don't we have to hurry?" Kyril asked. "We only have an hour to get back, and less time than that until the curfew bell rings." He took a step down the new tunnel in front of them, not knowing which direction to go. His part in the plan was later, once they obtained the book. Jordan was their guide.

"We have plenty of time," Jordan said firmly. "Humor me!"

"But…" Kyril glanced around the dark tunnel with plans to just start walking, but Jordan was the only one to know which way.

"Fine," Kyril growled. "I jumped off a wall thinking I could fly. There, are you happy? Now, which way are we going…or have you forgotten about the mission?"

He expected both to start laughing, but neither did. They stood, watching him pace, with surprised looks on their faces.

"And transporting?" Jordan asked. "Did you feel it then, too?"

"Yes," Kyril whispered back.

Jordan appeared deep in thought for a moment as if trying to understand the implications of Kyril's experiences.

Altia nodded her head. "He's the missing piece that Gamal spoke to us about."

Jordan's eyes flared at Altia's words. "Altia!"

She closed her mouth. What were they talking about? They couldn't take their eyes off of him. Was something wrong? Was his hair sticking up?

"What did Gamal say?"

Altia opened her mouth to speak, but Jordan shook his head at her and spoke instead. "That is none of your business right now, Kyril. Gamal has a brilliant mind and is always searching for ways to…ah…help Targon."

Kyril noticed that both of his companions seemed very uncomfortable talking about Gamal.

"I deserve to know if it's about me," Kyril said.

"Wizard Targon has been looking for a missing piece to his plan and Gamal has been helping him," Jordan said with tight lips.

"What is it?" Kyril asked.

"It's not a what, it's a who," Jordan added. "Someone that has unique abilities."

"Who is it?" asked Kyril carefully, not knowing if he wanted to know the answer.

"You, Kyril," Altia blurted out, excitement written across her face. "If you were feeling a presence in your mind and you can now transport, you must be the answer to his plan. Isn't that wonderful?"

Kyril's stomach felt like someone slugged it and he leaned over and retched.

"Kyril!" Altia said. "That's so gross."

"Now hurry up, we're behind schedule," Jordan said in a clipped voice. "No more of this talk of who is special or not. So far, I'm not seeing anything important in front of me but a fearful apprentice. Come on, we need to be careful."

"We're just stealing a book, what could go wrong?" Altia said, joining Jordan up front.

"Well, at least I know I'm not going crazy," Kyril admitted to himself as he picked up his pace behind the other two followers of Targon.

But crazy or special, Kyril was far too deep in this mess now for him to back out. He had a horrible feeling that he was only at the beginning of his troubles.

CHAPTER FIFTEEN

The tunnel lightened up the farther they went, so Jordan eventually extinguished the light. Now they needed to stay closer to the walls and creep more slowly from shadow to shadow.

Suddenly, Altia grabbed both Jordan and Kyril and pulled them back into a small recess with a door in it. Just as Kyril was going to ask what she was doing, two guards walked down a hallway at the end of the tunnel.

The three waited for a few more moments, listening to the retreating footsteps of the two guards. Before continuing their mission, Jordan brought three masks out of a small pack he was carrying on his back. Kyril handled the silky-smooth material in his hands before sliding it over his head.

The mask was tighter than he thought it would be. He pulled and tugged until the holes for his eyes and nose lined up. It was tight and uncomfortable. He looked at the other two and moaned, realizing they all appeared quite ridiculous—but also quite disguised.

They edged out of their hiding place and approached the aisle where the tunnel ended. Torches lined the length of the stone walls, and the floor turned from dirt to stone. Bits of old crates and other discarded items littered the edges of the underground hallway.

"This is where you stay, Kyril," Jordan said, pointing to the crossroads. "Warn us if someone approaches. We should be less than ten minutes."

With those words, Jordan and Altia ran in stealthy silence down the hallway, leaving Kyril alone and exposed if anyone came by. He backed up against the wall and continued to peer right and left for anyone else.

With his heart beating loudly, Kyril wondered again why he was there at all. They didn't need him along. Standing guard was just a menial task to give him something to do. But Wizard Targon had insisted. Did Targon know that Kyril had passed information about the mission to his handler? Was this a trap?

It had been a strange encounter the night before. He'd found a secluded place behind the academy and had activated the magical communication device again. Kyril spoke to his handler once again through the artifact, who appeared as a faded hologram and had a disguised voice.

Reaching into a pocket inside his dark burgundy cloak, Kyril fingered the artifact. It fit snugly in the palm of his hand, round at the base, but rising up into a triangle. Thoughts of the exchange the previous night made him wonder again who his handler was. The way he spoke and the words he used seemed familiar to him, making Kyril think his handler wasn't old—maybe even his own age.

Hearing a noise, he jerked his head to his right and squatted down behind a stack of crates. Peering through the slats, he watched carefully, but no one materialized. He needed to pay better attention. For whatever reason, he was chosen to spy on Targon. He needed to do his best to get into the wizard's good graces. If the emperor suspected that Targon was up to something, he must have a good reason. Kyril needed to try harder.

Still squatting down, Kyril looked back down the hall in the direction that Jordan and Altia had gone. They should be coming back soon. They were to secure a book from someone in the palace. Kyril wondered if his handler and those he worked with would do anything with the information he had shared with them.

Kyril ground his teeth in frustration again at being put in this position. He sat in stark silence, trying to be vigilant, when all of a sudden, he heard shouting. Standing up to hear better, he realized it was coming from the direction where Jordan and Altia had gone. Should he go to their aid? What if they were in trouble? Although…wasn't that what he had given the information to his handler for, so they *would* get in trouble?

Kyril grunted. He hated playing both sides. It wasn't fair to him. He didn't want anyone to get hurt. Targon, Altia, and Jordan had all been nice to him so far.

Flashes of light flew down the hallway as Jordan and Altia came running as fast as they could. At the same time, Kyril heard a sound behind him and turned his head. At the opposite end of the hallway came the two guards they had hidden from earlier. Both pulled their swords and sprinted toward Kyril.

"Stop right there!" one of the guards shouted.

Kyril turned back towards his friends, and saw a man chasing them. The man—obviously a wizard—lifted his hand, and fire flew from his fingertips, barely missing Jordan as he ducked just in time. Behind the wizard ran more guards.

Altia ran next to Jordan, an ancient book held tightly in her hands. Kyril didn't know what to do. He froze in place trying to think of a plan, but his mind shut down. He wasn't trained for these types of things. He clenched his fists and closed his eyes just as one of the guards came within a few yards of him.

"Grab him, and I will get the others," said one of the guards.

Kyril desperately tried to close the chaos out of his mind, and as he did so, he felt the mark on his hand and wished he was anywhere but there. A sudden bright light made him open his eyes. It swirled all around him and he knew what was going to happen only a moment before it did.

Jordan and Altia knocked one of the guards down as they reached his side.

"Run!" Altia shouted at Kyril as she pushed into him.

But instead, he grabbed his friends' hands, and suddenly the light flashed a brilliant white around them. The two guards, one on the ground, put their hands up to block the glare.

The light went out, and Altia and Jordan crashed into Kyril, knocking him to the ground. When he got up all three of them were now farther down the tunnel away from the guards in the hallway.

"So, that's what transporting is." Altia stumbled nervously on her words.

Kyril pushed a bout of nausea away and before he could say anything, he heard someone groan. He was still somewhat blinded from the flash, and it took him a moment to see a crumpled heap in a small, carved-out hallway to his left.

"Kyril, we need to get away," shouted Jordan.

The two guards, now joined by the others, were running toward them down the tunnel. They only had a few more moments before they would clash again with them.

"We have the book, let's go," said Altia.

But Kyril looked closer at the man on the floor. There was another book next to him that appeared identical to the one that Altia held in her arms.

"There's another book," Kyril said.

Jordan stopped and turned around. "Another one? This wasn't part of the plan."

The yells of the guards grew louder, then more shouts came from the other end of the hallway. Kyril turned in that direction and saw three people running toward them. In the semi-dark tunnel, he couldn't tell who they were until one shouted out.

"Hasani," Sylvie yelled. "Hasani, are you here?"

Kyril groaned. What was Sylvie doing here? This was getting bad. And who was Hasani?

As if in answer to Sylvie's call, the figure on the floor stirred and tried to sit up. Kyril deduced it must be Hasani. From Kyril's angle the dark-skinned man seemed familiar to him.

Jordan and Altia jumped out to meet the rushing guards.

"Take the book," came a raspy whisper from the tunnel. The voice was also in his mind. Kyril darted his head around. In the shadows behind the man on the ground stood another figure. This one leaned against the wall as if he was hurt.

"Let's go!" Jordan yelled out from behind Kyril.

Kyril peered closer in the darkness toward the strange figure. He reached his hand out and thought really hard. Not normally one to be able to do much with his magic, he was actually surprised when the mark in his hand flared to a brilliant light once again. If he had had more time, he would have been excited about what he had just done, but the yells and threats and strange people around him were excitement enough. Jordan was right. They needed to leave.

The figure stood with a black hooded cloak around him, so Kyril couldn't tell if it was friend or foe. The man seemed to stumble in pain, then reached over the body on the ground, grabbed the book, and thrust it into Kyril's hands. As the man did so, the light in Kyril's palm winked out leaving him blinking in the darkness once again.

"Take this and leave the other one," he whispered, his voice soft and snakelike.

The two books appeared identical to Kyril, but with the new book in hand he turned back to Jordan and Altia, who were now fighting groups from both sides. Wizard's fire flew through the air from the right—Kyril surmised coming from Sylvie—while swords thrusted at them from the left. Joelle came pushing through with a staff spinning in precise motions in front of her. Altia had to back away.

Jordan appeared to have more skill and training, but the sheer numbers and strength of their opponents was pushing him back on the defensive more and more. Soon the three of them would be overran and caught.

After a quick flash of light, Kyril turned back around and watched as the figure who had given him the book took a few steps farther back into the dead-end hallway.

"Do as I said!" the man said with vehemence as he winked out of existence. Just before he did, Kyril saw the outline of a dark medallion in the bright light. Kyril suspected he had transported somewhere else and was caught for a moment wondering who else other than him had the ability to do so. Could it have been Targon? If so, why did he send them there on the mission?

Nothing made sense to Kyril. Altia's yells forced him to move into action. Leaving the other man on the ground, he now ran toward Altia and Jordan, keeping his voice quiet—he didn't want Sylvie to know it was him.

Standing next to Sylvie was an older woman that Kyril recognized from the library but whose name he couldn't place at the moment.

"Get the book!" Sylvie yelled to Joelle while pointing to Altia. Joelle somehow had moved around behind Altia and Jordan, her staff now swinging with a bright light around her head in quite a skilled fashion. It surprised him to see the healer fighting, but at second glance it appeared more defensive than offensive.

With one hand, Joelle reached toward the book in Altia's hands.

"No!" Jordan shouted. "Don't let them have it!"

Kyril didn't know whether to trust the hooded figure or not, but he didn't have much choice at the moment—not if they wanted to get out alive. He took a few quick steps closer to Altia, and with his back to Sylvie, spoke in a low voice to Altia and Jordan.

"Give it to them," Kyril said firmly—more out of fear than anything else.

Before an answer came, a guard broke through their perimeter and thrust a knife in Kyril's direction. He jumped back quicker than he had supposed he could, but still ,the blade grazed his arm, tearing through his cloak and drawing blood. The sting of the wound made him yelp out in pain.

"Keep the book, Altia," Jordan roared. "He needs it. That's our mission."

Kyril understood who "he" was—Wizard Targon. He wasn't sure what to do, but he had to trust his instincts for a moment—so reached over to Altia and tore the book from her hands, took two steps and thrust it into Sylvie's hands, while keeping the other book in the shadows of his cloak. With the mask on there was no way she could recognize him.

Sylvie's eyes widened at now having the book thrust at her. Her fingers scraped against Kyril's palm as she grabbed the book from him. Kyril pulled back, but Sylvie cocked her head and stared at him for a moment.

"What are you doing?" Jordan shouted at Kyril and tried to grab the book back.

Kyril moved to intercept Jordan. As he did so, a blast of wizard power barreled toward them from another wizard who had joined from the palace side of the hallway. Kyril and Jordan dove to the side, Altia falling to the ground beside them. Jordan scrambled up and helped Altia and then ran over to Kyril's side.

"If you know how to do that trick again, now would be a good time," Jordan hissed at Kyril. "This mission is a total loss thanks to you."

He wasn't sure how he had transported before, but the last two times it had seemed to happen under stress and need. Sylvie, Joelle, and the other lady had stopped once they had received the book, but the other guards and the accompanying wizard moved in once again. Kyril didn't know what was such a big deal about these books. People were getting hurt and going crazy over them.

All Kyril wished was that he could be back in his own room and sleeping in his warm bed. The now familiar light from his palm flared around them once again. Kyril took one last glance back behind them, to where Sylvie stood with stern eyes glaring directly at him. Her lips then parted and although Kyril couldn't hear her words, he knew what she said.

"Kyril."

And then Kyril found himself tumbling into his own bed. Jordan and Altia fell on top of him. His three roommates screamed out loud and jumped up. Two of them had apparently already been lying in their own beds. Lights flashed out from palms as everyone summoned a way to see and prepared to fight.

All of a sudden Tal had a sword in his hand.

"It's me! It's me, Kyril!" he shouted.

Tal skidded to a stop and the other two joined his side.

"Where did you come from?" asked Sayid, his young, dark eyes wide and afraid.

Jordan finished untangling himself from the others and stood up, facing Kyril's three roommates. They cowed back a step at the hard glare on his face.

"There will be no talk of this, you understand?" Jordan spat, his usual fine features marred by anger and frustration. "You are apprentices, and if I ever hear of this, you will be kicked out of the school immediately."

Kyril didn't think Jordan, even as a full wizard, had that kind of power, but Targon probably did. And Jordan reported to the powerful wizard.

With those words, he crooked his finger for Altia to follow him. Before they left the room, Kyril ran to the door and pushed the book he held into Jordan's hands.

"What…?" Jordan struggled to speak. "I thought you gave the book to Sylvie?"

"I did, but this is the one we wanted," Kyril said, clearly not understanding for sure what had happened, and not actually in the mood to argue. "Just take it and give it to Targon."

Jordan glowered at Kyril, yanked the door open and Altia followed him out.

"Be sure that I will tell Targon everything that happened tonight, Kyril," Jordan spat on his way out. "You put us all in danger and changed the plan. That is not your place. Rest assured, you'll hear from him."

Once the door slammed closed, Kyril fell back onto his bed and groaned.

CHAPTER SIXTEEN

Late in the afternoon, two days later, Sylvie sat with Joelle and Hasani under a tree in the academy gardens. The enormous building afforded them additional shade as the sun moved farther west throughout the day. A summer storm had come in during the night, bringing with it much-needed rain and cooler, more pleasant temperatures. A rare summer day that wasn't so hot and humid.

The wound on the side of Hasani's face from when he had been attacked had healed nicely due to Joelle's healing, as had a few cracked ribs. The three were discussing the events of that night.

"But you never saw who attacked you?" Sylvie asked.

Hasani shook his head. "No. I went to retrieve the Codex for you, and someone attacked me from behind. It was dark…"

"Dark, because you weren't supposed to be down there, were you?" Sylvie said, a bit harsher than she had intended. But seeing someone she was sure was Kyril at the scene of the fight had shaken her more than she cared to admit. She hadn't seen him in the last few days, except for once from a distance. He was avoiding her and the impending confrontation that would surely come.

"You are right, Sylvonna," Hasani said, his eyes worried. "But I knew it was important for you."

Joelle put a hand on his arm. "That's fine, Hasani. You did nothing wrong."

Sylvie raised her eyebrows at Joelle, but the healer only frowned back. Not wanting to fight with her friend, she pushed on to the next question.

"Can you tell us anything about the man that attacked you?" Sylvie asked.

"I was able to stab his leg with my knife before he kicked it away from me," Hasani said. "He wore a dark hood over his head. He grabbed the book from me and pushed me down into the tunnels. I tried to fight back, but my mind seized up…"

"So, it was a wizard of the mind, then," Joelle said with a puff of air. "Who could it be?"

Sylvie thought about it. "Targon." She didn't like the influence he was having on Kyril either.

"I can't believe that," Hasani said. "He's a respected wizard. Anyway, what use would Targon have for that book?"

"That's what we have to find out." Sylvie jumped up. "They failed and we still have the book. So, we need to look through it and find out what someone might have been looking for."

The three were quiet for a moment, and Sylvie plopped back down.

Finally, Hasani spoke again. "It wasn't Targon."

"How do you know?" Sylvie asked.

"My attacker was too short," Hasani said, "and more broad-shouldered." He scrunched his eyes up for a moment as if trying to remember. "When we heard noises in the tunnel, his concentration slipped for a moment and I tried to see his face, but he moved back into the shadows and I couldn't." Hasani sat brooding for a moment as if disappointed with himself. "I tried to get away, but he had something in his hand that seemed to give him more power."

"What was it?" Joelle's eyes went wide. "Do you know what color it was? How big? What was he doing with it? That might give us a clue to who it was."

Sylvie chuckled at Joelle's multitude of questions but waited for Hasani to answer. He appeared to be thinking hard and pushed a few braids away from the side of his face before he continued.

"I…I…I'm not sure, exactly. It was dark."

"But you're a wizard, you could have made a light," Sylvie said, now more impatient than ever to figure out what had happened.

"Sylvie!" Joelle said with a shake of her head and fire in her eyes. "Be nice. Hasani already said his mind was being controlled."

"It had to be a powerful wizard to do that for so long," Sylvie said with a huff.

"Don't you think I know that?" Hasani shot back with the first stern words Sylvie had heard from him. "I may be an apprentice, but I am not a weak wizard by any means. I work in the library and my mind is sharp. This man had a power over me that…he shouldn't have been able to have."

Sylvie lowered her head for a moment. "I'm sorry."

Hasani took a breath and smiled, his bright white teeth standing out in his smooth, dark brown face. "I think it was a medallion that he was holding. But it was dark, and I couldn't be sure. When the others attacked, he was distracted, and I pushed him away. It flew and he scrambled for it, forgetting me for a moment. That's when I tried to run, but I only took a few steps when my legs stopped working and I fell over."

"What?" Joelle and Sylvie said at the same time.

"It was like my mind just told them to stop…and they did. He took something from his waist and hit me in the side of the head with it…something hard." Hasani's hand went instinctively to the side of his head where his wound had been.

"But I fixed it for you, Hasani," Joelle said, smiling broadly at the exotic man from the south. She pushed some wild strands of red hair out of her face with one hand while touching the side of his head softly with the other.

Sylvie almost rolled her eyes. Joelle was a complicated woman to figure out at best. She flirted with most men and chatted incessantly about nothing…but she was a marvelous healer, and Sylvie had to admit, a very good friend. With a deep sigh she waited for Hasani to continue his story.

"The next thing I knew, I heard another man behind me. I heard you calling for me, Sylvie, and tried to sit up. When I did, I was kicked in the head and then in the ribs by whom I can only assume was the same man. When I came to, both of you and the librarian were hovering over me and calling my name."

"And the man that hit you was nowhere to be found," Sylvie stated.

Hasani shook his head. "He was gone with the book…or so I thought."

Now it was Sylvie's turn to shake her head. "It doesn't make sense. He couldn't have gotten past us. It was only us three, some royal guards, and three others they were chasing in the tunnel. There was no other man."

"I didn't make this up, Sylvonna." Hasani's dark eyes sparkled at her.

"Oh, I believe you," Sylvie said. Then she scrunched up her face and thought for a moment. Why had the three thieves—if that's who they were—given her back the book after all that trouble? And had it really been Kyril under the mask?

"Hello," Joelle said, and tapped Sylvie on the shoulder. "Where are you, Sylvie?"

"Sorry," Sylvie said. "Just trying to reason things out. By the way, I didn't know you were so talented with the staff."

Joelle blushed bright red. "My father taught me when I was younger. It's for defense only. After all the healing I've done, I couldn't stand to hurt someone on purpose, but my father thought it would be good to be able to defend myself."

Sylvie nodded her head, but she was still trying to solve the problem of why everyone seemed to want that book. "We need to see that book again, Hasani."

Hasani threw back his head and laughed. "Good luck with that. You have to bring it up with the head librarian. I should have never given it to you the first time. The Western Codex is a very rare book.

"But you can get it for us again," Sylvie said.

"I'm afraid not. I'm not allowed down there for a while." Hasani's face fell. "I'm back to bookshelf restocking duty for the time being."

"Oh, Hasani!" Joelle tried to comfort him as they both stood up and joined Sylvie. "How horrible."

The three headed back toward the academy, passing a few other students on their way into the building for dinner.

"There has to be a way," Sylvie mumbled.

Before getting to the building—and almost as if on cue—a voice called out from a few dozen feet away. When she turned in that direction, she saw Prince Zaidan walking toward her. Others in his path moved to the side and bowed their heads to the young prince.

"Sylvonna," said Zaidan, "might I have a word with you?" Zaiden caught sight of Joelle and Hasani and smiled at them. "Greetings. I hear much about the famed healer from the Realm and the studious scholar from Mahli."

Sylvie smiled at his smooth manners. Joelle's face was almost the color of her hair once again.

"Prince Zaidan, you are too kind," Joelle said, fumbling over her words.

Hasani gave a quick bow and stayed quiet.

"I'll talk to you two later," said Sylvie, and with a quick eye roll toward the prince, said, "I might have found a way to see that book after all."

Hasani coughed, obviously caught off-guard by Sylvie's inference of using the prince for their benefit.

CHAPTER SEVENTEEN

Kyril had stayed in bed the day after his escapades, feigning illness. He'd told his roommates he didn't want to see anyone. They themselves had kept their distance from him and he could hear them whispering when they thought he was asleep. They were surely talking about how he, Jordan, and Altia had popped into their room unexpectedly the night before. They were certain it was Jordan's doing, which was fine with Kyril. He already didn't have a lot of friends. If rumors starting spreading, he was sure he would be thought of as even more of a freak.

He had expected Sylvie to come by, but she obviously was afraid of him now and didn't want anything to do with him. At the least he would have thought that Joelle would have come by and checked on him—she didn't like having people sick on her watch. But no one had come.

However, late in the afternoon on the second day, a knock had sounded on the door. When the knocking hadn't stopped, he reluctantly arose from his thoughts and answered the door. It had been Altia. She was pleasant to him, but didn't stay for any idle chatter. She delivered a verbal invitation to meet with Targon for dinner once again. Now he stood looking down at himself. He once again wore an expensive cloak—but this time, it was one that Targon had given him previously. He found his heart pounding with excitement to see the wizard once again. Though he hoped he wouldn't be in too much trouble.

Questions raced through his mind about his recent adventure under the palace . Why had Hasani—if that was the name of apprentice on the ground—been there in the tunnel? Who had been the man that had handed him the book? And most importantly, what was in that book? No, the most important question was how had Kyril learned to transport? It was not a common wizard power.

With a shake of his head, he cleared the never-ending questions out of his mind and finished pulling on his boots. He wasn't going to let uncertainties ruin his evening. Just before leaving, he heard what sounded like a scratch on the door. He listened for a moment as he finished getting ready, then opened the door to walk to Targon's rooms. On the floor at his feet was a note. Kyril groaned internally and stuck it in an inside pocket of his cloak, promising himself that he'd read it later. He was sure it was from his handler. Theirs was a relationship he was beginning to truly despise.

After walking down the hallway, he came to the double doors leading out of the building. As he moved his hands to push them open, he saw through a small window three young men on the other side of the door—and the middle one was Bale Nabhani himself. His dark skin glistened in the setting sun, his broad nose twitching at the sight of Kyril.

Kyril was determined to just ignore them. But they had other ideas. As Kyril pushed on the door they held it closed from the other side. He pushed it harder, but only taunting laughs met him from the other side of the etched glass. Anger welled up inside of him and he tried not to let his palm flare up again. Taking a deep breath, he turned around and decided to go in another direction. He wanted to get fresh air, but he could take a roundabout way through the halls of the academy.

As soon as he turned, he heard the door crash open behind him, and the taunts began.

"Hey apprentice, where you going in such a hurry?" Bale said. "I heard you were too sick to go to classes. Maybe you're finally embarrassed enough of your puny powers to stay away."

"Go back to your village and let us lead Gildan," said another young man next to Bale. Kyril thought his name was Gabriel. He had recently become a full wizard and it was rumored he had secured an apprenticeship with a powerful governor in the east.

Kyril kept walking, but his fists began to clench. Others in the hallway turned to watch the three men and their taunts, but Kyril tried to ignore them. However, someone pushed him from behind and he tripped and fell to the ground. Glancing up, he saw all three of them glaring down at him.

It wasn't fair. Why did they treat him like this? He was a citizen of Gildan just like they were. It wasn't his fault he came from a poor village and his family had all died. He felt the sting of tears in his eyes and he twisted his head to the side so they wouldn't see.

"Look, Gabe, Bale," said the third man. "He's crying."

"Oops, Mikal, I guess you tapped his shoulder too hard." Bale stepped around to Kyril's side, bent down, and lifted Kyril's chin. "You'll never be *anyone*, Kyril!"

"Neither will you, Bale," Kyril spat. "You are just jealous of my wizard powers."

"Jealous of *you?*" Bale laughed deep and loud as a small group formed around them. "I've got an important position working for the palace now. I don't need to be a wizard…a word that is far above your feeble abilities. Soon, I'll be in a position to get rid of you once and for all. Your power is pathetic."

And then, Kyril lost it.

He brought his marked hand up, and the power flared bright, pushing Bale hard. The man went flying a dozen feet in the air and landed hard on his back against the stone floor. Kyril stood back up, the mark in his hand still glowing a bright white.

"Kyril!" came a voice from behind him.

He turned around and shook his head. He couldn't deal with this right now. Sylvie was walking toward him, her pale face bright red and seeming to barely be holding in the anger. With three quick steps she came up next to him.

"You know that using power like that is against the rules," she snapped, and studied the scene around her. "What's going on here?"

Gabe stepped forward and spoke in a haughty voice—as if he shouldn't have had to explain things to her. "Kyril accidentally tripped. When Bale reached down to help him up, the crazy apprentice used his power on him. Now, look at Bale!"

Everyone in the hallway turned their attention to Bale, who was still sitting on the floor with a dazed stare on his face.

Sylvie's eyes narrowed toward Kyril and filled with a multitude of questions.

"Really?" Kyril snapped. "You believe them?"

"I don't know what to believe about you anymore," Sylvie said.

"Give it to him, Twig," called out Bale as he slowly stood back up. "He's crazy and a danger to all of us here at the academy. He should be banned from the school."

Sylvie shook her head. "Don't think I'm so naïve to believe you didn't provoke him. All of you"— she waved her hands at Bale, Mikel, and Gabriel— "need to treat others with more respect."

"You have no authority here," Mikel said. "You're from the kingdom of Arc."

"Arc or not," Sylvie said firmly, "I am a part-time instructor here and your superior as a wizard, and you *will* heed my words." She spread her arms to her sides and the floor underneath them began to rumble. "There are no rules about me using my powers."

Kyril backed away from Sylvie, wondering what was going to happen. The candles in the sconces shook and Sylvie's eyes flashed a brighter blue. He, along with the others, gasped at the amount of power she must be holding back.

Pointing her finger at Bale, she said commandingly, "Go and see Joelle for a healing. I better not see any of you pulling these types of pranks again."

Bale straightened up. "I don't need a healer." He moved stiffly, his back obviously hurting. "But you can believe I am reporting Kyril's flagrant misuse of magic."

"No need for that," Sylvie said, her eyes returning to their normal blue as the ground stopped shaking. "I will take him myself."

Sylvie reached for Kyril, but he pulled his hand back. "You're letting them go?" He couldn't believe it. "I didn't do anything."

"You broke the rules by using magic."

"I thought you were my friend," Kyril snapped at her. "But you're just like all of them. All you mighty nobles and rich families think you can control everything. Well, you're wrong."

Sylvie reached toward Kyril once again, but he brought his hand out in front of him and waved it around. He could summon his powers now. A bright light escaped his palm and enveloped him. Thinking of Targon and his dinner party, the light flashed around him, and he found himself bumping into a chair in front of a dining table.

The room grew quiet as Kyril glanced around. There were about ten others present, including Jordan and Altia. The latter had her hair braided beautifully down one side. Suddenly a loud clap came from beside him, and then two and then three.

"Well done, Kyril," Targon said. "Well done, indeed. Jordan has been telling me about your amazing powers."

Jordan didn't join in Targon's accolades, his face instead holding what Kyril thought might be a hint of jealousy.

Others, including Altia, however joined in the clapping. Kyril felt embarrassed at first, but then, gazing at their happy, friendly faces, he smiled broadly.

"Quite an entrance indeed," Targon said, walking to his side. "Come and sit down. We were just ready to eat. Come and tell us more about yourself, my good friend."

Kyril could hardly contain his smile. His heart was bursting. These people truly did like him. He surely didn't care about Bale and his associates. Even Sylvie had turned against him.

"Thank you," Kyril said with a short bow of his head to their host. "Thank you for having me here tonight."

CHAPTER EIGHTEEN

The meal consisted of piping hot strips of spiced beef smothered in brown gravy, rice, roasted zucchini, and fresh pineapple. Along with the food, there were ten other young wizards and apprentices present, a few of which Kyril knew from classes—all of which were wizards of the mind. None appeared to be from any noble family—at least ones that had any strong influence in Gildan. Having grown up in a much smaller town than the capital city, Kyril hadn't paid much attention to the ruling families, outside of knowing who the emperor and the mayor of his own town were.

Once he had arrived in the capital city, Kyril had noticed many more nuances about certain families with noble ties, Bale Nabhani being one of them. Some of the noble families employed wizards, but it seemed that many did not and ruled only due to family histories and longtime nobility.

Kyril took a few bites of food, only to eventually glance up. He caught Altia studying him from across the table. He blushed and turned his attention back to his food. She appeared to be studying him, trying to figure him out. Her eyes were accented tonight by dark blue eyeliner. He didn't think he was that hard to figure out. He was just a poor boy from a small city with a minor aptitude as a wizard of the mind. Well, at least he had been. Now, he wasn't sure what his abilities really were anymore.

He rubbed his fingers across his scars. He wondered if the medallion itself was still in his family's old barn. Thoughts of the medallion made him peek down the table at Targon himself. The man seemed to sense Kyril's attention and nodded his head and smiled. Kyril smiled back and wondered what he had done to get into the wizard's good graces.

Kyril hadn't been this happy in a long time. The only thing marring the experience was Gamal, Targon's scribe. He sat dutifully next to Targon, and although did the wizard's bidding from time to time, his eyes seemed to stay fastened on Kyril's every move. The man's red birthmark seemed to throb with a beat of its own and there were times that Kyril swore his eyes changed color. Even though Gamal was a scribe, he must have been a wizard of the mind if Targon kept him around, as he seemed to be a part of Targon's trusted group.

As dinner finished, the door opened, and a group of musicians entered. They sat up in the far corner, and as the dishes were cleared away by servants, began to play a lively tune. There were three men and two women, all dressed in colorful clothes. The women were wrapped in various layers of silk wound tightly around them, leaving the shapes of their bodies very apparent. Kyril flushed and turned away. As he did so, he caught Targon's eyes once again.

The wizard stood up from the table and beckoned Kyril to join him. Kyril glanced around the room, surprised that he was the only one being summoned away. He followed Targon to his study while glancing back over the room. Everyone was enjoying the music. Jordan even had one of the female apprentices out dancing across the floor, while others joined in clapping their hands to the rhythm. Laughter and enjoyment filled the room.

Kyril stepped through the doorway. As the door closed, the sound of the festivities faded in the distance. Targon motioned for Kyril to join him at a set of chairs.

Kyril let out a puff of air as he lowered himself down.

"Eat too much?" Targon said, his lips curving into a knowing smile.

Kyril nodded. "Yes, that was one of the best meals I have ever eaten."

"You didn't grow up with much, did you?" Targon asked.

The question was unexpected but did not bother Kyril.

"No." Kyril shook his head. "My father provided enough for us from his carpentry, but we never had much extra."

"And did you think that was unfair?"

Kyril thought a moment. "I never thought about it before. It's just the way it was."

"But others had much more," Targon said. "The mayor of your city, the nobles, and especially those here in the great capital. Didn't that bother you?"

"Well…" Kyril flushed for a moment, then lowered his head. "I was teased often, though I don't know if it was for my lack of wealth or just for who I was. I was small and skinny with not many friends."

"And do people still tease you now, Kyril?" Targon's voice grew a bit louder.

Kyril's head snapped up toward Targon. Had the wizard already heard about his altercation with Bale and his friends, all the way on the other side of the school? He thought once again about how he had thrown the bully far across the room, and a new feeling of pride filled his chest.

"I don't believe they will any more, sir," Kyril said.

"Good. Good." Targon leaned back and ran his fingers down his short beard. "I was once like you, Kyril, believe it or not. I grew up far away from the splendors of the capital city. I told you before that I had three older brothers who liked to pick on me. My mother was a minor wizard of sorts, and my father ran a boarding house for visitors."

Targon's eyes seemed to drift further away as he recounted his childhood. "They are all gone now."

"Gone?" said Kyril without thinking. Then he realized what Targon meant. "I'm sorry."

Targon smiled, but it did not reach his eyes. "It is for the better. My parents were old and my brothers, well…" Targon spread his arms to his sides. "They learned that having rich friends didn't help them much in the end."

Kyril swallowed hard, wondering what had happened.

"I'm glad to hear you have things under control, though."

Kyril thought about Bale and then Sylvie. "I'm not sure they are under control."

"Oh?" Targon said. "Is there something I can do to help?"

"Help *me*?" Kyril shook his head. "Why would you care about me?"

"I like you, Kyril," Targon chuckled. "Like I said, you remind me of my own struggles. You have abilities that are unique, yet somehow familiar to me. Don't you think others should treat you better?"

"I wish they would," Kyril said, "but that's not how things are."

Targon stood and his voice boomed. "But that's how they will be, Kyril Siravan."

Kyril stood, as much in surprise as in fear. The wizard's eyes went dark and his visage grew angry.

"Wizards, especially those of the mind, should never be treated badly," Targon continued. "We have been given our abilities for a reason. They are a gift. We are meant to be in charge. We have the knowledge and abilities to lead far better than those who only inherit their titles and wealth!"

Kyril only nodded his head in agreement. It did kind of make sense.

"Will you join us?" Targon said.

"Me?" Kyril was surprised. "How could I help?"

"Ah." Targon smiled, and this time it did reach his eyes. "You have no idea yet how special you really are."

CHAPTER NINETEEN

Sylvie sat alone at a small table in the corner of the library leafing through the Western Codex, but she couldn't find what she was looking for. The librarian came around the corner for the third time that hour. She glanced at the book, then Sylvie, scowled, then went on her way.

The older scholar wizard had not been happy having to give up something that had just been stolen, but when the prince had intervened on Sylvie's behalf, the librarian had had no choice.

A few minutes later, a sound behind Sylvie caused her to look up and over her shoulder.

"Joelle! Where have you been?" Sylvie asked. "I've been waiting here for an hour."

"Shhh," said a group of students from a table nearby.

Joelle's hair flew around her with a life of its own. She pushed back an unruly curl from her forehead and plopped down on a hard-wooden chair opposite Sylvie. She groaned after hitting the chair too hard.

Joelle sat uncharacteristically quietly, her head held low.

"What's wrong?" Sylvie asked.

Joelle slowly looked up, then turned toward the other table, then back to Sylvie again.

"Not here," she said in a low voice.

Sylvie glanced at the nearby students. They didn't seem to be paying them any attention.

"Is that the book?" Joelle asked, changing subjects.

Sylvie sighed. She would have to wait until later to get the information from her friend. Just then, Hasani walked around a shelf and stood at the edge of their table. Joelle jumped in surprise. The woman was nervous and worried about something.

"Hasani!" Sylvie said. "Don't sneak up on us like that. Are you busy?"

Hasani frowned, but then shook his head, his braids flapping around his face. "Well, the librarian has been keeping me busy these days with all sorts of menial tasks—but I have a break now, so I thought I'd come over and see if you found anything else."

Sylvie shook her head. "Nothing new, but…"

"What?" Hasani said.

Joelle also leaned closer, her anxiety forgotten.

"I can't seem to find the page on the medallions you showed us," Sylvie said.

"What?" Hasani reached his hands toward the book. "May I?"

Sylvie nodded and Hasani pulled the heavy tome toward him. He flipped through a couple of pages slowly, then quicker and quicker. He then closed the book and ran his hand over the front cover, turned it over and did the same to the back. His face scrunched up and he closed his eyes for a moment as if trying to remember something.

"This isn't the same book," he finally said.

"What?" Sylvie said, a little too loudly. The apprentices at a nearby table stared angrily at her, but she paid them little attention this time. "What do you mean? Of course it is."

"She's right, Hasani," said Joelle. "When we chased your captors through the tunnel, we caught up with them and one of them handed us back the book."

Sylvie's stomach twisted at the thought. Had it been Kyril who had given it back to her? She had touched his hand and felt his scars. But maybe she had been mistaken. Others had scars on their hands, didn't they?

"Believe me, it's not the same book," Hasani said, more firmly this time. "I know these books. They are my life. The covers may be the same, but the weight is different. There are fewer pages in this one, and the script is different; Written by a different hand. The language is more recent."

Sylvie glanced at the dust cloth in his hand.

Hasani drew his hands back behind him and gazed down in embarrassment. "It's only temporary…me cleaning up around here. Soon I'll be back as a librarian."

"I didn't say anything," Sylvie said, trying to apologize for any offense he had taken at her. "But I don't understand. The thieves in the tunnel gave the book back to us before they left, and we returned it here to the library as soon as we could."

"Then why can't you find what you are looking for in it?" Hasani shoved the book back at Sylvie. "Where are the pages we were reading before?"

Sylvie grabbed the book back in her hands and almost fell backwards.

"Hasani!" Joelle said, putting a soft hand on his arm.

Hasani took a deep breath. "I'm sorry. I'm sorry. But I'm not used to this kind of thing. The library is organized; I know all the books. The only time they go missing is when a student forgets to return them. But this book…" He waved his hand at Sylvie. "Or the book it *pretends* to be, is not one that can be checked out."

"Hasani," came a voice from behind him. "What are you doing chatting? Get back to work." The librarian stepped up to them with a stern expression on her wrinkled face.

Hasani shrugged and tried to return to his normal cheery disposition, covering up his recent frustration. "Sorry, ladies. Duty calls." He waved the dust cloth in front of them and turned down another aisle, ceremoniously taking great care to make sure the librarian saw him dusting off the old books.

"It wasn't his fault," said Joelle to the librarian. "We had a question."

The librarian sighed. "He's a good boy. He just gets distracted sometimes, that's all."

"But he knows the books, right?" Sylvie asked.

"Of course he does," beamed the librarian. "Best apprentice I have ever had. Those Mahlians have an aptitude for remembering things. He really is quite amazing." She glanced down the aisle at Hasani. "But he shouldn't have been down in the basement by himself with that book, so I had no choice but to put him on chores for a few days." She glanced down at the book in Sylvie's hand and frowned. "Are you done with that, my dear?"

"Why is it so important?" Sylvie asked. She didn't want to give away what Hasani had said about it.

"All the books kept in the basement are rare. Only one or two of each copy exist in all the world," the librarian said. "They are usually about magic or history. This one is about ancient magic artifacts."

"Could it ever be forged?" Sylvie asked.

The librarian frowned and her eyebrows furrowed. "Why would anyone want to forge it? Now, you women are wasting my time. With Hasani busy cleaning I've got twice as much work to do. If you are done with this, I'll take it back. Prince's orders or not, it shouldn't be up here in the open."

Sylvie slowly handed it back. It didn't have the information they were looking for, anyway. Joelle cleared her throat and Sylvie turned her way and shook her head. For some reason, she didn't want to share that it may be a forgery yet.

The librarian walked away, and Joelle fell in step with Sylvie as they left the library. It was late anyway, and she had some preparation to do for a lecture the next day. When they arrived at their rooms, she bade farewell to Joelle, but her friend didn't seem to want to leave.

"Can I come in for a moment?" Joelle asked.

Sylvie shrugged. "Only for a moment, Joelle. None of your ramblings. I have things to do." She smiled as she said the words and Joelle didn't seem to take offense.

She closed the door behind them and guided Joelle to a small sitting area. The room was smaller than those of most of the older wizards, but Sylvie didn't mind. It was more space than she'd ever had in the Arc Wizard Conclave. This was the first time she'd had her own personal room. Growing up, she'd shared with an older and younger sister.

The room was tidy and neat. A bed sat against one wall, with a dresser and desk opposite. Over a small fireplace on another wall hung a beautiful painting of the Superstition Mountains. Except to cross over on her way to Gildan, she hadn't been able to spend any time there recreationally. She hoped to do that this summer, but time was quickly getting away from her.

They sat in two of four stuffed chairs that circled around a small table with two books and a vase in its center. Joelle fidgeted with her hands, her eyes downcast. Sylvie was just about to say something when Joelle looked up and the floodgates opened.

"Oh Sylvie, I don't know what to do," she began. "There was a break-in at the palace two nights ago. A book was stolen from the emperor's own study. A fight broke out. A group of guards chased people down into the tunnels and then…"

Sylvie's eyes went wide; she was beginning to understand the implications of where they had been on that night.

"Then…" Joelle continued, her green eyes flickering back and forth. Her hands sat wringing in the lap of her light blue cotton dress. "Then…they found a knife that had been involved in the fight. One of the guards had nicked one of the attackers. Because of the masks they didn't know who it was, and well…you know how they escaped."

"The flash of light," Sylvie said.

Joelle nodded. "They brought the knife to me because of my abilities. They wanted to know whose blood it was. Normally I can't get that specific—well, at least not yet. As my powers grow, I may be able to. It's hard to know for sure, as most other healers don't have this ability, so I don't know who to ask. I…"

"Joelle!" Sylvie cut off her friend's rambling.

"Oh right." Joelle smiled, a pale blush running over her freckled face. But then she went quiet.

"And, could you tell whose blood it was?" Sylvie asked.

"Like I said," Joelle said, "it's not usually that exact, but…"

"But?"

"But the blood was very similar to someone I had just recently treated," Joelle said.

"That's good news. Who was it?" Sylvie smiled. "Did they catch the person?"

Joelle shook her head. "No, it's not good, Sylvie. Not good at all."

"I don't understand."

Joelle stood up and paced back and forth a few times.

"Joelle, what's wrong? What did you find out?"

"It's Kyril's," Joelle blurted out. "It's Kyril's blood."

So, it had been him in the tunnel after all. What was he involved in? She shook her head, at a loss for words.

Joelle plopped back down in her chair. "You don't seem surprised."

"I…" Sylvie said, worried about her friend. "I thought I felt his scars when he handed me the book, but I didn't know. I hoped it wasn't. It's strange that two books were stolen that night. One from here and one from the palace. Do you think they were switched somehow?"

"I don't know, Sylvie," Joelle said. "I'm more concerned for Kyril. What is he doing?"

"Targon," Sylvie said. "It has something to do with Wizard Targon. He's been gathering other wizards of the mind to him—apprentices and wizards alike. He's up to something."

Joelle opened her mouth to respond, but then a knock sounded on the door.

Both women looked at each other before Sylvie arose and headed toward the door. She opened it and found two palace guards standing there.

"Sorry to bother you, Wizard Sylvonna, but we are looking for Healer Joelle," said one of the men, peering past Sylvie. "Have you seen her?"

Joelle stood and came to the door. "Yes."

The man smiled at her. "The captain of the palace guard would like to see you. Have you discovered anything about the blood?"

Joelle turned to Sylvie, her eyes wide and afraid. "Just a moment—I'll be right there."

Joelle walked back into the room to grab a small bag she had brought with her. Sylvie joined her at the chairs, their backs to the door.

"What do I do?" Joelle whispered.

"Are you sure about the blood? Positive?" Sylvie said.

Joelle hesitated a moment. "Fairly certain. It's not an exact science."

"Healer, we need to hurry," the guard said.

"I have to tell them what I know," Joelle said. "If not, they could kick me out of the academy. I am learning a lot more here from the books in the library and doing a lot of good. I don't want to go back to the Realm yet. I'm afraid."

"Go and say what you must," Sylvie said. "Just make sure they know you're not one hundred percent sure. Kyril will have to live with his own mistakes, but something doesn't feel right here. First Kyril, then the books. I'm going to do some digging around."

"Just be careful," Joelle said as she walked back to the door and joined the guards.

Sylvie watched them leave down the hall. It was time to talk to the prince once again.

CHAPTER TWENTY

Kyril was still standing in Targon's office. The great wizard had just finished telling Kyril how special he was. Walking closer to Kyril, Targon put his hand on his shoulder. Kyril felt a small tugging at the back of his mind, similar to when his mind had convinced him he could do impossible things. Had that been Targon all along? Had he been trying to communicate with him, or test him? Before he could think any more about it, the door opened, and Gamal stepped inside.

The sensation at the back of his mind surged for a moment, and Kyril stumbled. Without taking his eyes from Gamal, Targon put his hand out and steadied Kyril.

Targon's eyes narrowed toward his scribe. "What is the meaning of this interruption?"

Gamal held Targon's gaze, a feat that Kyril was impressed with.

"The academy captain, a guard, and a wizard are here," Gamal said, his eyes never leaving Targon's own. "They are asking about Kyril. What should I tell them?"

Asking for him? Kyril groaned. It must have to do with Bale. He glanced up at Targon, wondering if the wizard would turn him in or not.

Targon thought a moment, then nodded his head. "We must show them who is in charge, Kyril."

The three walked out of Targon's office. The music had stopped and Kyril realized the presence he'd felt in the back of his head had also receded as soon as Gamal entered the room. He watched both Altia and Jordan move behind some other guests, and Gamal silently joined them—with a slight limp. Targon led Kyril forward.

The crowd parted, and Kyril stopped. The visitors were not who Kyril suspected they would be. It was not Sylvie with academy guards, but instead, Joelle with two palace guards. With a hand on his back, Targon encouraged Kyril forward.

"May I help you?" Targon said. "Is there such urgent business that you would interrupt my social gathering?"

One of the guards bowed his head. "We are sorry, Wizard Targon, but we come from the palace on pressing business."

Targon waited in silence for them to continue. Kyril wiped a bead of sweat from his forehead.

"There was an altercation in the tunnels below the palace the other evening. Intruders stole a book and clashed with some guards." The captain talking turned to the other man. "Halcon here was one of them."

Targon shook his head. "How unfortunate indeed. But how does this affect me?"

Kyril felt Joelle's eyes on him and glanced at her once, but then turned away. What could she know about him being in the tunnels? When she, Sylvie, and the librarian had arrived, Kyril's face had been covered by a mask. He surmised that Sylvie might know something…but had she told Joelle? He took a half step back, but Targon glanced down at him with a barely perceptible shake of his head, and he stopped moving.

"It seems that there was some blood on the edge of Halcon's knife that may belong to Kyril Siravan."

Blood? Kyril's stomach fell and he abruptly felt nauseous. It was then that he remembered Joelle's ability.

Out of the corner of his eye he caught Jordan and Altia moving a bit closer to hear better. What would they do? Would they turn him in to save themselves?

Targon frowned at Joelle for a long moment. "I wasn't aware that we could tell a man's identity that surely."

The captain motioned for Joelle to come forward. "The healer recently treated Kyril, so she was familiar with his blood."

Targon peered down at Kyril but said nothing before looking back up. "When was this exactly?"

"Two nights ago, right before the final evening bells," said Halcon. They were the first words he had said. "Another guard and I were attacked by three people. They wore masks and stole a book from the palace."

Targon chuckled. "Masked people stealing a book? How did they get away?"

"There was a bright light and they just…ah…disappeared," said Halcon.

"Just…disappeared?" Targon waved his hands in the air. "Just like that? Three people in masks."

Halcon nodded, but his tanned face flushed darker.

"Well, I'm sorry for this misunderstanding. Apprentice Kyril was here with me the entire evening. I have been tutoring him and some of the other young wizards and apprentices," Targon said. "My way of giving back, you know."

"But the blood, sir. The healer says it's his." The captain pointed at Kyril.

Targon's face grew darker and he took a step toward Joelle. Standing much shorter than the wizard, Kyril felt sorry for her. Her green eyes went wide, and fear crossed her face.

"This is not an exact science, is it?" Targon asked her.

"No sir, but..." she stuttered.

"I've never heard of anyone pinpointing an exact person...unless that is a new ability you have, my dear."

Joelle took a step back and tried to appear brave. "No, it is not new, but I do have a more fine-tuned ability than many others. I can tell where a person is from, whether they are male or female..."

As she spoke, she picked up steam and Kyril almost smiled. Even in the midst of trouble, the woman could talk a person's ear off.

"...I know I am young, but I treated Kyril earlier and I was able to get a sense of his blood. When the palace had me test the blood on the knife, it felt...familiar."

Gamal moved closer to Joelle, and as he did, Targon reached over and touched Joelle's shoulder. "But you can't know for certain, can you?"

Joelle opened her mouth as if to rebut his words, but instead only shook her head, lowered her eyes, and whispered, "Not for sure."

Targon pulled his hand away and turned back to the two guards. "There. Now, I'm sure this youthful healer from the Realm is good at her healing craft...I've heard wonderful stories about her. But come now, Captain, I am a wizard of

Gildan with some standing. If I say the boy was with me, that should suffice."

Kyril watched as Gamal stepped back away from Joelle. The captain turned to Halcon and then back to Joelle. The healer's eyebrows were furrowed, but she said nothing. Finally, the captain gave a slight bow to Targon and waved at the other two to follow.

"I am sorry to bother you, sir," the captain said with a look of frustration toward Joelle before turning back to Targon. "You have my apologies. Of course, your word is stronger than a young healer's conjecture."

Joelle, the captain, and the guard left the room and closed the door behind them. The room stayed silent, and all eyes turned to Kyril.

Targon slapped Kyril on the back. "Now that's the way to handle authority, Kyril. You just need to be firm with them. I'm sure you were nowhere near the tunnels, were you?"

Kyril's eyes darted toward Jordan and then back again. "Uh…no, of course not," he said weakly. It was an easy lie to cover up. "Why would I be in the tunnels?" he said more loudly.

"Well then. That's all settled." Targon smiled and turned back toward the musicians. "Please continue."

Soon, music filled the room once again and the crowd dispersed as if nothing had happened.

"Thank you, sir," Kyril said.

Targon put his arm around Kyril. "Oh, no. Thank you, Kyril. Thank you for choosing your side wisely."

His side? What had Kyril just done?

Someone called Targon away and Kyril was left standing alone for a moment. He gazed around the room slowly. Smiles and laughter filled the air. A few others nodded their heads in his direction, and Altia turned from Gamal and beckoned Kyril over with a crook of her finger. Bright golden nails caught the sparkle of the nearby candles, and a smile filled her face.

Kyril started walking toward her, when he met Gamal coming towards him.

"You need to be more careful, young apprentice," Gamal said. "Your carelessness could ruin our plans."

Kyril's emotions, so close to the surface after the recent occurrence, surged in anger at the scribe. Gamal had no right to ruin Kyril's good mood. The man was only a scribe as it was. He opened his mouth to speak, but from across the room, Targon called instead.

"Oh, Gamal!" Targon waved a hand toward them. "Kindly let Kyril enjoy the evening and come and help me with something more deserving of your attention."

Anger flashed across Gamal's eyes. The man seemed to barely hold his temper in check. But with one last glare toward Kyril, he smoothed his features and turned and moved swiftly to Targon's side. He nodded his head to his master. Words were exchanged, and although Kyril couldn't tell for sure, neither man seemed to be in a good mood as they headed back to Targon's office.

"Kyril!" Altia yelled, trying to get his attention.

At the sound of her voice, Kyril forgot all about Targon and his scribe, and joined in with his new friends.

CHAPTER TWENTY-ONE

Kyril arrived back in his room that night right before the final bell rang. His roommates initially only gave him obligatory grunts in greeting—all except Sayid.

"Been out with that strange girl again?" Sayid asked.

"She isn't strange," Kyril said, defending Altia. "She's my friend."

"Does Kyril have a girlfriend?" Sayid teased. "What about Sylvie? Does she know?"

Kyril leaped toward Sayid and grabbed the front of his shirt. "Why don't you just leave things alone that you don't understand?"

"Hey, Kyril," Tal said from across the room, "leave him be. You know he didn't mean anything by it. He's only teasing you."

Kyril let go of Sayid and spun around to face Tal. His fists hung clenched at his side. "I'm sick of your kind telling me what to do!"

"My kind?" Tal asked, confusion spreading across his face. "I'm just like you, Kyril, an apprentice wizard of the mind."

"You're nothing like me. You grew up with wealth and privilege and think that gives you the right to be in charge." Kyril took a step toward Tal, who had the sense to back up.

Putting his hands out in front of him, Tal, as was his way, kept his voice soft and calm. "That's not true at all, Kyril. I take my future responsibilities very seriously. One day, I may rule the province after my father, and I assure you—I do care about my people."

"*Your* people?" Kyril puffed, but relaxed his fists.

Behn jumped in to calm the situation. Standing up from his desk and moving between Kyril and Tal he spoke to the others "It's getting late, just go to bed. Kyril, enough of this. We are not against you here. We're all just apprentices trying to make our way through the academy."

Tal nodded and turned back to his bed. Kyril took them both in for a moment, then glared at Sayid before the younger boy headed off to his own bed.

Behn turned the lights off and Kyril lay in the darkness, staring up at the ceiling.

"Kyril," Tal said, "you've been listening to Targon too much."

Kyril shifted in his bed, ready to jump up in defense of his mentor. His palm throbbed a bit and he thought about what Targon had said: Kyril was special. The thought put a smile back on his face and he relaxed.

"Be very careful," Tal whispered in the dark.

Kyril ignored him and turned his thoughts to the events of that evening. He had bested Bale and spent the rest of the evening with those who truly appreciated him. Targon hadn't punished him for the events in the tunnel but had instead protected him and welcomed him fully into his group. It had been one of the more enjoyable evenings of his young life so far. With a smile on his face, he drifted off into a fitful sleep.

***

The next morning, Kyril's roommates left in a hurry, leaving him all alone for a few minutes before breakfast and his first class. He finally took his clothes off from the night before and changed into a fresh outfit. As he put the old clothes in a pile to be cleaned, a small slip of paper drifted to the floor.

A flash of terror crossed over Kyril's face. He had all but forgotten about the note that someone had slipped under his door before he had left his room the night before. With trembling hands, he picked it up and read it.

"Tonight, at dusk. Need more information."

Kyril groaned. It didn't need a signature for him to know who it was from: his handler. His heart raced and he glanced around the room nervously. Because of Targon's gathering, he had missed the appointed time. Originally, he'd been miffed that he didn't know who his handler was—it didn't seem fair to give him such an assignment without any recourse of who to go to for help. But now he was glad that his handler didn't know who he was either. At least he hoped that was still the case.

At breakfast he sat at a table with Jordan, Altia, and a few others of Targon's group, as was his habit lately. Jordan had been more standoffish since the experience in the tunnels, but the others had warmed up to him now. Throughout his meal he continued to glance around the room, wondering if his handler was there at the school or somewhere else in town. Working through the holographic device had only given him a vague identity, and he had always worn a hood, so he didn't really have a means to identify him. But an itch in the back of his head made him feel as if someone was watching him.

"Kyril!" Altia yelled, trying to get his attention.

Kyril jumped and turned back to the group.

"What's the matter? You're all jumpy and distracted today."

"Nothing," Kyril mumbled. Thinking of his handler and his mission made it hard to look the others in the eyes. He felt like he was being torn in two.

From behind him he heard a burst of laughter, and then a crash. Everyone at his table turned their heads around. Sylvie stood in the middle of the hall, looking down at her food splattered all over the ground.

"How clumsy of me, Twig," said Bale, his usual followers standing behind him. "I didn't see you there."

Sylvie glanced back up and caught Kyril's eye. Her own blue ones were filled with embarrassment and frustration, but then upon noticing Kyril, she tilted her head and something else passed between them. Was it sympathy?

Kyril pulled himself away from her eyes and went back to his food.

"She should stand up to him," said one of the other women at their table. "It's people like Bale that make Targon's point clear. We should be the ones in charge."

"She won't stand up to him," said Altia. "She's just on borrow from Arc. She doesn't have the guts. Everyone around here just bows and stoops to people like him."

Kyril wanted to defend Sylvie. He had seen her stand up to Bale before. She wasn't as weak as they said. But he was. He was pathetic, and with the negative conversation about Sylvie around the table, he kept his head down and hurriedly shoved his food in his mouth.

Out of the corner of his eye he watched as Sylvie, with a sweep of her hand, gathered all of the mess from the floor up into the air. The broken dishes mended themselves and landed back on her tray. She then proceeded to walk to the trash can, where she dumped the food, and with head held high, left Bale and his friends snickering behind her.

A few grunts of praise rang around the room, but those at Kyril's table were less forgiving, and instead sat around talking about how they would have handled the situation differently.

"When I'm a full wizard, I won't stand for that!" said one of the other boys at the table. "What about you, Jordan? You're not an apprentice anymore."

Jordan smiled broadly and leaned forward conspiratorially. The rest of those at the table bent their heads closer to hear Jordan's words.

"Soon, my friends," Jordan said. "We must have patience. If we act too soon, then we will tip our hand. I promise you that before the week is over, things will be different."

Kyril thought he saw Jordan glance at him as he said the last words. But then he turned back to the group and lowered his voice to barely more than a whisper. "A mutiny is coming soon. And you will all be rewarded. Then, people like Bale will be put in their place forever."

"That I'd like to see," Kyril mumbled without thinking.

Jordan slapped him on the back and offered the first smile to Kyril in days. "That you will, Kyril. That, and so much more." Jordan's eyes grew fevered as he continued. "Wizards of the mind will rule Gildan."

In the back of Kyril's mind, he thought about their emperor. He was a wizard of the mind. But Kyril didn't think that was the leader Jordan had in mind.

Soon, they all left for class and Kyril joined other apprentices and non-wizards in a weekly class on current events. It was his least favorite class. He didn't care what went on in the workings of the kingdom; he was just trying to get a hold of his wizarding abilities. Others in the class who were not wizards, including Bale, usually contributed to their professor's topics more than the wizards did.

Partway through the class, the door opened, and in walked another apprentice. She handed a note to the professor and he peered out over the class.

"Kyril Siravan," he said.

Everyone turned his direction, and he groaned at the attention. Face flushing, he stood up and walked to the front of the room. The professor handed him the note, and Kyril glanced down at it. Would it be his handler reaching out again? If so, wasn't giving it to him in the middle of a class a bold move? He didn't know what to do.

"Hey dummy, you going to read it or just stand there?" Bale's voice rang out over the classroom. Snickers followed.

Oh, how he hated that man. He thought about the other night and how he had thrown him across the room. Maybe he should do it again? No, Jordan had told them to wait, and besides, he needed to learn to control his temper.

"I'm to take Apprentice Kyril to the headmaster's office," said the young woman who delivered the note.

Headmaster? Then this wasn't a note from his handler.

The speaker waved his hand at them and shooed them toward the door. "Then be off. I don't enjoy my lecture being interrupted."

"Hope we see you again, Kyril," Bale said with a snicker. The man had a gleam in his eyes and a wicked smile on his face. "I've heard that the headmaster is not very tolerant these days on using magic against others…especially those in much higher stations than you."

"Which is about everyone here," piped up one of his friends.

The class laughed again as Kyril followed the woman out the door. It closed behind them, and the laughter faded as they walked down the hall. Kyril kept his head down and walked next to the young apprentice.

"I'm Helena," she finally said.

Kyril nodded his head at her. He didn't want to be rude. It wasn't her fault. "I'm Kyril." Then he mentally hit himself. Of course, she knew who he was; she was the one who had been sent for him.

He fumbled around with the folded note in his hand before finally becoming curious enough about what it said that he opened it. He'd expected to see a command to attend the headmaster, but Kyril stopped short and stared at the writing.

Tonight. Don't miss this one, or trouble could ensue.

His heart pounded hard and he stopped walking.

"Who gave you this?" Kyril called ahead to Helena.

She shrugged and stopped.

Kyril grabbed her by the shoulder. "Who? This isn't from the headmaster, Commander Brashir."

"Ouch. You're hurting me," Helena said and tried to pull away, but Kyril held her firm. "I never said it was from him," she said as she pulled hard and broke away from him. She rubbed her arm with her other hand.

A few wizards passed them in the hallway. One stopped.

"Everything all right here?" he asked Helena, eyeing both her and Kyril.

She hesitated for a moment, and then nodded. "Fine. Just going to the headmaster's office."

The other wizard turned around a few feet ahead when he noticed his companion had stopped. "Hey—you're the one from the fight the other night, aren't you?"

Kyril held his lips tight and didn't say anything.

"I don't question that you are going to the headmaster's office for that," the female wizard laughed. "I don't relish your punishment."

"Punishment?" Kyril mumbled.

"Oh yes. For using magic against another—and especially a noble with strong connections," the first wizard said, shaking his head. "Good luck with that." He waved his hand at them. "Now stop dawdling in the hallways and get going."

They two wizards turned and continued down the hallway. Kyril grunted at Helena and started walking the other direction. She took a few steps and caught up with him.

"I don't understand," Kyril said. "You give me a note that's not from the headmaster, but you say you are taking me to see him?"

Helena let out a puff of air. "I am taking you to the headmaster. He wants to see you." Helena appeared a bit flustered and stumbled on her words a bit. "The note's from someone else."

"Who?" Kyril prodded.

But Helena, with jaw held firm began walking again and Kyril hurried to keep up.

CHAPTER TWENTY-TWO

Five minutes later, he sat alone in a row of three chairs in a small waiting room outside of the headmaster's office. Helena had left without entering the room. He heard raised voices in the office, and hoped it wasn't about him. The small room where he sat had one window, letting in a bit of morning sun. Beside it was one painting on the wall—a view of the city of Gildan from a nearby hill at nighttime. All the domes of the city were lit, forming a colorful kaleidoscope over the city.

The city of Gildan still overwhelmed Kyril. Having grown up in a small village in the meadowlands to the west, he had only traveled once to the capital city as a child. He didn't like the crowds. It was rumored that Gildan held more wizards per capita than any other city on the western continent, which made him nervous. He had never been around wizards or magic much growing up. Periodically, a traveling fair would come through and a few minor magicians would put on a show, but that was the extent of his knowledge of magical things…at least until he came to the academy.

The outside door to the waiting room opened, and a young man a year or two older than him entered. His short hair was lighter than Kyril's and he sported a sparse goatee. He wore the colors of a wizard of the earth, which brought unbidden memories of Sylvie to Kyril's mind. He had hurt her but wasn't ready to deal with those feelings yet.

"Ah, you must be Apprentice Kyril," said the young man. "I'm Cyrus, the headmaster's apprentice."

Kyril's heart jumped. This man might know who his handler was…or maybe he *was* his handler. Maybe that's where the note came from? He jumped out of his seat. Cyrus flinched, clearly surprised by the sudden movement.

"Sorry," Kyril mumbled. "Was the note from you?"

"The headmaster wanted to see you…" He glanced back over his shoulder as shouting in the other room grew louder. His face grew worried. "I wouldn't want to trade places with you."

"But the note!" Kyril was not going to be distracted. "Where did you get it?"

Cyrus face grew impatient. "What do you mean, where did I get it? I work for the headmaster and he wanted to see you. Just sit down. I'm sure he'll be with you soon."

"But the note wasn't from him, it was from…" Kyril didn't know what to say. If Cyrus didn't know anything about his handler, he didn't want to say something wrong.

Cyrus waved a hand in the air, walked around the desk, and sat down. "Look, Kyril. I know you must be afraid to see the headmaster. But it's your first offense, and you are young. I'm sure it will be fine. As you can see," he said, peering down at his paper-strewn desk, "paperwork is not my forte. The note came from the headmaster."

Kyril was getting frustrated. The note was from his handler. "But Helena said…"

"Who's Helena?" Cyrus's face grew red. "Now look here, Kyril. Sit back down and stop bothering me. I've got things to do."

"What do you mean, 'who's Helena'? She's the apprentice that came for me." Kyril didn't move. He needed answers.

Cyrus threw up his hands in the air. "What are you talking about? I don't know anyone named Helena. I sent…"

Just then, the door slammed open and the headmaster stuck his head out. The man's brown eyes burned brightly. "Kyril!" He lifted his thin arm, from which his blue robe hung, and crooked his finger. "Now, in my office."

Kyril caught Cyrus watching him. But he only tilted his head and motioned Kyril to follow. Walking behind the headmaster, he felt short. The man was at least a foot taller than him, and his hair was greying at the edges. His sandals slapped hard on the floor. Without looking, he waved his hand and the door behind Kyril slammed closed on its own.

Before the headmaster, Commander Brashir turned around to speak to Kyril, another man who was already in the office came forward.

"Kyril!" Targon said with a bright smile on his face. "So good to see you again."

Kyril glanced from the headmaster to Targon, trying to figure out why they were there together.

"What's that in your hand, Kyril?" Targon asked as he moved toward him.

Kyril panicked and shoved the note from his handler deep inside his robes. "Nothing. Nothing, sir. Just my summons to see the headmaster." He needed to change the subject—and quickly—even if it brought his punishment on. Being caught with that note, however it had come to him, could be very dangerous. "Why am I here?"

The headmaster sat down behind his immense desk. Unlike his apprentice's, it was neat and tidy with hardly a scrap of paper on it. He motioned for Targon and Kyril to sit down in two chairs opposite him. Kyril did so and then wiped his brow with the sleeve of his robe. It was getting hot in the room.

"Kyril, there was a disturbing display of magic the other day against one of our students that I hear you were involved in." Commander Brashir got straight to the point. "Is that true? Did you use your wizard powers against another student inside the academy?"

There was no use hiding what he had done. "Yes." His voice squeaked, but he was proud that he held the headmaster's eyes without turning away.

"You do know that by doing so you broke a multitude of rules. One, use of magic to that degree by an apprentice is forbidden without a wizard overseeing it. Two, use of dangerous magic is forbidden inside the academy at all times. Three, use of magic against another student or faculty is also against the rules." The headmaster held his jaw firm. He obviously was taking things very seriously. "For any one of these infractions, let alone three, you could be expelled, or at the very least given work detail."

Kyril nodded his head. He had heard of work detail before. Young apprentices or wizards who disobeyed the rules were taken out of school for a time and sent around the kingdom to do manual labor without the use of their wizard powers.

"But, sir…" Kyril began his defense. The accusations were true, he couldn't deny that, but there was provocation on Bale's part. "Bale…"

He didn't get any further in his explanation before the headmaster leaned forward and cut him off. "I'm fully aware of Bale Nabhani. It was his father, the Minister of Housing and close friend to the emperor, that brought this to my attention. Can you imagine how embarrassing it was for me to have to try and defend one of my wizard students to such a man?"

Kyril cringed, and this time did look away from the man. His face was red, and his dark eyes squinted furiously at him.

"With the complaint of the minister and with so many witnesses, I can't overlook this, Kyril. I know that you don't have a home to go back to, but I can't have my apprentices flagrantly breaking my rules."

Kyril's heart fell. He was going to be kicked out of the academy, and the headmaster was correct: he didn't have anywhere to go. What would he do? His magic wasn't strong enough to sustain him in any type of trade. Thoughts of his magic made his palm begin to tingle and heat up. He groaned, and Targon glanced his way, first at Kyril's face and then down to his hands. They sat in his lap, blocked from the headmaster's eyes by the large desk. His scar began to glow again and Targon shook his head at Kyril, then took the attention of the headmaster to himself.

Targon stood up and Commander Brashir's eyes followed him while Kyril tried to get his magic under control. He closed his eyes for a few moments and calmed himself down.

"Where are you going, Targon?" the headmaster snapped at the wizard.

Targon walked to a window and peered outside at the scenic view. The palace sat off on a small rise to the north. "I fear you care more for the nobles than your students, Commander."

"How dare you." The headmaster stood up, his face growing red. "I've been leading this university for twenty years and have produced many fine students—our current emperor, Mezar Alrishitar, included."

"Then why do you let boys like Bale and his friends get away with the things they do? You know that you wouldn't let any of the wizard students treat others like they do. You empower them by not stepping in and doing something about it."

Kyril opened his eyes, his power now back under control, and expected the headmaster to be furious at Targon's words. The opposite, however, was true. The headmaster fell back into his chair and rubbed his bony hands over his wrinkled face. Targon glanced at Kyril, nodded his head and smiled, and then sat back down. It had all been a distraction for Kyril's sake.

"Sir?" Kyril prodded weakly. He really did need to make his case. He couldn't get kicked out. He needed to learn more about his powers. Something was different about him now. He had changed. The mark of the medallion had done something to him.

The headmaster looked up and waved his hand to stop Kyril's words. The man didn't seem interested in hearing Kyril's explanation. Instead he stood and loudly proclaimed Kyril's sentence.

"With regard to your punishment, Kyril Siravan, Wizard Targon has agreed to supervise that. You will be under his care for the immediate future. You will be allowed to attend classes in the academy, but you will sleep, live, and eat under his tutelage and not engage with any students unless supervised by him. Is that understood?"

Kyril sat, his mouth wide open and speechless, and didn't know what to say. He glanced at Targon and a wide smile filled the wizard's face. He turned back to the headmaster who was still awaiting his answer. The man didn't appear very happy, but he'd made his decision, nonetheless.

"Yes, sir," Kyril said, squeakily. "I understand."

He really didn't. Why had he let him off the hook, and why was he allowed to still attend the academy? And why would Targon take him in?

"Well then!" Targon stood and motioned Kyril to join him. "We'll be off then." He bowed his head to the headmaster. "Glad to see we could come to a measure of agreement."

"Don't push it, Targon," the headmaster said, as he too stood up and walked them to the door. "I will not be able to save him again if he breaks the rules."

Kyril realized that the yelling he heard earlier had definitely been about him. He was sure that the headmaster had wanted to kick him out of the school.

He fell behind the two as he glanced around the office for the first time. He stopped when he saw a tapestry on the back wall next to the door. A man with similar coloring to his own, but with much taller and broader stature, stood garbed in burgundy wizard robes. A vague representation of a castle stood off in the distance. But it wasn't the castle or even the man that held his attention.

It was a medallion that hung from the man's neck.

CHAPTER TWENTY-THREE

The medallion in the tapestry appeared almost identical to the one Kyril's mother had owned. The one he'd tried to get during the fire that killed his family. The one that had given him the mark on his hand. He would never be able to get that day out of his head. It had been the worst day of his life. He remembered the searing pain from the hot medallion and the first time his unique magic had appeared.

He was hit again by the feeling he needed to go home and find the medallion for himself. Maybe then he'd get answers to his rising powers. He hadn't seen it since putting out the fire.

Wiping a tear from his eye, he didn't hear Targon return for him.

"Kyril." Targon reached back and tugged on his arm. "What are you doing?"

Kyril kept his attention on the medallion for a second longer. Targon turned to see what had caught his attention, and a small gasp escaped his own lips.

"Come!" Targon pulled Kyril more forcefully.

They left the headmaster's office and passed by Cyrus. The apprentice gave Kyril a strange look as he left with Wizard Targon, then shrugged and went back to work.

They headed toward Targon's suites on the far side of the academy grounds.

Kyril glanced up at Targon a few different times. Each time, the wizard appeared to be deep in thought and Kyril didn't want to interrupt him. Eventually they came to Targon's door and entered the room that they usually dined in. It was empty at the moment.

"Thank you, sir," Kyril spoke up. The wizard deserved his thanks—he was the reason he hadn't been expelled, after all.

Targon was quiet, then blinked a few times as if returning to the present, and then smiled broadly. Running his hand over his stubbled salt and pepper chin, he nodded his head. "You are most welcome. You'll be better off here, anyway."

"Here?" Kyril asked as he took in his surroundings.

Targon walked over to the far side of the room and opened a door. At the end of a hallway he opened another and Kyril peered inside. It was a small room, but not too cramped. A bed sat on one wall underneath a square window. A washbasin sat on a bureau of drawers, and an old worn desk sat in the corner behind a wooden chair.

Targon opened his arms wide. "No one has used this for quite some time. This will be your room now. You will live with me."

Kyril didn't know what to say. It was much more generous than he thought he would get. A few tears come to his eyes once again and he turned his head away to avoid the embarrassment.

"You are excused from your classes for the rest of the day. I will send a servant to fetch your things from your old room, but the rest of the day is yours until dinner time. After dinner we will talk more."

As soon as Targon left the room, his scribe Gamal walked down the hall past Kyril's room. The man stopped, took a step back, and peered into the room. Confusion covered his face as his eyes bore into Kyril's.

"And what are you doing here?"

"I...I..." Kyril stuttered. The man truly did scare him. "I'm staying here for a while."

Gamal's eyebrows rose high onto his forehead. "Hmmm. Interesting," he said, as a barely visible grin turned up his lips. It was more of a sneer than a grin, but the man did seem pleased. "Very interesting indeed."

Kyril didn't know what to say. But apparently Gamal wasn't waiting for an answer, because he was soon on his way again. Kyril sat down on the edge of the bed and bounced up and down a bit. It was a good, firm bed. He thought about what he would do with the rest of his day. He hadn't been outside the academy grounds for a while—well, except for in the tunnels underneath the palace, but that didn't count. There weren't any rules against leaving, but most students, especially apprentices, were usually too busy to do so.

He walked out of his room, shut the door behind him, and made his way down the hall, through the large dining room, and into the hallway. Instead of turning back toward the school, he headed to a door that led outside.

In short order he was outside the academy grounds and walking the short distance toward Gildan. It was a hot day, and once in the city he tried to stay close to any shade provided by the large palms and tall, three-story houses that existed in this part of the city. The cobblestone streets were clean. A few merchants and servants crossed his path, but it was a relatively quiet time of day in the city.

Kyril continued wandering randomly until he found himself in the market district. Here, the noises were louder, the colors brighter, and the crowds thicker. He jingled a few coins in his pocket as he went in search of something to eat.

A trio of men wearing fancy silk robes walked by him, one bumping into him quite hard. When Kyril turned toward them, they looked him up and down, and seeing his apprentice robes they sneered, then turned to each other and started laughing.

Kyril felt his ire build once again. This was what made Targon's plan so enticing. If these strangers knew the powers he had, they would treat him with more respect.

Finally, a heavenly smell drifted past him. He stood up on his tiptoes to find its source. It was a few carts away from him.

He fished a coin out of his pocket and paid for a delicious smelling wrap. Biting into the warm bread, a mixture of pork and mixed vegetables filled his mouth. He reached up with his other hand and wiped a drizzle of spicy white liquid off his chin. With a smile on his face, he wandered a bit more through the market.

Eventually he found himself standing in front of the construction site of a new building. He licked his fingers clean and gazed up above him. The building was at least four stories tall with a dome rooftop. The dome was only partially finished, the outer shell not yet complete. He wondered what would occupy such a grand building. Was it someone's house? He could hardly understand that. He had grown up in a small home with only three rooms. The kitchen and sitting room with a serviceable fireplace had occupied half the house, and the other half had been split into two bedrooms: one for his parents, and one for him and his sister. Because of his father's carpentry skills, their house was even larger and nicer than many in his village in the meadowlands.

A cracking sound in the air above him tore him from his thoughts, and he brought his vision back into focus. High above him, a substantial piece of stone was falling, and was tumbling down the wall toward him.

"Watch out!" yelled a man from above, but in the few moments it took Kyril to figure out what was going on, he realized he wouldn't be able to move before the rock hit him. Instead, he crouched over, covered his head, and waited for the smashing of the rock.

But it never came.

After the point in time that it would have surely hit him, Kyril slowly opened his eyes and tilted his head up. Floating directly over him, only about ten inches above, was the dusty-colored stone.

"You might want to move out of the way, apprentice," came a voice from behind him.

Kyril jumped away, and the rock then proceeded to crash to the ground. Kyril had to put his hand up to block a few stray chips, but he was safe and unscathed.

"Are you all right?" came the voice again. It was a young voice, not much different than his own.

Kyril turned around and caught the eyes of a young man about six feet behind him. He had just finished lowering his arm from stalling the rock above Kyril's head. He was around the same height as Kyril, with a full head of dark black hair. His features were small, and his eyes and smile appeared amused, but friendly. It was then that Kyril noticed the golden band on his wrist.

"Prince Zaidan!" The words slipped from Kyril's lips. Then, remembering protocol, he bowed his head low to the emperor's youngest son.

"Are you all right, My Prince?" shouted a man from above.

Zaidan waved his arm and smiled. "Yes, I'm fine. No problem here, Jorell."

"Thank you, My Lord," said Kyril, realizing that the Prince must be a very skilled wizard of the earth to have stopped the rock so steadily above his head. "I didn't see it until it was too late."

"I'm just glad I was here, Kyril," Zaidan said.

"You know my name?" Kyril blurted out.

A hefty man came up behind him. "Zaidan remembers everyone's name in the kingdom. Despite him being a wizard of the earth, his young mind is quick."

Kyril stood staring at the man. He was huge for a Gildanian. He wore a sleeveless shirt with leather armor over it, his biceps bulging out. The man stood at least six inches taller than Kyril, and most likely weighed at least as much as the prince and him together. The man's face was expressionless as he looked Kyril up and down.

Zaidan laughed. "This is my guard, Naji. He takes care of me."

Kyril stood there not knowing what to say, and still surprised the prince knew his name.

"Come with me, Kyril, I would like to show you something," said the prince.

Kyril glanced around, thinking it was maybe a joke, perhaps another teasing by the nobles…but there was no one else close by.

"What is it?" Kyril asked.

Naji gave Kyril a mean glare, and Kyril decided he shouldn't be asking questions of the prince.

"It's fine, Naji," said the prince with a wave of his hand. "Kyril must be worried about getting back to the academy."

The prince had given him a way out without shaming him. No one had ever treated him this way…well, except for Targon.

"Maybe another time," Zaidan continued. "It's a book I think you might find interesting."

"A book?" Kyril asked. What kind of book would the prince have that would be interesting to him?

As if to answer Kyril's unspoken concern, the prince smiled. "One from my father's study; it's a very old book about medallions."

Kyril's eyes snapped wide open, and he felt the scar on his left hand begin to grow warm at the mention of a medallion. *Oh, no, no, no.* He couldn't have his power escape right now. He needed to leave.

Kyril gave a short bow and began to walk away. "I really do need to go." he said. Then so as to not appear rude, he added, "Maybe another time."

"I'll hold you to that, Kyril." The prince grinned as he spoke his name again—something that still caused Kyril concern.

With that, Kyril took off running, clenching his left fist as he did so. As he neared a corner, the prince called out to him.

"Give Targon my greetings."

Kyril almost tripped on a loose stone as he turned to look back at the prince. How had he known about Targon? He needed to get out of there fast. The prince waved at him and Kyril took off around the corner. He ran for three blocks until he finally stopped behind an inn. Glancing around, he brought his hand out in front of him. The lines on his palm glowed faintly, but he kept them from being seen. He was getting better at controlling his power.

Closing his eyes, he tried to slow his heart rate and clear his mind. He thought about Targon and the room he had given him. All of a sudden he heard a scream, and something drop, and he opened his eyes and found himself in his room. A servant was standing open-mouthed in front of him. A small box of clothes—Kyril's clothes—was on the floor in between them.

After recovering from a moment of sickness he tried to smile at the servant. "Hi, I'm Kyril. Nice to meet you."

CHAPTER TWENTY-FOUR

Sylvie hadn't been able to see the prince for the past two days, and her own classes and guest lectures had kept her from researching anything else about the missing book and the medallions. And now, she heard that rather than getting punished for using magic against another person in the academy, Kyril was living in Wizard Targon's quarters—a consequence far from punishment.

"Sylvie!" said Joelle. "Sylvie, are you listening to me?"

Sylvie peeked up from a book that sat in her lap—one that she hadn't been paying any attention to. Joelle stood in front of her, her long hair almost hiding her face as she leaned over and poked her hand against the book Sylvie was holding.

"Sorry," Sylvie said with a sigh.

"Thinking about Kyril again?" Joelle began chattering away. "You should just leave it alone, Sylvie. You don't owe him anything. He can take care of himself. In fact, it might be good for him to be trained by someone like Targon. Maybe Kyril will be able to learn more that way. Everyone knows how weak of a wizard he is." Joelle paused to take a breath.

Sylvie tried to speak up, but Joelle rolled on past her.

"Now, I know you're going to tell me that he's in trouble and that Targon is not good for him, but Sylvie, you and I are not from here. We have to be careful. Sylvie…are you listening?"

Joelle stomped her foot hard and Sylvie realized her thoughts had run away with her once again. Jumping up from her chair, she put her hands out in front of her, pleading Joelle to stop.

"Joelle! You've told me this a dozen times in the last two days. But aren't you curious? Something is happening to Kyril, and it has to do with that mark in his hand. The mark of a medallion."

Joelle let out a quick puff of breath and stepped closer to Sylvie. "Of course, I'm curious, but I'm not as brave as you are. You have the powers of earth at your command. What if we're caught looking into something we're not supposed to? What if we get in trouble? What would I do then? I can't heal myself!"

Sylvie put a hand on her friend's arm. Joelle's face was red, and she appeared flustered. "I'm sorry, Joelle. I didn't realize you were so worried about this."

"Well, I am," Joelle said, her voice growing quieter. "Magic artifacts scare me." She looked down as if embarrassed by the admission. "There are still a lot of people in my hometown that don't like magic. I'm comfortable with my healing, but not much more."

Sylvie put her arm around Joelle. "I didn't know. I'm sorry. In Arc, magic has long been accepted and practiced. I discovered my abilities when I was quite young and grew up knowing I would be trained at the Wizard Conclave."

"I went to the wizard school at White Island for three years. It was better for me there than at home in Belor," Joelle said as she pulled out of Sylvie's embrace. "I just want to concentrate on my healing abilities."

Sylvie sighed. "Then you won't like what I'm about to do."

Joelle's green eyes went round in anticipation.

A few other students walked by and the two stopped talking for a moment. Then, Sylvie motioned Joelle out of the study hall with her. They walked silently down a hallway and outside to the back of the school—close to the earth wizard practice yards.

"I can't sit by and do nothing, Joelle. I just can't." Sylvie peered around to make sure no one was listening. "I need to get to the basement of the library and find more books."

Joelle groaned and her eyes flickered around. "Sylvie, didn't you hear anything I was saying earlier? We are guests here. If we get caught, there is no one to help us."

"We won't get caught," Sylvie said. "There have to be more books about the medallions. Kyril's powers are growing stronger and he doesn't understand them. I'm afraid what Targon will do to him."

"I can't go with you," Joelle said. "It's not right."

"Joelle!" Sylvie said in frustration. "Isn't it right to try and help Kyril?"

Joelle swung her head from side to side, her long hair floating back and forth around her face. She looked torn inside. "I'm not trained to fight like you."

"But you are powerful," Sylvie said. "A wizard of the heart is the mightiest of wizards. You can do more than heal. I've seen you use your staff."

"I'm not going to use my abilities to break the rules or steal something," Joelle said. "That's not what they are for. And I don't like fighting. I've trained in order to defend myself, but that's all. After healing so many people, I just can't stand the thought of hurting anyone."

Sylvie paced back and forth for a few moments. Her friend wasn't seeing reason in this. Sylvie didn't want to break rules either, but if there was a problem, then it was up to her to find out what it was. There was something about the medallions that she needed to find out. Something inside was driving her.

"Don't think of it as breaking the rules or doing something wrong, Joelle," Sylvie said. "Think of it as doing something for the greater good."

"Isn't that what every rogue wizard or leader says? Isn't that what Targon talks about?" Joelle's freckles stood out on her face. "'The greater good' is just another excuse to break a rule or a law for someone's own purpose. It's not for the greater good; it's for *your* good."

Sylvie felt like Joelle had slapped her in the face. There was only one last argument she could try. She'd tried to keep him out of it, but she couldn't any longer.

"Prince Zaidan Alrishitar has asked me to look into these things and keep my eyes open," Sylvie blurted out.

Joelle's eyes went wide once again, a definite trend since they had begun talking that day. "What do you mean? Why would he ask you to do this? You aren't even from here, and he's only a boy." She put her hands on her hips and a frown covered her face. "Are you making this up to get your way?"

Sylvie shook her head. "No. No, Joelle. I'm not. He's the one that gave the librarian permission to get us the book the other day—the book that turned out to be a fake. I've met with him. His family is concerned about someone trying to recruit others to undermine the emperor and the laws of Gildan. He told me to keep an eye out for things that appeared…other than normal."

Joelle dropped her arms to her side, relaxing the slightest bit. "But isn't keeping an eye out for things different than breaking into a secure part of the library?"

"It's all in the way you approach it, I suppose," Sylvie said with a smile. "I'm not doing anything of harm. I'm going to read a book. "

Joelle let out a small chuckle. "You're determined to do this, aren't you?"

Sylvie nodded.

Before anything else could be said, a woman burst out the back door of the academy. Sylvie knew her as one of the older healers in the academy. She taught classes and helped in the healing center when needed.

"Healer Joelle," the lady said, trying to catch her breath. "I'm glad I found you. There's been an accident and we need you in the healer's room."

Joelle trotted over to the lady, with Sylvie close behind.

"What happened?"

The lady turned and started running back into the academy. Joelle and Sylvie followed.

"We don't know for sure, but three wizards have been hurt," the woman called over her shoulder. "Two fell into a sinkhole and one was hit by runaway horses."

Joelle gave Sylvie a worried look.

Soon they arrived in the healing center and Sylvie stood back as Joelle raced forward. An assistant gave her a towel to wash her hands with, and then with speed belying her small frame, she moved with hurried steps to each patient, first determining what was wrong, and then giving orders to others in the room.

Sylvie was amazed at the efficiency of the operation. The same woman that was afraid of a magic artifact and to bend a few minor rules a few minutes ago was not timid in her own environment. And although she and her team moved swiftly around the room, there was a calmness that began to settle in. In fact, it was something that Sylvie had felt before when she had come here with Kyril. A tingle ran down her arm as she caught a quick glance and smile from Joelle.

It was then that Sylvie realized the true extent of a wizard of the heart. Joelle could not only heal physical wounds but had the ability to smooth emotions and make people calmer and happier. It was incredible. She herself, just being in the same room, felt a renewed sense of energy and clarity of thought. She felt happy and content and had to actually cover her mouth with her hand to keep from laughing.

Of the two wizards who fell into a hole, one was a man with a broken arm and a very bruised face. The other, a woman had a deep gash in the side of one leg. Blood also stained the side of her shirt. Her breathing had slowed, and the healers gathered around her first.

The third man lay off to one side, a bloody gash down the side of his face. He held his shoulder but appeared conscious and interested in what the healers were doing with the other two. Sylvie thought she recognized him—a young apprentice of royal nobility.

Sylvie put it together as she walked over to him. "You're one of Kyril's roommates, aren't you?"

The man nodded. "I was. My name's Tal, but Kyril's moved out."

Sylvie nodded. "Yes, I heard. So, what happened?"

"It was the strangest thing," he said. "My father was in town staying at an inn after meeting with the trade minister. I was going to visit him and was waiting at the side of the road for a carriage to pass, when..." Tal groaned for a moment and grabbed his shoulder.

Sylvie leaned closer, and with a wet cloth dried some blood from the side of his face. "Does it hurt much?"

Tal nodded. "My shoulder does. My face, not as much."

"So, how did you go from watching the horses to being trampled by them?"

Tal appeared nervous speaking about it. "I'm not sure. A thought came to my mind that I could beat the carriage across the street, so I stepped out in front of it. "

Sylvie pursed her lips. This sounded awfully similar to Kyril's experience of jumping off the wall the other day. "You're a wizard of the mind, aren't you?"

"Yes," Tal said. "Well, an apprentice still. But yes, of the mind. Why?"

Sylvie thought for a moment. "Did you notice anything strange about Kyril the past few days?"

Before Tal could answer, Joelle walked back up to them.

"Sylvie, what are you doing with our patient?" Joelle came up behind Sylvie and pushed her gently to the side. "We need to heal him, and then he needs to rest. Stop pestering him with your questions."

"I...uh..." Sylvie stumbled over her words.

"I know what you were doing," Joelle said, without looking at her. She was leaning over and running her hand gently over Tal's shoulder. She closed her eyes and Tal shuddered a few times. "Just relax. You'll be fine," Joelle said soothingly.

Sylvie was standing so close she too felt the power wash over her and felt her body relax. She rubbed her eyes, feeling tired.

"Sylvie?" Joelle leaned back up from helping Tal. "Why don't you go and get some rest? I'll talk to you later."

Sylvie nodded. That was a good idea. She was feeling kind of tired. She walked toward the door but stopped once to turn back to watch Joelle and the rest of her healers at work. With a hand on the doorframe, she realized that Joelle had manipulated her feelings with her powers of the heart.

Shaking her head to clear her thoughts, she left the room. She couldn't sleep right now. There were things to do! And if Joelle couldn't help, she would have to take matters into her own hands.

CHAPTER TWENTY-FIVE

Sylvie had a three-hour break before her next lecture—this was with a group of younger apprentice wizards and involved a few minor demonstrations of moving small objects while harnessing the power of the earth. She needed little preparation for that.

As she moved farther away from the healing center, her energy returned, and she felt more invigorated. Joelle, in her healing as a wizard of the heart, helped her patients to relax. Being in such close proximity to her patients, Sylvie also felt the effect. She allowed herself a small smile at her friend's amazing powers. Sylvie herself could use her growing powers to move objects, reconstruct things, even speed up the growth of plants. This was along with the normal powers of any wizard to form mage lights or balls of fire, open doors, and other smaller things that involved outward influence…but Joelle could affect a person's thoughts and feelings.

There was one ability that she had been experimenting with lately that gave her an idea of how she could get back to the library's underground rooms without being detected. She bit her bottom lip with her upper teeth and a plan began to form, but it would have to wait until evening—she would have better luck in the dark and with less people around.

As her mind worked on the problem of getting into the library's basement, her legs carried her outside. When she stepped out the door, she was instantly hit with a wave of hot, humid air. The sky was cloudy, and in the distance, a grey, churning mass was approaching from the east. Soon it would be raining.

Sylvie picked up her pace and walked through the academy grounds. Normally she would have stopped to appreciate the gardener's work. The tall palms, shorter greenery, and multitude of flowers and water fixtures were much different than the desert she grew up in. The only greenery in Northern Arc, besides an occasional oasis, was on the western slopes of the Superstition Mountains—a place far from the capital where she had attended the Wizard Conclave. There, sand, cactus, stubby trees, and rocks ruled. It was a harsh kingdom to live in sometimes.

She didn't consciously know where she was going, but halfway to the palace, she realized what she was intending to do. She hadn't seen Prince Zaidan in a few days. She wasn't sure what to tell him or how to share her worries about Kyril or suspicions of Targon, but she needed to speak to him.

The road to the palace began to turn slightly upwards. She passed tall, three-story homes with gates in front and domes on the top. Most were made from a smooth cement of some sort. Small palm plants lined the walkway next to the cobblestone street. A few vendors walked with their carts, yelling their daily specials to the citizens of the area, most of whom sent their cooks, bakers, or maids out to buy what they needed. It was too hot for the nobles to go outside during the middle of the day in the summertime.

A few glanced her way, giving her strange glances. A thin, blonde woman wearing wizard robes was not a normal sight for this part of town. She wasn't afraid, though. Gildan was known as a safe and clean city—however, as the events of earlier that day came to her mind, she began watching her step more carefully. It sounded like the accidents with the three wizards were sudden, and quite suspicious. Could someone be targeting wizards?

Soon, she approached the palace and walked for a block next to a tall iron fence. At various intervals, towers had been erected to watch out for any danger. Guards manned these watched towers and hardly paid a young woman any attention.

Coming to the main gates, she stopped and spoke to a captain. He nodded his head in deference to her station as a wizard. The man was of age to be her father, yet stood trim and fit, wearing tight leather armor over an obviously toned body. His hair was dark and short, and he wore a small goatee. His smile was friendly, but his stance showed he was serious about what he did.

"Wizard, what brings you to the palace today?" he said. "We don't have any visitors from the academy on the schedule."

Sylvie smiled, knowing that her dimples would show on each side of her cheeks. "I'm sorry to bother you, Captain. I have business with Prince Zaidan today."

The captain's smile dropped slightly. "I'm sorry, but the prince is not in the palace this afternoon."

Sylvie scrunched up her face, trying to decide what to do. She had not expected that he wouldn't be there. But then, why had she thought he would be? Of course, there were other tasks for him to attend to. He was the second heir, but a prince, nonetheless.

"Would you happen to know when he will be back?" Sylvie asked. "He discussed something of importance with me the other day and asked for my input." She added the last part hoping to convey the importance of her being there. Maybe the captain would give her a snippet of information that she could work with. "It is quite urgent."

The captain turned and glanced at the palace, pursing his lips and furrowing his forehead as he did. He was obviously thinking things through.

"I am Wizard Sylvonna Hickory from Arc, by the way," Sylvie said, trying to make him feel more comfortable with her presence. She tilted her head just a bit and smiled.

The captain threw back his head and laughed. "I know who you are, Wizard Sylvonna. There are not many from Arc here in the city. You do kind of stand out."

Sylvie felt her cheeks warm and she absently touched her blonde hair. She hadn't realized that she was known in the city.

"We have all heard of the powerful young earth wizard from Arc," the captain added.

"Thank you." Sylvie bowed her head. "But I do need to speak to the prince. Can you please let him know I came asking for him?"

The captain put a hand to his chin and seemed to be deciding something. Another guard walked past and nodded toward the captain. After he was gone, he lowered his voice and leaned in closer to Sylvie.

"He went to the southern part of the city, where the accidents happened this morning," the captain said. "To be honest, he should have been back by now. I don't want to make a scene—you know, young men do wander sometimes, and he is a good boy. But if you could check on him, I'd be most grateful. I don't want to tell the emperor that he hasn't returned."

Sylvie could see the man's predicament, and realized it was also his way of letting her know where the prince was without disobeying orders.

"I would be happy to," she said with another smile. If she walked quickly, she should have enough time to find him, talk to him for a few minutes, and then get back to the academy for her lecture.

She gave the captain a small bow and he did the same in turn, then she started down a road toward the other side of the city.

Halfway there, a few drops of rain began to fall, and she picked up her pace. Three blocks later, farther from the palace, the houses were smaller. Now, most of them were two stories, with the bottom floor being a shop or business of some type. The colors were more muted here than in the neighborhood closer to the palace, but the streets were still kept clean, though now the cobblestone had turned to hard-packed gravel.

The wind picked up and the rain began coming down harder. She opened her mouth and laughed with glee. She loved the rain. It was one of her favorite things about Gildan compared to her desert city, where only occasional flash floods roared through during the summer. There, they had to catch their water in cisterns, and collect it from a few smaller streams from the mountains on either side of the desert.

With the sound of the rain, she hadn't been paying as much attention to her surroundings as she should have. Turning a corner, a man ran into her, knocking her hard to the ground. He stopped for a moment and looked her up and down but didn't take any time to help her back up.

"Run," was all he said to her. "You're not safe here."

Sylvie didn't understand what the man was saying. Her backside was bruised, and she slowly stood back up to ask more questions, but he was already dozens of feet away. Instead she continued walking down the street. Even in the rain, a considerable crowd had formed in front of a storefront. It was hard to see through the crowd, but it appeared that an overhang had fallen, and someone was trapped underneath.

"Help!" she heard someone yell.

Without thinking, she pushed through the crowd to find a woman lying on her side, crushed under the weight of a dozen boards.

"I'm not strong enough," the woman said, seeing Sylvie. She struggled for a moment, and the boards shifted slightly on their own.

The woman was a wizard, but not likely an earth wizard. Sylvie stepped forward, rain still running down her face, and lifted her hands up in front of her. The boards began to shake and then lift up off the ground. Sylvie dug deep inside of herself and brought more of her power up. The boards lifted higher, then up and over the side of the crowd, settling back down on the ground a dozen feet away.

Sylvie leaned down and put her hand out for the woman. The woman reached for her hand weakly, then it fell to the ground and she closed her eyes with a loud sigh.

"No. *No,*" Sylvie said. Glancing around for help, she pointed toward some stronger-looking men. "You there, help her to the academy. Healer Joelle will see to her."

The two she pointed to were dressed more finely than the rest and held umbrellas. They shook their heads and started to back away. Sylvie couldn't believe the lack of help. Much of the crowd began to disperse.

"Won't anyone help?" Sylvie surveyed the situation and furrowed her eyebrows at the spectators. "What happened here?"

"I'll not touch her," said another man. "Wizards are getting hurt all over the city today. I'm not getting involved."

"They think they're better than us, and now they are being punished," said another woman. "I say good riddance to them." She turned and walked away.

Had she been inside the academy for so long that she didn't know what was happening in the city? The animosity between wizards and non-wizards was a much bigger problem than she thought. Deep in her own thoughts, she hadn't noticed three men move closer to her.

"And you're one of them," said the first one, a man just older than Sylvie herself. His hair was tied back in a ponytail and he wore all back clothes.

"Yes, I'm a wizard." Sylvie stood her ground. "And if I don't help that woman there," she said, pointing to her, "she may die."

"She got her punishment for thinking she is better than us," said another man, this one barely Sylvie's own age.

"Get out of my way," Sylvie said, walking around them. "If you won't help, I'll have to do it myself." Using her power, she could carry the woman to the academy. It would be difficult, but she thought she could do it.

As she walked past the group, the third man, larger than the other two—in fact, larger than most she had seen in Gildan—moved to block her. His skin was pale and his hair much lighter; most likely, he had a parent or grandparent from the Realm.

He put his hand on her arm and clamped down hard. "You need to leave."

The man was hurting her, and she tugged on her arm to get it away, but he held on tightly. With only a moment's thought, she drew power from the dirt and rocks under her feet. She stomped down hard, and the earth shook around them. The man in front of her stumbled to stay on his feet. In the process, his grip weakened, and she pulled her arm away.

The man with the ponytail moved in to grab her, but she put her hand out in front of her, and with a blast of air pushed him back a dozen feet to the ground. Now the younger one drew a knife from his belt and thrust it toward her. She jumped high and kicked out at him, knocking the knife out of his hand, while simultaneously using her hands to gather in the rain around her and shove it all at once at the man who first tried to grab her. It hit him hard in the face and he swallowed a bunch of the water. He scrambled to keep from falling to the ground, but eventually he did, gagging and coughing.

With the three on the ground, the remaining crowd retreated inside the nearest storefront. Sylvie grunted in anger, then approached the woman on the ground. Waving her hands around in front of her once again, she lifted the woman up in front of her, forming a cushion of air underneath her. With the storm raging around her, pulling the additional air she needed was actually easier.

Standing there for a moment with the woman hovering a few inches above her arms, she turned around with disgust at the storefront where the people had retreated out of the rain and away from the confrontation. A man walked out of the store with a sword in his hand and approached her. She wasn't sure if she could fight him off while still carrying the woman.

A shout came from down the street behind them, and the man turned. Sylvie tried to see around him. Through the rain came a young man with dark hair plastered to his forehead. The familiar gold wristband shone brightly, glowing in the stormy day.

The man with the sword looked back at Sylvie, then over toward the approaching man before kneeling down on the wet ground on one knee.

"My Prince," the man said with a bowed head.

Others inside the store echoed the greeting. The three on the ground stirred, but only one rose far enough to kneel before the prince.

Prince Zaidan peered at the three on the ground, then back to Sylvie with raised eyebrows.

"I can explain," Sylvie said to the prince, "but for now, I need to get this woman to the healers."

Zaidan nodded his head, but his eyes were darker than normal, and he didn't appear very happy. "This doesn't look good, wizard Sylvonna."

"I…" Sylvie was going to say it wasn't her fault, that they attacked her. But with the three men on the ground and her still standing, and because she was a foreigner there and a wizard to boot, now was not the time for explanation. Instead, she glared at Zaiden in her frustration of being accused unjustly.

"Well, are you more of a man than these three are?" she said glaring at those that had attacked her and the man that brought the sword out. "Will you help me carry this woman to the healers, or are you going to make me do it alone?"

Zaiden's eyes went wide. She was sure he was not used to being talked to that way. But at the moment, Sylvie didn't care.

"Of course, I will help, Wizard Sylvonna," Zaiden said. "Marna is one of my people. I care about all my people."

At first, they carried her together, and Sylvie only had to use a bit of her powers. Soon, however, they met two guards heading their direction, and Zaiden ordered them to carry the woman instead.

Walking next to Zaiden and following the guards, Sylvie glanced over at him. He turned and met her look at first with a frown of his own, then a small smile began to spread across his face.

"You really took all three of them down?" Zaiden asked.

Sylvie shrugged. "It wasn't that hard." She gave a small smile of her own that only lasted for a moment, then turned to a frown. "But I thought I would be safe in your city."

Zaiden shook his head. "Something is not right in Gildan. Strange things are happening."

Sylvie saw something move out of the corner of her eye—a shadow of a man in a doorway. He was broad-shouldered, but short, and pulled up a hood over his bald head.

"Sylvie!" Zaiden prompted her attention.

"I'm sorry, I just saw something suspicious," Sylvie said, turning back to the spot. But no one was there now. It was as if he'd just vanished.

"Where?" Zaiden asked.

Sylvie shook her head. "I don't know. But you are right, something is not right in Gildan."

CHAPTER TWENTY-SIX

"This is an outrage!" Wizard Targon Quereshi informed the group in front of him. "An attack on wizards will not be tolerated."

Kyril was surprised at the vehemence in his mentor's voice. Glancing around the room he spotted Jordan, Altia, and other followers. They were clearly riveted by Targon, and their heads were nodding in confirmation of his words. Standing near the back of Targon's dining room was Gamal. When Kyril turned and saw him, he was staring back at Kyril as if he had already been watching him for a while. The man's eyes bore into his own, and Kyril was forced to turn away. He wondered why Targon kept such a creepy man around.

"As a longtime wizard myself, I have pled my case to the nobility of Gildan, but they have not taken this threat seriously," Targon said, continuing his speech. "We must rise up and protect our own."

Kyril sat, engrossed by the speech; a strange sense of pride building in his chest. Targon was right. He was now wondering if the piece of the building that had fallen toward him the other day had even been an accident after all. And had the prince only saved him as a ploy? In the past two days, there had been eight incidents involving wizards being hurt in the city. Maybe Targon was right; maybe they did need to take things into their own hands.

"I have set up a command post outside the city on one of my estates," Targon said. "Any wizard who would like to, can take refuge there, but..." he held up his hand for emphasis, "make no mistake who is in charge. The wizards of the mind are the only ones working to solve this problem. You here have chosen to stand with me already. You will be my eyes and ears among the wizards. We will build a force to be reckoned with—but that force must be loyal to us. Who is with me?"

Targon's voice rose in challenge, and the fifteen or so people in the room cheered their acceptance. Kyril himself smiled at the thought of being a part of something so grand and important. Targon motioned for them all to go find recruits and let others wizards know of the gathering place. As the others began to leave, his mentor called Kyril over to him.

"Have you settled in here well?" Targon asked.

"Oh, yes," Kyril nodded. "Your staff has been very friendly to me." He caught Gamal glaring at him once again and pushed the sour scribe from his mind.

"Good. Good." Targon placed a comforting hand on Kyril's shoulder. "You will always have a place by my side, Kyril."

"Thank you, sir." Kyril beamed at Targon. He was still amazed at his good luck in gaining the wizard's attention.

"I have an important task for you," Targon said.

Kyril still didn't understand why Targon cared about him so much, but he was happier than he had ever been since his parents and sister had passed away. No one had accepted Kyril so unconditionally and treated him so well. He owed a lot to Targon already and would do whatever the wizard wanted.

Something important tickled the back of Kyril's mind. Thoughts of his handler came to his mind, but he pushed them to the side. His handler and those working with him obviously didn't understand the type of man Targon was. There was nothing to tell them. The wizard wasn't doing anything wrong; he was only fighting for their rights.

"Come with me." Targon's words snapped Kyril out of his musings.

Targon walked toward his office and Kyril followed. Only Gamal remained in the room, and the man had a sly smile spreading across his face as he nodded his head to Targon. Maybe he should tell his handler about *that* man. There was definitely something wrong with him—but Kyril didn't have anything concrete to share. He'd missed his last two meetings with his handler and hoped he didn't know he was now living with Targon.

The office always appeared the same: clean and neat. However, Kyril's eyes were drawn to an ancient book on a small table. It was the book that had been thrust upon him in the tunnels under the palace. At the time, he'd thought the man that had given it to him might have been Targon, but if so, why would that be?

"What's the matter, Kyril?" Targon smiled at him. "Is something wrong?"

"No." Kyril shook his head a bit to clear his thoughts. "Just thinking about that book there."

"Ah!" Targon's eyes lit up. "That's what I wanted to show you. Come and sit down." Targon picked up the book and joined Kyril, sitting on a sofa next to him.

"This book is going to change your life," Targon said as he opened the heavy cover.

"Change my life? A book?" Kyril said. He didn't understand.

"This book is about you," Targon said.

"Me?" Kyril sat up straighter. "How can that be? This book looks as old as my grandparents."

"Oh, much older than that," Targon said, a smile spreading broadly across his face. "This book is the Western Codex and goes back far before anyone we know was alive, almost back to the founding of magic here on the western continent."

Kyril was confused. "Then how can it be about me?"

Targon began flipping through the pages. Kyril saw glimpses of artifacts—most of which had no meaning to him. Some of the words he could decipher, but most he could not. He had studied some ancient artifacts in his classes and knew that some could augment a person's wizarding skills in various ways. But he still didn't know what this had to do with him.

Targon stopped on a page about three-fourths of the way through the book, and Kyril gasped out loud. Without thinking, he brought his left hand out in front of him and turned his palm upwards. Tracing it with the fingers from his other hand, he glanced back and forth between his palm and the book. The pattern was the same. Three concentric circles with 6 lines coming out from the center. Three of the lines ran to the edge of the medallion and formed smaller half circles on the outside of the relic. He finally glanced up at Targon's smiling face.

Targon nodded. "Yes, Kyril, it is the same pattern on your palm. I told you this book was about you."

"But what does it mean?"

"Do you trust me, Kyril?" asked Targon, lowing his voice a bit. "If I am to share this with you, I need to know that you trust me."

"Yes, of course I trust you," Kyril said without hesitation. He couldn't believe that the medallion sitting on the page in front of him was identical to the one that his mother had owned.

"Where is the medallion?" Targon asked. "Is it in your room?"

Kyril's face dropped and he shook his head. "I don't have it. It was my mother's."

Targon's expression grew dark and he snapped the book shut—but not before Kyril spied two other medallions on the same page. All held the same mark, but all three were different colors. One was gold, like his mother's, one was silver, and one was bronze.

Before Kyril could think any more on the matter, Targon stood up and glowered down at Kyril. "I thought you said you trusted me, Kyril. How can I help you if you don't tell me the truth?" The man's voice was soft, but so full of venom, Kyril shrunk back on the sofa.

"I'm sorry, Wizard Targon," Kyril began. He didn't want Targon to be angry with him. "I do trust you. But I don't have the medallion."

"Then how did you get that mark?" Targon pointed to Kyril's palm.

"There was a fire. Remember I told you my family was killed." Kyril didn't want to talk about it, but he had no choice and so he pushed forward, his voice growing angry. "I grabbed the medallion to remember my mother by, but it burned my hand and I dropped it. I suppose it's still there somewhere in the meadowlands."

Kyril didn't know what else Targon wanted from him. A few stray tears formed in the corners of his eyes and he wiped them away in embarrassment. Targon paced the room for a few more moments, stopping in front of his own black medallion. He picked it up and fingered it a moment. Kyril noticed now that the pattern was the same as his, but the black medallion had not been shown on the page of the book—at least, not as far as he could see before it was shut.

"I need that medallion, Kyril," Targon said through clenched teeth. He put his own medallion back carefully on the shelf and then walked back over to Kyril. He sat down once again, took a deep breath, then turned to Kyril.

"I'm sorry I became angry," Targon said, visibly relaxing. "It's just that the attacks on the wizards have gotten me so worried for our people. Will you forgive me?"

Forgive him? No one had ever asked Kyril to forgive them before—at least no one with such a high ranking as Targon.

"Of course, Wizard Targon," Kyril said. "There is nothing to forgive. You are an important man with lots on your mind. I'm just a poor apprentice. I understand."

"Do you? Do you really understand what I am doing here, Kyril?" Targon asked. "Maybe it wasn't right to bring you along with me. I may have made a mistake. I don't want you to get hurt, Kyril."

Kyril sat stunned in the silence following Targon's words. *No!* Targon couldn't give up on him. He was just beginning to feel like he was a part of something, and to have friends. What could he do to help Targon?

"Please don't give up on me, sir," Kyril said quietly. "You've been so nice to me. Everyone has been. I can't lose all of this. I don't want to leave. I'm with you." And Kyril meant every word he said.

"Being a part of this grand plan is more than just being nice, Kyril," Targon said. "We have been overlooked for far too long. It's time for us to unite and show the nobles and those who look down on us what we truly are."

"I know, sir," Kyril said, his voice becoming stronger. "I understand. Like you said. We are alike. We've both been treated badly in our lives. I want more than that."

"Do you really?" Targon said, his smile returning.

"Yes." Kyril meant it. "What can I do for you?"

"I need you to go to your hometown and find that medallion," Targon said. "I need it. We need it."

Kyril nodded. He already felt the need to do so at some point, but now with Targon's direction, he would go immediately. "Yes, of course. I will leave tonight."

Targon chuckled. "I think in the morning will be soon enough. I have one other favor to ask you first."

"Anything."

There was a knock on the door, and Gamal poked his head in. Kyril felt Targon tense up next to him. His scribe always seemed to interrupt him at the worst times. The wizard stood up as Gamal strode into the room. He glanced around the room, his attention lingering a bit longer in the direction of the black medallion.

"Gamal, what is the meaning of this?" Targon asked.

"Just wanted to make sure everything was all right with our young friend, and that you didn't need anything," Gamal said with a smug smile.

"I am fine," Targon said. "Kyril has agreed to do a favor for me."

"For you?" Gamal tilted his head, his eyebrows shooting up on his bald forehead. "You mean for *us*?"

Targon stumbled a bit on his words. "Yes, of course, I mean for us. For the cause."

"And does young Kyril have what *we* need?" Gamal asked.

Targon's visage fell a bit. "He does not, but he knows where it is."

Gamal's lips turned down and he put a hand on Kyril's shoulder. "I hope he finds it soon." The hand squeezed and Kyril tried not to wince. "It's almost time."

Targon nodded his head. Kyril glanced from Gamal to Targon and wondered what it was almost time for.

"As I said, we are fine, my good scribe," Targon said, emphasizing Gamal's position. "Now if you will excuse us, Kyril and I were just finishing up our business."

Gamal gave a short bow and left with a mock smile. After the door closed, Targon let out a deep breath.

"If you don't mind me asking, sir," Kyril said, "why do you keep Gamal around? He isn't a very nice fellow."

Targon laughed and slapped Kyril on the back. "No, he isn't."

The question was left unanswered, and Kyril decided it wasn't any of his business who Targon employed. Gamal must have had impressive skills as a scribe.

"Now the other favor?" Targon said, glancing at the door and lowering his voice.

Kyril nodded.

"I need you to teach me how you teleport."

CHAPTER TWENTY-SEVEN

Sylvie had never been overly adventurous as a young child. However, as she grew up and found out she had the powers of an earth wizard, she began to have more confidence in herself. Leaving home at twelve years old, she lived most of the year at the Wizard Conclave in the kingdom of Arc. There, she progressed quickly, surpassing many older students in the first year. The ability of magic and wizardry appeared randomly in people most of the time in Arc, but she surmised with two of her grandparents being wizards she had inherited her abilities from them.

The High Wizard of the Wizard Conclave, Danijela Anwar, become her mentor and Sylvie would do anything to have her praise. Passing her wizard test at fifteen was not unusual, but the way she had done it—with more finesse and power than many—had earned her high marks and allowed her to travel here to Gildan to continue her studies while being a guest teacher of other young apprentices.

She now used some of those abilities as she snuck through the library. It was late at night, past the time of the first bell and just before the second. Most of the apprentices had headed to their rooms for the night, leaving only a few wizards finishing up.

A shuffling sound came from the other side of a bookshelf from where Sylvie stood. Backing up against the shelf, she rooted her feet firmly to the floor and brought up her powers. She had been practicing this ever since the prince had helped her past the block in her mind. Bringing the power up through the floor and the shelves and into the books, she wrapped it around herself until she became one with the bookshelves—virtually disappearing.

Standing perfectly still, she watched an older wizard with two books in her hand hobble past her. All the woman saw were the shelves of books around Sylvie. Holding her breath, Sylvie maintained the illusion until the woman passed by. She let out the breath, and if someone had been looking, it would have appeared that she'd just solidified from thin air. Peering around the shelf, she didn't see anyone else between her and the set of stairs that led down to the basement rooms.

By the light of the few remaining candles, she snuck across the shadowed room, taking care to stay as close as possible to other objects. If she needed to, she could hide herself again, blending in with the objects. It took very little power for her now that she knew how to do it.

She stepped on the first stair. The stone staircase was hard and smooth under her slippered feet. A few steps down, she heard a voice from up above. She didn't have anywhere else to hide herself.

"Hasani," said the librarian. "You've done enough for tonight. Thank you. You'd better get to your room before the final bell."

"You're welcome," Hasani said. "I will be back tomorrow after my classes."

Sylvie couldn't see them yet, but their voices were definitely growing louder.

"When you come in tomorrow you can resume your normal duties, Hasani," said the librarian. "I suspect you have learned your lesson about sneaking into areas where you are not supposed to be."

"Yes, madam, I have," Hasani said. "I assure you, I have."

The two came around a corner and Sylvie shrunk back farther against the wall. She hoped the darkness down below would keep her from being discovered. She backed up one more step, but only hit the marble with half her foot. She slipped, and even though she caught herself, she grunted, a sound that echoed clearly in the library.

The librarian and Apprentice Hasani came around the corner. The librarian's back was to Sylvie, but Hasani peered right down the stairs at her—and his eyes opened wide.

"It sounded like it came from below," the librarian said as she began to turn around. "I'll go and check."

Sylvie slid back as far as she could on the stairs and quietly lay down on her stomach without being noticed. Hasani looked her direction and stared into the darkness, then drew the librarian's attention away.

Sylvie concentrated, then pulled a small breeze into the library—just enough to blow out a few of the candles on the other side of the library.

The librarian jumped. "Did you feel that?" she asked Hasani as she wrapped her arms around herself. "I'll check on those after I look downstairs."

"You check out the candles," Hasani said with a hand on her back. "I'll check down the stairs for you. I know your legs must be tired."

"Such a nice boy you are, Hasani," the librarian complimented, but then her voice turned sterner. "Just check the door to make sure it's locked. Don't go through it."

"Don't worry about me," Hasani chuckled. "I've learned my lesson. I'll check and then head out."

Sylvie watched the librarian walk away before Hasani turned and headed down the steps.

"What are you doing here, Wizard Sylvonna?"

Sylvie stood up as he approached her, and a thought came to her mind. "I could use your help."

Hasani shook his head, his braids swinging around his face. "You heard the librarian. I'm only to check the lock on the door and then I'm going to my room. I'm done being a custodian for the library."

"But it won't take long," Sylvie said pleadingly. "It'll go much faster if you're with me."

"With you…where?"

"I need to look through the books downstairs," Sylvie said. "I need to find something else about the medallions. Please, Hasani, there's something wrong going on, and I need to figure it out."

Hasani sighed, glanced up the stairs for a moment and then back at Sylvie. "You know what happened last time I was down there." He rubbed his head where he had been hit.

"But I'll be there to protect you this time," Sylvie said. "I am a mighty earth wizard." She said the last with a smile and punched Hasani softly in the arm.

"You are at that!" Hasani said. "You saved a wizard yesterday in the city while fighting off a group of ruffians!"

"Oh, you heard?" Sylvie asked, feeling a little sheepish.

The candles started blinking off around the rest of the library.

"Come on, we need to hurry before it gets too dark to see!" Sylvie grabbed Hasani's hand and pulled him down the stairs. He almost tripped once, and Sylvie had to stop him from falling. Reaching the bottom of the stairs, the last candle up above went out, plunging them into pitch darkness.

"She thinks I'm gone already," whispered Hasani.

"Good," Sylvie said.

She could hear Hasani fiddling with the door handle. "It's locked. Now what do we do?"

"You're a wizard, Hasani. Can't you open a locked door?" Sylvie asked.

She could almost sense Hasani shaking his head in the dark. "That's not my specialty. I remember things, think through problems, and can summon fire if needed, but I haven't picked any locks."

Sylvie smiled, though she knew Hasani couldn't see her. "Good thing you have a wizard of the earth with you, then." She put her hand out and wrapped it around the doorknob. She felt the powers in the earth guide her to the metals in the lock mechanism. Pushing forward her will, she moved the pins in the lock, and subsequently a faint *click* was heard.

She slowly turned the handle and pushed the door open. A weak light from somewhere in the basement rooms filtered through to them—enough that Sylvie could see Hasani's worried face. She pulled him through the doorway and then closed the door behind them. They went down a short hallway to the familiar place where she and Joelle had been only a few days before with the head librarian.

Eventually, they came to the small sitting area, where multiple doors lined the room, leading into the smaller rooms where the books were stored. A lone torch flickered on one of the walls, sending dancing shadows throughout the area.

"Where to?" Sylvie asked.

Hasani stood staring at the room that he'd been taken from before without speaking.

Sylvie put her hand on his arm, and he jumped a bit. "Sorry, I didn't mean to startle you. You won't be kidnapped this time. I promise."

Hasani arched an eyebrow at her and only grunted. "I'm going to be in so much trouble."

"Which room?" Sylvie asked with a smile and a wave of her hand.

"I don't know!" Hasani's voice rose in pitch. "I've never even been in some of these rooms. I'm only an apprentice librarian, remember—these books are some of the most ancient and priceless in all of Gildan, and I suspect on the western continent!"

"Relax, Hasani," Sylvie said, trying to comfort him.

Hasani let out a deep sigh and took a few labored breaths. "I'm sorry. I'm not usually like this. It's…all these attacks on wizards, a book that disappeared, and talk of these medallions—you have to understand, I'm a scholar. I'm not like you, Sylvie. You're brave, resourceful, and if I'm being honest, a little reckless." He smiled at that.

Sylvie laughed. "Joelle thinks the same, but I just can't leave it alone. Kyril is my friend, and somehow, he's mixed up in all of this. I need to help him. It's the right thing to do."

Hasani nodded "I trust you, Sylvie. But if I get caught down here, I'm not sure they'll let me stay here in the library or in Gildan. They might kick both of us out and back to our own kingdoms."

"Do you miss it?" Sylvie asked. "Mahli?"

Hasani's lips turned down for a moment. "Sometimes, yes. The tall snow-covered mountains are breathtaking. And I do miss my family."

Sylvie nodded. She agreed with the last part. Ever since she had gone off to the Wizard Conclave, she had only seen her family for a few days each year. Neither her older nor younger sisters had any wizarding powers, but when she was with them they treated her no differently than they did each other.

Hasani began walking toward one of the rooms, and Sylvie followed.

"But you know what I miss the most?" Hasani said.

Sylvie shook her head.

"The dragons." Hasani's grin was infectious.

Sylvie had seen a dragon and its rider only once since her arrival in Gildan. It had been Dragon Rider Liam, the son of the king of the Realm. It was magnificent. The other dragons tended to stay in the southern kingdoms.

"You've met Bakari, the famed Dragon King?" Sylvie asked.

Hasani nodded his head. "Yes, being from Mahli himself, I've seen the Dragon King multiple times with his brillliant blue dragon. What I wouldn't give to fly on a dragon someday." He opened one of the doors, stepped inside, and brought up a small mage light in his hand.

"I agree," Sylvie said, "but for now, we need to concentrate on finding something that will tell me about the medallions.

"What do you think I'm doing?" Hasani asked with a sly grin.

"But…?" Sylvie waved her hand around. "You've been talking about other things…"

"I *can* think about two things at once," Hasani laughed.

"Wizards of the mind," Sylvie grumbled, and shook her head. But she smiled back at Hasani.

"I've been thinking back through the catalogue of records that I've studied." Hasani walked to a tall shelf and began running his fingers over the spines of the ancient tomes. "Even though I haven't been in all these rooms or seen all the books, I have read and studied about them and how they are organized. This room here focuses on the timeframe of about 400 years ago."

Sylvie gave him a bewildered look and he continued talking and searching at the same time. Every once in a while, he would pull a book down and thumb through its pages carefully for a few moments before placing it back in the exact same spot on the shelves.

Sylvie couldn't make any sense of the hundreds of books around her. There were tall books, small ones, and thick ones. Some were leather bound, others held together with string or metal rings. Some had colored covers, but most were brown or black.

"A little over 400 years ago, King Anikari formed the Realm. At that time, Gildan was already a flourishing city, although the kingdom didn't extend much farther than the city itself. Your kingdom, Arc, was basically a bunch of warring tribes divided from the Realm and Gildan by the Superstition Mountains."

"But why are you searching here?" Sylvie asked.

Before Hasani answered, she heard a small noise outside of the room. She put her finger to her lips to quiet Hasani and took a few steps to peek out into the sitting room. She stood still and listened for a few moments. When she didn't hear anything else, she walked back into the room.

"I guess I'm just jumpy," she said. "Now, why are we in here?"

"Because of this." Hasani pulled down a large book and placed it on a small table in the middle of the room. Its cover was worn, black leather. Gold writing was scribbled faintly across the font, but Sylvie couldn't tell what it said from her perspective.

Hasani reverently opened the two-inch-thick book, and ancient dust wafted by Sylvie's nose. She had to look away for a moment to keep from sneezing.

"Around the time of the founding of the Realm, Anikari was a great wizard. Much of what he could do and what he knew has been lost through the years, but I remember two things about that time period."

Sylvie moved next to Hasani as he carefully turned the brittle pages. She was anxious to find out what Hasani would find in the book, but she needed to have patience and let the scholar go at his own pace—something she'd learned years ago in the Wizard Conclave. Although a wizard of the heart usually jumped headfirst into things with their emotions, a wizard of the earth still made decisions much more quick than a wizard of the mind. She took a deep breath and waited it out.

"Ah," Hasani said as he turned a page.

Sylvie leaned over and saw a sword. It was gold and beautiful with strange writing on its blade. But it wasn't a medallion. She let out a deep sigh.

"Hasani?" Sylvie asked, staring to lose patience and wondering how long they had been down there.

"King Anikari's sword," Hasani said.

"And why are we looking at a sword?"

"Patience, dear earth wizard." Hasani smiled and his dark eyes reflected the mage light that now sat above the book.

Oh, great, Sylvie thought. *Now he's more relaxed, when I need him to hurry.*

"The current King of the Realm has possession of the sword. But there are also stories of other ancient magical artifacts that Anikari controlled," Hasani began, going into teaching mode as he held the book open in his hands. "Three medallions for example. Each with very special powers. It is rumored that when they are used together, they bring balance to the magic.

"Really?" Sylvie leaned down. Now she was interested. "Where are they?" She reached forward to turn a page of the book in her haste.

Hasani slapped her hand away. "Be careful!"

She pulled back but flashed a frown at Hasani. She needed to find out what was in the book.

Unexpectedly, what sounded like someone crashing into a door made both of them jump. Hasani dropped the book to the table and let out a sound of frustration.

"Cut the light!" Sylvie ordered Hasani.

Instantly, they were in pitch darkness.

Sylvie moved quietly to the door and closed it as far as she could, leaving only a slit to see out of. She could feel Hasani close behind her, his breathing hot and quick against her neck. Faint voices came from behind a door on the far side of the waiting room—the door that led to the tunnels under the palace.

Again, without warning, a light appeared in the waiting room, and two figures stood smiling at each other.

"Kyril, my boy," said Targon, "that was amazing!"

Sylvie sucked in a quick breath and backed away from the door, bumping into Hasani and stepping on his foot as she did so. He muttered something quietly and she flung out her arms to grab hold of him to keep from falling.

"Someone's here," said Targon.

CHAPTER TWENTY-EIGHT

Kyril stumbled a bit, but Targon grabbed his arm and kept him upright. He didn't feel as sick as he had on previous times of transporting. After a moment of quick disorientation, Kyril peeked around the dim room. Only one small torch sat lit in a wall sconce. They were in a sitting or waiting room of some sort. The walls were smooth stone, and a few groupings of chairs and tables sat around the small space, with multiple doors leading off to each side.

This was the first time he'd ever transported anywhere he hadn't been before. However, Targon had described the place to him in detail. It had taken many tries. Kyril had at first gotten them to the tunnels just outside of the door, as he'd been in those tunnels before when they were retrieving the book…though he had miscalculated a bit and they had bumped into the solid door itself. He ran his hand over a spot on his hip where there would definitely be a bruise.

Targon now stood in the center of the room and turned his head slowly around. He was listening for the source of the sound they had just heard. The place appeared deserted to Kyril, but Targon was much more experienced than him, and appeared to be taking it seriously.

Targon turned back to Kyril, patted him on the back, and smiled. "You really are an amazing wizard, Kyril."

"But I'm only an apprentice," Kyril said, turning to the side to hide the blush creeping up his face.

"Well I'm sure that won't be for long," Targon said. "The things you can do are much more powerful than many wizards."

"Really?" Kyril asked enthusiastically. "You think I could be a full wizard soon?"

Targon laughed. "Oh, yes. But we need to progress quickly in our plans. You are leaving for your hometown in the morning, right?"

Kyril nodded.

"Good, good," Targon said. He took a step toward one of the doors, stopped, and tilted his head to the side. "Something is not right here."

Kyril looked around. He didn't notice anything.

"There are books here with many secrets, Kyril. Secrets that should not be hidden, but shared with all wizards, especially wizards of the mind. For only we can truly decipher them. I never knew they hid so much from us." Targon put his hand on a doorknob of one of the rooms—the door was slightly ajar.

The torch flickered for a moment, and he removed his hand and turned the other way.

"Kyril, bring up a mage light for us," Targon instructed.

Kyril groaned internally. Doing outward magic was not his forte. He concentrated hard, and a brief sputter of light appeared above his palm.

"Use the power of the medallion and feel its power inside you," Targon coaxed as he brought out the black medallion in front of Kyril. "Feel the power in my medallion. Use that."

Kyril didn't like how Targon's medallion made him feel; something inside him wanted to push it away. Instead, he thought hard about the scars on his hand and felt the power there. A white light shot out from his palm and headed straight toward Targon's black medallion that hung around his neck.

Targon dove to the side and the light barely missed him, smashing instead into a chair on the other end of the room. Kyril took a step back as Targon stood up. He was afraid of what Targon would do—he had almost injured his mentor. However, when Targon stood up, a gleaming smile filled his face.

"Your powers recognized *my* medallion," Targon said.

Was that what happened? Kyril wondered. It had felt more like his power was trying to destroy the black medallion. But now, sitting in the air between them, was a mage light of brilliant white.

"Your powers are astounding," Targon said. "We need to find out more information about the medallions; that's why we are here, Kyril. Don't you want to know what other powers the medallion has? How much more will we be able to do once we get the actual object in our hands? The book we have was vague on their purpose, only explaining that there were three of them—well now four…" Targon fingered his own black one and became lost in his thoughts for a moment.

Targon walked to another door, turned the handle, and slid inside. Hundreds of books lined the shelves around three sides of the room. Kyril wasn't overly keen on reading but did appreciate the amount of knowledge that must be there.

"But there are too many," Kyril said. "We can't read them all."

"I'll stay here, you go to another room," Targon directed. "We'll stay all night if we need to."

Kyril groaned and Targon's eyes flashed at him.

"Sorry."

Targon pursed his lips and nodded. "There are sacrifices we all have to make, Kyril. But they will soon all be worth it."

Kyril turned and walked away, listening to Targon talk to himself. Entering one of the other rooms, he gaped once again at all the books. He tried not to groan and let out a quiet sigh instead. Walking to one of the bookshelves, he began scanning the titles on the spines of the books and, every once in a while, pulled one out and flipped through it.

Over the next few hours, Targon and Kyril moved from room to room. Kyril actually was beginning to find some interesting things. His mind now full of new information—history, artifacts, science, and wizardry. He wondered if he could retain the information. Some wizards of the mind had the ability to recall almost everything they had ever seen or read.

There were now only two rooms left; Targon went into one and Kyril into the other. It was the one with the slightly open door. It felt heavy and wouldn't move at first, so Kyril pushed harder.

It felt as if something was behind it. He was about to turn and call for Targon when it gave way and he crashed through it, falling to the floor next to a small table.

"Kyril, is there a problem?" Targon asked from the other room.

Kyril turned toward the doorway, and as he did so he found himself staring straight into the eyes of Sylvie and Hasani—the young man he had seen unconscious on the floor of the tunnels the previous week. His dark eyes held Kyril's, while his long braids swung softly around his neck.

"Kyril?" Targon called out again, and Kyril could hear him take a few steps on the hard stone floor.

"I'm fine," Kyril said loudly, his voice cracking. "I'm fine. Just tripped."

"Well it's getting late, so finish the last room," Targon said.

Sylvie closed the door behind her until only a slit remained once again.

"Watch out for us, Hasani," Sylvie said.

Hasani stared at Kyril for a moment, then nodded and took a step toward the door.

Kyril gazed around the room and his eyes fell on an old book open on the table. He couldn't see it clearly, but it appeared that a sketch of a medallion stood on the open page. He took a step toward it, but Sylvie blocked his way.

"What are you doing here, Ky?" Sylvie whispered, her hands on her hips and short blond hair bobbing around her neck. Her jaw tensed and her eyes flared.

Kyril took a step back, and she moved into the space he had just vacated. She poked him hard in the chest. "What are you messed up in, Kyril?"

Kyril shook his head. "Nothing," was all he said.

"Nothing?" Sylvie said with a hiss. "After all this time, that's all you've got to say for yourself? *Nothing?* You've ignored me and Joelle, moved out of your room, and now popped into the basement of the library with a dangerous wizard!"

"He's not dangerous!" Kyril jutted out his chin in defense of Targon. "He wants to help us. We're just searching for information." Kyril's eyes went to the book on the table.

"Information about what?" Sylvie reached over and closed the book.

Kyril only scowled at her. "What are you doing here in the dark after hours where *you're* not supposed to be?

Sylvie blushed, glanced at Hasani out of the corner of her eyes, then let out a deep sigh. "All right. So, we're both not where we are supposed to be. Why don't you tell me what you are searching for? Maybe we can help each other."

Kyril turned his head toward the door. Targon would be done any minute. He looked back at Sylvie. She gazed intently at him, but her eyes held concern—maybe she *could* help him. She was his friend. Maybe she would listen to him and Targon.

"Targon has big plans, Sylvie," Kyril said with excitement. "If you would just listen to him…"

"Kyril," Sylvie said, her eyes changing from concern to pity.

And that angered him.

"Kyril!" Targon called. "Find anything useful there?"

Kyril regarded the book on the table once again and took a step forward. Sylvie blocked him.

"Do the right thing, Ky," Sylvie said.

Memories of times he'd spent with Sylvie flashed through his mind. For the past year, she had been one of his only friends—and from another kingdom, at that. His own people teased him, shunned him, and Bale and his noble friends mercilessly treated him like scum. But never Sylvie.

She put a hand on his arm and smiled, and Kyril became very confused. She had been his friend, but Targon had offered him so much more. Sylvie had chided him on using his powers against Bale, but Targon rewarded him by bringing him into his own household. And now he was helping Kyril master his powers. For that, Kyril owed the powerful wizard much.

"Kyril," Targon said again, his voice this time sounding much closer. "Come, it's time to go."

Kyril looked into Sylvie's eyes once more and saw her concern there. He glanced at the book, and then at the door. He brushed Sylvie's hands off his arm, left the book where it was, and turned and rushed out the door, almost knocking over Hasani in the process. Slamming the door behind him, he almost ran into Targon.

"You alright?" Targon asked, glancing at the room where Sylvie was hiding. "Did you find something in there?" He reached a hand toward the door.

Kyril moved to intercept Targon, grabbed a hold of his arm, and turned him back around with more force than he intended.

Targon glared down at him. "What is the meaning of this?"

"You wanted to learn how to transport, didn't you?" Kyril burst out. He was angry—at Sylvie, at Targon, but most importantly, at himself. He was a mess and he knew it. But it wasn't right to let Sylvie be caught in the middle of his problems. "It's your turn. Try it now!"

Targon tilted his head and scrunched up his eyes. "What's with you, Kyril?"

"I'm just tired," Kyril lied—well, it wasn't a total lie. He was exhausted. That's what happened every time he transported. He got tired and sick.

Targon seemed to accept the explanation. He proceeded to put his hand on his black medallion, and gripped Kyril's left hand with the other.

"Take us back to your office," Kyril said, as power burst from his own hand.

Targon concentrated for a moment, then blackness flared from his medallion. It collided with Kyril's own white light and he felt a terror that he had never felt before creep into his chest. It was vile and seemed to want to slide through his soul. Fighting it all he could, he clenched his teeth and thought about Targon's room. The two transported, crashing into Targon's sofa a mere moment later.

Kyril pulled his hand from Targon's and leaned over, breathing hard. His stomach roiled and he felt sick again, more than at any time before.

"I did it!" Targon said with excitement. "I transported."

Kyril didn't know if he actually had, or if Kyril himself had done all the work, but right then, he didn't care. He bolted from the room and ran down the hallway toward the kitchen. Just as he arrived, he leaned over and heaved. Over and over, his dinner went spewing over the tiled kitchen floor. Finally, it stopped, and Kyril wiped the sweat from his brow.

His cramped stomach loosened and Kyril felt better. He shivered thinking about Targon's black medallion. It was surely evil. With jumbled and confused thoughts running through his mind, he grabbed a mop and cleaned up his mess.

After dumping the waste water out back, he proceeded to his new room. He spied a pack in the corner—all made up for his travels the next day. With a sigh, he lay on his bed without removing his clothing and fell asleep.

CHAPTER TWENTY-NINE

Late the next morning, Kyril found himself on the outskirts of Gildan, walking on a road that went west toward the Superstition Mountains before splitting into three branches.

The day was already hot, and Kyril wiped his brow and took a drink of water from his waterskin, but it gave little relief. A few clouds skirted across the sky, but they didn't block the sun nor would they bring rain anytime soon. A few crows flew high overhead and cawed at him, but he paid them little attention. To his left were flatlands and to his right were rolling hills, both currently brown due to the dry season. A few copses of trees were scattered here and there. Even though he was stuck in the heat without shelter, he tried to make the best of it; it wasn't anything he hadn't grown up with.

Thinking of home gave him a slight pause in his step. He had debated numerous times that morning about whether he was doing the right thing or not. When he'd come to Gildan almost two years before, he had left the difficult memories of his family and childhood behind. Becoming a wizard and trying to fit in with others at the large academy had been his goals. He had failed at both miserably.

I am neither a strong wizard, nor do I have many friends.

"Hey, move on over!" came a voice behind him.

Kyril turned around and noticed two horses leading a cart of goods down the road heading in the same direction he was.

He stepped to the side and watched the man pass by. If Kyril had had a horse, getting to his hometown would be much quicker. As if in answer to his own thoughts, the cart ahead of him slowed down and eventually stopped.

A middle-aged man with a thin beard and even thinner mustache stood up and waved back at him. Kyril picked up his pace and jogged forward to see what the man wanted.

"You seem a bit out of place all alone out here, young man." The man turned a compassionate face down toward Kyril. "You need a lift somewhere?"

"I'm going to the meadowlands just south of Salish," Kyril said, knowing that the man was most likely taking one of the other two fore heavily traveled roads.

The man smiled and rubbed a hand down one side of his beard in thought. "You runnin' from something? I don't want any trouble."

"Oh no, sir," Kyril said. "I attend the academy in Gildan and am on an errand to my hometown."

The man's eyes lit up. "A wizard, huh? Going back to visit your home." The man's head nodded up and down as if he was coming to a conclusion about what he was thinking.

"Something like that," Kyril mumbled, not correcting the man about either him being a wizard or visiting a home—neither was entirely truthful, but neither was completely a lie.

"I could use someone like you," the man said.

Kyril gave him a questioning look.

The man laughed. "A suspicious one, huh? Well, my name is Zane. I can take you where you're going if you don't mind stopping at a few villages on the way to sell my wares. I could use some help setting up and taking down."

Kyril was still perplexed, and he guessed that Zane could tell. The man turned toward him and pointed down. Kyril followed his finger.

"Got a bum leg that doesn't work as well as it used to," Zane said. "So, I figure a young pair of legs could help me set up and take down, while your being a wizard would be an added bonus to protect me from any potential bandits that want to take advantage of me."

"Not sure how much good I would be in an attack," Kyril admitted. "I'm only a wizard of the mind, and weak at that." Thoughts of the power he could yield with the mark of the medallion came to his mind, but he pushed them aside. Those powers were untrained and untested.

Zane laughed. "Well I'm not so good in a fight either. Between my growl and your small bite maybe we'll keep troublemakers at bay. What say you?"

Kyril shrugged. "Why not?"

"Good. Good." Zane sat back down and patted a spot next to him. Kyril climbed up, put his pack in a small space behind the seat, then sat down next to his new traveling companion.

They moved west quickly, but the sun followed them and was soon in their faces. Kyril tried to shade himself but to no avail.

"We'll be stopping in an hour," Zane said. "The horses can't work all day in this heat. And there's a nice village up ahead. We'll set our wares out for the evening market."

Kyril wondered what kind of wares the man sold but didn't want to pry. He figured he would see soon enough.

"If you want, you can sit on the back of the wagon and enjoy a bit of shade," Zane said with compassion.

Kyril smiled. "That would be wonderful."

"Not used to being outside so much at the academy, I guess," Zane said. "Busy studying all day and spending time with your friends?"

Kyril lost his smile. He thought back to how he had treated Sylvie the night before. And ever since he had moved in with Targon, Jordan had begun treating him differently— perhaps it was jealousy. Even Altia seemed preoccupied in the last day or so; Kyril got the feeling she was also ignoring him. He surmised he didn't have many real friends right then. Well, except for Targon. He treated him well, no matter what Kyril did. And now, Zane. Maybe he just got along better with adults.

Without any more words, Kyril jumped off the slowing wagon, then hopped onto the back. Sitting on the wooden tail gate, it felt good to have the sun out of his eyes. He gazed back down the road toward Gildan, its domes and walls now lost in the far distance. He leaned back and was about to put his hands behind his head and close his eyes when he spotted a small dust cloud in the distance. He thought he could spot a single horse and rider but didn't think much else about it as he fell asleep. Many travelers used this road.

* * *

Dreams took Kyril back to that fateful day in the meadowlands. Smoke rose up in the air around him and fire engulfed his house. He felt someone watching him this time and turned around in his dream, but all he saw was a puff of black smoke. Through the smoke he thought he heard a wicked laugh.

He screamed for his family and searched around frantically for something.

The medallion, came a voice came in his head.

It was a voice that wasn't his—though it was familiar—speaking to him as if from a distance, but he couldn't put a finger on who it was. He ran to the burned-out house and glanced over the glowing cinders and charred belongings for anything that would help him make sense of the situation.

He spied his mother's medallion, and the voice spoke to him again.

Ahhh, I finally found it.

"Who's there?" Kyril spun around listening for the voice. But once again, no one was there—except in his mind.

Bring it to me, Kyril.

Something pushed against the voice in his head. He was having a hard time telling what was real and what wasn't. But there was a strong urge to pick up the medallion and bring it back to Gildan. A silent warning flashed in the far recesses of his mind, telling him this wasn't real. It was more like the time he thought he could fly.

"But I can fly—kind of," he spoke to himself as he remembered transporting around the school.

The scene in front of him wavered and he saw the school again. He saw Bale teasing him and Sylvie rescuing him.

"No!" he screamed out loud, and the burning house of his family came back.

What was happening to him? It was as if someone was trying to take control of his mind. He tried to push the presence away again, but it picked up energy and shoved back against him. He found himself in the tunnels under the palace. A man lay on the floor—Hasani, the librarian apprentice, he now realized. And another man stood in front of him giving him a book, the black medallion hanging around his neck. As his hand reached out to hand him the book, he noticed the red ruby ring on the man's hand for the first time.

The scene wavered and he was back at the fire at his old home once more. Something glittered in the fire. Something round. His mother's medallion. He carefully walked over to the burning embers.

Pick it up.

Without thinking, he leaned over and grabbed hold of the searing medal medallion. It scorched his palm before he could shake it out of his hand. The smell of burning flesh filled the air and he stuck his hand out in the air in front of him and shook it to stop the fire from spreading. A sudden wind responded to his need.

He knew next that he would shove his hand in the water bucket in the barn. That would be the last time he saw the golden medallion.

But the vision stopped and a chuckle sounded behind him. He twisted his head around. Someone was there. Or were they just in his head? In Kyril's mind, a hand reached out toward him. The same hand that had given him the book; the hand with the ruby ring.

He recognized that ring from somewhere. His mind flashed back over the last week as he tried to remember everyone he had met.

Give it to me! came the voice again.

Kyril screamed and fell to the ground as darkness began to close around him. He thrust his hand out in front of him and yelled.

Someone began shaking him and shouting his name.

"Kyril!" said Zane. "Kyril, wake up!"

Kyril left the flames and the hand with the ring and the school and found himself staring up into Zane's eyes. Kyril's hand was out in front of him and was glowing a brilliant white. Zane stepped to the side but put a hand on his shoulder.

"You were yelling in your sleep," Zane said. He paused to glance around. A few passersby glanced their way, but then continued walking.

Kyril took a few deep breaths and the power receded. Zane stood next to him and handed him a waterskin. Kyril drank greedily, clearing the last remnants of the dream from his mind—though he wondered how much of it had been dream and how much had been real.

After a few moments, Zane's eyes grew hard. He grabbed Kyril's left hand and turned it over, the scar facing upward. "Who are you, really? And what in the emperor's name is that?"

Kyril cringed under his glower and tried to pull his arm away, but Zane's strong hands held it firm. Anger flared up in Kyril at first, but then he softened. Zane had done nothing but befriend him. The man didn't deserve his wrath.

Kyril took a deep breath and blew it out slowly. "That is the mark of a medallion. I am Kyril Siravan, a lowly wizard apprentice with no friends and no idea what to do."

Tears filled his eyes and he brushed them away, but more took their place. Zane, still standing next to him, hopped up on the back of the wagon and put his broad arms around Kyril shoulders.

"Tell me what's wrong," Zane said in a soft voice.

For the first time, Kyril told someone everything. From the first time he had touched the medallion, to the teasing at school, to someone trying to influence his mind. He told Zane about his handler, about Targon befriending him, about the strain of having to push his friends away to do what he needed to do. And eventually, about him needing to find the medallion.

By the time they were done, the sun had lowered behind the trees and more people were roaming around the small village.

Zane only nodded, then stood back up and motioned for Kyril to take the tarp off the wagon.

"Let's get set up, shall we?"

Kyril rubbed his red eyes, stood up, and proceeded to help Zane set up his wares for the villagers.

CHAPTER THIRTY

The rest of the evening was a blur to Kyril. Villagers came excitedly to see Zane's newest products, which Kyril learned were a mixture of jewelry, trinkets, dinnerware, vases, and other decorative items. Most of the items appeared used to Kyril, but that didn't seem to bother the villagers.

When assistance was needed to set up tables, box the wares up, or carry things, Kyril would help out Zane, who mostly sat on a wooden crate behind the long table they had set up. Otherwise, Kyril sat off to the side by himself in front of a small cook fire. He wasn't there for warmth, but to feel the comfort of the light of the fire. It was soothing and helped him to gather his thoughts.

Many of the things he'd told Zane Kyril hadn't even understood himself until he'd said them out loud. He was frustrated with everyone: Sylvonna and Joelle for their kindness, Bale and his friends for bullying him, Jordan and Altia for taking to him so fast and then seeming to back off when he became closer to Targon.

Targon! He didn't know what to think of the wizard. The man had shown a fondness for Kyril that he hadn't felt since his own parents. Memories of them once again caused him to swipe at his eyes.

Targon had taken him under his wing, protecting him from Bale and his friends. He was supportive and encouraging of his growing powers, and eager to learn more himself. He gave Kyril a room in his own suites. No one had ever done so much for him. But his handler—a man he hadn't spoken to for days, whose face he had never seen—wanted information on Targon. Like he was someone bad.

Kyril kicked a log from the fire and sparks flew up in the air.

"Careful there," said Zane, who'd come up behind Kyril. "We don't want to catch the town on fire."

Kyril smiled at the man's joke. "Sorry."

"Nothing to be sorry about," Zane said. "You've had a rough time of it, from what you've told me."

"I don't know what to do," Kyril admitted. When Zane didn't say anything, Kyril continued. "I think I'm in big trouble. There's no way to please everyone."

"There never is." Zane shook his head. "Sometimes you just have to choose sides and hope for the best."

"But why should I have to choose sides?" Kyril asked. "I'm a nobody from a small village. What should my actions matter?"

Zane raised a bushy eyebrow at Kyril. "I think you might not be giving yourself enough credit." He glanced down at Kyril's hand. "You have some sort of power I've never seen before. Surely, that makes you a somebody."

Kyril stood up, feeling frustrated, and paced back and forth a few steps. The sun was setting now, and most of the people who visited Zane's wares had gone home for dinner. Kyril's stomached rumbled, reminding him that he hadn't eaten in a while either.

Zane pointed his head toward his wagon. "There's a pack of food in there. Bring it here, and while you feed and brush down the horses, I'll put something together for us."

Kyril nodded and did what Zane asked. The horses were pleased to dip their noses into a bucket of oats. Kyril stood and watched them eat, finding himself jealous of their simple life. A life, he feared, he would never have. Eventually he joined Zane again in front of the fire.

After eating a plate of dried meat and a few roasted vegetables, he leaned back on his elbows. He turned his palm over and studied the familiar scar.

"I've never heard of a power like yours before," Zane said.

Kyril shook his head. "Wish I never had either. It's a curse, I tell you."

"What can you do with it?"

Kyril glanced around to make sure there weren't any townspeople close by. His hand flared white for a brief moment, and he suddenly found himself standing at the back of the wagon.

Zane scanned the area looking for where Kyril had gone, finding him a second later. "By the power of the emperor, I've never seen such a thing. What do you call that?"

"Transporting," Kyril said with a lopsided grin as he walked back toward Zane.

"Can you do anything else?"

Kyril shrugged. "I know that my base wizard abilities are stronger when I use the mark in my hand, but I'm not sure what else I can do. Targon says that once I get the actual medallion, I will be able to do a lot more. His medallion…" Kyril stopped, wondering if he had said too much.

"His medallion?" asked Zane, sitting up straighter. "You mean your mentor Targon has a medallion?"

"Forget it," Kyril said, standing up collecting their dishes to clean. "I shouldn't talk about things I don't understand."

Kyril walked to a nearby well, pulled some water up, and began rinsing off their dishes. He turned once and saw Zane staring at him with a determined, almost hungry gaze. Kyril didn't know what to make of it. Did the man believe anything Kyril told him? Probably not. He wasn't sure what to believe himself.

After pushing Zane's wares up to the front of the wagon, the two settled down for the night in the back atop a thin layer of hay. Kyril fell asleep and hoped he didn't have any more nightmares.

* * *

Early the next morning the two travelers found themselves on the road once again. They rode in comfortable silence for a while before Zane started asking more questions about Kyril's magic and life at the school. Kyril didn't feel like talking, but he shouldn't be rude to the man that was helping him get to his destination, so he answered as simply as he could.

"And this friend of yours, Sylvie," Zane began, after Kyril had told him about her stopping Bale's attack. "She is another of Targon's followers?"

Kyril laughed. "Oh, no. She's been a friend to me and treated me well…at least until recently. She doesn't understand what Targon is trying to do and she doesn't know about my new powers. Well, she must suspect something; she's smart and won't let things drop."

"Is she powerful?" Zane asked, seemingly curious about everything having to do with the Wizard Academy and the wizards themselves.

"Much more than I am," Kyril said with a grin, then paused and thought for a moment. "Well, at least she was. I'm not sure what will happen when I find the medallion. She's a good person, but…"

"But she just doesn't understand what you're feeling," Zane added. "Things are different, and you have new friends now."

Kyril nodded, more to stop the conversation than in belief that he did have friends. The father he traveled away from the academy, the more clearly he had begun to think.

Later that night, they stopped at another village, and Kyril continued to help Zane with the setup and selling of his wares. He made a decent number of transactions before the people headed back to their homes for their evening meals.

The town was eerily quiet. All of a sudden, Zane's horses neighed loudly as two other horses galloped around the side of the wagon. Both carried riders—men in their twenties with long, shaggy dark hair and cloths covering the lower halves of their faces. One of the men jumped off his horse and landed on his feet between Kyril and Zane.

Zane's hand went to his waist where his knife was, but Kyril had nothing to defend himself with, and took a step back.

"You stay right there," the bandit demanded of Kyril, before turning back to Zane. "How much gold you got there, old man?"

Zane's face went red and Kyril found himself clutching his hands into fists.

When Zane didn't answer, the man slapped him hard across the face. Then he leaned down and ran his hand over the remaining goods on the table. He snatched up a few of the larger, more expensive-looking items, then turned his attention back to Zane.

"Where's the gold?"

Zane stayed quiet once again, but a quick glance under the table gave him away. The bandit laughed and leaned over. Poking his head under the table, he grabbed a leather bag and brought his head back up.

"Hey, look what I found, brother," the bandit said to the man still sitting on his horse.

"That's not yours," Kyril found himself staying as he stepped back closer to Zane. He wasn't sure what he was doing, but Zane had agreed to take him to the meadowlands in exchange for some help; he couldn't just sit idly by.

"Is that so?" the bandit asked. He flicked the leather pouch up into the air toward his brother. But it never made it there.

While the pouch was in mid-flight, Kyril, without thinking, thrust his hand outward and thought about pulling the bag back toward him. After only a brief flash from his hand, the pouch sat in Kyril's outstretched hand instead of with the bandits.

Well that was new!

The man on the horse jerked in surprise, and the one on the ground rounded on him. He reached out toward the bag, but before he knew it, Kyril was instead standing on the other side of the attacker, behind Zane.

"Why, you little trickster," the man said. "An abominable wizard, I see." He thrust his knife into the air toward Kyril. "We'll see how you do against a blade."

Kyril, his palm still glowing, and feeling power flowing through his veins, saw his mother's medallion clearly in his mind. The gold metal shimmered on the ground, reflecting what Kyril thought must be the sun.

"Summon the power," a voice said in his mind. "Use it to attack!"

The second bandit leapt from his horse and joined his brother. The two came at Kyril. Zane, with his slow leg, wasn't much help. One of the bandits circled around behind Kyril. It was hard to keep track of where they both were. As if planned, the two came rushing him at the same time, knives drawn. Kyril waited until the last moment, then clearly thought about the wagon. In a blinding flash, he found himself standing on the seat of the wagon.

The two bandits couldn't react in time and collided with each other, their knives held out in front of them. Each stabbed the other and fell down. At about the same time, some villagers arrived to see what was going on, led by the constable. With a wave of his hand, the constable called over two other men to help him lift the bandits up, tie their hands together, and march them away. Blood leaked down their shirts and onto the dusty ground as they were dragged off toward the town jail.

Zane let out a puff of air and glanced nervously over at Kyril, who fell to the ground in sudden exhaustion. His head swam for a brief moment and his stomach felt like it would explode, but somehow, he kept it all together. A few minutes later, he climbed up on his knees and handed the pouch of gold back to Zane.

Zane gave him a lopsided smile and then barked out a laugh. "Well, I've never been protected so well before. You certainly have earned your keep, Kyril."

Kyril couldn't stop smiling. He had actually fought off two bandits! He, little Kyril Siravan. Maybe he was somebody after all.

CHAPTER THIRTY-ONE

Sylvie tried to stay as far back on the road as she could manage while still keeping Kyril in sight. She had been following him for three days now on a borrowed horse, and was nearing where she'd learned his hometown was. After watching his escapades with the bandits the night before, she wanted to confront him and ask him what he thought he was doing. He was an untrained apprentice throwing around uncontrolled magic without any discipline; he frustrated her to no end. But she still intended to help him.

She peered over her shoulder, and not for the first time since departing Gildan, she had the feeling she was being watched. But as of yet, she hadn't glimpsed anyone.

"But that doesn't mean they aren't there," she mumbled to herself.

Dark, low clouds had been gathering all day, blowing in from the Blue Sea in the east. They were trapped by the Superstition Mountains, and visibility was dropping. Another summer thunderstorm was sure to start soon.

After the encounter with Kyril in the library basement, she and Hasani had finished glancing though the book they'd found. It hadn't had as much information as she'd hoped it would. It had mentioned that three medallions were created, one for each of the magical disciplines of the earth, mind, and heart. But there had been no clues as to where they were now or what kind of powers they held individually. Though, as Hasani had mentioned, the book had hinted that together, they could bring a binding of peace.

A sound from behind alerted her, and she twisted around in her saddle, but it appeared to only be the wind picking up and blowing some branches of large oak trees standing off to the side of the road. When she came back around, though, her horse reared up in the air at two people standing in front of her, and she was thrown to the ground. She moved her hands to try to cushion her head from the fall but wasn't successful. Her head bounced off the ground and she blacked out.

When Sylvie came to, she was sitting up and tied to a tree. She struggled for a moment at the rope and was just about to use her magic when the two figures from earlier stepped in front of her. One held a sword at her throat.

"Jordan," Sylvie sighed. Everyone knew the good-looking wizard of the mind. His long, black hair was held back in a ponytail, as was his usual style. His dark eyes sparkled as if he held a secret that she did not.

Standing next to Jordan was Altia. Sylvie didn't know much about the apprentice but had learned her name once Kyril began spending time with Targon and his followers. Her eyes—highlighted by blue eyeliner, scrutinized her.

"Well, look at what we have here," Jordan sneered, but even a sneer from Jordan didn't diminish his good looks. "Twig, I think I've heard you called before. A wizard from Arc is a long ways from home out in the countryside of Gildan."

Sylvie hated it when people called her "Twig." It wasn't her fault that she was thin or that her last name was named after a tree. But she tried to remain calm and not dignify his taunt with a response. He was a full wizard as was she, but she surmised that as a wizard of the earth, she was most likely more powerful. However, he did have a sword pointed at her throat.

"Don't even think about it." Jordan glanced from Sylvie to Altia. "There are two of us."

Sylvie shrugged. "So, Jordan and Altia, to what do I owe the pleasure of your company today? Is there any law against a ride in the countryside?"

"Quite a long ride from Gildan," Altia said with a menacing snarl.

"I had some time off, and it's so hot in the city I thought to spend some time in the mountains."

"Likely story." Altia snorted and stood back up. "You're following Kyril."

Sylvie opened her blue eyes wide and feigned innocence. "Kyril Siravan? You mean he's out here too?"

As quick as lightning, Altia slapped Sylvie across the face.

Sylvie's face turned warm and her eyes watered at the pain. "Apprentice," she addressed Altia, "you do know it is a grave offense to strike another wizard."

Altia stepped back and seemed momentarily shocked at Sylvie's words. She turned to Jordan with questioning eyes.

"Don't worry about that," Jordan said. "Targon will vouch for you. No one in Gildan will believe a young wizard from Arc over a influential wizard from Gildan."

"Are you sure he will?" Sylvie went on, following a hunch. "Seems that Kyril has become his darling now."

Altia moved forward with a hand outstretched toward Sylvie, but Jordan stepped in to intervene. "The plan moves forward, regardless of Kyril—or even Targon."

Hearing his talk of Targon surprised Sylvie. Jordan was the wizard's nephew. Had they had a falling out of sorts over Kyril?

"Then why are you so intent on following Kyril?" Sylvie asked.

"Because he doesn't know what power he holds," Jordan said through gritted teeth.

"And you do?" Sylvie said.

Jordan took a deep breath and let it out slowly to regain his composure. With a sneer of a smile, he waved his sword around in front of Sylvie. "Let's not make things harder than they need to be. As a wizard yourself, you will be given a place of respect in our society."

"But the wizards of the mind will be the rulers?" Sylvie asked, assuming full well what Jordan would say.

"Exactly," Jordan said with a broad smile. "I'm happy to see you are understanding."

"Now, if I'm part of your protected class of citizens, being a wizard and all," Sylvie continued, while she began slowly pulling more of the earth's power to herself, "then why are you worried about where I am going or what I am doing?"

"Because not all wizards believe in our cause," Altia said, speaking up for herself.

"And what does Kyril believe in?" Sylvie taunted.

Altia's face grew dark and she stepped closer to Sylvie. "That's what I intend to find out."

"Targon seems to trust him," Sylvie said. She could tell Altia would be the one to slip and give her the answers she sought. Soon, Sylvie would push her right where she wanted. "I think you're jealous. You've been with Targon from the beginning. Now Kyril comes along with unknown powers, and Targon takes him in and tells him things he isn't telling you."

"He is not!" Altia actually stomped her foot.

Sylvie smiled. A wizard of the heart could have easily manipulated Altia's emotions, but even Sylvie was making headroom.

"Then why are you following him, Apprentice?" Sylvie mocked with a sneer. "Either you don't trust him now, or you want the power he has. Either way, Targon and Kyril have left you out of things."

Altia brought her hand up to hit Sylvie, but Jordan reached out and grabbed Altia's hand before she did. "Enough, Altia! Can't you tell she's goading you?"

Altia only grunted at Sylvie. "Then what are we going to do with her?"

Jordan glanced down the road. There was no sign of the wagon that Kyril had been traveling in. Sylvie guessed they needed to hurry and decide what they were going to do with her, or they would lose his trail. While Jordan was looking away, the tip of his sword dipped, and Sylvie burst the rope that held her and kicked up toward him. The edge of her foot clipped the point of the sword and it flew from his hands.

Jordan appeared to stay calm, but Sylvie knew he was thinking about what to do—that's where wizards of the mind drew their power from. Taking advantage of the pause, Sylvie raised her hands up high in the air, and the ground around Jordan and Altia shook.

Jordan grabbed a branch from a nearby tree to keep from falling, and Altia stumbled a few times but remained on her feet. Bringing her own right hand up in front of her, she summoned a ball of fire and threw it at Sylvie.

"That could get you expelled from the school, dear Apprentice," Sylvie said.

"Targon will protect me," Altia said with a glance toward Jordan.

Jordan didn't seem so sure anymore.

"He saved Kyril!" Altia stuck her chin out in defiance. "And he'll save me too!"

"I fear that Kyril means more to him than you," Sylvie said.

Altia turned to Jordan for help. He just shrugged.

"I don't know, Altia," Jordan said. "Maybe we should just let her go. We need to find Kyril and get back to Gildan."

Jordan appeared more nervous and less confident than Sylvie would have guessed. He continued to watch the road and shuffle his feet. The things she'd said had gotten to him too— he was just better at hiding his emotions.

"No, Jordan," Altia said. "You're a full wizard, do something!"

Jordan's visage grew darker, and his hesitation seemed to leave him. He waved his hands intricately around in the air and then pulled them back toward his body with a quick thrust. Suddenly, Sylvie found herself rising into the air and weaving toward him. As soon as she left the ground, she felt her powers lessen considerably.

Jordan laughed. "Took me a bit to think of it, but it worked. Without the touch of the earth, your powers are no match for ours."

Sylvie grunted, but wouldn't admit defeat.

Altia moved over next to Jordan and grabbed his hand. Power flared up around them and flared toward Sylvie. Once it reached her it made her immobile—she couldn't move anything on her body except her eyes and mouth.

"No one will ever know what happened to you, Twig," Jordan sneered, his once beautiful face now marred by his internal ugliness. "My uncle will be a great and powerful leader of Gildan, and no one will be able to stop him. The prince's birthday party will be a time of change in Gildan. It's just too bad you won't be around to see our rise to power."

Sylvie grunted, but realized she had just been given an important nugget of information. She reached out around her with her senses, trying to find a source to draw from, but the few particles of dust in the air were not enough for her. It was something she had studied but had not mastered yet.

"I guess as Targon's nephew, you fancy yourself as some sort of prince in his new regime?" Sylvie asked.

Jordan laughed out loud. "Oh, I've been promised much more than just being a prince. I've been part of his plan my entire life, and you're not going to mess this up for us."

"What about Kyril?" Sylvie said. "Isn't *he* messing it up for you? You're after him to get his power, aren't you? But you don't know how." Sylvie was just guessing, but it didn't hurt to keep stalling.

"He doesn't deserve the attention from Targon," Altia spat. "He's too afraid to use the power he has. But with a little coaxing, I think he might share it with us."

"You mean a little threatening?" Sylvie asked, already knowing the answer. "Maybe he won't want to share it with you. Maybe when he returns to the city, he will be too powerful to stop. He will rule by Targon's side and forget about you two."

Altia picked up a jagged rock by her foot, and with a grunt, threw it at Sylvie with all her physical strength. The rock hit Sylvie on the shoulder and pain exploded through her. But she noticed that Altia's magical hold on her waned just a bit.

Altia, seeing she'd hurt Sylvie, picked up another stone—this time with her wizard powers—and flung it toward Sylvie. Sylvie tried not to smile; Altia had given her a way to supplement her powers. As a wizard of the earth, that's what she did—use the power in rocks, the ground, the trees around her. Without being able to move her body, she commanded the rock to slow, and it did. Altia pushed against it and it nudged closer to Sylvie, but she used the rock's internal energy upon itself, and it moved slowly, as if the air was water.

Altia gasped with effort and threw another stone and another one—her wizard powers now solely focused on pelting Sylvie.

"Altia, stop!" Jordan shrieked. "I can't hold her much longer myself!"

"I'll kill her first."

A dozen rocks hurled through the air toward Sylvie at the same time, but then skidded to a stop in the air, mere inches from her. They now swirled around her, forming a rock wall, protecting her, and Sylvie felt her limbs begin to move again. The barrier of rock was too much for Jordan, and he dropped his arms in exhaustion. Sylvie's full powers were restored. Using the power of the rocks she held herself in the air for a moment longer.

Thunder shook the ground and lightning flashed in the sky—it was a normal thunderstorm and not Sylvie's doing, but she could use the power of it anyway.

Drawing energy from the incoming storm and with a grunt of sheer will, she punched her fist forward. The rocks around her shattered into hundreds of pieces and shot out and away from her body in a wide arc.

Altia screamed and dove to the ground, covering her head as she was hit by dozens of sharp shards. Jordan took off running, but as Sylvie landed on the ground, she stomped hard, and a wave of ripples rolled through the now wet ground.

Rain began to fall, and the wind swirled around them, making the ground instantly muddy and slippery. Immediately, Sylvie's clothes were soaked through. The cool rain in the opposing heat felt good—and more importantly, the water held power.

Jordan fell backwards. He thrust his hands out around him and threw a burst of air at Sylvie. But this time she was ready for it. Circling her hands in the air, she formed a clear but wavering shield of water and wind. It spun around and absorbed Jordan's wind, then spat it back at him.

The sky grew dark and amidst the deafening thunder, rain exploded around them. Altia still lay on the ground barely moving, but Jordan tried to stand once again. With one last swipe of her arm in the air, Sylvie knocked him back a dozen feet, the back of his head thumping into a nearby tree. Sylvie cringed, hoping that she hadn't done any more damage than daze him. She was not a killer.

She was sure they would not say anything back in Gildan about the encounter as they would have to explain why they were away from the academy as well as admit that a wizard from the Kingdom of Arc had bested them.

Sylvie searched for her horse, who had trotted away in fear of the sounds of the storm. She whistled for him and soon he came running back to her. She pulled herself onto the saddle, and with one last look in the direction that Kyril had gone, she turned and instead headed back to Gildan. Her meeting with Jordan and Altia had told her something very important. She needed to get back and warn the prince of Targon's plan before his birthday—in three days.

Kyril would have to fend for himself for now.

CHAPTER THIRTY-TWO

Kyril thought they would have stopped and found shelter during the heavy rainstorm, but ever since he'd saved Zane, the older man seemed to have a renewed sense of energy in getting Kyril where he needed to be. In fact, they didn't even stop that night for Zane to set up his wares. Kyril was worried that the man thought of him as more than he actually was and hoped he didn't have any other expectations of Kyril.

The way Kyril had transported around the bandits had both frightened and surprised him. He was gaining more control of his powers, but he also felt a few moments of indestructibility…and he knew that was dangerous. Also, in the midst of the fight he had felt something else: a faint voice in the back of his head, urging him to draw more of the power into himself. The feeling reminded him of the dream he'd had a few nights before.

Zane had sent Kyril to the back of the wagon under the tarp to escape most of the rain, insisting he was fine staying up front with a poncho covering his body. The horses plodded on in the mud, obviously used to the varied weather patterns in Gildan.

Under the tarp, with the persistent rain pounding overhead, the air began to become stifling hot. Kyril could feel the humidity in the warm air and it was becoming harder and harder to breathe. To distract himself, he thought about the medallion. Thinking about it brought up images of his parents and younger sister. He couldn't ever remember his mother wearing the medallion. It was kept in a special lacquered wooden box in the front room on a shelf near the fireplace. Periodically, he had caught his mother holding it up and gazing at it wistfully.

When he asked about it, his mother told him that it had belonged to his grandmother, and her grandfather before that, and then went back further than anyone could remember. Even at times when the family struggled to put food on the table, his mother never considered parting with the medallion—a beautiful piece of golden jewelry that could have fetched a nice price. She had said only that it wasn't hers to sell, that it needed to stay in the family until the right time.

"Kyril!" Zane said from the front seat.

Kyril wiped water from his eyes—telling himself it was only the rain, but his thoughts of his family had made him more emotional than he thought they would. He guessed being in such close proximity to his hometown brought these feelings to the surface.

He poked his head out of the tarp and glimpsed sunny skies to the east. A few drops of rain were still falling, but the summer storm would soon be over, bringing with it an increase in the stifling humidity. He jumped down off the wagon, splashing mud all over his pants, and ran up to the front. Grabbing a side board, he pulled himself back up on the bench next to Zane, then looked out in front of him.

Instantly a lump formed in his throat as he looked down the short incline of the road that led into the meadowlands.

The sun poked out and sent shimmering diamonds of rain over the fertile valley of grass and cattle. Scattered throughout the valley were clusters of homes interspersed with farmlands, while off in the distance stood the main town—Haram. It was little more than a few thousand people, but to Kyril, who had lived out in the countryside, it was always the big city to him.

He laughed out loud and Zane peered curiously at him.

"I used to think Haram was so big," Kyril said, "but compared to Gildan, it's little more than a village."

Zane smiled back and put a hand on the boy's back. "So, this is where you grew up?"

Kyril nodded, a small lump forming deep inside his throat.

"Ever been farther north to Salish?" Zane asked.

"No." Kyril shook his head. "Never been anywhere until I went to Gildan. I didn't know if I'd ever come back here. It's beautiful."

"That it is," Zane said as they reached the valley floor.

Kyril gaze longingly up toward the tops of the Superstition Mountains. They were as comfortable and familiar a sight to him as anything in the world. He had grown up hiking in their foothills with an occasional excursion with his father up farther into the mountains when he went hunting. Today, the top half of the mountains were still covered with billowing rain clouds.

Now in a melancholy mood and full of apprehension, Kyril guided Zane toward where he used to live. Turning down a narrow lane, he passed by familiar neighbors. The nostalgic feelings rising inside of him were almost too much. At one point he thought about bolting and running north, never to return to here or Gildan again, but then he came to a portion of a broken fence and motioned to Zane to turn once again. The road here was full of holes and rocks, a sign that it didn't get used much. Off ahead of him sat a familiar copse of trees.

That's where they headed.

Passing over an old bridge that seemed to barely hold the cart and the horses, they proceeded on. Wild bushes grew in close on either side and they scraped the sides of the wagon. Zane furrowed his brows at him.

"Just a bit more," Kyril said in a mere whisper.

Zane stopped the cart and Kyril hopped down. Despite the time, and even with the recent thunderstorm, the scene in front of him, of the ragged remains of his childhood home, was little changed from the memory burned into his mind. Burnt by fire and shame and loss and pain. And power.

It was here that he had first seen and felt what he now knew were the effects of the medallion. From the book Targon had, Kyril had learned that the medallion was an ancient artifact with immense power. That was why the great wizard Targon wanted it—to use it to unite the wizards behind him and to stop the persecutions that had been on the rise lately. Thinking of those that had teased him here at home fueled his anger and drove away any remaining tears.

He wandered to where the front of the house used to be. He spied a few cobblestone steps now buried mostly under decaying wood, left behind from his burned-out home. Turning to his right, he spotted the barn, still standing, and in not much different shape from when he left. He closed his eyes for a moment and relived what had happened once again. The medallion had been lying in the middle of the ruins—had dropped out of its protective box when the house had burned down. He pushed his mind outwards, concentrating as hard as he could, and tried to picture where the medallion could be.

After it had burned his hand, he'd ran to the water bucket in the barn. But he could remember nothing after that until waking up in Haram at the home of the town healer. He had never been back to his property again.

He opened his eyes and wandered over the grounds, crisscrossing the area back and forth over and over again. He kicked at the wreckage with his feet and rummaged with his hands to no avail.

"Aarrgh!" Kyril yelled walking back out of the broken down barn. "It's not here."

Zane hopped down from his cart and joined him in the middle of the ruins. "Are you sure?"

Kyril rounded on him, feeling anger from head to toe. "Yes, I'm sure. It's not here. All this way and it's not here!"

His left hand began to grow warm, and Kyril turned it over and stared at his palm as it began to glow brighter. He pushed it out in front of him as he dug deep inside for all the power he possessed. He used the concentration exercises that he had been taught as an apprentice wizard of the mind and tried to picture what he was searching for.

That's how his wizard discipline worked. A wizard of the heart used emotions, a wizard of the earth used the world around him, but wizards of the mind used their own mind. It was the most limited discipline, because it depended completely on one's own ability—an ability that to Kyril's frustration he currently had limited access to.

Kyril breathed deeply and removed all else from his mind. He thought of the medallion—how he had seen it in his mother's hands dozens of times. *Find it!* came a voice—Kyril didn't know if it was his own or someone else's.

He felt his arm raise up in front of him, and through his eyelids he could see a bright flash. At the same time, Zane gasped.

Kyril slowly opened his eyes. He was surprised to see that daylight was waning, the sun already behind the mountains. How long had he been standing there like that?

Escaping from his outstretched palm was now a brilliant bright light that snaked out in front of him as far as he could see. In his mind, he pictured it going down the lane back to the main road and farther toward the town.

"It's in Haram," Kyril said with certainty.

Zane let out a puff of breath he must have been holding. "You sure?"

"Yes," Kyril said. He was positive. "Someone has taken it from here. Someone that knew about the accident—maybe even someone that caused it."

"Well, let's get going before it grows dark," Zane said. "A night in a nice inn would be a change of pace."

"You don't have to do this," Kyril said. "You've done enough."

Zane glanced down, almost embarrassed. He seemed to be deciding on something. Finally, he turned around, and without looking at Kyril, walked toward the cart. "Come on, before I change my mind. I need to see this thing through."

The light in Kyril's hand receded, and Kyril felt a moment of disorientation as he simultaneously saw what was physically in front of him and where the light was leading.

He growled in frustration. That was his mother's medallion, and someone had taken it. He wasn't going to leave until he got it back. "It's not theirs to have."

And with that thought his hand flared up once again, before dying back down to its normal scarred form.

CHAPTER THIRTY-THREE

It was late in the evening when Kyril and Zane arrived in Haram. They were still wet from the rainstorm earlier in the day and Kyril was feeling an exhaustion that he believed was from his use of his power.

Before they went searching for the medallion, Zane talked Kyril into finding an inn, getting the horses settled, changing clothes, and getting a bite to eat. After asking several locals for directions, they were led to a medium-grade inn. It was three stories tall and freshly painted. Sitting on the large porch in rocking chairs were four older men, smoke swirling around them. They nodded their heads toward Zane and Kyril, and the two entered inside.

The room was bright, lit by candles and lanterns everywhere, include two crude wooden chandeliers hanging from the ceiling. Kyril's burgundy cloak clinging to his body drew a few stares from the local crowd, but they quickly resumed their own conversations.

"May I help you?" asked a young woman about Kyril's age. Her long, wavy hair reminded Kyril of Joelle's, but it was light brown instead of red. By the woman's coloring, Kyril guessed she wasn't full-blooded Gildan. Closer to the border with the Realm and its southern city Denir, the meadowlands south of Salish had many citizens of mixed nationalities. "My name's Lynzie."

"We need a room and a hot meal," Zane said as he peered around the room. "Looks like a crowded place."

Lynzie smiled. "Our mayor has been invited to the young prince's birthday, and he leaves tomorrow. Tonight, the town celebrates our mayor's good fortune."

Kyril remembered Targon talking about the upcoming party and that he wanted Kyril back before then.

"Hey, how about a fill-up over here?" yelled a patron rudely.

"Sorry," Lynzie said to Kyril and Zane. "Take a seat, and I'll be with you in a moment."

"We were hoping to change first," said Zane.

"Of course. Of course," Lynzie said. She pointed upstairs. "The owner's up there now. Just find him and he'll show you to a room. Most of these people aren't staying the night here." With that, she turned to meet the demands of her customers.

Kyril watched her walk away, finding himself mesmerized by the sway of her hips and her long hair. He felt a light tap on the back of his head, and he turned to find Zane smiling at him.

"What?" Kyril said.

Zane chuckled and led them upstairs. After finding the owner, they procured a room and began digging through their packs for something dry to wear. Kyril laid his cloak out, hoping it would dry soon; for some reason, he felt more comfortable with it on.

He walked to the single window and tried to see outside. The glass was thick and the lights from the town sparkled and streaked through the glass in the darkening night. His eyes lifted, and he found himself giving his attention to what appeared to be a larger building on the edge of town. He wiped the dirty, foggy window with his sleeve—which wasn't much cleaner—and tried to discern more clearly what he was looking at. He put his hand up to the window and felt his palm warmed to the touch.

"That's where it is," Kyril said.

"Where?" Zane asked as he joined Kyril at the window.

Kyril pointed. "That building there. Where the mayor and his family live."

Zane grunted. "You sure?"

Kyril rounded on him. "Why do you always ask me if I'm sure?" He knew his momentary temper was unnecessary, but he was hungry and wet.

Zane only laughed and tousled his hair. "It's good to be sure about things, don't you think?"

Kyril pursed his lips and stayed at the window for a moment longer. Perhaps Zane was right. It *was* good to be sure about things. There hadn't been much surety in his life since his family had died. Targon was beginning to bring some stability and assurance, and now maybe Zane. Still deep in thought, he began to change his clothes as Zane did the same. Kyril didn't know why the man was still helping him. He guessed he still wasn't used to people actually being nice to him.

With a puff of air and short chortle, Kyril realized people liked him now because of his growing powers. He shrugged to himself. If that's what it took, then he would take it for now. Over time, hopefully people would like him for who he was— or who he would become.

After changing, he splashed his face with water from a small basin and tried to clean up any other obvious mud splatters. Raking through his thick black hair with his fingers, he figured he was presentable enough to head downstairs.

Zane raised one eyebrow at his fastidious attention to his appearance but said nothing. Kyril felt his cheeks redden as he moved to the door. When they arrived back downstairs, they found a small table in the back and settled in.

Soon Lynzie came over to serve them. As she set the table, her eyes flickered to Kyril before she blushed and turned back to her duties. His stomach flipped and he couldn't think of what to say to her. With a sigh, he instead took up a glass of water and drank it slowly.

The meal soon arrived and instantly Kyril's stomach growled in response. He hadn't eaten well since leaving Gildan. The roast beef, summer squash, and freshly baked bread went down quick and left him feeling heavy and tired. Letting the meal sink in for a moment, he was about to tell Zane that they needed to go find the medallion when a trio of musicians started up a lively tune and everyone started clapping and tapping their feet.

Zane excused himself for a moment to go relieve himself outside. While he was gone, Kyril leaned back in his chair and took a few minutes to enjoy the music. It was the first time he'd felt relaxed in a long time—so much so that he almost thought twice about just staying here and never returning to Gildan and the academy. But what would he do? He didn't have any other skills. He turned his palm over and looked at it a moment. *Or do I?*

He heard the door open and glanced over. It was Zane. He stopped Lynzie for a moment, leaned over, and whispered something to her. Her light brown eyes opened wide and she looked over at Kyril and blushed. It seemed to Kyril that Zane then gave her something, but he couldn't tell. Probably just paying for the food. He shrugged and turned back to the musicians. A man with a nice tenor voice was singing while two others, a man and a woman, played the lute and a string instrument that Kyril hadn't seen before.

Zane returned and took a deep drink of his ale, then leaned back with Kyril, enjoying the evening.

"We should leave soon," Kyril said. "We need to get the medallion."

Zane nodded his head without saying anything, then turned and gazed out over the room. Soon Lynzie arrived and took their dishes, then returned with a sweet apple pie. Leaning down in front of Kyril, she whispered, "I've a break for a few minutes. How about a dance?"

Kyril almost choked on a swallow of water. Zane only grinned. He'd obviously heard Linzie's words.

"Go on, you deserve some fun," Zane said.

"But…" Kyril pleaded softly. They really needed to go.

"Later is better," Zane whispered. "When it's quiet."

His words made sense to Kyril, and he let Lynzie pull him up from the chair. Here seemed to be someone that liked him for who he was. She didn't know about his wizard powers.

"Take your time," Zane said. "I'm going out to check on the horses and get some fresh air."

Kyril glanced around the now raucous room. The crowd was enjoying the music; many were up and dancing. He'd never been left alone in a place like that before. Overwhelmed, he decided he should just go outside with Zane, when Lynzie elbowed him.

"Come on," she said. "I want to dance."

"I'm not very good," Kyril said, not wanting to admit how poor he really was. He'd only danced a few times at academy events with Joelle and Sylvie. Thinking of them made him regret the way he had treated them. But it was for their own good. They needed to stay away from what he was doing—whatever that was.

"Why so melancholy, Kyril?" Lynzie asked as they entered the dance floor and faced each other.

"Just a lot on my mind, I guess," Kyril said. They bowed to each other as the song started. Kyril took her hand in his and put his right arm around her waist.

Holding each other at a fair distance apart, they danced in circles around the floor following the flow of others. Kyril stepped on her feet a few times, but she only laughed and pulled him along.

"You're good," Kyril said at the end of a song.

"I work here most nights and get a few minutes of break," Lynzie said, her chest heaving with the effort of the lively dance.

The musicians slowed it down, and after glancing around the room, Lynzie pulled Kyril in closer. He felt his cheeks warm and he wanted to dry off his sweaty hand, but he couldn't.

"Are you from around here?" Lynzie asked.

"I used to be," Kyril answered. "Lived at the entrance of the meadowlands, south of here."

"And now?"

Her eyes sparkled in the flickering light of the candles and her light brown cheeks were flushed with the excitement of the dance. Kyril thought he had never seen someone so beautiful in his life.

"I live in Gildan," he said, "at the Wizard Academy."

She stopped dancing for a moment, and Kyril thought he saw a flicker of fear cross her face…but before he could figure out if that's what it was, she smiled up at him.

"How exciting that must be," she said with a husky voice, and pulled him closer.

"You have no idea," Kyril mumbled.

Soon that song was over, and another started up—this one more lively again. During this dance, the couples changed partners throughout the song, but each time, Kyril longed to have Lynzie back as his.

Then the musicians played a humorous song in which the audience joined in for the chorus. Kyril laughed out loud at the story of a man who kept getting caught in his lies. He was tempted once more to stay here with Lynzie forever. He could find some kind of work to do; he wasn't too old to become a tradesman's apprentice.

Song after song, the two of them twirled across the floor. All of a sudden a loud noise shook the building, and everyone stopped to listen.

Thunder. And then silence.

"Lynzie!" called a man from the other side of the room.

She was breathing hard, but her lips parted into a smile that caught his heart. "I've lost track of the time, it seems. I need to get back to work. They'll all be leaving now."

"Leaving?"

"By the sound of that thunder, quite a storm is coming," Lynzie said. "They'll be rushing back home before the rain gets too bad. It's not safe to be out on an evening like this."

All of a sudden, Kyril remembered why they were there. How could he have forgotten? Lynzie leaned over and gave him a soft peck on the cheek.

"Thanks for the dance," she said, then she was off cleaning up tables.

The musicians packed up, and before Kyril had even left the dance floor, the room was half empty, with the remaining gathering up their belongings and saying goodbye to friends. Kyril searched around for Zane and realized he hadn't seen him in a while.

He went back to their table and waited as he watched Lynzie work. A monstrous crack of thunder followed a bright flash of lightning. It was only a brief warning before the rain crashed hard into the sides and top of the building. At the same time, Zane came running in from outside.

Kyril stood up and noticed Zane shove his hands deep in his pockets, then he glanced back up and smiled and smiled.

"Where've you been?" Kyril asked, then looked around to make sure they wouldn't be overheard. "We were supposed to go out, you know."

Zane shook his head. "Not now, we aren't. It's not safe for anyone out there."

As if to emphasize his point, lightning lit up the room, with thunder following closely behind.

"Have a nice time dancing?" Zane's eyes lit up with amusement.

Kyril couldn't help it—he smiled back. "Yes, I did. I didn't realize how much time had passed, though."

Zane shook his head toward the stairs. "Might as well head up to the rooms and get some sleep."

"But…?" Kyril asked without saying anything else. The room now only contained a few people—those he presumed were actually staying there that night. Lynzie and a few other workers were busy cleaning the place.

"We'll have to figure it out tomorrow," Zane said as he headed up the stairs. As Kyril followed him, he noticed something red seeping through the right sleeve of Zane's shirt.

When they were in the room, he also noticed that Zane was limping a bit.

"What happened to you?" Kyril asked.

Zane only shrugged. "Slipped on a wet rock and fell down. Nothing too serious."

"But you're not muddy at all!" Kyril said.

Zane looked himself up and down and laughed. "You're right, Kyril. What do you know? Not sure how I managed that."

Kyril grunted. "First thing tomorrow we go and find the Medallion."

"First thing," Zane said. "I promise."

CHAPTER THIRTY-FOUR

Kyril was woken early the next morning by the rumble of hooves pounding the road outside of the inn. By the sound of it, there were dozens of horses. Sitting up in bed he looked over at Zane, who seemed to still be sleeping.

"Zane, wake up," Kyril said, and he shook the man once before moving over to the window to see what was going on. "Something's happened."

Zane groggily got out of bed and joined Kyril at the window. There was indeed a small company of guards riding through town. Looking as far as he could see through the blurry glass, Kyril watched as some of them veered off into side streets. Soon, the yells of men and woman were heard.

"Get dressed and packed," Zane said urgently. "We need to leave."

"Leave?" Kyril asked. "But we need to find the medallion, remember?"

With his back to Kyril, Zane's posture stiffened for a moment before he finished ramming his belongings into his pack. "Do you even know where it is?"

"It was near the mayor's estate when I first checked," Kyril said. "Maybe I can try again."

Zane turned to him and shrugged. "Go ahead."

Kyril frowned. Zane was acting strange. Something wasn't right, but he couldn't place what it was. Before he could do anything more, a pounding on the door made them both jump. Zane pulled a knife and reached the door first, then opened it slowly.

Lynzie poked her head in, and with hardly a glance at Kyril, spoke to Zane. "The mayor's daughter has been kidnapped. They are closing off the roads in and out of town."

Kyril glanced at Zane and then back to Lynzie before sighing. *Another delay.* Was everything out to get him?

It was then that Kyril noticed the tears in Lynzie's eyes.

"Do you know her?"

Lynzie nodded. "She's a sweet girl just a bit younger than me. It's said she disappeared during the night sometime."

"I'm sorry," Kyril said. He knew what it was like to lose someone. He put a hand on her shoulder to try and comfort her, but she remained stiff in his presence. "Maybe we can help search for her?"

That brought some light back to her eyes.

Zane nodded in agreement. "Let's go, Kyril. Take your things with you. We might have to get out of town quick."

Kyril wondered what Zane was talking about.

Zane seemed to sense his curiosity. "I mean, once they unblock the roads…we may have to leave to finish our journey…?"

"Yes, of course," Kyril said.

They grabbed their belongings and headed downstairs. Lynzie ran to the kitchen and returned with a small loaf of bread and some cheese.

"Here, take these," she said, shoving them into Zane's hands.

Kyril reached out his hand to grab hers. After the wonderful night before, he didn't want to leave without saying something. When he touched her hand, she stiffened. He caught a quick glance at Zane who gave a small nod of his head, and he returned his attention to Lynzie.

Zane walked to the door to give them some privacy.

"Lynzie, I don't know what's wrong," Kyril said worriedly. "We had such a wonderful time dancing last night. I thought that maybe…well…" He stumbled, trying to figure out what to say. He wasn't used to speaking to women about his feelings.

"You mean you thought that meant something?" Lynzie said, her face reddening but her eyes flickering around the room nervously. "Don't you think I dance with other men?"

"Well, I guess, but…" Kyril stuttered again. This wasn't going well. He hung his head. "I'm sorry, I thought you had a good time."

Lynzie let out a small sigh and her face softened a bit. "I did, but that's all it will ever be."

Kyril understood. She liked him too but he was leaving.

"Kyril, let's move," Zane said, more impatient than usual.

"Well, it was nice to meet you," Kyril said.

Lynzie glanced at Zane and then back at Kyril and smiled, tears glistening her eyes. "I'm sorry, Kyril." She turned and ran back off to the kitchen.

Kyril decided he would never understand women. He walked over to Zane, and together they went outside. Within moments, a company of three guards rode over to them. One leaned down with a paper in his hand.

"Have you seen this woman?" the guard asked them.

One the paper was a crude sketch of who Kyril assumed to be the mayor's daughter. Her hair hung long over her shoulders and her facial features were small. But it wasn't the girl's face or hair that caught Kyril's attention. His hand involuntarily went to the spot on the paper where a medallion hung around the girl's neck. The medallion he was searching for.

My mother's medallion!

The guard snatched the paper back. "Have you seen her or not?"

Kyril felt dizzy and his left hand began to warm. Zane put his arm around Kyril's shoulders.

"We're just passing through," Zane said.

Kyril hid his hands inside his cloak and tried to take deep breaths to calm his nerves.

"What's wrong with him?" one of the other men asked.

"My nephew isn't feeling well," Zane lied for Kyril, who couldn't seem to see anything around him except for the sketch of the medallion. It burned in his mind and he doubled over to try and stop the light from escaping.

It was too much, and his hand came out in front of him, shooting white light down the street and around a corner.

One of the horses neighed loudly and reared up on its hind legs.

"A wizard!" exclaimed the leader of the three men. "Why didn't you say so?"

"Only an apprentice," croaked Kyril, who sat watching the white light racing away from him. He knew where it led—but they did not.

Zane tried to gain control of the situation and grabbed Kyril and pulled him away. "Sirs, he is not well-trained. Being sick, he can't control his magic. I need to get him back to Gildan."

"Well, get things under control," said one of the guards. "We can't have him hurting people."

Zane slapped Kyril on the side of the head. "Cut it out, nephew! You don't want people to get hurt, do you?"

Kyril frowned at Zane as he shook his head. He fought for self-control over his powers. His forehead dripped with sweat and his stomach churned with the effort. The light finally vanished, and he hung his head low.

The three guards whispered amongst themselves but then rode off. Kyril waited until they were farther down the street before turning on Zane.

"Why did you hit me?"

"I was saving you from being taken in by them for questioning," Zane said. "You need to learn better control."

"That's what Targon says," Kyril grunted.

"Smart man," Zane said. "Now, let's go."

"Go where?" Kyril stood his ground. "I saw where the light led. That's where the medallion is."

He began to trot around the front of the inn toward a side alley that led back to the stables. Zane followed behind.

"It went this way," Kyril pointed, "but I don't know where it went after that." He brought his hand up in the air to try again.

Zane smacked his arm back down. "You can't do that again. It'll be a beacon for those guards."

"But the mayor's daughter must have the medallion, somehow," Kyril spoke as quickly as his mind was reasoning things out. "Someone obviously kidnapped her last night, not knowing what it was…" He paused for a moment as sudden thoughts came to him—pure intelligence. It was the first time he felt what other wizards of the mind explained happened to them when figuring things out. "Maybe someone did know what it was and took the girl before I could get to the medallion.".

Zane pulled Kyril closer to the stables where their horses and cart were being held. "I think we need to get out of here, Kyril. You can come back another time."

"No!" Kyril stood his ground once they were inside the doorway of the stable. He looked up and down the small alleyway. There was no one else around. "I'm going to try it once more. Just for a moment. It's close by. I can tell."

Zane grunted in frustration and began hooking up his horses back to the wagon. "You do what you want, Kyril. But I'm leaving with or without you. I got you here and that's what you wanted. I need to get back out of town before they close the roads."

"What about your wares?" Kyril asked. "Don't you need to sell them?"

Zane took a moment to answer. When he did, his voice was harsher than Kyril had heard before. "Don't tell me how to run my business, Kyril. I need to get back to Gildan."

Kyril shrugged with frustration but wasn't going to be deterred by Zane's strange turn of personality. He closed his eyes for a brief moment and pictured the medallion in his mind, then lifted his hand out in front of him. This time, without much effort on his part or hesitation from the magic, the usual white light shot out from his marked palm.

But instead of racing down the street like he suspected it would, the white light bent itself around Kyril and slammed into the front of Zane's wagon.

"Zane!" Kyril yelled, things suddenly falling in place. "What have you done?"

"Fine!" Zane said as he finished hooking up the horses. He hobbled over to the front of the wagon and pulled up the seat. Fishing his hand around inside, he pulled out a small wrapping of burlap.

The light from Kyril's hand rested on Zane's hand.

"Can you turn that thing off?" Zane spat.

Kyril only had to think of what to do, and it now happened instantly. The light blinked out and Kyril took a step closer to Zane and held out his hand.

"What were you going to do with this?" Kyril snapped at Zane. "Sell it before I got it?"

"I did it for you, Kyril," Zane stammered. "I didn't want you to do anything foolish or get hurt."

Kyril was surprised at the sentiment, but something was off. Zane was still acting strangely.

"Take it," Zane said gruffly.

Reaching out his hand tentatively, Kyril wrapped his fingers around the burlap bundle. His pulse quickened and he felt a small surge of energy. With shaking fingers, he unwrapped the package, almost dropping the medallion in the process.

He held up the medallion by the chain and watched the morning sun sparkle off the gold as it spun slowly around. Tears came to the corners of his eyes as recollection of home and his mother threatened to overtake him. This was the only tangible memory he had of his family.

Kyril glanced up at Zane but couldn't read the expression on his face—it was almost one of hunger. He then moved the medallion in the air over his left palm and lowered it onto his outstretched hand. The cool metal sent a jolt of power into the mark on his palm, and his hand flared up once again. Closing his fingers around the edge of the medallion, Kyril shut his eyes and took in a deep breath.

With that breath came a flood of power, memories, and knowledge. In his mind, he found himself standing on a small hill at the edge of a city. Four people stood in front of him. One was dressed like a king; the other three sat on their knees in front of him with bowed heads.

Kyril's senses seemed heightened as he glanced around at his surroundings, the four not seeming to notice he was there at all. A slight breeze ruffled the hair of the three on the ground, a brown hawk flew over them high in the sky, and a few stray sounds from the city reached him at the foot of the hill. Looking back at the man standing in front of the three, Kyril noticed his strong grey eyes, firm jaw, and brown hair. A gold-lined blue cloak swayed around him and a crown of gold sat on his regal head.

The man cleared his throat and all three turned their faces to him, adoration in their eyes.

"My Lord," said one, a man of middle years, his hair and skin darker than the rest.

"King Anikari," another one said while bowing her head. She was a woman with fair hair and skin.

Anikari! Kyril shook his head in disbelief. He was alive over 400 years ago in the Realm.

"It has been an honor to serve you, great wizard," said the third, another woman, one of wild red hair, which reminded Kyril of Joelle.

King Anikari gazed on them fondly and raised his arms for the three to stand back up. "Wizards, power must always have a balance. That's why we have four disciplines of power—you three represent three of them, and of course the magical creatures, the fourth. To keep that balance, I give each of you a token of my appreciation."

The king pulled three medallions out of a pocket inside his cloak. All three appeared to have an identical pattern—matching Kyril's own that still sat in the palm of his hand. Each wizard came forward one by one, and King Anikari slipped the chains of the medallions over their heads.

"A gracious gift indeed, My Lord," said the man, now wearing the gold one. "I can feel the power already augmenting my own."

"You now have the power to transport," said Anikari with a broad smile. "Use it wisely and only when in dire need."

Turning to the blonde woman, the king placed the silver one around her neck. "And you will have the power to read events and portents from the earth around you. Careful not to burn yourself out."

Kyril crinkled up his nose wondering what that meant and what good it would do to read the rocks and dirt. But before he could reason it out more, the red-headed woman came forward and received the bronze medallion. She curtsied to Anikari and wrapped a slender hand around it.

"And your power will be the power to read the emotions and intents of others," the king said. "A personal power that must be used with all care."

Then facing all three he continued to give instructions. "Keep them safe," Anikari said. "In the wrong hands their combined power could be very dangerous indeed. Now, go your separate ways and keep the balance in the world of magic. Besides their specific abilities, they will also augment your own wizard powers, and together will create a mighty force. Above all the rulers of our great kingdoms, this power of balance must prevail. Pass these medallions down to your descendants, for one day when the balance of power is threatened, they will be needed again."

The three wizards bowed to Anikari and then the man in the middle—the one with the gold medallion, took the hands of the two women and in the blink of an eye disappeared— transporting, Kyril determined, back to wherever they were needed.

King Anikari remained standing alone for a few more moments. He turned and gazed out over the city and whispered, "I name you Anikari, and here I will build my castle and my kingdom for the people I love."

Kyril felt something pulling at him, and in a blinding streak of light he stood once again in Haram in the stables behind the inn with Zane still in front of him. Kyril blinked his eyes a few times to reorient himself.

Shouting was heard close by around the corner and Zane ran to the wagon.

"Hop on, Kyril!" he shouted. "We need to leave now."

Kyril shook his head to clear his thoughts. He was still trying to make sense of what he'd seen. But with additional urging from Zane he joined the man at the front of the wagon. Zane pushed the horses hard as they pulled out of the yard of the inn and took a small back dirt road back west toward the mountains.

"Why are we going this way?" Kyril asked.

"We need to get away from the city and then circle back around toward Gildan. They will have closed the roads by now searching for the mayor's daughter."

Kyril nodded. Still clutching the medallion in his hand, he felt a renewed sense of power flowing through him. Recent events started clicking into place, and his priorities began to shift and swirl around in his mind. The medallion gave him a renewed sense of purpose and place in the world. It was exciting and terrifying at the same time.

"Zane," Kyril said finally, "how *did* you get the medallion?"

Zane was silent for a long stretch, and in that silence, Kyril heard a faint moan coming from under the tarp in the wagon.

"What is that?" Kyril asked, turning around in his seat. "It sounds like a person…" He stopped and leaned toward Zane.

Zane had the good sense to appear worried.

"You didn't…?" Kyril asked.

Zane still said nothing, but he clenched his jaw tighter.

Kyril threw his arms up in the air. "It's the mayor's daughter, isn't it? *You* kidnapped the mayor's daughter!"

CHAPTER THIRTY-FIVE

Sylvie rode hard to get back to Gildan as fast as she could. She needed to find the prince, and she Jordan and Altia wouldn't be too far behind. Skidding to a stop in front of the school, she left her horse with a stable boy then ran to find Joelle.

Her friend was in the healing center with a crowd of people lining the edges of the room. Some lay on makeshift beds, others sat on the floor, while a few stood leaning against the walls. The group seemed to have separated themselves across the two sides of the room. One side wore wizard robes, the other side did not.

Coming up behind Joelle, Sylvie tapped her on the shoulder. "What's going on?"

Joelle jumped and turned slightly but continued working on healing a man's broken arm. "Where have you been?"

"I…I've…" Sylvie glanced around and lowered her voice. "I was following Kyril, and…"

Joelle held up a hand. "Not now," she said, nodding her head toward the group standing in front of her, waiting to be healed. "Give me a minute and I'll meet you outside."

Sylvie didn't have much time. She needed to warn the prince, but she wanted to let Joelle know what was happening and to find out where all these injured people had come from.

Leaving the building she paced back and forth on a walkway beside the academy. A few other wizard apprentices roamed the gardens, but most had stayed inside due to the hot weather. The storm had cleared away the previous night, but that just made things more humid now.

She was about to go back inside when Joelle stumbled out of the nearest door. Sylvie led her over to a bench and sat down next to her.

"Are you all right?" Sylvie said. "What happened in there?"

Joelle nodded her head. "I'll be fine. I just need some rest and food. I don't go back for another two hours. Since you've been gone, more fighting has erupted in the city. More wizards were targeted, and now some of them have been fighting back. It's a mess, Sylvie. Why would they be doing this? I don't understand."

"Let me guess. It's Targon leading the wizards charge against the nobles and populace," Sylvie said.

"Yes," Joelle said. "Well, against the nobles and those in authority at least. Those outside of nobility or wizardry so far haven't been affected directly. He has set up a safe house for wizards and stirred up a group of wizards that are demanding retribution. They have called to have more control in Gildan and for many of the leaders of Gildan to step down."

Sylvie gasped. She didn't think they would be so bold. "And the emperor and his children?"

Joelle shook her head. "I don't know. I'm not privy to that information. But tomorrow night is a party for Prince Zaidan's fifteenth birthday. Many of the high-ranking nobles and wizards are invited…as are we." Joelle smiled weakly. "If I can get away from all the healing. I'm just so tired."

Sylvie raised her brows at her friend. She hadn't heard about being invited to the party.

"The prince came asking for you and delivered the invitations personally," Joelle said, blushing. Her lack of wordy explanation of the matter proved how tired she really must be.

"I bet that caused quite a ruckus," Sylvie chuckled. Then growing more serious, she put her hand on her friend's arm and brought her up to speed on what had happened to her. "I'm worried about Kyril," she said in the end. "He went in search of the medallion that marked his hand. I'm afraid of what that means for him and for the company he has been keeping. Things seem to be racing out of control."

"There has definitely been a shift in the balance of power here, Sylvie," Joelle said in a serious tone. "I'm wondering if it may be too dangerous here in Gildan for us anymore."

"You're thinking of leaving?" Sylvie asked with concern.

Joelle nodded. Her eyes were downcast, and her long hair hung over the sides of her face. "Something is telling me to go back home. There is something there I need to do."

Sylvie only nodded in agreement, and she and Joelle sat in silence for a bit. On her ride back to Gildan, Sylvie had had plenty of time to think about everything that was happening. Early that morning, she too felt a strong impulse to go back home to Arc. "I need to get something to eat and regain my strength," Joelle said, lifting herself slowly off the bench.

Sylvie smiled. "Of course, you are exhausted. But I must see the prince—something horrible is being planned for the night of his party. That only gives us one day to prepare."

"Us?" Joelle said, her green eyes resuming their normal sparkle.

"Yes, us!" Sylvie said with a sly grin. "You, me, Hasani, the prince. It's going to take all of us to help save Kyril and put down this rising rebellion."

Joelle sighed. "I guess you're not letting me out of it this time, are you?"

"No, I'm not," Sylvie said. "Go eat and get some rest and heal as many as you can but keep some strength for tomorrow. I'm afraid that before the prince's birthday is over, we will need your abilities."

* * *

Less than an hour later, after cleaning herself up as well as she could and donning a clean blue cloak, Sylvie sat in a comfortable, red, stuffed chair in a hallway in the palace. She was amazed at the splendor and riches that met her eyes. Far more extravagant than her own kingdom's headquarters, this place screamed ancient wealth and prosperity.

Gold-lined artwork, marble floors with traces of gold, tapestries larger than the walls of her own room, and mahogany railings and stairwells were only a bit of the evidence she saw. Each doorway was an arch with intricate detail carved into its moldings.

Two guards stood next to her in front of the emperor's doorway. They'd told her that Prince Zaidan was meeting with his father and would come out soon.

After another quarter of an hour, one of the heavy, ten-foot-tall doors quietly opened. Sylvie stood up as both the prince and his father—the emperor—exited the room.

Surprise crossed the prince's face, then he smiled. "Sylvie!"

The emperor himself turned to Sylvie. She gave a deep bow. "Emperor Alrishitar."

The man was more handsome than she remembered—she'd met him once when he visited the Kingdom of Arc and the Wizard Conclave. His deeply tanned face held intelligent brown eyes and a smile that highlighted his bright white teeth. A golden crown sat atop his thick hair, and a flowing robe of gold-lined burgundy hung from his slender but toned frame.

"Wizard Sylvonna Hickory," the emperor said. "It is nice to meet you again. How is the High Wizard, Danijela Anwar?"

"She is fine, My Lord. At least the last time I saw her. I've been serving here in your wonderful academy for a while now, so I haven't seen her in some time." Sylvie mentally slapped herself. She was rambling on like Joelle. She took a deep breath and tried to calm herself.

The emperor didn't seem to notice but only smiled and laughed. "Oh, I remember your high wizard when she was just a young girl…about the age of my son here. She was quite the feisty one—and powerful."

Sylvie joined in his amusement. It was true: Daniela Anwar, despite her small stature, had been one of the mightiest wizards of the western continent for most of her life.

"Did you need something?" the emperor asked.

Sylvie looked from him to the prince and then back at him again. "I have some news for the prince, but given the situation, if you have the time, you might want to hear it also."

Zaidan's eyes grew worried, and the emperor nodded his head. "If it's about this rebellious uprising, I would welcome some news. Nothing seems to make sense." He ushered her and his son back into his office.

If the hallways of the palace seemed overly opulent to Sylvie, then the emperor's own office was overwhelming. It wasn't only the richness of the surroundings—made of the best materials available—but the pulse of power that seemed to come from every artifact in the room almost overwhelmed her.

Prince Zaidan led her to a chair and gave her a nod of understanding. "This room can be a bit much sometimes to those that have strong wizard powers. My father collects artifacts."

Sylvie nodded and sat down with the prince and emperor. The two nobles stared at her and waited for her to begin.

"I've heard that something bad may happen at the prince's party," Sylvie started.

The emperor's eyes softened when they glanced at his youngest son before turning back to Sylvie. "Where did you hear this?"

"West of Gildan, from two followers of Targon," Sylvie said. "A wizard and an apprentice."

"Why were you outside of the city?" The emperor frowned with concern. "Don't you have classes to teach at the academy?"

Zaidan who gave a quick nod of his head, and said, "I've asked Sylvie to keep an eye on things at the academy for us, Father. She must have had a reason to leave."

"Is that so?" The emperor gave his son a curious glance. "I don't remember asking you to do this, Zaidan. We have people already in place in the academy. You could have jeopardized our operations."

"I was only trying to help." The prince held his head high with a stubborn pout on his face. "I knew we could trust Wizard Sylvonna, so I recruited her. You never specifically forbade me from doing this."

The emperor leaned his head back and Sylvie saw a small twitch at the corner of his mouth. "Very well." He brought his head back level with the other two. "I must admit, our handler has not been able to contact our inside man recently—and that worries me."

"I'm afraid Wizard Targon is behind this," Sylvie said. "He intends to take control and only have wizards of the mind running things. No more nobles."

"Well, good thing I am a wizard of the mind," the emperor mumbled, but worry creased his forehead. "These attacks don't make sense. Why would the nobles attack the wizards? I can hardly arrest Targon for protecting the wizards, if that's only what it is. We have no other proof of his underlying deeds, unless our inside spy comes forward."

After a moment's silence, Sylvie spoke again. "Sir, there is one other thing. I'm not sure if it's related, but…"

"Go on."

"I overhead Wizard Targon and an apprentice speaking," Sylvie began, trying to keep Kyril's name out of it for now—though she didn't know how long she could, given the circumstances. "They were searching for a book containing more information on three medallions and…"

Emperor Alrishitar jumped up so fast that Sylvie let out a squeal and refrained from leaping out of her seat herself. Zaidan, though, was instantly up, hands ready to defend some unseen enemy that it appeared his father was reacting to.

"Father?" Zaidan said. "What is it?"

The emperor stayed silent for a moment longer as if thinking things through, then with a wave of his hand he commanded, "Leave us."

Sylvie stood up. The power of the emperor's voice brokered no argument. She could see his hands shaking as she took a step toward the door. She didn't know what was going on, but she would leave the two to talk things out.

"Not you, Sylvonna, but the prince."

Zaidan's eyes went wide. He looked to Sylvie and then back to his father again. He opened his mouth to contest his father's words.

"No arguments, Zaidan," the emperor said, his voice growing more tender. "You will understand in time. Go and find the spymaster and his handler and wait outside the doors for me. Also check on your sister."

Zaidan, in respect for his father's position, and with only a small furrow of his brows to show his disagreement, bowed slightly and left the room. Sylvie was much impressed by his grace and control.

CHAPTER THIRTY-SIX

After he was gone, the emperor paced his room for a moment and ended up next to a bookshelf. He rested his hand on an empty space between two large books. Sylvie turned slightly to watch him but waited for him to speak first.

"A book was stolen a few days ago," the emperor said.

"I know," Sylvie said quietly. "From below the library, but we recovered it. That's where I first saw a drawing of the medallion. But when we looked through it again the original pages were missing, almost as if they had never been there at all."

"What does this book look like?" the emperor asked. "The one you say was returned. And what did you read in it?"

"Its cover is old, dark brown leather. There is a symbol on the front that is a crown with a sword across it." She paused to arrange her thoughts. She didn't want to get in trouble for going back to the library's basement, but she sensed that this was more important. "The librarian and Hasani called it the Western Codex. I searched other books to find more information about the medallions, but they didn't say much other than that the medallions are very old, powerful, and I had assumed now lost, but…"

The emperor put up his hand to stop her momentarily. "The book you describe belongs to me." He pointed to the empty spot in the bookshelf where his hand was resting. "It was stolen a few days ago, and I suspect it was used to replace the Codex taken from the library. Both books have identical covers, but slightly different contents. Mine is more of a summary and leaves out many details—it's more to show and share with others in my office here. The other—the Western Codex—was supposed to be safer out of prying eyes and held in a very secure room in the library's basement. If you say you saw it that was definitely a breach of security."

Sylvie winced and hoped that Hasani wouldn't get in too much trouble.

"Someone very powerful must have stolen it," Emperor Alrishitar continued. "There were spells on it that should have stopped the holder from leaving the confines of the library with it. It is a dangerous book that contains not only information about these medallions you speak of, but of other potent magic. Magic that could be used to destroy us all. We must find that book!"

Sylvie let out a small puff of air. This was serious. "I read in it that there are three medallions and I've heard they can bring balance to magic."

"Yes, but with that balance comes a propensity for power—more than one can control sometimes," Emperor Alrishitar said. "But these medallions haven't been seen in a very long time."

Sylvie's heart sank. She knew what she needed to do but didn't know if she could live with herself for doing it. Kyril was her friend, but this was much bigger than both of them. She opened her mouth, paused, and shut it again. Her eyes darted around the room as she took in more of the ancient artifacts in the possession of their great emperor. She glanced back at him and he stood staring at her, not in anger or frustration, but in anticipation.

"Go on, Wizard Sylvonna," he said with a twinkle in his eye. "You know more than you are saying; that is why you are here."

"Well…" Sylvie paused, then cleared her throat and spoke louder. "I think I know who has, or at least had one of the medallions."

The emperor's eyes grew round and he walked toward her to stand only a few feet away. He wasn't a tall man, and Sylvie didn't have to look up much to see him, but his eyes held so much power that she had to turn away.

"Go on," he said with a voice that brought a steadiness to her that she didn't have before. "Tell me what you know."

"There is a young man at the academy, an apprentice who bears the mark of the medallion on his palm. It is a scar, burned there somehow." As Sylvie spoke, her confidence grew. "I'm afraid he went west to his hometown to find the actual medallion. I tried to follow him, but two of Targon's followers stopped me and I returned to warn you of trouble."

"And what is this man's name?" the emperor asked.

Sylvie hesitated a moment. But he had brought this on himself by not letting Sylvie help him. "His name is Kyril. Kyril Siravan, an apprentice wizard of the mind."

Sylvie didn't know what to expect from the emperor, but it was not the chuckle that now escaped from his lips. It didn't seem like a laughing matter to her. She waited for an explanation, but none was forthcoming. She presumed that kings and emperors held many secrets.

"Nothing you have told me or that I have told you must leave your lips unless I give you permission," said the emperor, his face growing serious again. "That includes the princess and prince; neither Liyyan or Zaidan are to know about the medallions, what they can do, or where they might be. This knowledge could put them in a very dangerous position."

"What about Targon and your son's birthday celebration?" Sylvie asked.

"I will take care of that," the emperor said. "I fear Targon may not be our biggest threat. I'm not sure he has the power to pull this building coup off. Someone else is pitting the wizards against the noble citizens and I think he is only taking advantage of the situation."

"But what can I do?" Sylvie asked. She wanted to help. "I am here to serve."

The emperor smiled. "I may yet have need of your strength. You are coming to my son's celebration, aren't you?"

"You're still having it?"

"Of course," Emperor Alrishitar said. "Why wouldn't we? That's where the trap will be sprung."

Excitement grew inside of Sylvie. She wondered what he had in mind. She would love to see Wizard Targon taken down. But then her demeanor fell. What would happen to Kyril?

She tried to hide her sadness from the emperor, but he was obviously astute at understanding moods. As he walked her to the door, he asked her what was wrong.

She shook her head, not wanting to bother the emperor with such trivial matters. But before he opened the door, she blurted it out anyway.

"It's my friend, Kyril," she said in a rush. "He's not a bad person. He's never had any friends, and Targon and his followers gave him attention. Please try to understand."

With his hand on the door he actually winked at her. "I think you shall see it will all work out, dear Sylvonna. The magic of all three medallions will find those that are true of heart and that can work together for the balance and good of all. Thank you once again for all your help." He pulled the door open for her. "I will see you at the celebration tomorrow."

Sylvie rushed out and bumped into someone on his way in.

"Twig!" exclaimed Bale Nabhani. "What are you doing here?"

Her fists clenched. Oh, how she hated that name.

"Now, Bale, her name is Sylvonna Hickory," said the emperor, to Sylvie's surprise. "She is a guest in Gildan and in my palace. You would not be showing disrespect to her in my home, would you?"

Bale's dark skin actually seemed to flush a shade darker. He bowed his head to the emperor and mumbled an apology. Bale slunk behind another older man with a blue cloak, and Zaidan. As a servant approached to shut the door, Bale turned around and gave Sylvie a murderous glare. She jumped in surprise and turned back around to continue on her way

"Don't bother with him, miss," said a guard after the door was closed. "He's always like that."

Sylvie smiled at the guard's kindness and continued walking down the hallway and out of the castle. The sun was setting, and the domes of the city began to light up. This was her favorite time of day in Gildan. She stood on the steps of the palace and gazed over the manicured wizard gardens. From her vantage point, she could see the patterns in the flowers and plants, sculpted trees, fountains that shot water dozens of feet in the air, and walls that cleverly and decoratively divided the gardens into the three magic disciplines. One level up, on a tier at the end of the wizard garden, stood the world-famous Garden of the Spirit.

In this garden, stunning and masterful sculptures of dragons, Cremelino horses, phoenixes, and other magical and mythical creatures in dazzling colors peered down through bushes. White mage lights surrounded this higher level, and power radiated from its position to not only the palace grounds, but all throughout the city of Gildan.

A feeling of peace and calmness settled inside her and she smiled before descending the rest of the steps down into the garden itself. But she was afraid that the peace was only a façade to what the next day might bring.

Leaving the gates of the palace grounds, her mind drifted back to the emperor's office. *What was Bale doing meeting with the emperor?*

CHAPTER THIRTY-SEVEN

"**D**on't be mad at me, Kyril," Zane said.

Kyril continued to ignore him. He could see the faint outline of Gildan up ahead. After discovering that Zane had kidnapped the mayor's daughter in order to get the medallion, he made Zane let the girl go on the outskirts of Haram before they left. That was two days ago, and he had hardly said a word to the man since then.

Shifting in his seat a bit, Kyril watched Zane out of the corner of his eye. He was still trying to figure out why Zane was taking him back to Gildan at all. The man didn't owe him anything. However, he had told Kyril that he needed to refresh his wares in Gildan anyway. Wares that he suspiciously hadn't stopped in any town to sell since leaving Haram.

Obviously, if Zane had pulled off the kidnapping, his leg wasn't as bad as he'd originally let on. But, Kyril couldn't help the small smile that crept onto his lips; he did have the medallion.

"See, it's not so bad, is it?" Zane asked.

"You should have told me," Kyril said.

Zane smiled. "Ahhh, the apprentice wizard *can* speak. I was getting worried that the beautiful, magical, gold medallion that I retrieved for you had taken your tongue."

Kyril let out a long puff of air. He could feel the coolness of the medallion on his chest. It was tucked under his shirt and made his entire body throb with power. Since putting it on, he felt a new sense of connection—a connection to the other two medallions he had seen in his vision. The only thing he knew about them was that one was to the northwest and the other to the northeast; most likely in Arc and the Realm. He felt their tug on him, as if each pulled him equally, creating a balance around him.

"What will you do when you get back to the academy?" Zane asked.

"I don't know," Kyril said. "I really don't know."

"Seems from what you told me before, your friend Targon has grand ideas for you, and now that you have the medallion…" Zane left the sentence dangling.

Targon would be expecting Kyril to come straight to him, and he figured that after all his mentor had done for him, he owed him that. But after that, he wasn't quite sure. It would depend on what Targon wanted to do next with him.

Kyril still wasn't sure all that he could do with the medallion, but he knew enough to know he was most likely dangerous. Anyone holding the power of the medallion might be a danger to those around them. His life had changed forever. And he had to admit, he had Zane to thank for part of it.

"Thank you," Kyril said, the afternoon breeze pulling his words away.

"What was that?" Zane asked, knowing full well what Kyril had said.

Kyril rolled his eyes and spoke louder. "Thank you for helping me find the medallion."

Zane chuckled. "Ah, it wasn't anything, Kyril. You seem like a nice enough fellow and all. It seemed my duty to help. Who knows, someday you may be a mighty wizard, and you might come back looking for your old pal Zane."

"Don't take things too far," Kyril said with a laugh of his own. "I fear there are dangerous times ahead."

Zane's face dropped and he took renewed interest in Kyril's thoughts. "What are you thinking?"

"I need to see Targon, and then I need to see Sylvonna Hickory," Kyril said, as much to himself as to Zane. He knew he had been unfair to her before. "She'll know what to do. I've not been a good friend to her."

"I'm sure Sylvie will forgive you, Kyril," Zane said, with one hand on the reins and the other one waving in the air for emphasis. "That's what friends do. Being an earth wizard from Arc, she probably doesn't have many friends in Gildan."

Kyril nodded absently as he thought about both Sylvie and Joelle. He would owe them an apology after all this was done. They would understand that he was working under orders from the emperor to spy on Targon. But then, Targon had taken him in and befriended him. There wasn't much to tell his handler. Although he had grand designs for power, Targon hadn't done anything to truly warrant the emperor's suspicion. *Yet.*

An alarm went off in the back of Kyril's mind. He whipped his head around and studied Zane. He had never told Zane that Sylvie was an earth wizard…or from Arc, had he?

He was about to ask when they approached the city gates. Of the two sides of the gate, only one was open, and four guards stood there, two on each side. Zane approached slowly.

"Purpose of visit?" asked one of the guards.

"I'm here to restock my wares to sell, and this man is a student at the academy," said Zane, glancing around nervously.

One of the guards went around the side of the wagon and lifted up the tarp. After searching for a few moments, he returned.

"Is there some trouble?" Zane asked the guard.

"It's the prince's birthday celebration tonight," the guard said, then turned and spoke specifically to Kyril with a frown on his face. "And you should not be out of the academy. You know the rules."

"Rules?" Kyril stumbled. Had someone turned him in? It wasn't exactly forbidden to leave the academy, although he should have told someone.

The guard rolled his eyes. "Where have you been, apprentice? There's been fighting between the wizards and the city folk again. The academy is under lockdown unless permission to leave is expressly granted by a high-ranking officer or wizard."

The fighting concerned Kyril. He didn't know what it meant. But he also didn't want to be in trouble. "Wizard Targon knew of my…task," he said after a short pause.

The guard's eyebrows rose and he turned to one of the other guards—an officer, by the color and style of his uniform.

The officer waved a hand, and two other guards approached from behind the city gate. "Please, escort this wagon to the academy and make sure that this apprentice gets inside."

Kyril was taken aback by the attention. Why would they want to provide an escort? Had Targon taken greater influence and they didn't want to anger him? Whatever the reason, the two guards walked side by side with the wagon as it rolled over the main cobblestone thoroughfare of Gildan. It felt more like they were being watched, than escorted.

After being out in the countryside, the city once again felt overwhelming to Kyril. It was warmer here than at the base of the Superstition Mountains, and he wiped the beading sweat off his forehead. Feeling the rough skin of his left hand, he brought it back down in front of him, palm up on his lap. He traced his fingers around the scar.

Pinpricks of light flared up and Kyril stopped touching it and closed his fist, hoping no one saw the light. The power was always so close now, just barely controlled. The closer they got to the academy, the stronger it pushed inside of him to get out.

He swooned to the side and barely kept from falling off the wagon as it pulled up in front of the academy.

"You all right there, Kyril?" Zane asked. His face softened a moment, but then after looking around a bit, it hardened and he turned back to Kyril. "Down we go now," he said more gruffly. "Quit your dawdling."

Kyril couldn't figure out what had gotten into the man. With firm resolve, he got his dizziness under control and hopped down off the wagon seat. After walking around to the back of the wagon, he grabbed his pack and hefted it up on his shoulder.

A crowd had grown in the turnabout in front of the academy. Cloaks of burgundy, green, and blue flew around him.

He concentrated on the coolness of the medallion against his skin to keep his mind focused. What was everyone staring at?

With growing heat in his left palm he glanced down to see streams of white light escaping from between his knuckles. The medallion now began to grow warmer against his chest.

"Kyril!" said a lone voice.

He stood up on tiptoes to see who'd called his name. *Sylvie!*

He shook his head. He couldn't see her yet. He needed to get to Targon first. Trying to ignore the crowd around him, he pushed through to the doors. On sudden impulse he realized he hadn't thanked Zane, but when he turned around to do so, he wasn't in the wagon anymore. Kyril scanned the grounds and found him off to the side, in the shadows talking to someone.

"Zane!" he yelled.

Zane turned around, but as the man's head moved, Kyril saw who Zane was speaking with. "Gamal?" he whispered, then turned his eyes back to Zane.

The man's face dropped in shame and he wouldn't hold Kyril's gaze any longer. Zane moved away, stepping back into the shadows with Gamal.

Kyril's head began to spin again. His medallion was pulling him toward the academy. Why was Zane speaking with Gamal? Bits of conversations that Kyril had had with Zane over the last five days flooded through his mind. He'd thought he had been lucky that Zane stopped on his way to the meadowlands and offered him a ride…but what if it had all been part of a plan? He had shared much with Zane about the situation at the academy, Targon, and of course, the medallion. A sick feeling formed in the pit of his stomach. Everything Kyril had said was being passed on to Gamal for some reason.

Zane used me! And Gamal might be more dangerous than he had originally thought.

With his head spinning, Kyril stumbled through the door but couldn't go any farther. Falling to the hard floor, he tried to keep the blackness at bay. But he couldn't. With power thumping in his chest, it overwhelmed him.

"Ky!" Sylvie yelled.

Then the blackness took over and he passed out.

CHAPTER THIRTY-EIGHT

Slowly the sounds around him returned and Kyril saw light behind his eyelids.

"Will he be all right?" Sylvie asked worriedly.

"I think so," Joelle said. "I did all I could for him. But…" She hesitated for a moment and her voice lowered. "But I feel something in him I've never felt before. A power that is strange, yet somehow not frightening—like it belongs with him."

"Belongs?" Sylvie asked. "What kind of power?"

"I think it's from the medallion," Joelle said.

There was quiet for a moment, then Kyril felt someone touch his shirt over where the medallion should have been…but it wasn't there!

He popped open his eyes and tried to sit up.

"Hold on, Kyril," Joelle said with a firm hand on his arm. "You've been through a lot."

Kyril looked from her to Sylvie and back again. Who had touched him?

"Where's the medallion?"

"It's in your pack," Sylvie said, pointing to it. "It's dangerous to have out in the open, Kyril. You should know that much."

"I need to see Targon," Kyril said, swinging his legs off the bed and onto the floor.

"No thanks to Joelle for helping you?" Sylvie asked, hands on her hips.

"You should rest," Joelle said, her green eyes boring into his. "What happened? Who was that man that brought you back? Where did you find the medallion?"

Kyril shook his head and almost laughed at her familiar chatter. "I'm fine, but…thank you." He figured Joelle deserved that. He actually did feel good. Better than he had in a long time. She was a very talented healer.

He stood and moved toward his bag across the room, but Sylvie blocked his way. Her eyes flashed at him and with a shake of her head, her hair swung around her shoulders. "Kyril, you must know what's going on here."

"I don't have time, Sylvie," Kyril said, pushing her out of the way. "We'll talk later." He tried to put on a reassuring smile. "I promise."

Sylvie stepped aside but still followed him towards his pack, a stern expression on her face. "Are you going to be at the prince's birthday celebration tonight?"

Kyril opened his mouth to say no, but a voice from behind him answered instead.

"Of course, Kyril will be there," Targon spoke. "This is going to be a very important evening for Gildan."

Kyril turned toward the door as he felt both Sylvie and Joelle stiffen next to him. Targon stood smiling in his burgundy cloak, a golden chain hanging around his neck, and jewels adorning his fingers.

"Nice to see you again, my young friend," Targon said. Taking a few quick steps, he came up next to Kyril, put his arm around his shoulder, and squeezed. "You made it back just in time."

"In time for what, Targon?" Sylvie asked. "You won't get away with this!"

"Get away with what, my dear…Twig, is it?" Targon smirked. "Isn't that what I've heard them call you?"

Sylvie's face turned bright read as she clenched her fists. "My name is Sylvonna Hickory. *Wizard* Sylvonna Hickory."

Targon gave a short bow of his head. "My apologies. I must have been misinformed. Now, come now, Kyril. We have plans to get ready for this evening."

"Plans?" Sylvie asked.

Targon peered down at Kyril's dirty traveling clothes. "Well, you don't expect our favorite wizard apprentice to go to the prince's party dressed like this, do you?"

"Well…I…" Sylvie was caught off-guard by Targon's news.

"I'm really attending the celebration?" Kyril asked Targon, his stomach buzzing with excitement. He'd never been to the palace before—well he had been in the tunnels underneath it, but that didn't count.

Targon laughed and patted Kyril on the back as he led him toward the doorway. "Of course, Kyril. You are my prized apprentice. It's our right to be there. It will be such a wonderful evening. I've been planning this for you for quite some time."

"Kyril?" Joelle called out as they left the room.

Kyril turned his head to see what she wanted. Then he remembered the bag with the medallion. Sylvie was standing guard over it.

"If the headaches come back again, just think of where your power comes from, and use it," Joelle said in a rush of words. "If you need me, I'll be there."

Kyril furrowed his forehead trying to figure out what Joelle meant. Since returning to Gildan, it seemed events were moving one step ahead of his ability to understand what was happening. He only nodded his head to appease her, and then reluctantly left the medallion and his bag to Sylvie's care and walked with Targon toward his quarters.

Before he realized it, they'd entered Targon's suite. Already gathered were approximately thirty other wizards and apprentices—all wearing burgundy cloaks, signifying they were wizards of the mind. Kyril glanced at Jordan and Altia. Each held multiple cuts and scrapes on their faces and necks. When Jordan took a few steps, he walked slowly.

Kyril tried to catch Altia's eyes but was only successful for a moment. And in that moment, he realized something had changed while he'd been gone. Her eyes turned hard before turning away.

"Uncle," said Jordan, who, despite his injuries, was dressed in his finery. His silk cloak hung down to his ankles, open in front. He wore black pants and a lighter blue shirt—all to the latest noble's fashion. "The party will begin soon."

Targon smiled at Jordan. "Yes, I know. Please find something suitable for Kyril to wear. He will be attending as my guest."

"Kyril?" Jordan's usual amenable behavior took on a dark tone. "*I'm* supposed to go with you."

"Now that Kyril is back, he will take your place," said Targon with a smile toward Kyril. "That is what I had planned all along."

Jordan's fists went to his hips and he snarled. "I've been with you since the beginning, Targon. Kyril is only an apprentice."

Targon put his hand on Kyril's back and Kyril found himself stiffening for a moment. "Oh, Kyril is much more than an apprentice. He is *my* apprentice and my charge. He is much more powerful than you give him credit for. Much more powerful than you."

Kyril felt uncomfortable with the praise, but once again he appreciated the uplifting words of admiration from the great wizard. However, Jordan didn't appear happy at all. His eyes flashed angrily at both Kyril and Targon.

"Tonight, we will formally declare our intentions to change the way of rule in Gildan," Targon continued, then turned from Jordan to speak to the entire assembled group. "All of you will be at your assigned areas of the city. When a blazing light flashes from the palace, you will deliver this message to everyone around you."

Kyril wondered what could cause such a bright light from the palace that they would all see it, and what message they were to deliver. As if to answer Kyril's questions, Targon continued to explain his plan.

"You will inform the people that over the next few weeks, the wizards of the mind will take over the political posts of the city." Targon's eyes glowed brightly and enthusiasm filled his face. "We are not here to cause harm; in fact, because of our superior ability to reason things out, think, and plan, the citizens of the city will see their lot in life improved dramatically. Remember, we are not threatening the right of the emperor—he is a wizard of the mind—but I will be proclaimed as the governor of the city of Gildan before the night is over."

The crowd stepped in closer, not wanting to miss any of their leader's words, but Kyril took a step back and turned his attention toward a side door that was opening. Out stepped Gamal, and Kyril remembered seeing him speaking to Zane. He stared hard at Gamal for any proof of what they had been discussing. The scribe caught Kyril watching him and gave him a knowing smile and a quick nod of his head.

A pounding began in Kyril's head once again. Absently he reached his hand up to the outside of his cloak, just over where the medallion should be. But of course, it wasn't there. He panicked for a moment hoping it was safe. But he could still feel a connection to it, and with that connection he pulled on its power. It surged through him, warming his hand once again. Pushing against the headache, Kyril watched as Gamal stumbled, knocking into the table and making a dish at the edge fall to the ground.

The sound quieted the room as Targon stopped talking and they all turned their attention to the recent ruckus. Gamal stood up straighter, his red patch in his forehead throbbing darker.

"Forgive me, my lord," he bowed to Targon, but nothing but vehemence filled his face when he moved his eyes slightly toward Kyril.

Targon chuckled. "It's only my clumsy scribe."

The room joined in his laughter.

Kyril watched at Gamal's eyes grow smaller and darker. Holding his jaw tight, he shook his head and backed up into the room where he had come from.

"Now, where were we?" Targon asked. "Oh yes. After we liberate Gildan from the nobles' rule, we will then move across the kingdom. All of you will receive your reward and a place of rule in our new empire. But make no mistake, by the end of the night, I will be the second most powerful man in Gildan."

The applause began immediately and filled the room. Only Altia and Jordan seemed to lack the same enthusiasm as the rest. Both had their eyes on Kyril more than on Targon.

"Now, off to your places!" Targon waved his hands. "And Jordan, bring some clothes for Kyril. We will be speaking in my office."

Jordan's eyes grew hard, but he nodded anyway. Targon put his hand on Kyril's back and led him into the now familiar office. After closing the door, he turned to Kyril with a big smile.

"You did it, didn't you?" he said with excitement. "You found the medallion!"

CHAPTER THIRTY-NINE

Kyril relished in Targon's enthusiasm and he couldn't keep the smile from his face. "Yes, I did, sir. I retrieved the medallion."

"Wonderful, wonderful!" Targon clapped his hands. "May I see it?"

"I'm sorry," Kyril said. "I don't have it with me."

Targon's face grew hard for a moment and he took a few deep breaths, but eventually smiled, though it did not reach his eyes this time. Kyril felt ashamed that he had disappointed his mentor.

"I'll go and get it!" he said.

Targon appeared to think for a moment but then shook his head. "No, there is still time before the party. I want you to wear it there for all to see."

"I…I'm not sure that would be good," Kyril said.

"Nonsense!" Targon smiled broadly. "You need to remember who you are, Kyril. You are special, and the entire kingdom needs to know that. For our plan to work they need to know the power we hold. We will have more power than them all." Targon's brown eyes grew bright and his face flushed with excitement.

However, all that Kyril could think about was the vision he had experienced when he'd first touched the medallion. The three medallions stood for balance—to protect the balance in magic. A balance that didn't exist in Gildan right now.

"Kyril," Targon prodded. "What's the matter?"

Kyril tried to keep his spirits up. He couldn't let Targon use him or the medallion to overpower the others. It wasn't right. But at the moment he couldn't figure out what to do. He thrusts his hands inside two pockets on his cloak, and froze. There was a piece of paper in one that he hadn't remembered being there before. Thoughts of his handler flew through his mind and his breathing quickened. This is what they had been worried about all along. This was why they had sent Kyril in as a spy. He groaned and peered down.

"Kyril!" Targon put his arm around him.

"I…I'm…sorry," Kyril said, stumbling to say something coherent. "I guess I'm just not feeling well. It's been a long journey."

Before Targon could respond, a knock sounded on the door. The wizard appeared perturbed to be interrupted but walked to the door anyway. Kyril saw Jordan's face in the doorway and heard an angry mumble.

"Just a moment, Kyril," Targon said as he closed the door and stepped outside.

Kyril could hear raised voices. He took a few deep breaths and began walking around the room to calm his nerves. When he passed by the black medallion, he reached his hand toward it, and unexpectedly a splitting headache drummed through his skull and he pulled his hand back. Evil washed over him, and he realized it was the mark of his medallion and its power that recognized the unbalanced nature of the dark medallion of

Targon's making. It was an abomination to what the three original medallions were meant to be. He moved away and walked toward the desk. A parchment lying on the side caught his attention.

After a quick flash of his eyes toward the door, and still hearing the arguing, he glanced down at the paper and began reading it. He gasped. The paper contained instructions, telling someone to kill the emperor in the coming days.

Kyril couldn't tell if it was Targon's handwriting or not, but either way —sitting on the desk like it was--his mentor must be aware of the plans. Why would Targon want the emperor dead? Unless…The thoughts that sped through his mind were too horrific to consider. Had he read Targon wrong all along? Targon had said that he didn't hold any animosity toward the emperor, but what if he had greater designs than Kyril had suspected.

The clarity of the thoughts in his mind were clearer than ever before. Kyril wondered if it was the additional power of the medallion. He was about to pick up the letter and read it again when he heard the door handle click. He jumped and moved back into the center of the room.

Targon came back in holding a handful of clothes. He gave Kyril a quizzical glance, turned to his desk, then shoved the clothes toward Kyril.

"We leave in an hour, Kyril. Bathe, change, retrieve the medallion, and meet me in front of the academy." Targon's eyes grew bright once again. "Tonight, you will meet the emperor and the prince. It will be a marvelous night."

Targon must have taken Kyril's silence as nerves. He slapped him on the back, then brought him in for a quick hug. "I am proud of you, Kyril, my boy. Don't be nervous."

Kyril felt an odd kinship toward the man as he left the embrace. He did care for Kyril, and that's what was going to make the evening so much more difficult.

Hurrying to his room, Kyril dropped the clothes in a pile on his bed, then pulled the note out of his pocket. It was indeed a summons from his handler instructing him to meet him at the first opportunity.

Fishing around in the bottom of a drawer, Kyril found the device he used for communicating with his handler. He bristled at the thought of the verbal lashing he may get. It had been a while since he had checked in.

Throwing the hood of his cloak over his head, and using a trickle of his power, he activated the device. After a brief moment, the silhouette of a figure materialized in front of him.

"It's about time," the man's voice began. "Do you know how important this assignment is? You're not having second thoughts, are you?"

Kyril had expected the response. "I...I...I've been gone for a few days."

"I don't want excuses," said the handler. "I want information. You'll get us both in trouble if we don't come up with something to help the emperor."

"I have something," Kyril said, then stopped as he heard heavy footsteps in the hallway stop at his door.

Kyril's heart thumped loudly. He could see a shadow under the door. Someone stood there, listening or waiting.

His handler began to speak again, but Kyril shut the device down and waited in silence. Finally, the footsteps moved away. He waited for a moment longer, then activated the device again.

"We have to meet in person," Kyril said quietly. "But I don't have time now."

"I need information," the disguised voice pleaded, and Kyril almost thought he could recognize it.

"It's important," Kyril said. "It's what you've been waiting for."

The words seemed to calm his handler down.

"Meet me at the prince's party tonight," Kyril said.

"Where?"

"I don't know where!" Kyril wined. "I've never been to the palace."

A brief laugh ensued on the other end and something tickled Kyril's consciousness once again. Something about the way the man spoke.

"Figures," his handler mumbled before giving directions. "Second floor balcony, on the west side. How will I know it's you?"

Kyril glanced at his clothes, then around the room. An old scrap of yellow material sat in the corner. "I'll be wearing a silk burgundy cloak, with yellow tied around my arm."

"Ah, a wizard of the mind," his handler said. "I'll be wearing black; all black. And you better have good information."

"Don't worry," Kyril said, beginning to dislike his handler even more. Here he was, trying to do a service for the kingdom, and his handler treated him like he was worthless. Also, by not wearing one of the wizard colors to such a function, Kyril realized his handler wasn't a wizard. Thinking of the power he now held with the medallion, he actually smiled at that last thought.

He clicked off the device and began his preparations to meet Targon.

CHAPTER FORTY

An hour later, as planned, Kyril stood waiting for Targon in front of the academy. Standing with him were a few dozen others—mostly full wizards, heads of the school, or other such dignitaries from the academy. Sylvie, dressed in her royal blue cloak, met him out front with his bag, sensing he might need it.

Around a corner, he dug out the medallion, put it around his neck, and tucked it in under his clothes. He stuffed the bag itself behind a bush to retrieve later…if there would be a later. He was sweating nervously and wondered what would happen to him when the emperor found out what Targon was planning

"Ky, you can talk to me," Sylvie pleaded.

The worry in her eyes almost make Kyril crack, but he ground his teeth and firmed his resolve. "I can't." He looked around at the growing crowd. "You can't be seen with me. Please go away."

Hurt filled Sylvie's pure eyes and Kyril had to turn in another direction. She didn't deserve such treatment. But he had to see this thing through and couldn't chance Targon seeing him with her at this point. The success of the coming evening depended on Targon trusting Kyril to follow the plan.

"Don't hate me, Sylvie," Kyril said under his breath as he walked away.

"I don't," Sylvie whispered behind him.

He wiped sweat from his forehead and adjusted his cloak, making sure the yellow arm band was tied on tight. He tried to blend in with the crowd when he heard a loud voice from up front.

"Kyril Siravan," the guard called.

With a deep breath, he pushed through the crowd to be met by three guards. Panic began to set in. Had they found out about him? Were they going to take his medallion?

"Ah, there you are, Kyril," said Targon, off to the side.

The guard furrowed his brow at the wizard, but took a step back, his duty obviously accomplished.

"What are you doing in the back?" Targon said. "We won't be riding with them, like a herd of cattle; we have our own carriage."

Behind Targon was the most beautiful carriage Kyril had ever seen. Its burgundy color was varnished with a shine that reflected the summer sun, which hung low now in the western sky. Six broad-shouldered midnight black Friesians were waiting to pull the carriage up the hill to the emperor's palace.

Despite the weight that bore down on Kyril's shoulders with what the night could hold, he couldn't help but feel a twinge of excitement as he stepped into the carriage and sat down opposite Targon. Onlookers from the crowd commented on the luxurious carriage and seemed to be arguing who the young man was that sat inside it with the famous wizard.

The carriage began to move forward slowly, when a loud voice called a halt. Targon leaned his head out of the window to see what was going on, but then with a huff brought it inside.

The door opened, and Targon's scribe Gamal stuck his head inside. His clothes were not as fancy as Targon's, and his cloak hung to his knees rather than to his ankles. Under his cloak, Kyril spied a shiny gold dagger. Black pants, a white shirt, and a grey vest completed the scribe's outfit. It was about as fancy as Kyril had ever seen Gamal dress, but it appeared more rumpled on him rather than lavish.

"Running late, I see." Targon rolled his eyes.

Gamal only glared, and then sat down next to his superior, glaring at Kyril all the while.

"So, you are actually bringing the young pup," Gamal said to Targon.

Kyril's face heated and he turned and peered out the window as they began their short journey to the palace.

"Kyril is one of us," Targon said with certainty. "I trust him."

Kyril groaned inside. The scenery did not seem so grand now with the hollow pit in his stomach. He wanted to jump out and run away to the Superstition Mountains and never return.

"We'll see," Gamal huffed. "Let's just hope he remembers his place."

Soon they joined a long line of carriages and a few people on foot walking up the hill to the palace gates. The palace domes were lit with brilliant lights and there was an excitement in the air that Kyril could feel. Emperor Mezar Alrishitar was well-liked by the people, and his daughter and son were known for following in his kind footsteps. His first wife, a woman from the Realm, had died in childbirth with their daughter, and the current empress, Zaidan's mother, was sickly and rarely attended state functions, but all were hoping to catch a glimpse of her this night.

Circling the wizard gardens, they waited their turn to reach the front steps of the palace. Kyril took the opportunity to glance out the window. Fragrant flowers in bloom caught his attention. They, along with other beautiful plants and trees, were organized by color around the garden, each representing the three disciplines of magic—blue, green, and burgundy. One particular fountain shot water in a thirty-foot arc to a shimmering pool of water.

Once it was their turn, a footman opened the carriage door and helped the three of them out of the carriage. Another servant walked with them up the stairs, and a few palace guards joined behind them—something that Kyril hadn't seen with others. There were definitely more eyes on Targon.

Kyril took his time studying the palace dome above them, then ran his eyes back down to the 20-foot-tall double doors that now stood open in front of them. They were ushered into a foyer, the likes of which Kyril couldn't have conceived in his wildest dreams. The entryway rose up three floors above him. Tapestries depicting historical scenes were lit by mage lights, and the eyes from the artwork on the walls seemed to follow Kyril wherever he went.

Men and woman were dressed in their finest clothes and gowns. A servant offered to take their cloaks, but Targon instructed Kyril to keep his on. Gamal, however, handed his over to the servant, which earned him a look of disdain from Targon.

"It might get in the way," Gamal said with a devious wink aimed at Kyril.

Kyril took a step back and walked next to Targon as they were led to a giant ballroom on the first floor. He didn't trust Gamal, but, at the moment, he wasn't Kyril's concern. The real threat was Targon, and Kyril needed to find a way to meet with his handler and give him the information. Seeing the guards shadowing Targon already, his handler must have sensed trouble and in turn warned someone.

A small orchestra played in one corner, while heaps of various sweet- and savory-smelling dishes filled tables in another corner. A small group of young nobles were dancing and socializing to the side of the orchestra, which made Kyril feel very self-conscious and inferior.

Targon squeezed Kyril's shoulder tenderly and whispered, "Don't fear them, Kyril. Soon everyone in Gildan will know who you are. Your power will be legendary. You will be legendary."

Kyril winced at Targon's warmth and wished for once that the wizard would demean Kyril or talk down to him. It would make it much easier to do what he knew he had to.

A group of two men and one woman walked up to Targon. They seemed to instantly dismiss Kyril's presence, but Targon had other plans.

"Ministers, please meet my young friend—a great wizard apprentice, Kyril Siravan."

Each in turn gave a short nod of their head to Kyril, and Kyril bowed back.

"Nice to meet you," he said, his voice squeaking a little.

"Can we talk in private?" the minister of public safety asked. "We need to work together to restore order to the city."

"Ah, yes. That would be wonderful." Targon stroked his short beard a bit as if in thought. "I do have some ideas that could bring a resolution to this nasty business of wizards being attacked with no provocation."

The woman in the group bristled. By the appearance of her gown, she was not a wizard herself, but from some high-ranking noble family. "There are rumors of a wizard causing the problems," she said, glaring directly into Targon's eyes.

Kyril watched Targon's visage grow darker. He obviously did not like being threatened. "Come, Kyril." He waved toward a far corner of the room. "Let's see what these three have to offer."

The first minister, a wizard of the heart—as many of the ministers were—narrowed his eyes at Kyril. "I'm not sure your young apprentice needs to attend with us. There are other things for someone of his age to do at this party."

Targon started to argue, but Kyril saw this as the opportunity he needed, and jumped in. "Actually, I am kind of hungry," he said.

The woman smiled and pointed over toward the food. "See, Targon, the young man would rather be eating and socializing with his friends."

Kyril bristled at the word "friends." He didn't have any of those. But then, out of the corner of his eye, he saw Sylvie and Joelle enter the room. They both were beautiful with gold clips in their hair, and long beautiful cloaks hanging over silk gowns. Joelle carried a decorative staff in her hand as she walked slowly next to Sylvie. The healer's mouth was held in a stern and tense position.

The third man must have seen where Kyril's attention had been for a moment, and he chuckled.

"Seems our apprentice here might want to spend some time with the ladies, Targon. Come on, we won't be far."

Arguing more at this point would have only made things seem suspicious, so Targon nodded his head and smiled—one that Kyril knew was very fake.

"Very well," Targon said to Kyril. "But don't go too far. We have a lot to do still tonight. And watch the company you are in." Targon's eyes briefly swept toward Joelle and Sylvie. "Stay with our own kind."

Kyril glanced at the three ministers, who appeared even more worried with Targon's words. But Kyril tried to play it all off. "I'll be all right. A bit of food would be wonderful."

The three walked away with Targon in tow, seeming more like a prisoner than a fellow powerful leader. Kyril caught Sylvie and Joelle watching him suspiciously and they each took a step forward, but he shook his head and they stopped, with questions still in their eyes.

Kyril walked among the crowd for a moment before finding a staircase that led upstairs. Making sure that Targon wasn't looking his direction, he ran up the carpeted stairs two at a time. At the top, a few other small groups stood around visiting, but they hardly paid an apprentice wizard any attention. Moving toward where he remembered a balcony being above the ballroom down below, he found a set of double glass doors. Gazing through them, he saw a broad-backed figure dressed in black hunched over the railing, peering out to the west. The sun sat low in the sky, ready to set in the next hour. A golden and orange hue filled the air behind the figure.

Opening the door slowly, he slipped out onto the balcony and glanced around to make sure they were alone. He cleared his voice and spoke softly.

"Sir, I'm here."

The figure stood up straighter with a sudden jerk and a tilt of his head, though he didn't yet turn around.

"I am your handler," he said in a voice that made Kyril stop walking and panic fill his breast.

Before he could do anything more, the figure turned around, his own black cloak flying in the air around him.

"Bale?" Kyril exclaimed. It was his worst nightmare.

"You?" Bale sneered, then threw his hands up in the air. "How did this happen?"

"It wasn't my choice, if you remember," Kyril said, staying where he was.

"You're going to mess this up for me, aren't you?" Bale said. "Such a pathetic man I've been given to work with. What did I do to deserve this?"

Kyril was tired of taking this from Bale. He remembered when he had thrown him across the floor at the academy, and actually smiled.

"What are you smiling at?" Bale said. "You think this is funny, don't you?"

"It kind of is," Kyril said.

"Why, you little…" Bale took three quick steps toward Kyril.

But Kyril was not defenseless. Without even thinking he brought his balled fist up in front of him and bright light shot out between his fingers. It was all he could do to keep his hand closed and not let out all the raw power that now raged through him. The move stopped Bale in his tracks.

"You are the type of person that brought this entire problem into existence," Kyril said. "You've taken a good and powerful man in Targon and turned him to do things he shouldn't ever do. In the end, you may get Targon, but know that it was you who made him into the man he is."

Bale's eyes went wide and he actually seemed afraid for the first time that Kyril had known him. Kyril said, "You want your first assignment as a handler to go well right?"

Bale only nodded.

"And I want this whole thing to be done with, so I'll tell you what I know, and you'll take it to those that can make things happen. People far more powerful than you or me. And when this is over, you will never ever tease me or my friends again."

Kyril took a step forward. His thin frame was no match for the bully in front of him, but at this point he didn't care. With the power of the medallion, Bale would never be a problem for him ever again.

Bale nodded his head and seem to understand the gravity of the situation. "Tell me what you know," he almost pleaded.

Over the next five minutes, Kyril shared the information he had and how the plan was going to unfold. Bale only listened and nodded, clearly surprised at the depth and amount of information that Kyril had gathered.

"Are you sure of this?" Bale asked in the end.

"Why does everyone always ask me that? Yes. It's all true," Kyril said. "I will do what I need to help you, but don't think I will enjoy this. When this is all done, I'll no longer be your spy or work for the spymaster's office." Kyril's voice grew softer. "It's cruel."

With a new hardness in his eyes, Bale gave Kyril a quick nod. "We will get him."

Bale moved toward the door back into the palace, leaving Kyril alone for a moment on the balcony. He gazed out over the beautiful city, the domes shinning like colorful beacons. But Kyril didn't notice anything of beauty at that moment.

"I'm sorry, Targon," he muttered to himself. "I'm really, really sorry."

CHAPTER FORTY-ONE

A half an hour later, after meandering around for a bit longer, Kyril stood once again next to Targon. He wiped a drop of sweat from under his sideburns as his eyes darted nervously around the room. He could feel the coolness of the medallion under his shirt, but it did nothing to alleviate the panic he was beginning to feel.

The crowd grew quiet, and in walked Prince Zaidan, arm in arm with his sister, Princess Liyyan. The emperor and empress walked a step behind them. Murmurs ran through the crowd at the sight of the empress. She had been ill and hadn't attended many state functions lately. All four were dressed in an assortment of purples and reds. The two women wore beautiful slim gowns, and the men wore matching jackets and pants under bright silky cloaks. The emperor himself wore a thin band of gold across his forehead, and the empress, a golden chain with a jewel in the middle, both denoting their ranks.

"So much power," Targon murmured from the side, and Kyril could see him almost shaking in excitement.

Mezar Alrishitar, emperor of Gildan, raised his slender arms to the sky. A brilliant display of color flew from his fingertips and began encircling the room high up on the walls. The lights then coalesced in the center of the ceiling and dropped down to the floor of the ballroom, where a golden cloth had been covering something. The cloth drifted away on a small puff of wind, revealing a brilliant ice sculpture underneath.

"A dragon!" said someone more loudly than they'd intended, and the crowd around them laughed, then joined in with their own words of astonishment.

The colors from the emperor's magic flew around the dragon, and soon encased the astonishing sculpture in a yellow-tinted wall of glass. The dragon was a brilliant white, holding a blood-red rose in its mouth. It stood proud, about ten feet tall, and sparkled with the lights of the room.

"This ice dragon will sit in the gardens of this palace in recognition of my son's birthday. May his heart be strong like a dragon, but his demeanor for his people as soft as the petals of the rose it holds. Happy birthday, Zaidan Alrishitar!"

His sister leaned over and kissed his cheek, and his mother and father surrounded him with a hug.

Kyril watched as dignitaries began to line up to wish the prince well on his birthday.

"Come now, Kyril," Targon said, motioning toward the end of the line. "Let them have their moment before it's our turn."

Kyril said nothing, but stiffly followed Targon to the back of the line. With eyes flicking around the room he spotted an increase of guards, but not as many as he would have hoped. Still, there would be more needed elsewhere before the night was done. He spied Joelle and Sylvie up near the front of the line. As visiting dignitaries from other kingdoms, he supposed they must have been granted a special place in line. As their turn ended, though, instead of walking away, they only took a few steps back, and appeared to be watching the room.

He caught Sylvie's eyes and she gave him a closely concealed nod of her head. Her lips twitched upwards just a bit. They knew! Somehow, they knew.

The line moved forward slowly and soon Kyril found himself and Targon only a few places away. His heartbeat quickened and he used his sleeve to wipe sweat off his forehead once again.

The emperor glanced up and held Kyril's eyes for a second longer than made him comfortable. They all knew. Bale had warned them of the impending danger, and now it would be up to Kyril to play his part and do what was needed.

Targon cleared his throat, peered down at Kyril, and smiled, his face radiant. He brought his head a bit lower and whispered in his ear, "This is what we have been waiting for, Kyril. And I myself chose you to be here as it happens. Ready your power. Ready the sign of light for all the city to see. Tonight, you will bring forth the power of the medallion and usher in a new era of leadership in Gildan."

Kyril said nothing, only nodded, then turned his face forward once again. He blinked a few times in quick succession to keep a tear from leaking out. Fortunately, there was only one person in front of them now. Whatever way things went tonight, it would be over soon.

"Thank you for all you've done for me, Targon," Kyril said in a rush but without looking at his mentor.

He saw Targon nod and smile out of the corner of his eye.

It was now their turn.

Kyril noticed that Sylvie and Joelle were not there anymore. He glanced around but couldn't find them. He turned back to the prince with a pounding heart.

"Wizard Targon," Prince Zaidan said with a small nod.

A servant escorted the empress and the princess farther back, while the emperor stepped closer to this son, concern etched on his face. Music drifted in the background, and Kyril could hear the clicking of utensils on plates and snippets of conversations mingling around the ballroom…but his eyes were on the prince himself. Did he know what was about to happen? If so, he hid it well—a trait that Kyril found himself admiring and wanting at that moment.

Before saying anything to the prince, Targon turned around and cleared his throat loudly. "Attention, everyone!" he called out, magnifying his voice with power.

Everyone stopped what they were doing; even the musicians stopped playing. A movement off to the side caught Kyril's attention. He would recognize the bald head of Gamal anywhere. Where had he been hiding this entire time?

Targon sidestepped a bit closer to the prince, and then in a snakelike fashion, snagged his wrist. A gasp filled the room as Zaidan struggled to get away. A dozen guards soon moved in.

"Stop, or the prince dies!" Targon said, gathering a large amount of power around him.

The emperor put a hand in the air and the guards paused. "What is the meaning of this, Wizard Targon? Let go of my son."

"Not until you hear my declaration," Targon began. "Today marks a new day in Gildan. For too long, nobles have ruled for no other reason than from some long-ago ancestry. As recent events have played out, we have seen new and relentless attacks on wizards…"

Voices rose in the room, arguing the matter. Targon raised his other hand for silence and waited until the voices grew softer.

"I believe Emperor Alrishitar to be an honorable man, but he has been too soft and has turned a blind eye. Why, my newest and most promising apprentice here has been mercilessly teased along with others, just because they came from poor or lowly backgrounds!"

Kyril tried to shrink into the shadows and avoid the attention, but it was not possible. Targon's words brought a swirl of emotion into his heart as he tried to retain some type of decorum in front of the crowd.

"What would you have done, Wizard Targon?" said the emperor. "Surely we can talk about things civilly."

"There has already been enough talk," Targon's deep voice boomed over the room. "Now is the time for action. I now declare that wizards will control Gildan, along with a newly-established wizard council. The emperor will rule at their whim. This is the way it is done in some other kingdoms, and it is time for us all, nobles, wizards, and citizens of Gildan, to realize that it is our right—the right of wizards of the mind—to rule. I will be the head of this council and I will be named as Governor of Gildan and second in command to the emperor."

The crowd broke into pandemonium, nobles and wizards alike raising their objections. The guards stepped closer and

Targon grabbed the prince from behind with his arms wrapped in front of him.

"To ensure this transition is as peaceful as possible," Targon said to the emperor, "Prince Zaidan will be taken and held until all is settled and signed into law. I have no desire to hurt the boy."

The emperor took a step closer to Targon. "You'll never get out of here alive, Targon."

"Then neither will your son!" Targon turned his head. "Kyril, it is time!"

Kyril couldn't meet his eyes but reached over and grabbed Targon's hand and prepared to transport them away. He shut his eyes to concentrate and brought up in his mind the location—a small building between the palace and the school, not far away, but far enough that Targon had thought the emperor and his guards wouldn't be able to find him quickly.

But Targon didn't know the plan had changed. And Kyril shifted his focus to a different place; this one much closer.

Kyril pulled the medallion out from under his shirt as white light burst from both his hand and the golden medallion itself. The crowd murmured and yelled. Using the strength of the medallion he now wore, he did what he had to do—though it brought him no satisfaction to do so. A flash of light wrapped around the prince, Targon, and himself, and in the next instant they were transported away—but not to where Targon had planned.

The three materialized in the wizard gardens of the palace grounds, just below the level of the Garden of the Spirit. Scarcely had they done so when four guards fell upon Targon and ripped the prince from his grasp. Targon fought back and raised his hands to attack, but one of the emperor's own wizards—one of many now in attendance—brought forth his own power first and wrapped a strong cord around Targon's arms, holding them to his body. He then forced the wizard to the ground. With a grunt, Targon complied.

Kyril stood off to one side and peered out over the small crowd. It consisted of two dozen guards and at least six other wizards. Bale stood alongside Sylvie and Joelle, holding a sword and appearing ready to pounce at a moment's notice.

"Kyril!" shouted Targon. "Get us out of here. We've been compromised."

But Kyril said nothing. Soon the emperor and more guards arrived, running as fast as they could from the palace doors.

"Targon, you are arrested for traitorous actions against the Empire of Gildan and my family," the emperor began. "Your crimes in this are punishable by death."

"I wasn't going to hurt anyone!" Targon yelled out. "I was going to let the Prince go once you placed me in a position of power."

"I've been told there is evidence to the contrary," the emperor said as he looked over at Kyril.

"Kyril?" Targon said in a whisper this time. "What have you done?"

Kyril let the tears fall from his eyes as he regarded Targon. Before he said anything, he transported away, returning back only a moment later. He struggled once again to stay standing when he returned. A nearby guard grabbed his elbow and kept him upright. He held a parchment in his hand in which he handed to the emperor.

"This says otherwise," Emperor Alrishitar said to Targon, his voice rising in uncharacteristic anger. "This order to have me killed, along with kidnapping my son, and plans you made to set yourself up as second to my command, amount to treason."

"That was just a contingency, your Highness," Targon begged. "I'm sure things wouldn't have gone that far. You must believe me."

The emperor looked from Targon, then to Kyril, and back again, trying to access the situation. In the moment of silence Targon turned his head toward Kyril.

"Why?" Targon pleaded for an answer while turning his eyes up toward Kyril. "I gave you everything."

Kyril sniffed back the tears and hung his head low. He couldn't bring himself to speak.

"Did they force you to do this?" Targon continued to Kyril.

Without warning, a hundred feet away on top of the outside wall of the garden, three people materialized.

"You were a fool, Targon, to put everything on this boy," sneered Gamal. His head reflected the nearby colored lights of the domes of the palace. "I told you not to trust him. Now, I have no more use for you."

"Master Gamal," Targon uttered. "Kyril has the medallion. We can still get it. I can still be of use to you."

Kyril himself just stood with open mouth staring from Gamal to Targon and back again. "Master?"

CHAPTER FORTY-TWO

amal reached up his hand to scratch his head, and even in the lingering twilight Kyril noticed the red ruby ring on his left hand. The events of the past two weeks began to make sense. It had been Gamal that was trying to push into Kyril's mind from the beginning. It was he who had given him the book in the tunnel under the palace, and he who had been influencing Kyril's mind as he searched for the medallion in the meadowlands. Gamal had been the leader of this conspiracy all along. He was the one out to get the power of the medallions. Targon, although guilty of many things, was merely a pawn in Gamal's plan—taking the external leadership role, while Gamal pulled the strings from the back.

With the black medallion hanging around his neck, Gamal let out a crackling laugh. and along with the two people on either side of him, floated down from the wall and onto the ground. As they did so, the emperor motioned for his guards to intercede.

Kyril squinted in the growing darkness to see who the others with Gamal were. Finally, they came closer, and he gasped with surprise.

"Jordan?" Kyril said, half to himself. "Altia?"

Altia shot him a dark look. "You've failed Kyril. Again. You'll never amount to anything."

"But…?" Kyril mumbled.

"But, what?" Altia said. "You thought I liked you? I might admit I was intrigued with you at first. I mean, why would Targon want such a weak apprentice like you? But then I saw the truth. Targon fancied himself for more than he really was. He overstepped and got greedy. It was always Gamal who was set to rule."

Gamal walked slowly but deliberately forward. A black iridescent power emitted from the medallion he wore, and a wall of power rose up in front of them. At the same time, Kyril felt his own medallion heat up in response.

"Yes, pathetic apprentice," Gamal added. "I am the true power here. Targon was just my puppet—a puppet that forgot who his master was. I've made a lifetime study of the power of the medallions and even helped him create this one. I've always been with him, guiding him, directing him. But when it came to you, he forgot his place."

Gamal held the black medallion out in front of him and a burst of black fire shot out toward the guards. They all yelled and dove to the ground to avoid being hit. A few were successful; others were not.

Back behind Gamal, Kyril spotted Sylvie and Joelle. They moved quietly. Joelle held her staff in her hands, red hair blowing faintly in the evening summer breeze, while Sylvie began waving her hand in various patterns in the air.

Gamal headed toward where Kyril, Targon, Zaidan, and the emperor stood. Another contingent of guards moved out in front of them. Two wizards raised their hands and shot out balls of fire at the approaching scribe. Jordan reacted first and knocked one of the wizards off his feet, then Gamal used his medallion to deflect the other wizard's fire away from him.

"I'll make you a trade, emperor," Gamal said. "The life of your son in exchange for stepping down from the throne."

"No," Zaidan shouted. "I won't allow it."

Emperor Alrishitar shook his head at the absurdity of the request. "You know I cannot do that, Gamal. I must protect my kingdom. My son knows his duty, as do I."

Gamal brought his hand up in front of him, and with a broad sneer gathered a dark force around him. It swirled around his medallion and then coalesced into the palm of his hand.

The emperor, a great wizard in his own right, gathered his own considerable power and made a force field around himself and those around him. Kyril watched as Sylvie and Joelle continued to creep closer; no one was paying them any attention.

Kyril opened his own hand, the mark of the medallion glowing brightly. He tried to figure out what Gamal's next move would be. It was not what he expected.

Gamal stood directly in front of the shield that the emperor had created; then, in a flash of darkness, he was gone.

Everyone gasped and glanced around. Kyril felt a small tugging of his own medallion pulling him to the side. He followed the instinct and jumped sideways, just as Gamal materialized next to him. His hand was outstretched toward Kyril's neck as he reached toward the golden medallion.

Kyril did the only thing he could think of. With only a quick thought he transported away from Gamal's hand and reappeared on the other side of the garden down along the blue delphiniums, petunias, and foxgloves of the wizard of the earth gardens. He still couldn't transport very far and was limited by places he could either see or had been.

He put his hand against a tree to steady himself for a moment. Before he realized what was happening, Jordan ran toward him and shot out a line of fire straight toward him. Kyril dove to the side, the fire singeing the edges of his cloak.

"Give Gamal the medallion and we will leave," Jordan shouted.

"What about Targon?" Kyril shouted back. "What about your uncle? I thought you loved him and owed him your allegiance."

"He lost my respect when he sided with you, Kyril," Jordan shouted. "Do you know, in all my years of following him, helping him, and being there for him, he never once let me live with him? But he did you. He loved you more than he loved me."

A lump formed in Kyril's throat as he spared a quick glance across the garden toward Targon. The man was still on his knees with two guards holding him. But where was Gamal? He turned around and his own medallion warned him just in time. Kyril dove to the side as Gamal once again materialized next to him.

"Get the medallion," Gamal yelled at Jordan. "I can't get close enough to him. His medallion is protecting him from me."

Balance, thought Kyril. His medallion was made to bring balance, and it was indeed responding to Gamal's which, as an abomination, tried to tear that balance away.

The young wizard Jordan drew a sword from his side and with power flinging from one hand and his sword in the other, he advanced on Kyril.

Kyril wasn't a very powerful wizard on his own, and he had only just learned to do a few tricks with his medallion. The only thing he knew how to do for sure was to teleport, and so he did—this time, materializing on the wall of the garden before Jordan could do anything. But the constant transporting was weakening him. He leaned over and barely stayed on his feet.

"Shoot now!" Gamal yelled.

From seemingly out of nowhere, a slew of arrows flew not only toward Kyril, but toward the emperor on the opposite side of the garden. He tried to transport again, but as he did so an arrow grazed his shoulder and he yelled out in pain. After falling off the wall and onto the ground, he tried to stand up, but couldn't. He thought it was his own dizziness, but then he realized the ground was shaking all around them.

Across the yard Kyril saw Sylvie, with her hands raised high, instantly erect a new wall of stone in front of the emperor and his son. The arrows hit the wall and fell safely to the ground.

With a blast of dark power, Gamal tore large chunks from the wall and a spray of shards flew through the air. Kyril tried to move once again, but the chips of stone tore into his arms. Before he could respond, Altia plowed into him from his left side and knocked him to the ground. The medallion swung around his neck and she reached toward the chain and began to pull at it.

"It's not yours, Altia!" Kyril growled.

The chain grew hot and Altia pulled her hand away with a loud yell. Jordan was now fighting against Bale and two other guards on the other side of the garden. Sylvie tried to overpower Gamal, while the emperor himself guarded and protected his son. But Gamal pushed forward slowly but steadily. They were no match for his hidden reserves of power that he must have put into the medallion over the years. He flung fire and lightning right and left killing or injuring all the other guards until only the two holding Targon were left with the emperor and his son.

Both Zaidan and Mezar Alrishitar were strong wizards of the mind, but the power of the black medallion made Gamal a formidable opponent. The man lifted his hand once again toward the emperor.

"Sylvie!" Kyril screamed. "Protect the emperor!"

But Jordan, after defeating the guards, had pulled her purposely farther away to fight with him. There was only one thing Kyril could do. He thought about the power of the medallion, and brief flashes of others who had held its power over the years came to his mind. The power of balance. He was the only weapon against Gamal's unnatural, evil, black medallion. He mustered all the strength he still had, and a blinding wall of light materialized around him as he transported once more.

As he did so—more slowly than normal, weakened from so many transports—he raced past Gamal as the man shot a bolt of black light from his hand. It flew forward in the air and Kyril saw that Emperor Alrishitar didn't have time to move away. Instead Kyril sped faster than the black magic and positioned himself between Gamal and the emperor.

He materialized only a moment before the dark bolt of black magic hit him straight in the chest. The pain was worse than he had ever felt in his life. Every fiber of his body cried out in shock and torture as the black light flailed around him. He staggered to stay upright, feeling the emperor behind him grab him under his arms.

He took what he figured would be his last breath—but at least he had died to protect the emperor.

But after a few deep breaths, he noticed he was still standing.

He turned to his side at the sound of a groan and saw Targon slumped to the ground, his breathing labored. His old mentor slowly turned his head up with astonishment filling his face. He was staring right at Kyril's chest.

"Ky!" Sylvie called out as she came rushing forward. "The medallion!"

He glanced down and saw the golden medallion hanging in front of his chest. It had taken the brunt of Gamal's attack.

"He tried to save you," Sylvie said. "Targon tried to jump up and save you, but when Gamal's spell hit your medallion, it reflected off and caught Targon instead."

Kyril fell to the ground at Targon's side and yelled in desperation, "Joelle!"

"Kyril, my boy," Targon said, lifting a weak hand onto Kyril's knee. "Did you really hate me so much?"

Tears trickled down Kyril's cheeks as moments of the past two weeks flashed through his mind. "No, Targon." He shook his head, barely able to speak. "No. Never. But…I have to know…" Kyril paused for a moment as he saw Joelle running toward them before returning his attention to his injured mentor. "Was it all just an act? Did you use me just to get the medallion for yourself?"

Kyril waited a moment for an answer. Targon's eyes closed and his chest drew a few deep ragged breaths. At length, his eyes popped back open and he held Kyril in a fierce gaze.

"No, it was not just all for the medallion, Kyril. I was blinded by the power and by Gamal's drive to get it from you, but I did care. I really did care for you."

Kyril broke out into a sob as Joelle reached his side. She put her hands tenderly on the man, but the emperor touched the healer's shoulder and drew her away. She looked up at his shaking head and a moment later, removed her hands from Targon.

When Kyril glanced up to see what was happening, he saw a mix of compassion and judgement in the emperor's eyes.

"Let him go," the emperor said.

"But, sir," Kyril wailed, his heart reaching out for his misguided mentor. "It wasn't his fault. It was Gamal…"

At that point everyone looked around for the man that had tried to attack the emperor.

"He disappeared as soon as you blocked his magic, Kyril," Sylvie said.

As if they both had just realized that Gamal was no longer with them, Jordan and Altia began running past the group and toward the garden walls to escape.

Sylvie brought her hands up, but Joelle was quicker.

"Let me," Joelle said, with a rare angry expression on her face.

She grabbed her staff, and in the blink of an eye, leapt ten feet. She came down in front of the two fleeing traitors and brought her staff around in front of her in a blurry arc in one direction and then another. With two *thumps*, both Jordan and Altia were lying on the ground.

Joelle stood over them, daring them to get back up. By then Bale and one other guard had recovered enough to take the two into custody.

Kyril glanced up at Sylvie, who stood stunned and surprised.

"I never knew she could do that," Sylvie said.

Kyril grinned a bit; he had no love for either of the traitors at the moment and was glad to see Joelle take them down. But the man he did love then took a shuddering breath and brought Kyril's attention back to him.

"Forgive me, Kyril," said Targon in a low voice. "I can see I let you down. I wasn't the great man you wished for. But I hope I taught you something."

Kyril, still kneeling on the ground, turned to the emperor with eyes pleading for his help.

But Emperor Alrishitar shook his head. "This is better than a traitor's execution. Whatever had been his real intentions; he did try to take my son. That alone sealed his fate.

But he did try to save you in the end and hopefully that will bring him—and you a measure of peace."

Though Kyril wished it wasn't so, he understood the emperor's judgement and turned his attention back to his dying mentor. "You taught me to stand up for myself. You, out of everyone I have ever known, gave me confidence and hope. I will never forget that." He paused to wipe his eyes. "Wizard Targon, because of you, I know that I am somebody."

Targon laughed, and then coughed up blood. "Oh, my boy…" The words came out slow and gurgled. "You are much more than you know. You are definitely…somebody."

The wizard's breath stopped, and his eyes froze in place.

Kyril felt a hand on each of his shoulders and glanced up to see Joelle and Sylvie watching him. Tears filled their own eyes. Prince Zaidan and the emperor lifted Kyril from the ground and stood next to him, providing what comfort they could.

His heart ached from the loss of Targon and what he'd done, but peering around him, he realized he did have friends after all. And maybe was indeed somebody.

CHAPTER FORTY-THREE

"**H**ere is the book that was stolen, Sire," Kyril said. "I was able to retrieve it from Targon's study. I am sorry for any part I played in it."

It was the morning after the Prince's party. Joelle had healed Kyril's shoulder and any of the other guards that she could the night before. Unfortunately, there had been a few that had not survived. Jordan and Altia had been taken into custody but there had been no news of Gamal.

The emperor reverently took the book and held it in his lap. He sat on a small golden throne in the throne room. Prince Zaiden stood on one side with his sister on the other. Due to the long lives of Gildan's wizard emperors, neither would likely sit on the throne in their lifetimes, but the crown would instead pass to a young grandchild or great-grandchild of Emperor Alrishitar.

Kyril glanced to his left and right and smiled at Sylvie and Joelle. A bit farther over beside Joelle stood Bale. His eyes kept flickering toward Kyril, but as soon as Kyril would notice, the first-time handler would look away. It was as if he was trying to decide something.

"The Western Codex holds much power in its information. Knowledge that, I'm afraid, Gamal Turami might now have, depending on how much time he had spent reading it." The emperor flipped through the pages as he talked.

"Prisoners Jordan and Altia have told us much of his doings. It appears he had planned the attacks on the wizards to rile up the other wizards and create tensions among the citizens of Gildan, both noble, lay man, and wizard. Once Targon was set up as governor of Gildan, he was going to have me executed. The note you saw on Targon's desk was actually from Gamal. Once Targon was elevated, Gamal would rule Gildan from the shadows using Targon as his mouthpiece."

Kyril nodded. It all seemed to make sense now.

"I fear it was Gamal and not Targon that tried to infiltrate my mind, as well as others," Kyril spoke up softly. With respect in their eyes, the others turned to listen to him. "He had been using the dark powers of the black medallion to find someone that would respond—and that someone he hoped would be the holder of one of the three original medallions. He has been searching for years. When I tried to fly or walk through a wall—" Kyril grinned and blushed a bit "—well, that was his doing. He thought he could get the medallion from me, not knowing for a while that I didn't actually have it in my possession. Though, strange as it may be, due to its mark in my hand, I still retained some of its power."

"Speaking of power," Sylvie said, "with the help of Hasani in the academy library, I've learned more about the medallions. Like the Codex says, there were three of them, but there is not any mention of where they went."

The emperor shook his head. "Well, I'm afraid there may be more that we don't know, than what we know. It will take a lot more studying. But that is not why I invited you all here today."

The room grew quiet as the emperor put the book down and Princess Liyyan handed her father a scroll. He unrolled it, smiled, then turned his attention back to the small group in front of him.

"Be it known that Wizard Sylvonna Hickory of the Kingdom of Arc, Wizard Joelle El'San of the Realm, Wizard Kyril Siravan of the Empire of Gildan—"

Sylvie let out a small gasp and looked over at Kyril. He furrowed his brow at her and wondered why she was interrupting the emperor.

"What?" Kyril mouthed.

"He named you a wizard," Sylvie said.

Kyril's eyes went wide as he turned back to the throne. The emperor smiled and spoke from the cuff, "Well, you certainly have earned it."

"Can we get back on track?" Bale said impatiently from the side.

Sylvie's immediate glare made Bale's face turn a bit pale and he took a step back. Kyril only smiled and turned back around.

Emperor Alrishitar cleared his throat and continued. "— And Bale Nabhani of the noble house of Nabhani, all have performed above and beyond their duty in securing the safety of the Empire of Gildan, Prince Zaidan, and the emperor himself. Their names will be honored among the heroes of our nation."

Even Bale smiled and joined in the excitement of the others, and he stepped back closer to the three young wizards.

Kyril was happy enough being named a full wizard and didn't let Bale's presence dampen his mood.

"As a reward for your services, I award you each one hundred gold coins," the emperor said, having to wait a moment for the gasp of the four to settle down. It was enough money to live on comfortably for years. "In the case of visiting wizards Sylvonna Hickory and Joelle El'San, you are granted access to our empire at any time, may use all of our libraries and centers of learning, and you and the leaders of your kingdoms are welcome at my table any time."

The two women smiled at each other.

"Bale Nabhani," the emperor continued. "For your first assignment as handler, you showed extreme patience, aptitude, and wisdom, even putting your own prejudices aside in the end to help secure the kingdom."

Kyril bit his lip to keep from smiling too broadly. The compliment was also a veiled censure to Bale's treatment of others, specifically to Sylvie and Kyril himself. But it appeared that Bale only heard the accolades. Bale took a step forward and the emperor continued reading the scroll.

"Because of your valiant service, you are now permanently in the employ of the kingdom and part of the spymaster's organization, a position of deep trust in protecting the affairs of Gildan."

The emperor then turned to Kyril and seemed to think for a moment before speaking. "Kyril Siravan, as an apprentice wizard, you went undercover to gather information, even at the expense of your personal safety and feelings, and provided the key to keeping the peace in Gildan. Your final sacrifice in placing yourself as a shield between myself and Gamal is an act I will never forget." The emperor's voice grew thick with emotion and he cleared his throat before continuing.

He paused, looking up from the scroll he was reading from, and peered into Kyril's eyes. "What will you ask of me, Wizard Kyril? I will give whatever boon you request of me, even a seat on my council, a noble estate, or land to rule. I cannot place a price on my life and that of my family."

Kyril was caught off-guard. He knew his cheeks were red with heat and he wiped sweat from his brow. Without thinking much, he reached up and wrapped his left hand around the medallion. It fit perfectly and felt right. A bright gleam of light began to glow, and he was reminded of the vision he had seen, when the medallions were first given to three wizards by King Anikari. He pictured each one of those wizards in his vision, and then glanced from his left to his right, and made a decision.

"Sire." Kyril took a deep breath and rushed forward before he changed his mind. "The three medallions were created to be used together to bring balance to magic. I ask permission to help gather those medallions, and to find Gamal and make sure that his black medallion is destroyed, and that he poses no other threat to Gildan or magic anywhere."

The emperor chuckled. "Not many people would turn down what I offered you, Kyril."

From the corner of his eye, Kyril could see Bale standing there opened-mouthed, with a dumbfounded expression on his face. "Well, I'll be…"

The emperor sighed and shook his head. "You have amazed me once again. So, let it be done!" he said.

A scribe to the side finished writing out the final proclamation of the emperor and then handed four scrolls to the emperor for his seal, who then in turn handed them to Kyril, Sylvie, Joelle, and Bale. All four grinned broadly as they placed the scrolls of recommendation into their pockets.

The two women laughed joyfully, and each took one of Kyril's hands. His medallion lit up and spread a golden color around Kyril and both young women. Through the medallion, Kyril felt a connection to both of his friends and to the other two medallions.

Everyone in the room gasped.

"I guess we know who might be helping you in this quest," the emperor said as he stood up and walked toward the three glowing wizards. In a rare gesture, the emperor of the Empire of Gildan gave a low bow of respect and honor to them.

Kyril caught Bale's eyes and received a quick nod of understanding from him before turning and smiling at both Joelle and Sylvie. Their eyes were bright and their smiles broad. Joelle let out a small giggle and the others in the room joined in.

Letting the power of the medallion fill him up, Kyril thought of where he wanted to go, and in a blinding white light, all three young wizards disappeared and transported away from the palace throne room, leaving the emperor, his son, daughter, and Bale staring at the empty space where they had just been moments before.

* * *

To continue the adventures of Kyril, Sylvie, and Joelle and their quest to find the remaining medallions and stop Gamal read **Search for the Medallions, Book 2 in The Wizard Academies.**

Other Series By Mike Shelton
The Alaris Chronicles

Read about how Roland, Bakari, and Alli first met

A magical barrier. Civil war. Power-hungry Wizards.

The fate of a kingdom rests on the shoulders of three young wizards who couldn't be more different.

As the magical barrier protecting the kingdom of Alaris from dangerous outsiders begins to fail, and a fomenting rebellion threatens to divide the country in a civil war, the three wizards are thrust into the middle of a power struggle.

When the barrier comes down, the truth comes out. Was everything they were taught about their kingdom based on a lie?

Will they all choose to fight on the same side, or end up enemies in the battle over who should rule Alaris?

Sign up on Mike's website at www.MichaelSheltonBooks.com and get a copy of the prequel novella e-book to The Alaris Chronicles, Prophecy of the Dragon.

Protect the youngest heir of the Dragon King. That is the mission given to Imari in this prequel novella to The Alaris Chronicles.

Mike Shelton

The Cremelino Prophecy

About 15 years prior to The Alaris Chronicles and a few
kingdoms to the north.

A Prophecy. A Powerful Sword. A reluctant wizard.

Darius San Williams, son of one of King Edward's councilors, cares little for his father's politics and vows to leave the city of Anikari to protect and bring glory to the Realm.

When a new-found and ancient magic emerges within him, he and his friends Christine and Kelln are faced with decisions that could shatter or fulfill the prophecy and the lives of all those they know.

Wizards and magic have long been looked down upon in the Realm, but Darius learns that no matter where he goes, prophecy and destiny are waiting to find him.

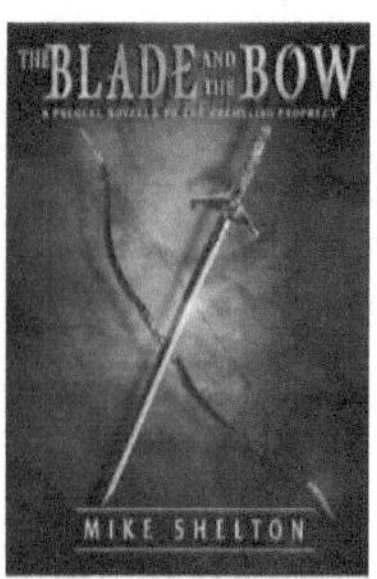

Sign up on Mike's website at www.MichaelSheltonBooks.com and get a copy of the prequel novella e-book to The Cremelino Prophecy, The Blade and The Bow.

Follow Darius and Kelln in one of their more fantastic adventures prior to The Path Of Destiny.

The TruthSeer Archives

On an island far out in the Eastern Sea join a new adventure of magic through the stones of power.

Everyone lies.
What if you could tell when they did?
What if this knowledge caused you immense physical pain?

Given a rare TruthStone, Shaeleen suffers immense agony with every lie she hears or tells. While struggling to control her new power and curb the pain she learns a powerful truth that could thrust an entire continent into civil war.

The stones of power protect the five kingdoms of Wayland - and have done so for two hundred years. Now those stones are failing and a dark power threatens to take control. With the help of her brother, and a young thief, Shaeleen sets out on a dangerous journey to gather and restore the power of all the stones.

The lies could kill her, but the truth could destroy a kingdom.

Will she succeed before the endless lies destroy her?

Mike Shelton

About the Author

Mike was born in California and has lived in multiple states from the west coast to the east coast. He cannot remember a time when he wasn't reading a book. At school, home, on vacation, at work at lunch time, and yes even a few pages in the car (at times when he just couldn't put that great book down). Though he has read all sorts of genres he has always been drawn to fantasy. It is his way of escaping to a simpler time filled with magic, wonders and heroics of young men and women.

Other than reading, Mike has always enjoyed the outdoors. From the beaches in Southern California to the warm waters of North Carolina. From the waterfalls in the Northwest to the Rocky Mountains in Utah. Mike has appreciated the beauty that God provides for us. He also enjoys hiking, discovering nature, playing a little basketball or volleyball, and most recently disc golf. He has a lovely wife who has always supported him, and three beautiful children who have been the center of his life.

Mike began writing stories in elementary school and moved on to larger novels in his early adult years. He has worked in corporate finance for most of his career. That, along with spending time with his wonderful family and obligations at church has made it difficult to find the time to truly dedicate to writing. In the last few years as his children have become older he has returned to doing what he truly enjoys – writing!

mikesheltonbooks@gmail.com
www.MichaelSheltonBooks.com
https://www.facebook.com/groups/MikeSheltonAuthor/
http://www.Twitter.com/msheltonbooks
http://www.Instagram.com/mikesheltonbooks